Requiem for a Reiver

John Michael Doyle

Requiem for a Reiver

Reiver: a marauder… a raider

(Little Oxford Dictionary)

Olympia Publishers

London

www.olympiapublishers.com
OLYMPIA PAPERBACK EDITION

A CIP catalogue record for this title is
available from the British Library.

ISBN: 978-1-78830-331-6

This is a work of fiction.
As such, it does not set out to present an accurate historic account of the times
and events included in the story. Some references to historic figures are
included but no resemblance to any other person living or dead is intended.

First Published in 2019

Olympia Publishers
60 Cannon Street
London
EC4N 6NP

Printed in Great Britain

Dedication

Dedicated to the memory of
James Mclaughlin – a small Scot with a large heart

Acknowledgements

My motivation for writing this book arose when I married an Elliott. Although Shireen comes from proud Yorkshire stock, she retains an interest in her Border heritage. Note that she spells her name with a double 't' i.e. 'Elliott', but there seem to be many variations in spelling, e.g. 'Eliot' and 'Elliot'. As most of my research sources point to 'Elliot' being the norm in the period in which the story is set, this is the form I have used in the novel.

My main research involved two excellent sources: George MacDonald Fraser's *The Steel Bonnets,* and Alistair Moffat's *The Reivers* with its accompanying DVDs from the ITV Border TV series. Many thanks to the people at the Eliott Centre at Newtowncastle for their help when I visited there, and, of course, I visited websites too numerous to list.

On the question of spelling: I have distinguished between the actual border and the Border Region by using capitals for the latter, i.e. 'the border' and 'The Borders'.

Chapter 1

The bitter wind whistled down from its frozen northern birthplace driving flurries of rain before it, and on this wild night in March, every raindrop struck home as if fired from a crossbow. The wind gathered strength over the snow-capped Lowland hills and held the vast expanse of the Anglo/Scottish Borders in its icy grasp, making the bleak Border landscape shiver in the cold. Sheep hunkered down in the heather and bracken. Cattle, held in rough winter enclosures close to the farmsteads, sought what shelter they could and turned their backs to the wind. Breaks in the scudding clouds allowed brief spells of watery moonlight to filter through.

On such nights, honest Border folk stayed indoors by their peat-fired winter hearths, aware that this weather could easily herald the arrival of some very unwelcome visitors. In other words, in this third month of the year fifteen hundred and eighty-eight, conditions were perfectly suited to raiding by the dreaded 'Riders'. The notorious Border Reivers.

***

Isabel Routledge sat alone in her sparsely appointed farmhouse. The modest little dwelling, and the few acres of arable land she farmed with her husband, stood close to Bewcastle in England, and within easy riding distance of the border with Scotland. Tonight, she was alone because her husband and son were serving as 'Border Watchers'. Appointed by Lord Scrope, Warden of the English West March, the watchers' task was to patrol the remote paths that traversed the moors and marshes on the English side of the lawless Border region. These routes, although rarely travelled by honest men, were highly favoured by the reiver bands and, from their inadequately sheltered hiding places, the 'watchers' were expected to raise the alarm should a band of 'riders' be spotted crossing the border from the Scottish side, or returning home laden with plunder from a raid in England.

Reiving, however, was not a solely Scottish occupation, and the watchers were just as likely to encounter bands of English raiders returning equally laden with plunder from Scotland. The March Warden realised that he would have extreme difficulty in persuading his watchers to report the presence of these latter reiver bands; most of them belonged to reiving families themselves.

John Routledge was not concerned about leaving his wife on her own on this particular night. He knew that the weather would certainly not deter the reivers, they could find their way unerringly over the boggy ground in the worst weather and on the darkest night, which gave them an advantage over the 'watchers'. Nevertheless, he thought that the proximity of his farm to Bewcastle, and the warden's men stationed there, would deter even the boldest raiders. He was wrong!

A brief glimpse at the moon told Mrs Routledge that it was after midnight, and she finally decided to go to bed. The only sounds were the roar of the wind and the splatter of raindrops against the tiny windows set in the earthen walls of her home. She had just begun making up the peat fire situated in the middle of the single room when the door crashed open. A burly, bearded, and heavily armed man burst in, and before she had time to scream, she found herself roughly grabbed by the shoulder, spun round, and hit on the back of her head. Knocked unconscious, she fell to the floor. Had she not been out cold, she might have noticed that her assailant was accompanied by two other intruders brandishing strange looking pistols, and who appeared to be little more than boys. All three quickly and efficiently searched the house for any other occupants and, finding none, they relaxed.

They ransacked the house and took anything that would be of use to them, but did not expect to find anything of great value. However, hidden in a dry corner they found three sacks of oats, and at this time of year, the grain was more valuable than money to them.

The woman groaned and appeared to be coming to her senses. One of the younger raiders picked her up and laid her on the crude bed already stripped of its rough coverings, and prepared to tie her up prior to taking her as a hostage for ransom.

The first raider, clearly the leader of the reiver band, took hold of his shoulder and pulled him away: "Leave her be," he said gruffly, "we're no' takin' prisoners this night."

The young man looked surprised but did not protest. The second young raider kicked a red-hot piece of peat from the fire in preparation for setting fire to the house, but again the leader stepped in and stopped him.

"I telt ye once, nae hostages and nae fires this night; the warden's men in Bewcastle will see it and take it to be a watchers' beacon. They'll be on us soon enough wi'out that."

The young man was clearly not happy about receiving such admonishment in front of his companion, but he had no option but to comply. Reluctantly, he replaced the turf on the fire.

The leader looked at the woman and was satisfied that she had passed out again, probably from fright, and could not raise the alarm for some time. He motioned the two young men outside with his lance. There, other members of the raiding party had rounded up what stock they could find, which amounted to very little: a mere six scrawny cows and two oxen. They took them anyway and, together with what they had stolen from the house, went to join the other members of the reiver band who waited a little way off with the rest of the night's plunder. This comprised a small mixed herd of nondescript farm beasts and a couple of pack ponies loaded with looted household goods, some of which they abandoned to make room for the precious oats. In a departure from their usual practice, tonight they had taken no captives to hold for ransom.

The leader, however, seemed satisfied with his night's work, and led his men, eighteen in all, north into the teeth of the howling gale and entered the wilderness of the Bewcastle Waste. From there, they would return over the border to Liddesdale and home.

Chapter 2

Alexander Elliot reined in his Galloway Nag, the sturdy, seemingly tireless, little mount favoured by the reivers for its ability to bear them sure-footedly across hills and bogs and, in a brief period of moonlight, he surveyed the results of his night's work.

The puny herd of twenty or so half-starved beasts represented the only livestock they had to show for their raid into the English West March. On another raid, this would amount to sparse pickings indeed, but it was the best that could be expected so close to the border. In recent years, the area had been virtually laid to waste by almost non-stop raiding, especially by the massive raids and counter-raids involving hundreds of 'riders', and mounted by both English and Scottish reiver bands who pillaged and plundered on both sides of the border. Those large reiver bands had, in reality, been small armies and, having taken part in a few of those raids himself, Elliot knew that that they were actively encouraged by those who sat in government in both Edinburgh and London. Added to that, The Borders had experienced several years of bad weather, and incessant rain invariably ruined crops before they were ready for harvesting. Borderers, therefore, were obliged to rely on their animals for survival, which made the sacks of oats stolen from Isabel Routledge very valuable indeed. Pickings for small bands of reivers had of late been disappointingly lean. Not that they were in the least inhibited by this; they simply raided further afield.

Tonight's raid, however, had not been carried out solely for plunder. It had been carried out by Alexander Elliot in retaliation for having his own cattle stolen, and one of his men killed, by raiders from an English reiver family, the Hetheringtons. In the complex interrelations between Border reiver families, the Hetheringtons were close allies of another English reiver family, the Fenwicks, and the Fenwicks, in turn, were involved in a long-running blood feud with his own family, the Elliots of Liddesdale. Alexander was an important chieftan, a 'heidsman', of this, one of the most feared of the Scottish reiver families and had he not retaliated against the Hetherington raid into his own land, he would have lost face among the other reiver chiefs and, more importantly, among members of his own family. As reivers, the Elliots were second in notoriety only to the Armstrongs, their neighbours and close associates in Liddesdale, a bleak, Lowland valley running roughly from southwest to northeast along the border just north of the Cheviot Hills.

Even though the pickings were meagre, in Elliot's mind the raid had been a success. A Hetherington heidsman and one of his men had been killed, both of them by Alexander's own lance. Normally he tried to avoid killing on a raid. To a man like Alexander, reiving was a perfectly legitimate enterprise but murder was a crime, except when committed in pursuance of a family feud. He did not know when, or even why, the feud with the Fenwicks and Hetheringtons had started, but that mattered little; Elliot family honour had been satisfied, and it did no harm at all to demonstrate that his family could raid with impunity wherever and whenever they chose.

Isabel Routledge had simply been unlucky. Her farm was on the raider's route home and they had stopped off to add something to their night's haul. Finding the oats had been an unexpected bonus.

Alexander, however, felt a sense of urgency. He knew that some English reiver bands were on good terms with certain officers of the law, and he suspected that the Hetheringtons were under the protection of one of the English March Warden's law officers, Richard Musgrave, the Captain of Bewcastle. Raiding with a small band so close to a village where the warden's men were stationed was a dangerous game, and he could expect the Hetheringtons to quickly organise a 'hot trod' expedition to apprehend him and retrieve everything he had reived from them. Under the hot trod system, the law not only allowed, but also actually compelled, landowners and other victims of the reivers to raise bands of armed men to follow the raiders and recover their stolen goods and livestock. In spite of the foul weather, he could expect a pursuit to be quickly organised, and, on this occasion, he guessed that the Hetheringtons and their friends, the Fenwicks, would have the support of the warden's men from Bewcastle. The pursuers and their official allies would attempt to get between his band and the border, and with this in mind, he resorted to the old reiver ruse of leaving some men to guard the route home to Liddesdale and set an ambush for any pursuers who followed him tonight. His carefully laid trap was set on the cross-border path the men on the hot trod were most likely to take when following him into Scotland and the effectiveness of the ambush would depend, not on the strength of the pursuers, but on their knowledge of reiver tactics. On several occasions, he, and relatively few of his men, had routed much larger enemy bands, and he was confident that they could do it again. They had the advantage of knowing the ground, and tonight the weather was a trusted ally. Moreover, on a night like tonight, the border watchers did not enter his thinking. With riders from so many factions involved, they would be more than happy to let sleeping dogs lie and avoid the risk of making dangerous enemies for themselves.

Even so, Alexander would be happy to get his band back to the safety of Liddesdale as soon as he could. Once there, and under the protection of the rest of the Elliot family and their associates, it would require a sizeable army to capture him.

He also knew the Captain of Bewcastle of old. He had little doubt that when the opportunity presented itself, the erstwhile law officer was as efficient a reiver as any and in the unlikely event of his arrest, Alexander doubted if the stolen property would ever find its way back to the rightful owners, and especially not those precious oats. Nevertheless, should he, or any of his men, be taken alive by officers of the law from either side of the border, they could expect nothing less than 'Jeddard Justice', which involved hanging first and a trial afterwards.

His concern, however, was not for himself – he fully expected to stretch a rope eventually – but for his two sons. The eldest, Malcolm, but known as 'Sandy' due to his hair colour inherited from his flaxen-haired mother; and Robert, known as 'Rabbie', dark haired like his father. Once well away from Bewcastle, he called a halt to rest the horses while he took a moment to look around at his sons.

Both were mounted and attired in a manner similar to their father. Each rode a Galloway Nag and wore a burgonet, a pointed metal helmet known as a 'steel bonnet'. For upper body protection, each wore a coat known as a 'jack o' plaite', a quilted leather jerkin stuffed with pieces of bone and other hard materials to deflect sword thrusts. They wore rough homespun trousers and stout leather boots, and Alexander was pleased to see that they had remembered to drape heavy homespun blankets over their shoulders to keep out the bitter wind. Like their father, they sported broadswords with basket hilts and long wicked-looking knives known as 'ballock daggers'.

He was pleased that Malcolm – he usually thought of his sons in terms of their given names – had, for tonight at least, the sense to wear his steel bonnet. Of late, his eldest son had taken to sporting a fancy Tudor cap, something he had picked up somewhere. Alexander smiled quietly to himself when he realised that Malcolm was simply out to impress the girls with pretty faces he had seen in Jedburgh. That was all very well at home, but on a raid, it did not provide a reiver with adequate protection for his head.

The rest of the reiver band were armed and clad in a variety of these pieces of equipment, although most of them wore 'skulls', simple steel caps, in place of steel bonnets. Unlike their father and most of the men, however, who carried long lances with the butt resting in a leather cup attached to their stirrups, Malcolm and Robert bore firearms. Each carried one of the latest model wheel-lock pistols. The guns were probably of German origin, and Alexander had presented them to his sons to mark their acceptance as fully-fledged reivers. He considered that there was no need for them to know where the weapons had come from, but they would have no doubts that their father had not acquired them legally. Although he had presented his sons with these guns, Alexander was beginning to have regrets. The thought of them bearing stolen firearms did not bother him in the least, but the manner in which they carried the weapons gave him cause for concern. Most reivers kept their pistols in leather holsters attached to their saddles until they needed them, but, with boyish bravado, his sons seemed more intent in showing them off, and were proudly displaying them for all to see. In Alexander's opinion, they were simply asking for someone else to come and take the guns away from them, and if the thief killed them in the process, it would be largely his fault for having given them the weapons in the first place.

Although only sixteen and fourteen years old respectively, in reivers' terms 'Sandy' and 'Rabbie' Elliot were fully grown men, and both had been 'blooded' before they had even reached their teens. On their last raiding foray, they had ridden with him and a large body of Armstrongs on a raid to the north, close to Edinburgh, the seat of Scottish government. Raiding in their home country of Scotland meant nothing to the reivers of Liddesdale; they struck wherever they thought the pickings would make it worth their while. Sandy and Rabbie had acquitted themselves well on that raid, and on returning home, he had presented them with the pistols. Nevertheless, they clearly still had much to learn.

Alexander also feared that he might have caused his sons to abandon the traditional reivers' weapons in favour of the pistols. Personally, he did not trust firearms, which he considered toally unsuited to the reiver's trade. Guns were clumsy, unreliable weapons, difficult to fire and almost impossible to reload by a rider on the back of a galloping horse. And they were useless if the gunner allowed his powder to get wet. He preferred to place his trust in his broadsword and in the ten-foot lance, with which he could spear a salmon without leaving the saddle. He supposed, however, that he had to move with the times. He had heard that even the English were replacing their deadly longbows with arquebuses and that, he thought, was a grave mistake on their part. The arquebus was a long-barrelled, clumsy weapon requiring a special rest to steady the gun in order to fire it with any degree of accuracy. That particular thought, however, served to cheer him, as a young man he had seen for himself how English bowmen had torn Scottish armies to pieces by loosing twenty arrows a minute with deadly accuracy from a range of several hundred yards.

Before getting his reiver band on the move again, he took a moment to talk to his sons. He did not admonish them for wearing the pistols so openly; with Robert especially, that would probably be a waste of breath. Instead, he gruffly told them to keep their pistols hidden in case of attack, and then use them to surprise the enemy. It could, he said, gain them a decisive advantage. Sandy instantly acceded to his father's order but, as he had done at Isabel Routledge's farm, Rabbie again muttered his displeasure at receiving such chastisement from his father in front of the other riders.

Alexander had long recognised that his sons possessed very different natures. Malcolm had inherited his mother's thoughtful approach to life and was inclined to think things through before acting, while Robert, on the other hand, resembled his father as a young man. He was prone to act first and think later. Nevertheless, Alexander hoped that his youngest son would soon learn to control his temperamental impulses, just as he had learned to do as a young man. He noticed that the one person Robert never seemed to argue with was his older brother, and it heartened him to see this growing bond between his sons. In his view, either one of them would be well equipped to one day take his place as heidsman. Like him and his father before him, his sons had been born into, and raised up in, a society that depended on reiving for its very existence and, for Alexander, it was not a question of right or wrong. To him, reiving was simply a way of life, and although he might be aware that it flew in the face of every law decreed by both church and state, he neither knew of, nor cared for, any other way of life. Consequently, he had brought his sons up to be reivers.

He was aware that his wife, Margaret, wanted something better for her sons and she had insisted on them learning to read and write. Malcolm, as usual, seemed to understand that reading and writing were skills worth learning, but Robert, as usual, had not taken readily to study. Their father knew that his wife entertained a hope that her sons, Malcolm in particular, would someday become 'gentlemen', and he suspected that Margaret was the one who had provided him with the Tudor cap.

At first, Alexander had been inclined to agree with Robert, and saw little or no point in teaching his children peacetime pursuits when peace never came to The Borders. He could not remember a time when his home and family had not been under threat from other reivers, or invading armies marching to the frequent wars between England and Scotland. His wife, however, shamed him into accepting her point of view by reminding him that he had not even been able to sign his name on the marriage contract when they had been married in the church in Jedburgh. For a reiver to be married in church was in itself unusual. Most preferred the traditional method of 'handfasting', where couples lived together for a year, and after that were partners for life. Although a basic education was available from the Kirk, reivers generally did not avail themselves of the opportunity. The Reformation was taking hold in Scotland just as it had done in England, but Borderers still held to the old religion – or as close to it as they had ever done. As a result, being the only literate member of the family, Margaret had undertaken the task of teaching her sons herself, and when possible, enlisted the help of the itinerant priests who sometimes secretly visited the area to say Mass for those few who wished to attend. In the end, she succeeded, and her sons learned the basics to the point where their father changed his mind and was proud of their achievement.

Satisfied that all was well with his sons, he turned to urge his men on as they chivvied the twenty-odd scrawny cattle into motion. Dawn was breaking as he led his reiver band out of the Bewcastle Waste and into the western fringe of the Cheviot Hills. Once through the Cheviots, they would be in home territory, Liddesdale. So far, he had managed to evade any organised pursuit and avoided falling foul of the Captain of Bewcastle, but he knew that tonight, a determined effort would be made to catch him. In this weather, it would take some hours yet to reach his tower house south of Hawick, but once he entered Liddesdale, he would effectively be on his home turf.

Later, he might be called to account at one of the 'Truce Days' – days set aside by agreement between the two governments for the March Wardens from opposite sides of the border to hold their Warden's Courts. These courts, set up to punish the wrongdoers and obtain compensation for their victims, met at regular intervals, but in common with most reivers, Alexander rarely took any notice of them.

The Hetheringtons, egged on by their Fenwick allies, would much prefer to retaliate in kind rather than lodge a complaint with the Warden of the English West March. In the event that they did lodge such a complaint, he would simply make a counter-claim with the Warden of the Scottish Middle March based on the initial raid by the Hetheringtons. In which case, he would appear before the Wardens Court at the next Truce Day, should he decide to turn up at all, as both plaintiff and defendant. Truce Days, in spite of being an attempt to bring order to the lawless Borders, rarely ran smoothly. There were usually so many complainants that the wardens could not possibly deal with them all, and so, rather than get involved in drawn-out arguments which were apt to lead to bloodshed, the opposing wardens were usually happy to adopt a 'common sense' approach and agree that the two 'bills' cancelled each other out.

There was, however, one snag to this plan. The Elliots' 'home' warden in the Scottish Middle March was Francis Stewart, the 5th Earl of Bothwell and Keeper of Liddesdale. Bothwell, known as 'Wild Bothwell', would spare no effort to bring one of the leading Elliots to justice, and Alexander felt that he might need some further 'evidence' to justify his actions. Isabel Routledge, however, had unwittingly provided him with a solution to his problem. Because her husband was a 'watcher', she would probably have her case for compensation heard comparatively quickly and she was almost certain to gain redress. Should that situation arise, Elliot would simply return the stolen cattle to Mrs Routledge as a sign of good faith, and that would be that. It was the real reason why he had not allowed his sons to commit the more serious crimes of kidnapping the woman or firing her house. The three stolen bags of oats, however, would present a greater difficulty, but returning the cattle, he hoped, would lend weight to his argument when he denied any knowledge of them.

Before he could think further, his thoughts were abrubtly interrupted by the sounds of battle coming from somewhere behind him. A hot trod had been mounted and had run straight into his carefully laid ambush.

Alexander knew instantly what he had to do. He quickly assembled his men, ordered them to abandon the cattle and directed two of them to take the packhorses, with the oats, home to Liddesdale by a different route. To a man, the vastly experienced reivers did as directed, but Rabbie began to question his father about leaving the cattle unattended. Alexander sharply told him to forget about that and turn his mind to what was to come. With the stolen oats safely on their way to Liddesdale, he led his riders at a gallop by a circuitous route that would take them to a spot behind the scene of the fighting. They came upon a mixed group of perhaps thirty or so Hetherington and Fenwick riders. Repulsed by the ambushers, they were regrouping. They were still in the process of gathering their strength when, with the element of surprise, Alexander and his Elliot riders charged into their rear. Sandy fired his pistol and one of the enemy fell from his horse;

Rabbie fired but missed. Their father yelled at them to retire and reload. He led from the front and speared a man with his lance then drew his sword. In the occasional spells of moonlight, a bloody, merciless, close-quarter battle developed with no quarter given, and none asked. The two Elliot brothers had reloaded, but in the melee, it was difficult to find clear targets. The Hetheringtons and their allies fought hard, but found themselves under a second attack from the Elliot men, who had set the ambush. After the first violent clash, both sides wheeled their horses and prepared to engage again, leaving several bloody corpses on the ground and a few wounded men limping away.

Most of the dead were undoubtedly Hetheringtons. The leader of the hot trod had been hoping that the warden's men from Bewcastle would come to his aid, but that never materialised. He carried on the fight for a while but, having lost several more men, one more of them to Sandy Elliot's pistol, he decided to retire under the cover of a flurry of rain.

The Elliots had won. They caught several loose Hetherington horses and departed the scene, taking the bodies of three of their own men and four wounded Elliots with them. The bodies of the enemy remained where they lay. Alexander was relieved that his opinion of how the Captain of Bewcastle would react, had proved to be correct. The English law officer had abandoned all thoughts of helping the Hetheringtons and had gone to help himself to the stolen cattle instead.

Alexander Elliot had little time for authority of any sort, but he knew how Border law enforcement worked, and how to use it to his advantage.

Chapter 3

Carlisle Castle was an ominously brooding presence in the bleak Border mist. The massive walls represented the bastion of power in the English West March, and housed the office of the March Warden – the man responsible for law and order in the March.

If the castle itself gave off an air of menace, then the castle dungeons appeared positively frightening, as they were designed to do. On this cold March day, the majority of the prisoners held there were men accused of reiving, all of them either awaiting execution or a trial which would inevitably result in their execution. Due to the high number of prisoners, all of the sparsely appointed cells were occupied, most of them packed to well beyond capacity, all except for one, which housed only a single prisoner. He sat on a pile of smelly straw totally at a loss to know how, as an officer of the law, he had managed to get himself arrested, thrown into prison, and be held there for several days without the benefit of an explanation. He was soon to find out. A guard came with orders to escort him to the March Warden's office.

Henry Scrope, 9th Baron Scrope of Bolton, was almost at his wits end. He had been Warden of the English West March and Captain of Carlisle Castle for over twenty years, and in all those years, he had never known Border lawlessness descend to its current violent depths. The reiver families had lived by plundering for centuries; raiding, looting, kidnapping and killing on both sides of the border, but the situation had rarely, if ever, been worse.

Scrope, appointed warden by Queen Elizabeth I in 1560, had instructions to put an end to the lawless activities of the notorious Border

Reivers, and one of his first actions was to propose a series of measures aimed at doing just that. He soon gained the cooperation of his fellow English wardens who, in reality, could hardly do anything other than lend their support to the Queen's appointee, but more importantly, several of his more diligent opposite numbers in the Scottish Marches had also seen the advantages of at least some of his proposals. Getting the governments in London and Edinburgh to agree on anything at all had always been fraught with difficulty, but lawlessness in The Borders had risen to such a level that the authorities could no longer ignore it until, eventually, both sides realised that they had to do something, if only to demonstrate their willingness to take the matter seriously. After much frustrating argument, Scrope managed to obtain agreements on measures to curb many of the less grievous offences, and to help in curbing the more serious ones. It was certainly not everything the new March Warden had hoped for, but it was something, and with these agreements in place, he somehow managed to keep a lid on the situation in the English West March; or at least as secure a lid as any previous warden had ever managed. As a result, there was a short period of relative peace while the reivers assessed, and came to terms with, the situation

Peace was as ever, inevitably, short-lived. Trouble flared up in Scotland when a long-running feud between the Elliots and the Scotts boiled over. Martin Elliot of Braidley raided into Scott territory and stole cattle. The Scotts retaliated by raiding into Liddesdale and killing several Elliots. Fearing that his family would be overwhelmed, Martin Elliot approached Scrope and offered to hand Hermitage Castle, seat of the Keeper of Liddesdale, over to the English. Scrope, who was beginning to get to grips with the ways of the reivers, and knowing that Hermitage did not belong to Elliot in the first place, wisely refused. But quick to spot an opportunity, the new warden persuaded Elizabeth's government to support Martin Elliot with money in return for confining his reiving activities to Scotland. For Elizabeth, this was merely a continuation of her father, King Henry VIII's, policy of causing as much disruption as possible in Scotland, and for Scrope it helped to ease the pressure on his scant resources by reducing, albeit by only one, the number of Scottish reiver bands plundering his March. The warden, however, soon realised that he was being somewhat over-optimistic. Forming an agreement with one Elliot did not mean that the rest of the family would follow suit, and there were hundreds of other Elliots left in Liddesdale who had not made any such cosy accommodations with the English warden. Moreover, Scrope's troubles did not end with the Elliots; there were plenty of other reiving families left to cause him just as many headaches. To make matters worse, the root of his headaches stemmed not only from Scotland but from England as well.

His superior in London was Lord Burghley, the Queen's Principal Secretary and most trusted advisor. Burghley was responsible for Elizabeth's finances, and his penny-pinching, added to the Queen's natural penury, resulted in the English March Wardens not receiving the resources necessary to carry out their duties with any semblance of efficiency. Little wonder then, Scrope thought, that many of them had turned to reiving themselves. As if that were not enough, Sir Francis Walsingham, Queen Elizabeth's feared spymaster, had just handed Scrope a virtually impossible task, but one that he must somehow try to carry out.

Stepping out of his reverie, the warden addressed the man standing respectfully in front of him, looking gaunt and unkept from his time in the Carlisle dungeon, and without the uniform and trappings of a Queen's Officer.

"Well now, Musgrave," he said casually, "this is indeed a pretty pass." The warden's tone was calm and even contained an element of familiarity.

"I fear that it is, my lord," Richard Musgrave replied as casually as he could. Under the circumstances, he felt that it was all he was required to say. He had been feeling more than a little apprehensive about this summons to the warden's office and feared that it might be the prelude to a trial; his trial. It was disconcerting to find Lord Scrope dressed in his formal best, wearing all of his medals and ribbons as if attending an audience with the Queen, and Musgrave only relaxed when he realised that Scrope was alone. There were no other law officers or witnesses, as would be required in a formal court.

What concerned Musgrave was that he himself was one of those Queen's Officers, one personally appointed by Scrope. In this land of reivers, the warden knew that his appointee was not above indulging in a bit of private reiving himself, but he also recognised that Musgrave had many other qualities that could prove invaluable in solving the problem handed to him by Walsingham. The warden knew him to be a brave and resourceful rider and, coming from an established family of English reivers, he knew The Borders and their ways. So, working on the principle that it was best to set a thief to catch a thief, Scrope had taken a calculated risk and appointed Musgrave as Captain of Bewcastle. As long as Musgrave performed his duties efficiently and did not stray too far out of line, Scrope reluctantly decided that he could afford to ignore most of his captain's extra-mural activities. Besides, for Border law officers to be reivers was all too common, and even many of the March Wardens, both English and Scottish, were nothing more than 'reiver lords'.

Scrope had an inherent aversion to using coercion. It went against his 'gentleman's code', and he considered it a tactic best left to the reivers, who were experts in such methods of persuasion. The Borders, however, was no place for such niceties and, like it or not, he was about to turn his officer's unofficial activities to his own advantage. That he was about to renege on the, albeit unspoken, arrangement he had with Musgrave, went against the grain, but try as he might, he could think of no other way of carrying out Walsingham's orders with any realistic prospect of success.

He opened his strategy by letting Musgrave know, in no uncertain terms, that this time the Captain of Bewcastle had gone too far. "You failed to intercept this latest Elliot raid right under your nose at Bewcastle, and you made no effort to apprehend the perpetrators on either side of the border."

Musgrave was only mildly surprised. He had served Scrope for long enough to know that the warden had ways of keeping himself informed on everything that happened in his March and so, he must have discovered what had happened in the Bewcastle Waste. Normally, his superior let such minor misdemeanours pass, but on this occasion, it appeared that he was not prepared to ignore it. On the other hand, while this interview bore no resemblance to a formal trial, he knew that it would be wise to proceed with care.

"No, my lord," he said with a perfectly straight face. "To begin with, the weather badly hindered the watchers and we had to be careful not to get caught in an ambush like the Hetherington hot trod riders did. In spite of that, we almost caught them, but they know their way through 'The Waste' too well and they managed to escape over the line."

"And at that juncture you abandoned the chase. Why?"

"Yes, my lord. Due to the reiver's ambush, the Hetheringtons could not continue with their hot trod, and I did not think it appropriate for me to cross the border without them. I believed that an uninvited encroachment by the Queen's Officers, who were not part of a hot trod, could be construed as an invasion."

The warden was clearly not impressed and his tone showed his displeasure. "You will have to do better than that, Musgrave," he snapped. "You know very well that it would not be construed as anything of the sort. You had every right to cross the border in pursuit of lawbreakers, but, as usual, it seems that you were more interested in stealing the raiders' ill-gotten gains for yourself than in apprehending a notorious reiver."

Scrope knew all about reiver ambushes, especially those set by the reivers of Liddesdale, and he knew that if Musgrave followed this particular Elliot band, he could well have ended up with a very bloody nose. Under different circumstances, he might have taken that into account, but not on this occasion. He had something else in mind for Musgrave's particular talents.

"You were not only perfectly entitled to follow the Elliots over the border, but it was also your sworn duty to do so. Your orders are to follow raiders wherever they lead you, even into Liddesdale. And, irrespective of whether you think that it presents you with an opportunity to help yourself to the stolen cattle."

He paused before adding: "But then you know this already, Musgrave!"

Musgrave was becoming increasingly concerned. Even though he was not facing an actual trial, here in the warden's office in Carlisle Castle, he felt completely out of his depth. The only defence he could offer was a feeble excuse. "I know nothing about the Elliots having any plunder that night, my lord."

"Rubbish!" Scrope retorted angrily.

The very mention of Liddesdale had done nothing to improve the warden's humour. That particular valley had been a thorn in the side of the authorities in both England and Scotland for two centuries, but Scrope feared that there was a danger of it becoming more than that. In his opinion, the quartet of reiver families living there, the Armstrongs, the Elliots, the Nixons and the Crosers, posed a positive threat to England, irrespective of whether some of them – currently it was one of the Elliots – at various times eagerly accepted financial support from an unsuspecting London government. Egged on by thoughts of Liddesdale, he thumped the table in frustration.

"Don't try to wriggle your way out of this, Musgrave. If you are wondering why I am making such an issue over a few stolen cattle, I can tell you that some of them belonged to Mrs Routledge, the wife of one of my senior watchers, and on top of that, the Elliots stole several sacks of oats from her as well. I will not stand by while one of my officers reives from his colleagues."

He caught the brief look of surprise on Musgrave's face at the mention of the sacks of oats, and thought that had his officer known about them, he would certainly not have abandoned the Hetherington hot trod.

Musgrave's heart fell. Scrope, he thought, was setting him up as an example of what happened to Officers of the Crown who got caught reiving, and he realised that he was in potentially serious trouble. As a man of The Borders, he was no stranger to tight spots, but he had always managed to find a way out of them. This, however, was different; having caught him red-handed, Scrope would have to act and the consequences could be dire. At best, he would lose his position as Captain of Bewcastle and the lucrative opportunities it afforded for some private reiving on the side; at worst, he could be hanged as a reiver; and all for a handful of scrawny cows. Had he known about the oats, things could have been different and he might have followed the Elliots, but he hadn't known, so he hadn't followed, and now he was in trouble with no discernible way out. It would be useless to protest, and all he could do was await the warden's verdict.

Scrope calmed down; he realised that his anger had as much to do with his being forced to use what he considered devious methods, as it had with his officer's behaviour. Nevertheless, they had been successful and he was confident that he had Musgrave where he wanted him. His officer now had no other option but to do as the warden ordered. He justified his use of coercion by reminding himself that, whatever else he might be, Musgrave was a more than competent reiver and completely at home in the lawless Borders. He knew the reivers and their ways, and was easily the best man available to carry out an unofficial mission into the Scottish West March; somewhere, an English warden dare not send an armed party except on an official hot trod.

Scrope had long ago concluded that the only way to deal with the reivers, was to fight fire with fire, and that meant mounting massive raids into Scotland, which amounted to a return to what had happened under King Henry VIII. 'Official' raiding into Scotland by large reiver bands had been positively encouraged and sometimes actually paid for by the king. Under Henry's daughter, Elizabeth, however, things were much different. In London, the enthusiasm for large punitive raids was as strong as ever but because of Elizabeth's noted penury, no money was forthcoming to support her wardens' efforts. Nowadays, the resources provided to the March Wardens were barely enough to administer their Marches efficiently while, much to Scrope's disgust, reivers like Martin Elliot of Braidley could still obtain financial support from London for raiding in their own country, and then renege on the agreement whenever they felt like it. Scrope had learned by experience that the Scottish reivers' need for financial support only arose when they were engaged in a blood feud with one of their rival families, and the thought caused his temper to smoulder again. Then there was a second political objection to sending a large party of armed men across the border. A new peace treaty, the latest in a long line of such agreements between England and Scotland, had recently come into force, and while these treaties were usually broken almost as soon as the ink was dry, in the current political climate, the English were reluctant to be the first to upset the applecart. As a result, officially sanctioned raids on the scale of those mounted during King Henry's reign, no longer received official sanction.

On their side of the border, the Scottish authorities employed so-called 'judicial raids'. These were expeditions led by one of the King's senior officers, and sometimes even by the King in person, to establish royal authority and restore order among his rebellious Borderers. The raids usually involved apprehending a few of the leading reivers and either hanging them on the spot, or carting them off to Edinburgh to hang later.

Judicial raids were generally successful, but they only happened when the level of reiving became such an embarrassment to the Edinburgh government that they felt obliged to act. Moreover, even successful judicial raids were rarely, if ever, followed up, and the reivers soon returned to their old ways, with Liddesdale invariably being the first to recover.

Now that James VI had taken his place on the throne of Scotland, and clearly had his mind set on becoming heir to the aging, and childless, Elizabeth of England, Scrope had hoped that judicial raiding would be intensified and help to ease the situation in his March. However, as nothing had happened yet, and seemed unlikely to for some time, Scrope had, albeit reluctantly, begun to fear that his hopes would never be realised. He reached the conclusion that neither England nor Scotland could hope to solve the problem of the Border Reivers separately. The only realistic solution to the problem was closer cooperation between the two countries, and that was something that had never happened in the past, but this time Scrope imagined that there was a glimmer of hope. A lasting solution to the problem of Border lawlessness might well come about when Elizabeth died, as she surely must before long, and James VI of Scotland replaced her to become James I of England. With the crowns united, the border would disappear and, while it might take a few years to complete the process, it would ring the death knell for the reivers. Scrope, however, dare not voice such a radical sentiment. Any mention of it would surely get back to Walsingham, whose spies were everywhere, even in his own English West March.

He sighed and turned his mind back to his immediate problem and the real reason he had incarcerated Musgrave in Carlisle Castle. "Is your family currently involved in a feud with any of the Scottish reiver families?"

Feuding among the reiver families on both sides of the border, was as much the bane of every March Warden's life as was their actual reiving. Scrope had long ago given up trying to understand how and why these inter-family feuds began, or indeed, how the reivers found time along with their stealing, killing and kidnapping, to raid each other with even more bloodthirsty enthusiasm. Nevertheless, feud they did and, as warden, Scrope tried to keep himself informed on who was feuding with whom, but it was not easy. The feud currently causing him most concern, was the one between the Elliots of Liddesdale and the English Fenwicks and their close associates, the Hetheringtons. None of the reiver families pursued a feud more diligently than did the Elliots, and Scrope suspected that this was what had been behind the recent audacious raid carried out under the nose of his Captain of Bewcastle. He knew that Musgrave's family were currently feuding with the Taylors and the Robsons, but this was an exclusively English affair and was not relevant to his immediate problem. He was also aware that the English Grahams were engaged in a cross-border feud with the Scottish Maxwells and Irvines. The Grahams were a cross-border family with factions on both sides and, as such, they were in a position to cause the maximum amount of mischief. Scrope would not mind in the least if the Maxwells wiped out the Grahams on their side of the border; he had been hoping for that particular outcome for nigh on the thirty years of his wardenship. For the moment, however, he was much more concerned with events in the Scottish West March, but if the Musgrave family were feuding with either the Maxwells or the Johnstones, it could have serious ramifications for his plans.

Scrope's abrupt change of direction came as a complete surprise and threw Musgrave even further off balance. Why would the warden want to know if the Musgraves were currently engaged in a cross-border feud, and what had this to do with his reiving the stolen cattle from the Elliots? Still, he was relieved that Scrope seemed to have temporarily dropped the question of the Routledge raid. Feuding, however, was a delicate subject for a reiver, and answering the warden's question required careful thought.

He stalled before answering: "I'm not sure what you mean, my lord."

Scrope recognised that Musgrave was struggling with the problem of family loyalty, and so he rephrased the question: "Is your family currently engaged in a feud with either the Maxwells or the Johnstones in Dumfriesshire?"

Although he failed to see what the warden was leading up to now, the rephrased question was one that Musgrave felt he could answer without breaching family loyalty, but he knew how well Scrope kept himself informed and it would be dangerous to lie.

"No, my lord," he replied.

The directness of the answer convinced Scrope that it was an honest one, but he knew how quickly these feuds could flare up, and he had no guarantee that the situation would remain as it was for long. Feuding was a fact of Border life, and even as March Warden, there was nothing he could do about it, so he put it out of his mind and carried on with his questioning.

"In that case, you would not consider it too dangerous for you to venture alone into Dumfriesshire?"

Musgrave had difficulty in disguising a huge sigh of relief. Scrope had something on his mind other than hanging. He suspected that the mention of 'danger' had nothing to do with his personal safety and everything to do with whatever scheme the warden was currently cooking up, but he had been handed a lifeline. Riding into Scotland with a group of armed men, whether on a legal hot trod or on a reiving expedition, was always a dangerous undertaking, but riding alone over the border, even if on the March Warden's business, did not involve the same level of risk. So, if that was what Scrope had in mind, he would jump at the chance. He could travel quietly and avoid arousing suspicion, and he had friends over the line who, while they would not appreciate him arriving with an armed band, would welcome him as an individual. Had it been Liddesdale, he would not have entertained the thought, but in Dumfriesshire, he should be safe enough, or as safe as anyone could ever hope to be in that turbulent area. He could not even begin to imagine what the warden had on his mind, but whatever it was, it must be better than facing certain execution for reiving.

"Not at all, my lord," he replied.

"And you know the area well?" the warden asked.

"Very well, my lord."

"As far west as Dumfries?"

"I have been further west than that, my lord," Musgrave said eagerly. He still had no idea of what Scrope was driving at, but was happy to keep the warden away from the subject of the Bewcastle raid.

"Good." Scrope seemed satisfied. "Now, if my information is correct, Lord Johnstone has been reinstated as Warden of the Scottish West March?"

"I believe he has, my lord," Musgrave agreed, and in the interest of trying to get the warden to come to the point, he offered a further comment:

"But I would say that he is finding the Maxwells extremely difficult to deal with."

For years, the wardenship of the Scottish West March had passed back and forth between the Maxwell and Johnstone families, depending on who happened to be on top in their long-running family feud. The centuries-old feud had flared up to new and even bloodier heights a few years previously, when Laird John Maxwell was warden. James VI came to the throne and had the former regent, the Earl of Morton, executed. Maxwell claimed that, as regent, Morton had promised him the earldom when he became king, so when James came to the throne and failed to appoint him as earl, he went on the rampage in east Dumfriesshire and slaughtered a force sent on a judicial raid by King James. He lost the wardenship, which passed to Laird James Johnstone and Johnstone, in turn, promptly used the position as a licence to begin murdering Maxwells. James issued a warrant for Johnstone's arrest and reinstated Maxwell as warden. The new warden immediately took up where he had left off and resumed raiding across the entire area. In the end, James could tolerate the situation no longer. He finally cornered Maxwell and sent him into exile in Spain.

As long as they confined their feuding and raiding to Scotland, it was not really Lord Scrope's concern, but Walsingham, the master spy, had discovered that Lord Maxwell was planning to escape from exile in Spain, and the news was causing Elizabeth's spymaster to have sleepless nights. It was common knowledge that Maxwell had been a staunch supporter of Mary Queen of Scots and had urged James VI to mount an invasion of England to rescue her from her imprisonment by Queen Elizabeth. In the meantime, however, Elizabeth had Mary beheaded, and Walsingham feared that Maxwell was now bent on avenging her with the help of King Philip II of Spain. If true, that spelled grave danger for England. He was convinced that there was something sinister afoot involving Maxwell and the Spanish, and he ordered Scrope, as the March Warden closest to Maxwell territory, to find out what.

The warden was well aware that, in typical Walsingham fashion, he had not divulged the whole story and the spymaster clearly knew much more, but Scrope could make an educated guess at where the heart of the problem lay. King Philip II of Spain had long been planning to invade England and replace Elizabeth with Mary Queen of Scots, and even though

Mary had now lost her head, Walsingham knew that the Spanish threat had not gone away.

As March Warden, Scrope was obliged to follow Walsingham's orders and find out what Maxwell was up to, but the question was how? In view of the diplomatic manoeuvring surrounding the delicate matter of Elizabeth's successor, he dare not send an 'official' English force into Scotland and neither could he approach the Scottish authorities for help. King James might already be aware of Maxwell's intention to return and, in Walsingham's devious mind, may even have sanctioned it. The matter required careful handling and Scrope decided that it was a task best entrusted to one man. He did not have complete confidence in his Captain of Bewcastle – Musgrave would certainly attempt to use the situation for personal gain – but there was no one else available with the necessary qualifications, and all he could do was spell out what the consequences would be for Musgrave if he failed to carry out the task.

For his part, Musgrave was having difficulty containing his curiosity. "So you want me to ride over to Dumfriesshire, my lord?" he prompted.

"Something like that." Scrope was still not prepared to offer a full explanation.

Musgrave tried a different approach. "Do I have a choice in the matter?"

"Indeed you do, Musgrave," Scrope told him with great deliberation. "If you refuse to do exactly as I say, then I shall be obliged to hang you as a reiver."

Chapter 4

In The Borders, the month of March gave way to April but the coming of spring brought no relief from the bitter weather. The incessant rain had stopped, sleet replaced the rain and, inevitably, turned to snow: and the wind continued to bite as ferociously as ever. This morning, the snow had ceased to fall but the sky remained leaden. To the south, the Cheviot Hills bore a heavy covering of white as did the lesser range of hills to the north, and there was more than a dusting on the Liddesdale valley floor.

Alexander Elliot stood on the roof of his tower house and surveyed the snowy Liddesdale landscape. He spoke briefly to the two men standing guard to satisfy himself that they knew their business, and was pleased to see that to combat the bitter cold, the sentries had wrapped themselves in coarse, homespun blankets.

In the weeks since the reiver chieftain had successfully trounced the Hetheringtons in the bloody affray at the border and led his men safely back to Liddesdale after his daring Bewcastle raid, nothing significant had happened, but Alexander knew that it did not do for a reiver to become complacent. As ever, there was danger all around and long experience told him that having successfully routed a hot trod, he must now expect the inevitable retaliation. Happily, on the ride back to Liddesdale, they had encountered no further trouble and he managed to get his wounded men and the bodies of his three dead reivers home – the defeat of the hastily organised hot trod mounted by the Hetheringtons had been bought at a price. Had the Captain of Bewcastle come to the aid of the hot trod, the cost in Elliot blood would have been much higher, but the English officer had simply not been able to resist taking Alexander's bait and had opted to help himself to the abandoned cattle instead. The Hetheringtons, therefore, had little option but to give up and return home to lick their wounds.

An added danger to reivers returning from a raid was falling foul of the Keeper of Liddesdale. The 'Keeper', the King's senior officer in Liddesdale, held an office equivalent to that of a March Warden. Under normal circumstances, he would not bother with a small group of riders who were not in possession of stolen cattle, but on this particular raid there had been a reiver ambush resulting in bloodshed, and Alexander knew better than to take chances. As a precaution, the men sent home with the stolen oats had alerted the rest of Liddesdale, and a large force of Elliots and their allies came to escort him and his men home. To Alexander's relief, the Keeper, never a man to take unnecessary risks, failed to put in an appearance.

The Keeper of Liddesdale and Captain of Hermitage Castle was, as far as Alexander was concerned, a man best avoided when returning from a raid, whether in possession of stolen cattle or not. The current holder of the office was Francis Stewart, 5th Earl of Bothwell, and he had little time for the Elliots. Apart from the trouble that the reiver family's widespread raiding caused to both him and his king, James VI, he bore a personal grudge against the Elliots that went back over twenty years. His predecessor as Keeper had been his kinsman, James Hepburn the 4th Earl of Bothwell, and in an attempt to impress his lover, Mary Queen of Scots, that particular Bothwell had set out to bring the reivers of Liddesdale to justice. In the process, he arrested several leading Elliots and locked them up in Hermitage Castle. Then, in what amounted to a moment of madness, Bothwell challenged Little Jock Elliot to single combat, and although he managed to shoot Elliot out of the saddle, the reiver was far from finished. Little Jock drew a dagger and badly wounded the arrogantly overconfident earl. To his lasting shame, the Keeper had to be borne back to Hermitage Castle in a cart, where he found that the Elliot prisoners had broken loose and occupied his castle. Obliged to negotiate or leave his castle in Elliot hands, Bothwell finally paid a substantial ransom to get his fortress back.

Bothwell lay recovering from his wounds for several weeks, and during his enforced convalescence, a very concerned Mary Queen of Scots happened to be on a visit to Jedburgh. When she heard of the incident, Mary immediately abandoned her regal duties and went to comfort her wounded lover, but on her way back to Jedburgh in foul weather, she fell from her horse into a bog and caught a severe cold. She, too, lay gravely ill for several weeks, which did not auger well for either of their futures.

The legacy of this ugly stain on the Bothwell name still lingered with the current Keeper of Liddesdale and, while he was ever wary of the Elliots, he rarely missed an opportunity to try to bring them to their knees. Alexander knew that Bothwell would definitely not pass up an opportunity to make war on all of the Elliots of Liddesdale, and even though he had not yet attempted to impose his authority, news of the audacious raid so close to Bewcastle would surely spur the Keeper into action. In addition, unlike the Hetheringtons, he could raise sufficient forces to attack a fortified tower house.

In common with many other reiver chiefs, or 'heidsmen', Alexander Elliot lived in a tower house known as a 'pele' tower. Set on a rocky hillock, the tower, built of solid stone, boasted massive walls four feet thick and stood several stories high. The ground floor served as a store with the living quarters on the floors above, and like all such tower houses, it included a right-handed spiral staircase built close to the wall and leading all the way up to the roof. In the unlikely event of an enemy forcing the entrance, the defenders would retreat backwards up the stair with their sword arms free and their left protected by the wall. Entrance to the tower was by double doors at ground level, the outer one being an iron grill and the inner constructed of solid oak reinforced with strips of iron. On top of the tower house, where Alexander now stood, a walkway supported by corbelling jutted out from the walls, and at the sight of an approaching enemy, a beacon lit on the roof gave a warning, or summoned help. Surrounding the tower, a 'barmekin', a wall two feet thick and six feet high, enclosed a compound to provide a safe haven for stolen cattle, or in times of trouble, for the heidsman's riders and their families.

Alexander kept a number of men as guards at the tower at all times, but when threatened with an attack, he could summon the rest of his reiver band and, if necessary, call on the other families of Liddesdale to bolster the defence. His wife, youngest daughter, and two serving girls, also lived in the tower, and unless there was danger of an assault by an overpowering attacking force, they were a permanent presence there. Born and raised in The Borders, they knew what was required of them and they were perfectly ready, willing, and able to fight alongside their menfolk.

Unless the attacking force possessed artillery, there were only two ways of capturing a pele tower. The first method was by 'smoking out', which involved forcing a way through the double doors, setting fire to the ground floor, and waiting for the smoke to force the defenders out of the upper floors before putting them to the sword. The second method required the attackers to climb up the walls, gain access to the roof, overcome the defenders stationed there, and drive a hole in the roof to gain entry. Neither of these methods, however, was easy to achieve, and both could be extremely costly in time and blood. If an overwhelming force armed with artillery attacked a tower, it would be abandoned, but first it would be stuffed full of smouldering peat, making it impossible for attackers to destroy it using gunpowder. Household items lost in the process were easily replaceable; most of them being plunder taken in raids in the first place.

Although crudely furnished, and devoid of luxuries such as carpets and decorations, compared with the houses of the ordinary Border families, Alexander Elliot's tower was comfortable in the extreme. Through centuries of warfare, Borderers had learned that unless they had the resources to build a tower house, building a permanent house was a waste of time. Why go to the trouble of building a solid house only to have it destroyed by an invading army, or even by fellow reivers? For the winter, they constructed houses built with whatever material lay at hand, clay, wood, or stone. Roofed with turf or thatch, they took only a few hours to construct. Having these rudimentary dwellings destroyed in an attack caused little disruption, and Borderers quickly rebuilt them once the raid, or the war, was over. In summer, they put their animals out to graze on the hillsides, and the people tending them lived in makeshift shielings. Larger border towns boasted more substantial homes built using solid oak beams lined with turf and these houses were, apart from the thatched roofs, much more difficult to burn. Even so, these householders, too, hastily abandoned their homes when invading armies or large reiver bands struck. Only 'official' buildings, and the houses of richer and more important landowners, were constructed entirely of stone, but even these were not immune from attack.

When raids by large reiving bands were imminent, Liddesdale families would run for the safety of their heidsmens' towers. Nevertheless, in times of extreme danger from invading armies, a common occurrence during the frequent wars between England and Scotland, the reivers' families fled west taking their beasts, and everything else they could carry, and lost themselves in the Tarras Moss, a desolate marshy area close to Liddesdale that provided an ideal hiding place until the danger had passed. They also employed this tactic during judicial raids when the authorities came to arrest the leading reivers – 'arrest' usually meant hanging without the inconvenience of holding a trial.

None of this, however, was in Alexander's thoughts as he took his leave of the guards and went down to the enclosure to talk to his sons. Malcolm and Robert – never referred to as 'Sandy' and 'Rabbie' within earshot of their mother – were in the compound, where they were supposed to be helping with the preparations for a possible attack. Malcolm seemed to be conscientiously doing as ordered, but Robert, much to his father's annoyance, seemed to be more intent on showing off his fancy pistol to impress the other men present. Alexander spoke sharply to his youngest son and ordered him to put his toy away, and he reminded both of them that they had to remain alert in case of an attack. Such an admonishment by his father in front of the other men, clearly did not sit well with young Robert, but he dare not argue with the heidsman. Satisfied that his message had struck home, Alexander relaxed and called his sons to a council of war with one of his most experienced riders, 'Big Jock' Elliot.

This old reiver was known as 'Big Jock' to distinguish him from the many other Jock Elliots – among the reiver families, names were repeated to the extent where at any given time, one could find a dozen 'Jock' Elliots in Liddesdale. Not that Big Jock needed anything to single him out; at six feet tall and built to match, his size alone was sufficient to distinguish him from most of his fellow reivers. He had proved his bravery and skill in battle on countless occasions and, if that were not enough, he was the son of 'Little Jock' Elliot, the man who had put the 4th Earl Bothwell firmly in his place. That alone was enough to ensure him lasting fame throughout The Borders.

Like his heidsman, Big Jock had seen it all, and done it all. He had followed the reiver's road for forty years and had ridden, plundered and pillaged on both sides of the border, not only with the Elliots, but also with the Armstrongs, the Nixons and the Crosers. He had fought in feuds with half a dozen English reiver families and most of the Scottish ones outside of Liddesdale, and Alexander always included him in his planning to take advantage of his vast experience as a reiver. Big Jock, Alexander knew, would not require him to go into long and detailed explanations. This experienced old campaigner would know exactly what his heidsman had in mind.

The covering of snow had improved the visibility, and while it helped him to spot an enemy from a greater distance, it was not entirely to Alexander's liking. He was aware that he was still prone to attacks from at least two quarters and the light would be of as much assistance to the attackers as it was to him, and more so in the case of the Hetheringtons. Even with the aid of the Fenwicks, they would not dare venture into Liddesdale in daylight, instead, and in true reiver fashion, they would ride at night when the starlight, enhanced by the whiteness of the snow, would produce conditions dear to a reiver's heart, clear moonlight. They might not attempt to attack a stronghold like Alexander's tower, but they would certainly use the light to plunder his lands and reive his cattle.

He sent word to all his riders to be ready to send their families to his tower if a raid seemed imminent, but he kept enough men in strategic locations to make life difficult for the Hetheringtons should they attempt a raid against him. Following the Bewcastle raid and the defeat of their hot trod, the Hetheringtons would be more intent on killing Elliots than in stealing cattle, and he was not about to afford them that satisfaction.

The danger to his tower from the Keeper of Liddesdale, who would certainly be able to gather sufficient force, if not to take the tower, then to make holding it a dangerous and difficult task, was a far more serious problem. It was, however, a distinct possibility, and he outlined to Big Jock and his sons how he planned to combat an attack by Bothwell. What he had in mind was a tried and tested reiver tactic. Instead of strengthening the tower's defences, then sitting back and waiting for Bothwell to attack, he would lay a trap for the Keeper of Liddesdale. It would require the cooperation of the rest of the reiver families in the valley, particularly the Armstrongs, but he would not have the slightest difficulty in obtaining it. He would simply be presenting them with an opportunity they would jump at. Big Jock immediately expressed his satisfaction, and as Alexander began to go into the details of his plan, his sons' resentment at their recent chastisement visibly turned to excitement. Their excitement, however, was short lived.

A shout from one of the sentries on the roof brought them abruptly back to the present. A band of riders was approaching. There had been no tone of urgency in the sentry's voice but Alexander immediately sprang into action. He climbed back to the roof to see for himself what the danger was, but relaxed as he instantly recognised the man leading a group of ten well-armed riders.

Martin Elliot of Braidley and his men, rode through the stout gate in the barmekin to be welcomed as old friends. The fact that Martin had once accepted English money, meant nothing to Alexander; given the same opportunity, any of the Scottish reivers would do the same. Having been at various times in the pay of the English, and having friends in important positions in Edinburgh, this particular Elliot had his ears to the ground on both sides of the border and he frequently picked up snippets of valuable information, all of which he readily shared with his fellow reivers.

After the usual greetings, the visitor came directly to the point. "Something is bothering Jamie and he's getting ready to ride."

Alexander's immediate thought was that James VI, colloquially known as 'Jamie', was about to make a judicial raid on Liddesdale, and that, on top of his other troubles, was something he could well do without.

Like all 'honest' reivers, he cared nothing for the authorities on either side of the border and he would have been pushed to name any influential person other than the actual monarch in either Edinburgh or London. All he knew was that he owed allegiance to neither, nor to anyone who did not bear the Elliot surname. As a young boy, he watched from hiding with his father as James V of Scotland hanged Johnnie Armstrong and several of his riders while they were supposedly under a flag of truce, and he doubted if the current Scottish monarch would be any more trustworthy. His boyhood memories also included the devastation wrought in the borders by Henry

VIII of England in pursuance of his 'rough wooing' policy to try and force through a marriage agreement between his sickly son, Edward, and the infant Mary Stewart of Scotland. These were lessons well learned and he trusted queens even less than he did kings. Only last year, Elizabeth of England had executed her own cousin, Mary Queen of Scots, for supposedly being involved in Catholic plots against Protestant England. Mary, having been deposed and imprisoned by her own people, sought refuge with her cousin, Elizabeth, in England, only to eventually lose her head. Catholic plots or not, in Alexander Elliot's world, executing a family member was treachery of the worst kind. The hated Hetheringtons exhibited a greater sense of family honour.

For reivers on both sides of the border, the family surname was their overriding concern. It counted for more than nationality, religion or social standing, and demanded complete loyalty.

Martin of Braidley, however, had not come to warn of a judicial raid. "As far as I know, we're not Jamie's main worry at the minute. I hear that Maxwell is set to come home, if he's not here already, and Jamie won't be able to turn a blind eye to that. He'll have to do something about it."

Alexander looked up in surprise. "Maxwell?" he said. "I thought that Jamie had him locked up in Spain?"

Martin was sceptical. "Jamie sent him off to Spain to get shot of him, but I doubt if the laird was ever locked up. I know Maxwell and that silver tongue of his, and I'll lay odds that he'll have talked his way out of whatever Jamie arranged with Philip of Spain."

"Och, so we have nothin' tae worry aboot?" Alexander said. Then after a moment of thought, he laughed and continued: "It might be better if Jamie did ride in here. He'd keep the Hetheringtons at home for a wee while."

The Scottish reivers were well used to judicial raids. These royal attempts at restoring order in the Scottish Marches usually resulted in killing members of the worst reiver families, hanging others on the spot, or taking some off to Edinburgh for hanging later. Over the centuries, the reivers had learned how to nullify the effects of the raids, and they never caused more than a temporary setback to their reiving activities. Moreover, as on this occasion, it was impossible for the authorities to keep news of an impending raid from reaching the ears of the reivers and there was always plenty of time to make well-practised preparations.

Alexander had seen it all before and survived, but Martin of Braidley was not finished. “Jamie is more worried about Maxwell at the minute, but that doesn’t mean he’ll forget all about Liddesdale.”

He adopted a conspiratorial manner and continued. “Maxwell will surely have had Spanish help to get home to Scotland and Jamie won’t like that one bit. It’s well known that he has his mind set on being crowned the next King of England when Elizabeth dies, and that can’t be far off now. The last thing he’ll want is for the English to get the idea that he has some sort of a deal going with Philip of Spain, so, when Maxwell comes home, and he will, Jamie’ll be all set to put him back in his place. After that, he’ll want to finish the job and turn his attention to us.”

International politics was something Alexander Elliot neither understood nor cared about. Whether Maxwell came home or not, or if he was in league with Spain, was immaterial to him, but if Martin Elliot of Braidley was concerned, then he would do well to be worried too.

Nevertheless, he still failed to grasp the core of the problem. “Why would he do that if Maxwell is the one he wants?”

“When Elizabeth dies,” Martin said, “and Jamie makes his move for the throne, he’ll have to make sure that The Borders are quiet. He’s bound to hit us sometime, and now is as good a time as any. At the very least, he’ll reinforce Bothwell so that he can hit us hard.”

Alexander now understood Martin’s concern. “So, when Jamie rides after Maxwell, he’ll send Bothwell tae attack us at the same time.”

Martin nodded. “That’s what I’d do if I was him, and I think he’ll hit you first. Having Alexander Elliot’s head mounted on a spike would do him a power of good in England, and force a lot of others to keep their own heads down. We’ll need to be ready, pal, and when the time comes the best thing to do will be for you to sit here as bait while the rest of us set an ambush for him. But, until we have some definite news about what everyone is doing, we can’t afford to take any chances.”

In spite of Martin’s worry about King James, Alexander was pleased that his original plan for dealing with Bothwell would be adopted; and without him having to do anything to set it up. Martin, however, still had one more worry on his mind, and he asked Alexander to help him clear it up.

"It all depends on Maxwell," he said. "Jamie's no fool and my guess is that he'll get Bothwell to strike here when he takes on Maxwell. We need someone to ride over that way to nose around a bit. He can let us know when the laird shows up in Dumfriesshire, and warn us when Jamie rides against him. That'll be the signal for Bothwell to hit us here."

Alexander noted that, in the present crisis, Martin Elliot of Braidley was clearly establishing himself as leader of all the Elliots of Liddesdale, but he could not fault Martin's reading of the situation, and in what was rapidly turning into an extremely complicated situation, Alexander knew that there was no one better equipped to lead them. He would do whatever Martin wanted.

Martin explained what he wanted and Alexander agreed. "I'll send Big Jock," he said.

Martin nodded. "There's no better man."

Braidley and his men rode off to alert the rest of Liddesdale and Alexander pondered over what he had said. He never wasted time thinking about the political intricacies involved, he left that to Martin of Braidley, and he had plans of his own to make. If Martin was correct, and he usually was, the Hetheringtons would be powerless to do anything, but Bothwell was an entirely different proposition. The Keeper would be more determined than ever to exact revenge on the Elliots and there was a real possibility that he would attack the tower, if only to impress King James. If the ambush by the rest of the Liddesdale reivers failed, defending his home would prove to be difficult and he might have to evacuate it. Should that become necessary, he would pack the tower with smouldering peat and, unless Bothwell included artillery in his force, which Alexander doubted because it would slow the attackers down, his tower would remain standing. The interior would inevitably suffer badly from burning, but would be easily restorable once the current emergency was over.

From what Martin of Braidley had said, Jamie and his advisers were intent on making a concentrated effort to put an end to the entire reiving way of life, but he doubted if the many reiver families outside of Liddesdale would agree to cooperate closely enough to defeat such an attack. Most of them were involved in feuds and they would look to their own interests first. Liddesdale, as always, would have to fight on its own, but they had coped before and would do so again. All the fighting men in the valley would join in the battle and if Bothwell burned their hastily constructed homes, then so be it, they would simply build some more. Their families would hide in the Tarras Moss and take their animals, and whatever they could carry, with them. They were reivers through and through, and expected this kind of emergency to arise from time to time. They would quickly recover.

As a precaution, Alexander decided to send his own wife, youngest daughter, and the serving girls to safety across the border where his eldest daughter was married to one of the Storeys in the English East March. There would be no objections; they were a reiver's family and knew what was required of them. He thought about sending Malcolm and Robert as escorts for the women, but changed his mind. He realised that he would be thinking of his sons' safety instead of concentrating on the business in hand. Besides, in spite of his having to issue occasional admonishments, his sons were fast becoming reliable reivers and had done well on the recent Bewcastle raid. Furthermore, for the current problem to be successfully solved, every man must be employed to the best effect.

Big Jock was to ride westward, try to discover when Maxwell came home to Dumfriesshire, and warn Liddesdale when the king rode against him. At that point, according to Martin of Braidley, Bothwell would ride against Liddesdale.

Alexander knew that Jock would have difficulty doing all of this by himself, and he had to have help. It could well prove to be a dangerous game, but he decided to send Malcolm and Robert to give support to the old reiver.

Chapter 5

Don Juan Martinez de Recalde was not at all convinced that sending Spanish soldiers to a desolate god-forsaken part of Scotland would serve any practical purpose. In his view, it was a misguided scheme doomed to failure before it started. A few years previously, he had landed a group of Spanish and Papal volunteers on the coast of Ireland to support an uprising by the Catholic Irish against Protestant English rule, but that expedition had ended in abject failure. The uprising had been defeated and his force massacred, and it was only by the grace of God that he had managed to avoid contact with Queen Elizabeth's navy and escape with his ship, not to mention his life, intact. His fear that the plan proposed by this Scotsman, Maxwell, could not possibly succeed, was based on practical experience.

The Irish expedition at least had the merit of being in support of a devout Catholic cause, but while the Scotsman professed a devotion to the Church of Rome, he was not a Catholic, at least as far as de Recalde understood the term. He simply could not bring himself to trust Maxwell, even if he styled himself as a 'lord, or 'laird'.

Lord or 'Laird' Maxwell he may be, but when de Recalde first met him in Madrid, he quickly reached the conclusion that the man was little more than a common brigand. Thrown out of Scotland as an outlaw by King James VI, he was, in de Recalde's opinion, motivated more by a desire for personal gain than by any semblance of religious zeal. Still, he had somehow managed to convince the ultra-devout King Philip II of his undying support for the Catholic Mary Queen of Scots and his true devotion to the Church of Rome. The fact that Mary was dead, beheaded by her cousin, Elizabeth I of England, seemed not to matter in the least to him.

Maxwell's scheme accounted for only a minor part of King Philip's great enterprise to invade England and depose the Protestant Queen Elizabeth, but, as second-in-command of a mighty armada, already assembled for the great crusade, de Recalde was responsible for organising every aspect of the plan.

From the very beginning, de Recalde found Maxwell frustratingly difficult to deal with. Feeling that he had the complete support of King Philip, the Scotsman demanded that everything be arranged exactly as he wanted it, and he questioned the Spaniard's every move. The relationship neared breaking point when Maxwell was adamant that he would not even consider allowing de Recalde to send a representative, or 'spy' as he termed it, to accompany him to Scotland. This was more than enough to convince de Recalde that his first assessment of the Scotsman's real intentions had been correct, and he refused to turn Maxwell loose on his own with Spanish money in his purse. It was only after he threatened to have Maxwell thrown in prison as a thief that the 'laird' relented. Maxwell was too anxious to return to Scotland and follow his own agenda, which included a return to his main occupation, reiving, to risk losing everything, and he reluctantly agreed to de Recalde's demand.

But, who to send, that was the problem? There was no question of involving the Spanish ambassador in Edinburgh. Diplomatic legations were extremely leaky places and Elizabeth's renouned spymaster, Sir Francis Walsingham, would certainly have agents in and around the Scottish Court. In addition, it was widely known that King James had designs on succeeding Elizabeth and would not welcome Spanish interference. Nevertheless, de Recalde was not prepared to send a sizeable band of troops to Scotland without a trusted Spanish representative to meet them when they landed. He had learned a harsh lesson about such ill-organised expeditions in Ireland and so, leaving Maxwell to fret about the delay, he searched for the right man to send to Scotland with him.

He finally settled on a man he knew to be completely trustworthy. Don Juan Cortez. Cortez was part diplomat, part soldier, part sailor, and he had served with distinction in the long-running war in the Netherlands. Furthermore, he had fought on the high seas against the English pirates and was, on occasion, something of a pirate himself. If need be, he could certainly defend himself, and he was not likely to be fazed by Maxwell's overbearing manner. Just as importantly, he would be well able to cope with the alien conditions he could expect to encounter in Scotland. Having been on a diplomatic mission to England, and although by no means an expert, he had learned something of the country and its people, and he had a reasonable grasp of the language. All of which made him the ideal man for the job.

Cortez, as a loyal Spaniard, did not hesitate to accept the mission. De Recalde briefed him as well as he could, and warned him of his suspicions regarding Maxwell, but could not shake off the feeling that he was sending Cortez to his death.

***

Meanwhile, hundreds of miles to the north, Lord Scrope's still somewhat confused agent, Musgrave, spurred on his horse at a dangerously reckless gallop over ground made rock hard by frost, as he approached the Scots Dyke. He crossed the dyke at breakneck speed and entered the northern section of the Debatable Land, and once over the dyke, he was officially in Scotland. He was extremely thankful that his mount had not slipped on the frosty ground and broken a leg, which would probably have resulted in death for the horse and broken bones, or worse, for the rider. Such an accident would have spelled disaster for his mission before it had started, so he reined in and turned to see where his pursuers were. They had halted at the border and, following what appeared to be a heated argument between themselves, they turned back without attempting to enter Scotland.

The Scots Dyke itself was little more than a ditch with the excavated earth piled up on either side and, as such, it did little to impede the former Captain of Bewcastle's progress. Just under five miles in length, the dyke was marked by stones set at each end, but its real significance lay in what it represented. It divided the Debatable Land in two.

The Debatable Land was a thin finger of land about twelve miles long. It ran in a roughly northeasterly direction and between the rivers Sark and Esk. Rarely more than five miles wide, it was extremely fertile, and had been a bone of contention between England and Scotland since the border between the two countries was first agreed in the early thirteenth century. The final agreement on how the Debatable Land should be divided was eventually signed in the mid-sixteenth century, when it was belatedly recognised that one way of achieving a measure of harmony in the troubled Border Region, was to separate the Scottish Armstrongs from the English Grahams. To mark the arbitrarily arrived-at boundary, the Scots Dyke had been dug, and the authorities in London and Edinburgh congratulated themselves on an agreement well made.

Meanwhile, the reivers on both sides of the border considered the dyke to be no more than a minor inconvenience and they carried on as they always had.

It was still early in the day and there was not a soul in sight, but Musgrave had the feeling that there were hidden eyes watching him. It was only to be expected. A lone rider crossing the dyke from the south was bound to arouse a deal of curiosity, if not suspicion, but he was confident that he was not in danger of attack from a band of reivers. Any reivers watching would, hopefully, have noted that he was unarmed and had been chased out of England by a band of armed men. They would know that the pursuers had turned back on reaching the dyke, which could only mean that they were a troop of English law officers, and for reivers, that would be enough. They would be more interested in why he had escaped from England in such a hurry and what he would do next, than in killing and robbing him of whatever he owned, which on the surface did not appear to be very much. Reivers, therefore, were not his most pressing problem. Instead, the greatest danger he faced came from the 'Broken Men'. These were bands of outcasts from the reiver families and, therefore, without the backing of a family name, or the protection of a heidsman. They were not welcome in any reiver family territory, and so they made their home in the Debatable Land. Owing allegiance to nobody, they preyed on everybody, and would see a lone rider as easy prey. They would kill him for his horse and the clothes he wore.

It had snowed again during the night, in recent years something quite common in The Borders, even in April, and a white carpet covered the whole area. Musgrave knew that he was leaving a clear trail, so he needed to vacate this area as soon as possible. He left the Debatable Land as soon as he could and rode into the low heather-covered hills stretching off to the west, where they eventually became the Galloway Hills. These foothills were ideal summer pastures and contained numerous now-deserted shielings. He decided to search for one where he could obtain at least some shelter from the weather and think seriously about what to do next.

Riding in this rough country would help him to minimise his tracks, but it was a risky business. His horse was sure-footed and experienced in these conditions, but it still required the rider to exercise extreme care to prevent the animal stepping in a boggy hole and breaking a leg. It slowed him down, but it was what any experienced watcher would expect a rider entering Scotland in such a hurry to do. He halted and looked carefully around, there were no obvious watchers but that did not mean that he was all alone in this barren winter landscape. He felt naked without the metal breastplate, steel helmet, and weapons that had marked him out as one of the English warden's men. His only means of defence was a knife known as a 'ballock dagger' nestling in a scabbard attached to his saddle, but that would not be very effective against a man armed with a lance. More than a weapon, however, he would have been glad of a reiver's jack and a large felt hat to keep out the cold. The garments he wore on leaving Carlisle: a heavy woollen shirt; light leather jerkin and homespun trousers, would barely keep out the worst of the bitter cold in daytime, and he could expect to suffer badly during the long freezing nights. He was grateful to have retained his stout leather boots, but his only other means of protection against the weather was the rough horse blanket tied to the back of his saddle. His horse would have to manage without it for a few nights, but the animal was a tough Galloway Nag and would cope better than its rider. Musgrave had left England in too much of a hurry to come properly prepared, but he was a reiver, he would survive.

It occurred to him that tracks in the snow would also work in his favour. They would tell him if any large bands of riders were in the area, from which direction they had come, and where they were going. It would help him to decide whether it would be better to avoid them.

Now out of the Debatable Land, he could dismiss one danger from his mind, and the further he rode the more his confidence grew. He was not yet certain whether he would actually see Lord Scrope's scheme through to the end; that would depend on what he found out about Maxwell, what the laird was planning to do, and who else was involved. And most important of all was the question of what profit there might be in it for him. Scrope had warned him that, having agreed to undertake this task, he must not return to England until he had satisfactorily completed it, unless he really wanted to face the hangman as a reiver, but he was able to put that unhappy thought to the back of his mind. He was confident that if he decided to return to England, even without having completed his mission, his reiver family and friends would protect him from any traps Scrope might have laid for him; but he would be careful not to let the warden take him by surprise as he recently had. He would never be able to regain the lucrative post of Captain of Bewcastle, and that, for Musgrave, was a major concern and required careful consideration.

These thoughts, however, had to be set aside. His reiver instincts told him that he could not expect to remain untroubled for long, and what happened next would depend on who was watching him.

***

In Spain, Laird Maxwell was extremely anxious to be back in his native Dumfriesshire. Following what was, in his opinion, his totally unjustified exile in Spain, he had immediately set about finding a way of escape. On arrival in Madrid, he had immediately picked up rumours that made him stop and think. A large fleet of fighting ships was under construction by King Philip II, and it did not take a genius to guess the purpose of such an armada. Spain was planning an invasion of England, and it presented the Scotsman with a welcome opportunity. The archetypical reiver, Lord Maxwell was one of the most feared raiders in the entire Border Region, and to supplement his ruthless nature, he was renowned for having a silver tongue. He had already inveigled two Scottish monarchs into appointing him as March Warden, both of whom soon came to realise that he was simply using the position to further his reiving activities and to pursue his long-running family feud with his neighbours, the Johnstones. Arrested on numerous occasions, he always managed to talk his way out of the hangman's noose. Yet despite whatever else he might be, he had been a staunch supporter of the deposed, and now beheaded, Mary Queen of Scots.

Having failed to persuade King James to mount an invasion of England to rescue Mary, he had vowed to avenge her himself, but before he could accomplish anything, he found himself an exile in Spain. As things turned out, it was a blessing in disguise. Maxwell somehow managed to charm his way into gaining an audience with Philip II and outlined for the king a scheme for landing a Spanish force in southwest Scotland to support the invasion of England. For his part, if he could return to Scotland, he would raise an army to support them. The king swallowed the bait and agreed that it should form part of the overall enterprise. He even supplied Maxwell with Spanish money to finance the plan.

The only concession he was obliged to make was to agree to de Recalde's insistence on his man, Cortez, accompanying him to Scotland. All that remained was a frustrating wait while arrangements for his journey home were set in place.

Chapter 6

"Ah ken who yon rider is." The problem of who the vaguely familiar rider was, had been perplexing Big Jock Elliott ever since they had watched from cover as Musgrave was chased out of England by a band of Lord Scrope's officers.

"And I ken why he would be leaving Carlisle in sich a hell o' a hurry wi' a bunch o' riders on his arse."

In the clear, cold, frosty air, visibility was excellent and they were able to watch from a distance. They temporarily lost sight of Musgrave when he left the flat farmland and rode into the low grass-clad hills, but they followed his tracks in the snow and he was again back in plain sight.

"Who is he, Jock?" Sandy Elliot asked.

"That's Musgrave, the Captain o' Bewcastle, an' he looks to be on his ain."

Sandy sat upright in surprise. "The same Captain of Bewcastle who nearly nabbed us a few weeks back? I thought he was locked up in Carlisle Castle for stealing our cattle."

"Aye," said Jock. "It's him right enough, but he's a canny wan, an' he must ha' broken oot. But why would he come here instead o' hiding wi' his ain folk, an' why would the warden's riders stop at the dyke when they were close tae catching him?"

As Sandy's brother, Rabbie, listened, thoughts of the Bewcastle raid were still fresh in his mind, and he still felt aggrieved about his father leaving the reived cattle to divert the Captain of Bewcastle's attention. To his mind, they could have kept the cattle and defeated the Hetheringtons irrespective of what the English law officer did, and now he saw a chance to redress the balance. As usual, he acted before thinking. He pulled the wheel lock pistol from under his jack and checked that it was properly loaded.

"That's the bastard that stole our cattle. Come on, Sandy, we'll make sure that he never gets the chance to reive off the Elliots again."

Big Jock held up his hand. "Hold yer horses, laddie, that's no' what we're here for. We'll follow him for a wee while tae see where he goes. Yer faither wisna bothered aboot a few beasties an' neither should ye be."

In The Borders, killing a lone rider without good reason or provocation, even one regarded as an enemy, invariably invited retaliation, and with everything else on his mind, that was not what Alexander Elliot would want, and it certainly was not what the heidsman had sent them here to do. He had taken Martin Elliot of Braidley at his word and dispatched Big Jock with his two sons to watch for any signs of Maxwell, and warn Liddesdale immediately they spotted King James and his army riding to apprehend the fugitive from Spain. The heidsman, however, had also told them to look out for any other strange happenings in the area. In The Borders, it paid to be aware of anything out of the ordinary, and in Big Jock Elliot's mind, a band of English officers chasing the Captain of Bewcastle out of England and then turning back at the dyke, certainly qualified as an unusual occurrence. His orders from his heidsman were to gather information and not get involved in side issues but, as one of Scrope's officers, Musgrave might just have some information about what Maxwell was planning.

Musgrave stopped and looked back, presumably checking to see if he had lost his pursuers, then waited as if considering what to do next. Although he was playing a part in Scrope's drama – his escape from Carlisle Castle had been a carefully staged ploy – there was little play-acting attached to him stopping to think the situation through. He was still undecided about whether he would follow Scrope's instructions to the letter, and he had to make sure of his ground before committing himself to any definite course of action. Besides, he was now certain that someone, he did not yet know whom, was watching him.

The two young Elliots looked questioningly at each other as Big Jock deliberately rode out into plain view, but he explained that he wanted to see if the Englishman bolted at the sight of them.

Rabbie was mystified. "If he runs, we might lose him, Jock."

"Nae matter," Jock replied. "As long as he does'na bother us, we'll let him be an' carry on wi' what yer faither sent us here tae dae."

Following Musgrave had led them into eastern Dumfriesshire, Johnstone territory, but for the moment at least, there was no bad blood between the Johnstones and the Elliots so they could carry out Alexander's orders just as well from here. But they must not stray so far west that they left themselves with a long ride back to Liddesdale with a report that the king was on the move.

Rabbie was clearly not satisfied with Big Jock's explanation, but had little choice in the matter. Away from Liddesdale, and out of his father's sight, he was determined to be his own man and not obliged to heed his heidsman's instructions, which stressed that he and his brother were to follow Big Jock's orders. He looked at Sandy for support but before his brother could join in the argument, Big Jock gave a grunt of surprise.

Musgrave had obviously seen them but did not attempt to run. Instead, he gestured towards a nearby shieling as if inviting them to meet him there. He had recognised the big man in the lead and decided that he did not pose a threat. Finding Big Jock Elliott so far from Liddesdale, and with just two companions, was just as mystifying to him as it was for Big Jock to find him crossing the dyke on his own. He wondered what reason three Liddesdale Elliots could possibly have for being in Dumfriesshire, and he decided that it might prove profitable to try finding out. Not that he really expected to extract much information from this particular Elliot. What he was sure of, however, was that Big Jock and his two companions were here for a specific purpose, and would not divert from it by starting a fracas with him.

Big Jock watched for a few minutes. "He wants tae talk wi' us," he said.

Rabbie brightened up and gripped his pistol. "We have the bastard now, Sandy."

Big Jock decided that it was time to assert some authority. Sandy and Rabbie Elliot might be his heidsman's sons, but their father had made him responsible for them. He spoke sharply. "Yer faither will want us tae hear what he has tae say first."

Rabbie scowled but said nothing. As Big Jock led them towards the shieling, he moved closer to his brother and spoke in a low voice. "Jock is getting too big for his boots and I'm fed up with taking orders from him, we should do for that bloody Captain of Bewcastle once and for all while we have the chance."

Sandy, who possessed a cooler head, had taken notice of his father's instructions. Like it or not, they had to take orders from Big Jock. "We can do for him anytime, Rabbie, don't worry about that, but we should see what he's doing here first, it might be something Da needs to know."

While Rabbie did not easily accept having to do as Big Jock told him, he was perfectly prepared to listen to his brother and so said nothing more. Nevertheless, he kept his pistol at the ready.

Musgrave sat on his horse, seemingly unconcerned as they rode up to the ramshackle shieling. Big Jock addressed him in friendly tones. "Good day tae ye, Mister Musgrave."

"I thought it was you, Big Jock," Musgrave ventured, by way of answering the greeting.

Big Jock sat quietly for some time before saying anything else. Eventually, he spoke. "Ye left England in a hell o' a hurry, Mister Musgrave, and wi' riders after ye."

Musgrave nodded. "I left in a hurry all right, Jock." He laughed. "And they damn nearly nabbed me before I got over the dyke," he added.

"I saw that," said Jock. "But they turned back at the dyke, an' Scrope's riders don't dae that very often."

Having made this pointed comment, he continued before Musgrave could offer an explanation. "I heard that ye had a falling out wi' the warden?"

"I did," Musgrave agreed.

Again, they sat in silence, but the shilly-shallying was proving to be too much for Rabbie Elliot. Woefully unable to control his impatience, he rode up and confronted Musgrave. "I know you, Mister bloody Musgrave, Captain of Bewcastle. You rode with the Hetheringtons when they followed us on a hot trod last month, but you got scared and stole our cattle instead." He laughed at Musgrave. "But you were nowhere near as clever as you thought you were. You got caught and locked up for it."

Musgrave held his temper in check. He could easily have told this belligerent young upstart that, whoever owned the cattle, it was certainly not the Elliots, but neither had they been his, so, instead of arguing with Rabbie, he pointedly ignored the young man.

This tactic did nothing to improve Rabbie's temper and he blindly carried on with trying to provoke the Englishman. "We know you broke out of gaol and now we want to know why you came here and where you're going. If you don't tell us, you won't be joining any more trods against the Elliots."

Musgrave still showed no emotion; as an experienced reiver, he had been in tight spots before. He never turned a hair as he looked at Big Jock. "Who is your big talking young friend, Jock?"

"He's Alexander's son," Jock told him.

Musgrave digested this. "Is he now? It's a pity Alexander didn't teach him to watch his tongue."

Rabbie, incensed at receiving such offhanded treatment, waved his pistol in the Englishman's face. "You watch your own tongue, Musgrave, or I'll blow your bloody head off, you bastard."

Musgrave continued to ignore him and carried on speaking to Big Jock. "The Alexander Elliot I know is man enough to fight fair with a sword or a lance. He never goes around threatening unarmed riders with a fancy pistol."

He spread his arms wide to demonstrate that he was indeed unarmed, except for the dagger attached to his saddle, which, he reasoned, didn't really count.

Big Jock was beginning to lose patience with Rabbie. This was not how he wanted this meeting to develop and, because of the young man's aggressive attitude, he was rapidly losing control of the situation. If they eventually had to kill Musgrave, he would do it himself, but quietly. It was best to avoid having the blame for the death of an Englishman laid at his, or any other Elliot's, door.

He rode over to Sandy and spoke quietly, but firmly. "Calm yer brether doon before someone sticks yon pistol up his arse. If he shoots a Musgrave out here wi'out a good reason, yer faither'll skin us a' alive. He has enough tae bother him wi'oot any mair bad blood."

Sandy, too, had been seething over Musgrave's treatment of his brother, but while in his heart he wanted to stand up for Rabbie, his head told him that Big Jock was right. Killing the Captain of Bewcastle was one thing, and although Musgrave probably no longer held that particular office, neither their father nor Martin Elliot of Braidley would thank them for diverting from their main task to kill the Englishman without first finding out what he was doing, alone and unarmed, on this side of the border. Such an action could easily initiate yet another cross-border feud, this time between the Musgraves and the Elliots, but in spite of this, Sandy wondered at the old reiver's general attitude towards Musgrave. In his view, no one had better reason to kill this Englishman than Big Jock Elliot. It was common knowledge in The Borders that several years ago, Big Jock had married, probably by traditional 'hand-fasting', and he had a son, but now both his wife and son were dead, burned to death in their home during a raid by English reivers led by Sir John Foster, Warden of the English Middle March. Big Jock had himself been on a raid into England at the time, but that made no difference to his quest for vengeance. Foster was more reiver than he was warden, but he enjoyed the favour of Queen Elizabeth, and under the circumstances, there was nothing Big Jock could do about it except wage war against all Englishmen. The fact that he was able to put all that behind him in order to carry out his heidsman's orders, made a lasting impression on Sandy; something he intended to point out to his brother.

In the meantime, if King Jamie rode west with a large army to apprehend Maxwell, someone would have to ride to Liddesdale with a warning for their father, and in that event, he would suggest to Big Jock that they send Rabbie. It would be no more than his brother's behaviour warranted.

Musgrave's remark about how his father would have reacted in a similar situation, left Rabbie at a loss to think of a suitable riposte. All he could think of was to wave his pistol and continue glaring at Musgrave, but the Englishman continued to ignore him and watched in amusement as Big Jock spoke to Sandy. He knew what was bothering Jock, but said nothing.

Sandy rode between his hot-headed brother and Musgrave. "Leave him be for now, Rabbie; you can't kill him here," he said firmly. "And there'll be plenty of other chances."

Rabbies's resentment of the Englishman who had simply dismissed him and caused him to lose face in front of Big Jock was, however, still evident. His pride had been badly hurt, but he knew that he had to follow his brother's advice. He glared at Musgrave with open hatred before backing away with Sandy.

In an attempt to regain control, Big Jock turned back to Musgrave. "For the Captain o' Bewcastle tae be kicked oot o' England in sich a hurry is something I ne'er thought I'd ever see," he said. "I thought that Scrope guarded his prisoners better."

Musgrave laughed. He knew that, in his roundabout way, Big Jock was asking how he had managed to escape from Carlisle Castle.

"I still have a few friends in Carlisle, Jock," he replied.

Big Jock nodded knowingly. It was a perfectly plausible explanation and he knew that probing further into Musgrave's escape, would be a waste of time. "So, what are ye goin' tae dae?"

"I don't rightly know, Jock, but I'll tell you this: I'd be able to think about it a whole lot better if I had something in my belly. I'm betting that you have something in that big bag there that would do the trick."

"Aye I have, right enough," said Big Jock. "And ye're welcome tae a wee bite."

It was out of the question to refuse to share food with someone who did not pose a threat. Border hospitality simply would not allow it, and over the years, Big Jock had learned that there were sometimes better ways of loosening a man's tongue than by threatening him with a pistol. A lesson he hoped that young Rabbie Elliot might soon begin to learn.

Big Jock and Musgrave dismounted and went into the shieling. Sandy and Rabbie had no option but to follow their lead. The construction of these summer shielings followed the same basic principle as most Border dwellings and took only a few hours to erect from whatever materials were available. Occupied by only a few people at a time, who took turns at caring for the animals put out to pasture for the summer, they were small and largely unfurnished. The summer occupants slept on beds made of straw and cooking generally took place outside, but there was provision to light a fire indoors when it rained and, for convenience sake, former occupants often left some rudimentary cooking and eating utensils behind when they departed for the winter reiving season. Unusually for a shieling, this particular one contained a table, an exceptionally well-made and expensive table, clearly reived from a prosperous home. The current 'owner' kept it here rather than in a farmhouse in the hope that it would not be reived or burned in the next raid.

Big Jock kindled a peat fire, retrieved some slices of salted beef from a bag attached to his saddle, and found a cooking pan and some tin mugs. Musgrave was surprised at the large amount of food Big Jock was carrying. These three Elliots were obviously prepared to be away from Liddesdale for some time and he wondered what they were expecting to do here in Johnstone territory, but he knew better than to ask. He made no comment but fetched a few handfuls of snow to melt down for water, and they set about making a thick broth from the meat and some oatmeal.

While this was happening, Sandy and Rabbie could only stand around with nothing to do. Rabbie was still clearly seething with resentment, but Sandy's developing reiver instincts eventually took control and he led his brother outside to care for the horses. Rabbie baulked at caring for Musgrave's animal and stood back while his brother fed it with the others from a small pile of hay stored with the peat against the side of the shieling. If they eventually killed Musgrave, he explained patiently, they would at least have a well cared for horse to show for it. They went back inside. Big Jock looked up from stirring the broth and nodded in silent approval. He served up the thick soup in the tin cups and produced some oatcakes from his bag. In spite of his resentment at having to share with Musgrave, Rabbie was hungry and ate with the others.

When the rudimentary, but nourishing, meal was finished, Big Jock resumed the conversation he had been having with Musgrave. "Weel, Mister Musgrave, are ye ready to tell me why ye rode here instead of hiding wi' yer friends in England? They were quick enough tae break ye oot."

Musgrave decided to stick to the story concocted by Scrope. "Like you said, Jock, I had a falling out with the warden over the ownership of a few cattle. I tried to go home when I got out, but Scrope was too quick for me, and made it too dangerous for my friends to help. They were happy to get me out of the castle but that was all they could do. After that, I was on my own and I had no option but to cross the dyke."

As an old reiver, Big Jock decided not to ask for further details. He had no reason to disbelieve the former Captain of Bewcastle, and he already knew about Musgrave's reiving and the fact that Lord Scrope had caught him in the act. The English warden had usually ignored his captain's misdemeanours in the past, but for some reason, on this occasion had decided to act and had Musgrave arrested, probably as an example to others. It was a story as old as the Borders themselves.

"So, what will ye dae th'noo?"

"I don't rightly know, Jock," Musgrave replied. "I can't go back to England for a while because Scrope will have posted me as an outlaw by now." He cast a glance at the two young Elliots. "And I don't think I would get much of a welcome in Liddesdale."

"No you wouldn't; if you come anywhere near there, you'll get your head blown off!" In spite of having received several hard looks from Big Jock, Rabbie simply could not resist saying something.

"I didn't think so," Musgrave laughed. "In that case, I suppose I'll have to head north or west."

"The Johnstones won't want ye any mair than we do. Johnstone is warden th' noo and he'll see nae reason tae help an English outlaw." Big Jock's voice actually held a note of empathy. He could see no reason for not believing the Englishman and he knew how difficult life could be in The Borders for a man on his own without family backing.

Musgrave nodded in agreement, but did not seem to be too concerned. "Before I had to take my leave of Lord Scrope, I heard that Maxwell might be coming back from Spain. If that's right, he'll be looking for riders so I might try my luck with him."

Rabbie Elliot could no longer contain his impatience. He had thought of a way of making his presence felt. He sneered at the Englishman. "Maxwell is coming back all right, but it won't do you any good, Musgrave. King Jamie will have him hung or back in gaol before you can get anywhere near him."

There was a stunned silence. Big Jock glared at Rabbie and even Sandy was appalled at his brother's lack of discretion. He gripped his brother's arm as tightly as he could and when Rabbie looked round in pain, Sandy held his finger to his lips in an unmistakable gesture for him to keep his mouth shut.

Musgrave had difficulty in preventing himself laughing at Big Jock's discomfort, but he decided not to cause the big man any more pain. "Well, it's good to know that it's true," was his only comment.

As far as Musgrave was concerned, Rabbie Elliot's impetuous outburst did much more than confirm Scrope's information regarding Maxwell's imminent return. The news had penetrated as far as Liddesdale, where they also seemed to know that King James was preparing to ride into Dumfriesshire with an army to send the escaped laird back to Spain, or more likely, to the gallows. He guessed that this might be the reason behind the three Elliots' presence on this side of the Debatable Land. For whatever reason, the Elliots felt that there was some danger to them in the situation and had sent Big Jock to watch, and warn them, if either Maxwell or the king was on the move. Musgrave, however, dare not voice his suspicions. If what he guessed was true, and Big Jock thought that he had worked out the Elliots' plan, Musgrave knew that he would be lucky to escape with his life. Big Jock would not allow him to warn Maxwell. Besides, to add weight to the story concocted by Scrope, he had come unarmed except for the dagger, and he could not go up against Big Jock's lance and the two-wheel lock pistols with that. And that was not the end of his troubles. If Scrope's scheme to get him into Dumfriesshire went to plan, some of the warden's officers would be arriving here shortly to add credence to the story that they were hunting him as an outlaw, and it would not do for them to find him with the Elliots. The wardens's riders would either have to arrest him and take him back to England, or kill Big Jock and the two youngsters to stop them reporting that Scrope's men had allowed him to escape. There would be bloodshed, and as he was virtually unarmed, Musgrave feared that much of the blood spilled would be his.

It was time to leave the comfort of the shieling, but he could not go without an acceptable reason. "In that case, I can't go anywhere near

Dumfries either. Between Johnstone and the king, Maxwell won't get much of a chance to do any riding and I'd only be heading into trouble."

He paused to think of what to say next. He looked at young Rabbie. The lad was obviously still full of resentment and itching to use his pistol, but was getting hard warning looks from his brother. He gazed at the bag where Big Jock kept his supplies. "I don't suppose I can stop here with you, Jock?"

He didn't wait for a reply. "I didn't think so."

He tried to give the impression of a man alone not knowing what to do next but, after another pause, he seemed to have had an idea. "With all that's going on, nobody will be doing any riding, and there might be some easy pickings north of here in Douglas country for a man that knows how to do a bit of reiving. Why don't you come with me, Jock? We could do well out of this."

"I canna," Jock replied, casting a glance at the two young Elliots.

Musgrave nodded his understanding. "Well, in that case I'll be on my way; I want to be well out of Johnstone's way before Scrope tells him that he has me posted, and he comes looking to claim the reward."

Big Jock sensed that he should not simply allow the Englishman to ride away, but he had to balance that with what might happen if he killed a Musgrave. In the end, he reasoned that as long as Musgrave kept riding north, he could do little harm.

"Aye," he said.

The Englishman mounted. The sound of hoofs on the frozen ground carried on the clear frosty air and gradually receded as Musgrave rode off, heading directly north.

Chapter 7

With Don Juan Cortez a constant and irritating presence, Maxwell sailed from Cadiz in a fishing boat ostensibly bound for the North Banks fishing grounds. He would have much preferred to travel overland on horseback to the Duke of Parma's headquarters in The Netherlands, take the shorter sea journey to England, and then ride to Scotland, but de Recalde would not hear of it. He still did not trust the Scotsman, and between Spain and the Netherlands, anything could happen. He decided that, confined to a ship, Maxwell was much less likely to cause mischief.

Eventually, after a hair-raising journey during which they survived a severe storm in the Bay of Biscay, they managed to avoid Queen Elizabeth's navy and sighted the south coast of Ireland. There, they transferred to a captured English pinnace for the last leg of their journey up the Irish Sea. After three days of battling against adverse winds, they sailed into the Solway Firth and entered the tiny harbour at Kirkcudbright. Welcomed at the little fishing settlement by a large band of Maxwell's riders with spare horses, they set off immediately for the laird's castle at Lochmaben. Cortez, ever conscious of the necessity for keeping Maxwell's return, and his presence in Scotland, a secret, became extremely nervous at the thought of their riding openly across what he regarded as enemy territory. Maxwell, however, was very much on home ground and back among friends. He did his best to assure Cortez that this was not Protestant England, but a staunchly Catholic part of Scotland where a Spanish invasion would be welcome. Cortez, however, remembering de Recalde's warnings, was not entirely convinced. Nevertheless, the welcome the returning exile received did help to calm the Spaniard's nerves, but not sufficiently to leave him completely satisfied.

He was still suspicious of Maxwell's real motives, and on arrival at Lochmaben, he began to pester the laird for more detailed information about what he intended to do to support the Spanish landing. For his part, the newly returned exile was not about to divulge anything at all about his real plans to someone he regarded as a Spanish spy, but Cortez was soon making such a nuisance of himself that Maxwell became increasingly frustrated with him. He only just managed to hold his temper by reminding himself that Cortez was nothing more than an interfering nuisance. One that would not prove difficult to dispose of once it became necessary to do so.

To add to Cortez's problems, in The Borders, late April did not always herald the beginning of spring and he was feeling the cold. His attire of doublet and hose was woefully unsuited to the climate, but it gave credence to his guise as a Spanish diplomat completely out of his depth in an alien environment, and the more he learned about Maxwell, the more important keeping up that deception became. In order to keep up the pretence, he ought to remain inside the castle, but it was also essential for him to go out into the bitter cold to keep track of what Maxwell was doing, and to learn more about this part of Scotland.

Lochmaben Castle, Maxwell's current base, was located in the northeast of somewhere called Dumfriesshire, and to Cortez's experienced eye, it appeared to be a solid enough fortress. It compared favourably with many he had seen in other parts of the world, and it was a much more substantial fortification than any he had expected to find in this country. In spite of de Recalde's warning about not trusting Maxwell, he could not help but be impressed by the laird's standing in this godforsaken part of the world. The man appeared to rule over a significant area and Cortez learned that, as well as the castle at Lochmaben, he was also master of two other similar fortresses at Langholm and Caerlaverock; places that the Spaniard had never heard of and with names he could barely pronounce. Although miniscule compared with some of the great Spanish castles, these fortresses provided proof enough of Maxwell's rank and influence in this part of the world. That, and the fact that hundreds of obviously battle-hardened fighting men were rushing to join their laird as soon as he set foot in

Scotland, was almost enough to cause Cortez to question whether de Recalde might have been mistaken in his initial assessment of Maxwell's character. Then something happened to rekindle the Spaniard's suspicions.

Without a word to Cortez, Maxwell rode off at the head of a large group of fighting men. He was gone for two days and, whatever its purpose, it was clear that the expedition was the result of forward planning. The Spaniard's suspicions were again aroused and he became increasingly concerned, and had he been riding with Maxwell during those two days, his concern would have risen to even greater heights. Maxwell was, at that moment, leading a band of close to two hundred riders laying waste to a large tract of territory belonging to the Douglases, the ancient and influential family of the Earls of Angus who boasted of powerful allies holding high positions at court in Edinburgh. Raiding Douglas lands would seem to be a dangerous game for the laird to be playing so soon after his return from exile, but Maxwell was taking a calculated risk. He was simply making a point. Laying a wide swathe of Douglas land to waste was sending a clear message to the entire Border Region; Maxwell was home and back in business. At pains to drive the message home, he looted and burned, reived hundreds of cattle, stole several valuable horses, appropriated carts and loaded them with plunder, and in the process, he spilled Douglas blood. Any semblance of resistance he met with extreme brutality, and he put several leading Douglases to the sword. It was reiving on a grand scale, and once word of it got out – something that would not take long in The Borders – more and more experienced riders would flock to join him.

Maxwell was, of course, aware that the Earl of Angus would retaliate, but by the time Douglas had gathered sufficient force, he was confident that he would be too strong for him. And, more importantly, strong enough to finally defeat the hated Johnstones.

Chapter 8

The day had well advanced by the time Musgrave left the shieling and rode north, as he had told Big Jock that he would. He set a fast pace and rode as hard as he dare on the frozen ground until he was certain that he was out of sight of the Elliots, and then slowed down. He carried on for a little longer in the fading light and then turned west. He was aware that he was leaving clear tracks in the snow, but that was unavoidable; all he could do was to put as much distance as possible between himself and the Elliots.

Night fell and he was obliged to slow to a gentle walk, and eventually stop or risk injury to his horse. The night was already bitterly cold and later the temperature would drop even further. He found shelter behind some boulders, dismounted, wrapped himself in the rough horse blanket, and used his horse's body as shelter from the wind. With his heavy coat and long mane, and with his thick tail turned to the wind, the tough Galloway Nag could tolerate the cold much better than his rider could, and Musgrave hoped that the animal's body heat would keep him alive while he waited for the moon to rise. Without it, he would freeze to death, and if he fell asleep, he would certainly die. He realised that he could not stay here all night, but soon the moon would rise and, even with the overcast sky, there would be sufficient light reflected off the snow for him to move on. The effort of riding over the frozen ground would generate sufficient body heat to ensure that he survived the night. It was an experienced reiver's tactic, tried and tested over many years. After what he calculated to be something under an extremely uncomfortable hour, his horse began to raise his head and sniff the air. At first, he thought that the Galloway Nag had smelled danger, but his reiver's instincts told him that was not the case, and the only other reason for the animal's behaviour was that he sensed a change in the weather. Musgrave was confident that conditions were due to improve, and soon. In the meantime, he had an opportunity to consider his options.

He had gleaned some useful information from young Rabbie Elliot's ill-advised outburst, and he could certainly make an educated guess at a good deal more. But useful to whom, and where did the most profitable use of it lie? He had to apply his mind to answering these questions before making his next move, and he realised that he had to answer them quickly. There was a possibility that, with the improving conditions, he would soon have someone on his tail; and this time it would be someone who was intent on killing him.

He did not think that he had much to fear from Big Jock Elliot. The old reiver had a specific reason for being in Dumfriesshire, and Musgrave guessed that he was there because Alexander Elliot needed someone to provide him with an early warning if either Maxwell or King James posed a threat to Liddesdale. The Elliots and their fellow reivers never left anything to chance and, with such a responsibility on his shoulders, Big Jock would never leave his post to come chasing after a lone English outlaw. Nevertheless, what the two young Elliots, especially young Rabbie, would do was nothing like as clear-cut. Rabbie Elliot clearly felt that he had something to prove to Big Jock and his brother, and Musgrave's easy dismissal of him had obviously caused his resentment to boil over. He had suffered a severe loss of face, and the only way he could regain his pride was by carrying out his threat to 'blow Musgrave's head off'.

The Englishman was not in the least worried about the actual threat. In itself, it meant nothing; he had bested Rabbie Elliot once and could do it again. Next time, however, the young hothead might have the backing of his brother, and that would increase the threat by a factor of two.

He was an experienced enough warrior to be confident that he could cope with both, but what really bothered him was the possibility that if he had to fight the two Elliots, he might end up killing or badly injuring one, or both, and that would certainly have consequences. As Captain of Bewcastle, he would get away with killing an Elliot if he caught him reiving; in that case, he could claim the protection of the law in the form of the March Warden. But killing one of Alexander Elliot's sons while he was ostensibly an English outlaw meant that there would be nothing Lord Scrope could do to help him when Alexander came seeking revenge. Not that it would matter much; in those circumstances, he would never get back to England alive.

He might well have vented his anger on Lord Scrope for having forced him into this position, or cursed himself for having fallen into the warden's trap, but that would be of little help. Nothing he could do would change the situation now, and there was no point in wasting time thinking about it. In The Borders, men in his position did not live for long if they concentrated on what might have been rather than dealing with the reality of the moment.

He examined his options. He could abandon all thoughts of going on to seek out Maxwell and return to hide in England, but that would mean giving up all thoughts of reinstatement as a Queen's Officer. If he went back, he would have to go to Carlisle with a concocted story for Scrope, and he would have to be extraordinarily lucky to get away with that. Future events would almost certainly find him out. A better option was to assess the solid information he already had and take that back to Lord Scrope. So far, he had confirmed that Maxwell was definitely coming back from Spain and may have already arrived, but Scrope would probably already know that. He had also learned that King James was planning a judicial raid into Dumfriesshire to teach Maxwell a harsh lesson, but it did not take a genius to know that this was bound to happen sooner rather than later, and Scrope was no fool. What the warden may not know, however, was that the king's plans were common knowledge in Liddesdale, and that the reivers there were already busy preparing for it. That would be useful information for Scrope, but was it enough to warrant him returning to Carlisle? Definitely not. What he had to offer would not satisfy Scrope, and certainly not Scrope's superior in London, the feared Sir Francis Walsingham.With nothing more than that to offer, Musgrave could expect to be ordered back over the border to discover Maxwell's real reason for returning from Spain, which was why he had been sent to Scotland in the first place. Bearing in mind the problem he had with the Elliots, going back over the Scots Dyke and then returning later, was a dangerous option. Young Rabbie Elliot would soon learn of his return and he would face the same problem attached to killing an Elliot as he did now.

His best option, indeed his only real option, was to carry on and try to find out what Maxwell intended to do now that he was back from exile. To have any chance of achieving that, he must leave now before the two young Elliots broke away from Big Jock and came looking for him.

When he had 'volunteered' to take part in Scrope's scheme and galloped over the Scots Dyke, things had appeared straightforward enough, but within a matter of hours everything had changed, and for the worse. The entry of King James into the picture had complicated matters. On a judicial raid against Maxwell, James would not waste time trying to distinguish between Maxwell's supporters and an English outlaw, and he would deal with both with equal severity. He would not even bother to ask whose neck he was placing in the noose.

Working on the premise that Maxwell was already back in Scotland, Musgrave thought that he could find him easily enough; he would be in his castle at Lochmaben. Of the other Maxwell fortresses, Caerlaverock was located to the south in the remote marshland by the Solway Firth, and Langholm was too far east, where it was vulnerable to attack by the Johnstones on one side and the king on the other. Langholm lay on the route King James would take from Edinburgh and, as such, it would be the first of Maxwell's castles he attacked. The reiver laird must know that the king could not allow him to flaunt his royal authority by returning from exile. He would expect James to come to arrest him, probably this summer, and it seemed clear to Musgrave that the returned exile must have some reason to be confident that he could deal with whatever the king threw at him. He had no idea of what Maxwell had in mind, but he knew something that Maxwell might not. He knew that James was already gathering his forces and was not going to wait for the summer weather, and that piece of information alone, Musgrave thought, would certainly gain him easy access to the laird's reiver band. But he was experienced enough not to play his trump card until he had to.

If he could join Maxwell's band without warning him, he would be well prepared to escape with his life, and hopefully a nice amount of plunder, when King James came riding into Dumfriesshire with fire and sword.

The Elliots would not be the only ones to have noted his flight out of England and word travelled fast in The Borders. Scrope would have sent word to the Scottish March Wardens that he had posted Musgrave as an outlaw, and young Rabbie Elliot would certainly not keep the news to himself. It would soon be common knowledge, and few would question whether he actually was an English outlaw. That alone, he hoped, would be sufficient to gain him entry to Maxwell's new reiver band and ensure that he got a share of the plunder.

The moon rose and bathed the snow-clad landscape in an eerie light. Musgrave remounted and pointed his horse's nose to the northwest and Lochmaben. He would have to be careful to avoid Warden Johnstone; telling Scrope that he would be welcome in Johnstone territory had been true at the time, but now, the possibility of having a price on his head changed everything. If it came to a choice between old friendships and a reward, however small, he knew that he would be the loser. But he considered that a chance worth taking when measured against what he expected to gain.

***

In Carlisle, Lord Scrope finished a letter to Walsingham informing him of the steps he had taken to discover Maxwell's reason for taking the highly risky step of returning from exile in Spain. The Scottish reiver lord must surely know that it was bound to incur the wrath of King James, but Scrope very much doubted that Sir Francis Walsingham would be satisfied with just that. He could expect the spymaster to pester him with more questions and criticisms. The very mention of Catholic Spain was enough to give Walsingham sleepless nights. Through his extensive spy network, he had known for some time that Philip II was planning an invasion of England, and he had stationed ships in the English Channel to warn of a Spanish invasion fleet; but that, Scrope thought, would not totally distract Walsingham's attention from the situation in Scotland.

***

In Liddesdale, Alexander Elliot was busy preparing to meet an attack on his tower house by Earl Bothwell. He could spare no more than a moment to think of his two sons, but he saw no reason for worry. He was pleased with how they were developing as reivers, and he had every confidence in Big Jock.

Had he known, however, that at that very moment they and their mentor, Big Jock, were involved in a highly dangerous escapade initiated by his youngest son, his confidence would have suffered a severe setback.

Chapter 9

As he watched Musgrave mount and ride off, Sandy Elliott, although not as consumed with hatred for the Englishman as his younger brother, was not convinced of the wisdom of simply letting him ride away. He had noted Musgrave's reaction, or more accurately lack of reaction, to his brother's rash outburst. He was sure that the Englishman had gleaned much more from it than was actually said, and Musgrave's rapid departure immediately following the incident tended to lend credence to the argument. Posessing a much cooler head than Rabbie, Sandy was concerned about what the consequences of his ill-advised outburst might turn out to be.

"Are you sure we should be letting him go, Jock?" he asked. "He'll have guessed what we're doing here."

"Aye, he will," Big Jock replied. "But there's nothing we can dae aboot it. We canna kill him here and we canna gang after him. We have tae stop here and watch for yon king, yer faither will need a' the time we can gi' him tae get ready for Bothwell."

Sandy accepted that Big Jock was right. Liddesdale was depending on them. "Ah well, maybe Maxwell'll do the job for us," he said.

"Ah would'na bet on it," Big Jock replied. "Yon Musgrave is a canny wan. Maxwell'll ken that he was hunted out of England and that Scrope has him posted as an outlaw, and he'll take him in wi' his riders jist tae rub Warden Johnstone's nose in it."

"And he'll warn Maxwell that Jamie is coming to take him."

Big Jock was not sure of what use that information would be to Maxwell, who would not expect the king to ignore his escape from Spain, and he decided that the laird receiving a warning of the king's intentions to attack sooner rather than later, would be no bad thing. It would help him make life difficult for James, and if the king was involved in a hard fight in Dumfriesshire, he might be reluctant to face another by going to Bothwell's aid in Liddesdale. Nothing else mattered more to Big Jock, neither nationality, nor king, nor religion, nor even personal survival, nothing other than Liddesdale and the Elliots who lived there.

He thought about saying as much to his two young companions but decided not to, that was not the real point at issue here. The Elliots simply did not divulge information about their activities in the way young Rabbie had; if they did, they would not have continued to thrive as reivers for as long as they had. Big Jock felt that Sandy had learned a good lesson but he was not sure about Rabbie, and he thought that he might have to have a word with the lad's father, his heidsman. That, however, was something he was loath to do. Alexander had put him in charge, and he knew that it had been a grave mistake on his part to assume that both youngsters would know how to conduct themselves in any given situation.

"Any road, it's a' ma fau't," he said to Sandy. "Ah should ha' let Musgrave be, and minded oor ain business."

Sandy, wisely, let that pass. "So, what can we do now, Jock?" he asked.

Big Jock was cursing himself. He had allowed himself to be diverted from his main task by getting involved with Musgrave, and although he felt that his heidsman would want to know about the lone rider, letting anyone at all see them in Dumfriesshire had been a basic mistake.

"We'll move north a wee way to anither shielin'. We have tae gang up there anyway because Jamie'll be ridin' that way. An' we have tae move soon. We canna let anybody see us here."

Rabbie had been standing in sulky silence at the entrance to the shieling with his fists clenched, watching in frustration as Musgrave disappeared into the snow-covered hills. He was still harbouring a deep resentment and trying to think of a way of settling his account with the Englishman. He desperately wanted to go after Musgrave, face him down with his pistol, force him to apologise for treating him with such distain, and only then would he shoot him. Knowing that, for the present at least, Big Jock would not allow him to, added fuel to his resentment but, gradually, he became aware that his brother and Big Jock were talking. At first, he tried to ignore them, but when he heard the name 'Musgrave' mentioned, he was compelled to listen and take notice of what they said. On a couple of occasions, he was on the point of interrupting but something stopped him. He became aware that they were genuinely concerned about the fracas between him and Musgrave, and it dawned on him that he might actually have put his father's plans in jeopardy. He began to realise that his rash attempt to impress Sandy and Big Jock by challenging the Englishman with his pistol, might have seriously backfired on him, but he was loath to accept any responsibility and latched onto the fact that Big Jock had said that he was the one to blame. He consoled himself with the thought that the others should have backed him up and it was they, not he, who had let not only his father, but also the whole of Liddesdale, down. Big Jock and Sandy should have allowed him to kill Musgrave while they had the chance. It helped him to convince himself that he had done nothing wrong and his hatred of Musgrave continued to dwell on his mind. It fuelled his burning desire to make the Englishman pay for making him look foolish.

He reached the conclusion that the only way to retrieve the situation, and restore his shattered pride, was to ride after Musgrave and prevent him from joining up with Maxwell, but it would not be easy to get away from Sandy and Big Jock. He would need to have a valid excuse, and it had to be an excuse that would satisfy not only Big Jock and his brother, but his father as well.

He was sharply aroused from his brooding by Sandy urgently shaking his shoulder. "Come on, Rabbie, we're moving north to a new shieling as soon as it gets dark."

Rabbie realised that there must have been more to the conversation between his brother and Big Jock than he had picked up. "Why are we moving?" He immediately regretted asking the question; it confirmed that he had not been listening.

Sandy knew that his brother's mind was elsewhere and he was tempted to tell him to wake up, but decided to make allowances. "Jamie will be coming that way," he said, "and we have to go at night in case anybody else sees us."

Alexander had already made his sons aware of the necessity of keeping away from prying eyes, and having his brother remind him of it, did nothing to lighten Rabbie's mood. He had not yet learned that it was best to keep his feelings to himself, but on this occasion, it was Sandy and not Big Jock telling him what to do, so he refrained from commenting. The main object of his spite was still Musgrave, but now he began to include Big Jock as well. He convinced himself that Big Jock had deliberately left him out of the discussion about what they planned to do next, and once the thought had crept into his mind, he made no attempt to dismiss it; as his mind continued to dwell on the subject, he even began to think of Sandy as being partly to blame. He was determined to prove himself to both of them, and the only way he could possibly do that was to prevent Musgrave joining up with Maxwell. He decided that at the first opportunity, he would leave them and go after the Englishman with a fully loaded pistol.

Sandy was becoming concerned about his brother's darkening mood, and it was easy to guess what was causing it. He could understand his brother fostering a deep resentment against Musgrave, he too still felt angry about the Englishman's attitude, but if Rabbie didn't soon put all thoughts of the incident behind him and turn his mind back to the task in hand, he would make things doubly difficult for them when King James marched to confront Maxwell. At that stage, all three of them would have to be fully alert if Liddesdale was to receive ample warning.

He knew his younger brother well enough to be able to think of a way of helping him. Rabbie needed something important to do, something to take his mind off Musgrave, and he approached Big Jock with his concerns. Big Jock nodded his understanding. He, too, was deeply concerned about Rabbie's attitude. He would have to rely on both brothers when King James put in an appearance and they needed to keep their minds firmly fixed on what they were here to do. Alexander's instructions were clear. As soon as they sighted the king, one man was to ride back to Liddesdale with the news. The other two were to follow Jamie to make certain that he actually did attack Maxwell, and then report back on his success, or otherwise. That would be the most dangerous part of their assignment as it would be all too easy to become embroiled in the king's battles with Maxwell and be killed or wounded in the process. To guarantee success, it was essential for all three men to remain alive.

"I was thinkin' o' letting him be the wan tae ride back tae yer faither when Jamie comes through," he said.

Sandy was perfectly aware of what his father's orders were and, under the circumstances, Big Jock's comment made eminent sense. He had been thinking along the same lines himself. The least experienced member of the party should be the one to carry the warning, but he was fully aware that, in his present uncooperative state of mind, his brother would not see things in that light. Rabbie would almost certainly regard Big Jock sending him back to Liddesdale as an indication that he was not to be trusted with the more dangerous task, even though it meant crossing the Debatable Land on his own. He might also complain that Big Jock was keeping him out of danger simply because he was the heidsman's youngest son, but in the end, it would not matter which; either way, it would serve to increase his sense of resentment. Sandy, however, hesitated before saying anything of this to Big Jock. The big man might agree with Rabbie and decide that the only alternative would be to send the more reliable older brother to take the warning back to Liddesdale, and that thought was not at all to Sandy's liking. Just like Rabbie, the excitement of the occasion was getting to him, and he was looking forward to seeing what happened when King James attacked Maxwell.

Big Jock suddenly interrupted Sandy's thoughts. He motioned urgently for the two to pay attention. "There's riders comin."

Alarmed by the urgency in Big Jock's tone, Sandy and Rabbie went out of the sheiling and looked towards where Big Jock was pointing. Neither brother could see or hear anything in the gathering gloom, but their instincts told them to heed the big man's warning. Big Jock grabbed his long lance and Rabbie took it as a signal to heft his pistol.

Big Jock shaded his eyes with his hand. "Riders comin' up frae the dyke," he said.

The shapes of several horsemen appeared against the backdrop of snow and quickly became more sharply defined.

"Who are they Jock?" Sandy asked.

"Maybe it's Scrope's riders looking for Musgrave?" Rabbie could not prevent a tone of hopeful anticipation from entering his voice.

"They might be," Big Jock replied. "They have nae cattle wi' 'em, so they're no' riders coming hame frae a raid. But oor tracks'll tell 'em that we're here, so we'll have tae wait and see who they are."

"I'll get the horses," Sandy said. Irrespective of whether the strangers were friendly or hostile, no reiver worth his salt would want to meet them on foot, and the approaching riders would not see anything untoward about finding them in the saddle. They mounted and sat patiently waiting for what they could see was a group of eight riders to reach them.

"What happens if they decide that we might have something worth reiving?" Sandy asked quietly.

"We'll have tae ride," Big Jock replied reluctantly. "We canna dae anything else. They look tae me like Scrope's men and we canna fight them any mair than we could kill Musgrave. We'll split up and meet back here after dark."

Rabbie's excitement was again getting the better of him. He held his pistol ready in his hand. "If it's Scrope's riders after Musgrave, we could go with them."

"We canna." Big Jock's tone betrayed his growing frustration with the young man. "An' dae like yer faither telt ye and hide yon thing until ye have a need of it."

Rabbie cast him a resentful glare. Twice he had been criticised by his father for showing off his precious pistol and he did not like Big Jock reminding him of it. He realised, however, that in the current situation, arguing among themselves would do nothing to help, but he thought that the oncoming riders might give him an opportunity of doing what he had convinced himself he should have done earlier. Kill Musgrave.

As the riders approached, neither side showed the slightest sign of alarm but both were ready for instant action. As they came closer, Big Jock could see that the four leading riders were clothed and armed as English law officers; undoubtedly Scrope's men looking for Musgrave. The other four he was not sure about, but they were obviously also well armed.

Big Jock sensed danger. He turned to the other two. "Get ready tae ride if there's bother. I'll gang north, Sandy, ye gang east, and ye, Rabbie, ride west."

They nodded their agreement. The approaching riders did not seem to be in any kind of hurry, but that, too, caused Big Jock some concern. He had no way of knowing that this was part of the English warden's plan to convince everyone in The Borders, and particularly Laird Maxwell, that Musgrave really was an outlaw. It was all part of a great deception, and the riders would make no real attempt to capture the fugitive.

Then Big Jock remembered how the first group of English law officers chasing Musgrave had given up at the dyke and his suspicions were immediately aroused.

Before he had time to think further, he noticed that the unidentified members of the oncoming group were talking animatedly with the lead rider. Without warning, they broke away from the warden's men, kicked their horses into a gallop and charged at the three waiting Elliots with lances at the ready and yelling at the tops of their voices. The rest of the group, taken by surprise, were slower to react and did not join in the charge. Big Jock reacted immediately. He realised what had caused these four men to charge at them. They had recognised him.

He issued a shout of alarm. "Watch yerselves, they're Hetheringtons!"

Big Jock knew that they must stand and fight. If three Elliots turned tail and ran from just four Hetheringtons, the whole Elliot family would lose face, but there was also the problem of Scrope's men. If they recognised him, they would have to take a hand. Under no circumstances could they pass up the opportunity to kill or capture such a notorious reiver.

There was no shame attached to retreating from the authorities, but first, they had to deal with the Hetheringtons. The odds were not quite even, but Big Jock thought that the two wheel lock pistols would make a difference.

"Stand where ye are and hide them guns until they're near enough for ye tae use them."

He held his lance at the ready and glanced round to ensure that the two others had heard and were complying. Sandy was doing as Big Jock told him. He was clearly tense, but he held the pistol hidden by his horse's long mane and his hand was steady, but there was no sign of Rabbie! Big Jock cursed and his heart missed a beat. In the failing light, Rabbie Elliot was charging straight at the Hetheringtons, waving his pistol.

Big Jock and Sandy had no choice but to ride after him. The sound of a pistol shot rang out. Sandy saw his brother wheeling away from one of the Hetheringtons who was slumped in the saddle. The man's arm hung limply by his side and blood dropped on the ground. Rabbie was frantically trying to reload as well as control his horse but the other Hetheringtons were almost on him with their lances. Sandy rode desperately to his brother's rescue, but Big Jock got there first. He speared one Hetherington rider from the side, but his lance became caught up in the Hetherington rider's jack. He abandoned it and turned his attention to the third enemy. This one was better prepared. He waited for Big Jock to come to him with his lance at the ready. It did him little good. Sandy rode up and fired at point blank range. Even in the twilight, he could hardly miss. The man, driven backwards by the force of the ball, fell from his horse. The wounded man had partially recovered and even though he had only one good arm, he charged at Rabbie who was still trying to reload his pistol. Big Jock rode after him, barged into him and knocked him out of the saddle with a backhanded swipe from the handle of his basket-hilted sword. The fourth Hetherington held back and waited for the English law officers to come to his aid.

In spite of young Rabbie's impetuous action, it was all over in minutes. The wheel lock pistols had made a difference.

Sandy was aware of the shouts raised by Scrope's men. He grabbed his brother's rein and forced him to ride away. Big Jock leaned down and retrieved his lance at the gallop before following. He yelled at the others to separate, and meet back at the shieling after dark. He knew that Scrope's men would concentrate on capturing him. The feud between the Elliots and Hetheringtons was of no interest to them, but they dare not ride back to their warden without having made some effort to kill or capture a reiver as notorious as Big Jock Elliot.

The three Elliots galloped off in different directions. The warden's men made the mistake of trying to take all three. One followed Rabbie and one went after Sandy, leaving two and the surviving Hetherington to chase down Big Jock.

Big Jock, remembering their original lack of urgency, suspected that the English warden's men would not make too strenuous an effort to catch him. They would make a show of following him but would soon give up the chase, and at that point, even the boldest Hetherington could not hope to take on Big Jock Elliot by himself. Soon, it would be fully dark, and he guessed that the officers would not wait for moonrise but go back over the dyke. The two riders chasing Sandy and Rabbie would be wary of those wheel lock pistols and, he thought, they would be under instructions to return to Carlisle tonight. He was now sure that Scrope's men had crossed the dyke simply to make a show of looking for Musgrave, and the Hetheringtons had decided to join in the chase. He decided to lead them on to the north to draw them further from the dyke. His ruse worked; after following him for a while, Scrope's men gave up the chase and he knew for sure that it had all been part of a clever plan to get Musgrave into the Maxwell camp as an English outlaw. In which case, Musgrave was indeed Scrope's spy.

The four Hetheringtons, Big Jock decided, were mere opportunists who had tagged onto the warden's men in the hope of partaking of a bit of reiving, and when they spotted the three Elliots, they couldn't resist the urge to slaughter them. Being at feud with the Hetheringtons, he would probably have done the same, but he could not afford to waste time thinking about that now. There was little daylight left, but he could still make out Scrope's riders joining up again and riding off towards the Scots Dyke. Although Big Jock's earlier suspicion about Musgrave being an English spy was correct, unless the Englishman posed a threat to Liddesdale, it made no difference to him. He had too many far more important matters to attend to; but to be on the safe side, he decided not to say anything to young Rabbie.

He made his way to the shieling, hoping that both his heidsman's sons were there. They were not. The Hetherington that Rabbie had wounded was nowhere in sight, he had somehow managed to recover, remount and ride home, presumably to get help. The other two bodies remained where they had fallen.

Sandy eventually made his way cautiously back and was relieved to find Big Jock already waiting for him.

"Where's yer brether?" Big Jock asked.

"I don't know, he should be here by now," Sandy replied. "The last I saw of him, he was headed west. But he shouldn't be long," he added hopefully.

Big Jock shrugged. "I hope tae God he won't be, we have to be awa' frae here soon. Every Hetherington in England will be heading this way, and we canna be here when they come."

They waited for a while longer but there was no sign of Rabbie. "I suppose he got lost," Big Jock said, more in hope than expectation.

Sandy shook his head. "I don't think so. Rabbie knows how to find his way around at night. He'll follow his own tracks in the snow like I did."

Big Jock considered this, but it was becoming increasingly obvious what had happened. "Yon young dunderhied is awa' after Musgrave."

Sandy, who was well aware of his brother's reckless nature, had to admit that it was the most likely answer. "We'll have to stop him or he'll get himself killed."

"Aye," Jock said sadly. "An if Musgrave or the Hetheringtons dinna kill him, yer faither and Martin o' Braidley will, an' me alang wi' him. Between us, we buggered their whole plan, but we canna dae anything th' noo. We have tae wait on the moon."

Chapter 10

The night grew gradually warmer, as Musgrave had thought it would, but it was still sufficiently cold to make him wish for daylight and the sun. Had he been riding with a troop of his men as Captain of Bewcastle, or on a reiving expedition with members of his family, the cold would not have bothered him in the least, but riding on his own with nothing to do but keep alert, allowed the cold to seep into his bones and cause him to become drowsy. He was cold and hungry and the smell of a peat fire from a local farmstead assailed his nose, tempting him to stop and seek some relief, but succumbing to tiredness and stopping to rest could mean losing his concentration, and that could mean death. There was nothing for it but grit his teeth and keep on. Whenever his mind began to wander, it required an effort to bring his thoughts back to the matter at hand, especially now that he had entered Johnstone territory where vigilance assumed even greater importance. Still, he was an experienced reiver and he had ridden like this before.

In the early hours, his persistence paid off. The clear night sky clouded over as he expected it would. The cold became less intense, but the visibility dropped perceptibly. It forced him to slow down, and although he still felt drowsy, he could look forward to some relief from the cold.

As he had told Lord Scrope, he had friends in the area and he seriously considered calling on them, but recent events meant that it posed too much of a risk. Once news of his flight from England and his posting as an outlaw reached Dumfriesshire, it would spread like a summer gorse fire. The people here, as elsewhere in The Borders, might live as farmers but their principal occupation was reiving, and even those he thought of as friends would not think twice about handing him over to the Scottish March Warden once they learned of his escape from Carlisle. As an English outlaw his capture would fetch a reward, not much of a reward, but enough to make it worthwhile for the little effort involved. Warden Johnstone would then sell him back to the English for a much greater price, but in The Borders, those were the rules of the game.

Scrope would probably release him, but would immediately send him back over the dyke to complete his task, and that, with the extra risks a second ride over the dyke would add to what was already a dangerous enterprise, was a chance Musgrave definitely would not care to take.

Suddenly, something jerked him into full wakefulness and his mind immediately refocused on the present. Without actually seeing or hearing anything, his inborn reiver's instincts told him that there was someone riding close behind him, and Musgrave trusted his instincts. Whoever it was could not be very far away and they were not making much of an effort to disguise their presence. At first, he thought that it was reivers returning from a raid, but as they drew closer and the sound of hoofs became audible, he knew that it was a single rider. There was no question of a reiver riding alone, and any other lone rider at this time of night would be unusual in the extreme. He knew that he himself was an exception to that particular rule, but encountering a second lone rider on a night like this could only mean trouble.

The stranger, whoever he was, must be following him and using his tracks in the snow as a guide. His best guess was that it was one of the Elliots, probably young Rabbie, in which case he had little to worry about, but if it happened to be Big Jock, he would have to be very careful indeed. He employed an old reiver ruse to determine which.

***

Following the fight near the sheiling, Rabbie Elliot was feeling extremely pleased with himself; he was convinced that he had killed a Hetherington with a single pistol shot, and had finally proved himself. Neither Big Jock nor his father could find fault with him now, and Sandy, too, would have to stop treating him as a younger brother.

Back at the shieling, he heard Big Jock telling them to wait, but only one word really registered in his brain: 'Hetheringtons'. The thought of killing a Hetherington drove everything else from his mind, and he failed to give a single thought to the fact that armed with just his pistol and a short sword, he was woefully unprepared for what he intended to do. This, he thought, is my chance to show them all. His blood was up, and without stopping for further thought, he rode straight at the four oncoming riders. He fired his pistol at the first man and turned away to reload.

While he was in the process of reloading, he heard the second gunshot. He looked around and saw Sandy holding a smoking pistol. Big Jock was there as well and there were two Hetheringtons on the ground, one of them with a lance sticking out of his body. It registered that the third Hetherington had merely suffered a wound in the arm and was still in the saddle. One of the men on the ground had clearly been killed by Big Jock but, in Rabbie's mind, there could be no doubt whatsoever that the other dead Hetherington was the one he had shot. He had proved himself a better pistol shot than Sandy and he decided to finish the wounded Hetherington off himself to drive the point home to his brother, but Big Jock had got there first and knocked the man out of the saddle.

In his state of high excitement, and without thinking, Rabbie had been ready to turn his pistol on Scrope's men who were now almost on them and ready to join in the battle, and had Sandy not pulled him back by grabbing his horse's bridle, he would have charged straight at the English officers. By now, both men were screaming at him to ride away and he came to his senses. He realised that he had little choice but to follow the others' example and ride for his life. Even his headlong dash failed to dampen the sense of complete self-satisfaction he felt at his imagined achievement. Had he been prepared to stop for a moment and think clearly, he would still not have been prepared to accept that Big Jock had actually finished off the wounded Hetherington rider for him. In his current frame of mind, there was no possibility of such negative thoughts clouding his thinking, and he galloped gleefully on.

After his initial mad dash, he looked back and saw that there was only one man chasing him, but the rider did not seem to be making any great effort to catch him. He thought of how good it would be to add another kill to his day's work and he began looking for a suitable spot to set a reiver's ambush, something he had learned from his father almost as soon as he was old enough to sit on a horse. Darkness was almost complete before he found a suitable ambush site but by then all sounds of pursuit had faded to nothing and he had to accept that his pursuer had turned back. He felt cheated and decided to return to the shieling as Big Jock had instructed, to receive the congratulations he felt he deserved for killing one of the Hetheringtons. Then, as he turned his horse around to head back, he noticed another set of tracks in the snow leading north.

Musgrave! This was too good an opportunity to miss. He dismissed all thoughts of returning to Sandy and Big Jock and decided to follow the Englishman's tracks. He found where they changed direction to the west and he realised that, in spite of what he had said, Musgrave was riding to join Maxwell. He could not be too far ahead and Rabbie saw what seemed to be a real opportunity to get his own back on the Captain of Bewcastle.

Born a reiver, he had received the best training possible from one of the best in the business, his father. One of his first lessons had been that riding in the dark on unfamiliar frozen ground, could be extremely dangerous and, in spite of his youth and impetuous nature, it had been a lesson well learned. He knew that Musgrave would be facing a similar problem and he had seen how lightly armed and clothed the fugitive was. Making such a hasty escape from Carlisle had left Musgrave only a ballock dagger to defend himself with, and not only that, the Englishman would soon have to stop and try to keep himself warm while waiting for the moon to rise. He, on the other hand, had come much better prepared. Like Big Jock and Sandy, he expected to have to spend several nights in deserted shielings so he wore a stout jack and had a rough woollen blanket rolled up and tied behind his saddle. He also had a large pocketful of oatcakes to sustain him while the Englishman would have to go hungry. He felt too that, unlike his quarry, and with care, he could keep going without waiting for moonrise. Then there was the fact that Musgrave was finding his way and, in the process, left tracks in the snow, clear enough for a blind man to follow. Rabbie believed that he held a distinct advantage over the Englishman, and as long as he could see Musgrave's tracks, he decided that it would be safe enough to keep on with the chase. Even so, he decided that it would be wiser to walk. Not only would it be safer, it would also give him a clearer sight of the tracks. He dismounted, wrapped his blanket around his shoulders, ate some oatcakes and, without a thought for the consequences, set off after Musgrave.

He found the place where the Englishman had stopped to wait for moonlight and he knew that he had stolen a march on his quarry. He remounted, confident that he could catch up with a cold and hungry Musgrave, kill him, and get back to Big Jock and Sandy by morning.

***

Musgrave sat and waited. The sound of the horse behind became more distinct and so, if he could clearly hear his follower, then his follower could hear him. He moved off, picked up his pace, and strained his ears to hear if the rider behind did the same. He did, and Musgrave knew that the man on his tail was not Big Jock Elliot. That old reiver would never have fallen for such an obvious ruse. Neither, he thought, would Sandy, who was much more likely to think before he acted. That left only the headstrong young Rabbie and it gave him a sense of relief. He would much prefer having to deal with the impetuous Rabbie than with the canny old Big Jock, or even the more cautious Sandy.

Whatever he decided to do about the youngster, however, he would have to be quick. He was certain that Big Jock would not be far behind. The old reiver would have missed Rabbie by now, and he simply could not allow Alexander Elliot's son to ride off on his own. He would have to ride after him. Not that young Elliot was in any great danger from Musgrave; the Englishman's reasons for not killing Rabbie had not changed since he rode over the dyke. Killing an Elliot was always a dangerous business, and killing Alexander Elliot's son in particular would certainly lead to serious consequences for both him and his family. His best bet was to lead the youngster a merry dance through these hills and then lose him before going on to Lochmaben and Maxwell.

The game of cat-and-mouse went on for a while, with Musgrave dictating the pace. He slowed down until his pursuer was almost on him and then speeded up. At intervals, he turned off the direct route northwest to Lochmaben, sometimes to the left, sometimes to the right, but always avoiding the scattered farmsteads. His plan was to frustrate young Elliot to the point where he gave up the chase, but Rabbie, demonstrating some of his father's persistence, kept doggedly on. Having previously witnessed the lad's shortness of temper, this surprised Musgrave.

The sky began to lighten and bathed the hills in a watery half-light. There would not be much of a false dawn and soon there would be some murky daylight. The change in the weather became more noticeable as the wind altered direction to come from the west and the cloud cover became denser. Musgrave knew that this wind would carry warmer air, which would cause the frost to give way to a fine mist and the visibility would deteriorate.

When he reached Maxwell's castle, he wanted to be completely alone. The laird would certainly have scouts in place who would get the impression that the second rider was actually there to support the first, and his pretence of being a lone English outlaw would lose credibility.

Time, he thought, to lose his pursuer for good and, if possible, do it while they were still in Johnstone territory. His nose located a farmstead and he turned off the track to his left. With the smell of burning peat acting as his guide, he drew close to where he knew there would already be a profusion of animal tracks in the snow around the farm buildings. His intention was to mingle his tracks with them and confuse the man following him. Any competent reiver would eventually pick up where his tracks departed from those around the farm, but it would take time and, in the meantimc, Musgrave would have doubled back in the direction Rabbie would least expect, and get behind his pursuer. By the time young Elliot managed to work out what had happened, Musgrave planned to be long gone. With the sunrise, a thaw would set in and the tracks in the snow would begin to disappear.

It was a good plan, one that had worked before, but almost as soon as he decided to set it in motion, it began to go badly awry. As he neared the farmstead, a cacophony of shouting mingled with screams shattered the silence of the hills and an ominous glow appeared in the sky accompanied by fingers of fire. There was clearly more than a peat fire burning. Musgrave dismounted and hid in a clump of gorse. He realised that he had stumbled on an event all too familiar in The Borders; a group of riders had descended on the farmstead in the early hours, stolen what stock they could find, ransacked the house and set fire to it before preparing to ride off. The thatch was soon fully ablaze, the loot loaded onto packhorses, and the reiver party was leaving, driving the stolen cattle before them. They were heading his way and he could see that it was a relatively small band, not more than twenty riders he thought. There could be little doubt about who they were and what they were doing. They were Maxwells, riding to join up with their recently returned reiver laird, and taking the opportunity of raiding a Johnstone farmstead on the way. They would take the spoils to Lochmaben as a homecoming present for Maxwell.

Musgrave quickly moved further back into the cover of some bushes to get out of their path, but then realised that young Rabbie Elliot would not be so careful. He could easily ride right smack into them and, in spite of everything, he was worried about the lad's safety. The Maxwells killing him was of no great consequence to Musgrave, but even though he was not to blame, given what had happened yesterday he doubted if the Elliots would see it that way. He expected Big Jock to arrive on the scene at any minute and he reluctantly decided that his safest course of action would be to warn the rash youngster before he ran into the Maxwells. It would also not do him any harm with the Elliots to have it known that he had saved Alexander's son from death at the hands of a band of Maxwell's reivers. He mounted and rode carefully away to avoid alerting the reivers to his presence and when he was sure that he was out of earshot, he picked up the pace and headed back to his original path, hoping to intercept young Rabbie.

He heard the sound of approaching hoofbeats and backed off the path. Wary of that wheel lock pistol, and the lad's propensity to use it, he wanted to make sure that he gained an advantage over the youngster. His pursuer came into sight, but to Musgrave's surprise, it was not Rabbie but his brother, Sandy.

He had thought that Big Jock would have been the one to come looking, but now he realised that sending Sandy first made sense. Realising that Rabbie would be more willing to listen to his brother than to him, Big Jock had sent him on ahead. The canny old reiver had not made the mistake of both of them riding together, but he would not be far behind. As far as

Musgrave was concerned, none of this mattered now. Rabbie was somewhere up ahead and in danger of running into a Maxwell reiving party. That he was an Elliot would not mean a thing to these men. When Rabbie blundered into them, as he was sure to do, their first thoughts would be to kill him on the spot. In a way, that would suit Musgrave; with Sandy to witness that he was not the one to kill Rabbie, he would not have to take the blame, but he feared that the Maxwells might be shrewder than that. It all depended on how young Rabbie reacted. If his first thought was to raise his pistol, he was dead, but if he recognised that fact and acted sensibly, the leader of the reiver band might consider it worthwhile taking him back to Maxwell as a hostage. It would make a nice addition to his offerings to the laird.

Musgrave had to admit, however, that in Rabbie Elliot's case, acting sensibly was a remote possibility, and his concern added an urgency to his tone as he rode out of hiding and quietly called a warning. Sandy turned round in surprise, and recognising Musgrave, came galloping back to the Englishman, levelling his pistol and demanding to know where his brother was.

Musgrave held up his arms in submission. "If he's not careful, the Maxwells will nab him. There's a band of them up ahead on a raid, and the young fool will ride right into the middle of them."

Sandy, taken aback, took a moment to think. "Why would you care whether the Maxwells get him? They have no quarrel with us. You'll have to do better than that, Musgrave." He meaningfully raised the pistol. "Now tell me what's really going on."

"Why don't we wait for Big Jock?" Musgrave replied calmly. "He'll be here any minute."

Sandy again showed his surprise, but while he was still thinking of a suitable retort, Big Jock rode up. Before Sandy had an opportunity to say anything more, Musgrave quickly explained about the reivers and his fear that Rabbie would fall into their clutches.

Sandy's anxiety for his brother was clear. "He's lying, Jock," he said. "I think he killed Rabbie himself and is trying to blame the Maxwells." As soon as the words left his lips, however, he knew that the argument did not stand up.

Big Jock made a quick mental assessment and decided that Musgrave was telling the truth. He grasped the gravity of the situation and immediately put everything else out of his mind while he searched for a solution. Dealing with the Englishman would have to wait. First, they had to prevent his heidsman's son falling into the Maxwell reivers' hands.

They were about to ride after the youngster when a pistol shot shattered the peace of the early morning.

Chapter 11

Juan Martinez de Recalde had little time to spare for worrying about how the Scottish element of King Philip's great enterprise was faring. As second-in-command of the mighty armada, he was fully engaged in preparing a vast assortment of ships for sea. Scattered across a number of ports, not only on the Spanish Atlantic coast but also at several points in the Mediterranean Sea, the fleet numbered well over one hundred vessels, and he had a myriad of details to supervise. Powder and shot had to be procured, allocated, and loaded. Copious quantities of stores had to be sourced, and loaded. Each ship was to have a unique station in the fleet, which required that every ship's captain receive an individual briefing.

This last item was, in de Recalde's opinion, of equal importance to all the others combined. King Philip's grand scheme for the invasion and conquest of England depended on the armada sailing as an integrated fleet with every captain knowing not only his own ship's unique station, but also the details of the overall plan. Most important of all, each one must be aware of his duty in every foreseeable event. In de Recalde's considered opinion, the senior commander should carry out such a vitally important duty in person, but he knew that was not practically possible. The man chosen to lead the great armada, the Duke of Medina Sidonia, was not an experienced admiral. King Philip alone had decided who should have overall command, and he had based his decision on rank and social standing rather than on experience. Much to de Recalde's dismay, the Duke had never before commanded a fleet of any size, never mind the greatest armada ever assembled.

To his credit, Medina Sidonia himself knew that he was not suited for such an important command, and when he received his commission he wrote to the king asking to be relieved, but once Philip had made a decision, he was not disposed to alter it. As a result, de Recalde was responsible for overseeing every aspect of Philip's great crusade.

He could have accepted the situation with an easier mind if he had absolute faith in ultimate victory, but he had misgivings; he had detected a major flaw in the king's plan. Philip had decreed that the armada would sail up the full length of the English Channel, link up with the Duke of Palma's army in the Netherlands, and then cover Palma's soldiers as they made the short crossing to invade England. To de Recalde, this was a recipe for disaster. They should launch the invasion as soon as they sighted the English coast. Battling their way through the relatively narrow English Channel while under attack by Elizabeth's navy, was fraught with danger. A more practical alternative, de Recalde argued, would be to take the Isle of Wight or one of the deep-water harbours on the English south coast. This would provide them with a secure base and tie down the English fleet as they tried to dislodge them. In the meantime, Parma could land his invasion force from the Netherlands on England's east coast, virtually unchallenged. He put his ideas to Medina Sidonia only to have them immediately dismissed.

While the armada remained in port, it remained effectively under the direct control of the king, and the commander's sense of duty forbade him from questioning Philip's orders, so, in spite of his fears, de Recalde had little choice but to keep his opinions to himself. Once at sea, however, and clear of the king's immediate influence, he fully intended to make his feelings known to Medina Sidonia in much stronger terms.

Then there was the scheme hatched by the Scotsman, Lord, or 'Laird', Maxwell, to land Spanish troops in Scotland and launch another invasion from there. To de Recalde, this seemed like a completely futile waste of time and resources. He had, of course, followed his king's orders and set the scheme in motion, but privately he had already given up the landing on the Solway coast as a lost cause. Once the armada was at sea, this was yet another concern he determined to raise with Medina Sidonia.

His conscience occasionally bothered him for leaving the man he had sent to watch Maxwell in a difficult, and highly dangerous, position, but he had chosen Juan Cortez for his resourcefulness and was confident that the experienced soldier would somehow manage to survive.

***

Like de Recalde, Alexander Elliot too, was a busy man. Preparations to deal with a punitive raid by Earl Bothwell demanded his complete attention. He had dispatched his wife, younger daughter and the serving girls to safety with his married daughter in the English East March, and given them a small escort of trusted riders. They had orders to ride swiftly and take a route that would keep them well clear of the Scotts on one side of the border and the Hetheringtons on the other. He retained enough of his men to form an effective defensive force for the tower and dispatched the rest to join Martin Elliot of Braidley, who was busily assembling a sizeable army of Elliots, Armstrongs, Nixons and Crosers to ambush Bothwell when the Keeper of Liddesdale rode to attack a seemingly lightly defended target, Alexander Elliot's tower house. Braidley had considered calling for help from outside Liddesdale, but with blood feuds rife among the other reiver families, he decided that this could prove to be more trouble than it was worth.

Liddesdale would, as usual, stand alone, and leave those outside to fend for themselves. With the Tarras Moss denied to them because of its proximity to King James's route to and from Dumfriesshire, the Liddesdale families dispersed into the Cheviot Hills.

Alexander's preparations were almost complete when Martin Elliot of Braidley rode up to the tower with some unwelcome news.

"I heard that Jamie's sending soldiers to Hermitage to reinforce Bothwell, so we'll have a harder fight on our hands than we thought."

Alexander's heart missed a beat. He tried to hide his anxiety but it was not easy. "Will Jamie give him artillery?"

If anything went wrong with Braidley's ambush, and Bothwell broke through with artillery, his tower would face a bombardment it might not be strong enough to resist.

Martin set his mind at rest. "I very much doubt it, but it would be better for us if he did. It would slow him down, and that would give us a better chance to ambush him."

The remark gave Alexander at least some relief. "So we have nothing to worry about," he said.

"Maybe." Braidley again sounded sceptical. "When Jamie hears that we gave Bothwell a bloody nose, he might decide to come and try to make us pay for it on his way back to Edinburgh when he's done with Maxwell."

A worried Alexander asked if they should change their plans, but Braidley felt that they could still cope. "As long as we get plenty of warning from Big Jock!"

"We will," Alexander assured him.

In spite of his anxiety, he had complete trust in any ambush laid by Martin of Braidley. It was a tried and tested reiver tactic, and in the past, the Liddesdale reivers had used it more successfully than most. It had worked before and he was confident that it would work again. Frequently outnumbered, the reivers had learned not to fight pitched battles against superior forces. Instead, they had perfected the art of laying a trap for their enemies. Alexander could already envisage the scene unfolding. The Liddesdale reivers would appear to be gathering at his tower. Bothwell would sense an opportunity and ride to attack, taking a direct route from Hermitage Castle. Once he was committed, and his force strung out in a long line, a group of Liddesdale men would make a show of attacking him head on, as if to prevent him reaching his objective. Bothwell would have to retaliate in force or lose face in front of his men. At the opportune moment, the rest of the reivers would spring from cover and set about slaughtering his rear. Caught between two attacking forces, Bothwell would become embroiled in a defensive battle where neither his cavalry nor his artillery, if he deployed it, would be of any real practical use. If the fight seemed to be going against them, the reivers could simply ride away, but by then they would have inflicted sufficient damage on the Keeper of Liddesdale to oblige him to abandon his attack and return to Hermitage Castle to lick his wounds.

Martin of Braidley left, and Alexander turned his mind to the changing situation. A second attack mounted by the king would complicate things, but he had every confidence that Liddesdale would once again survive. Much depended on getting ample warning of the king's approach, but he had complete trust in Big Jock. For the first time since they left the tower, however, he wondered if it had been wise to send just two men, Malcolm and Robert, with Big Jock. At the time, three men acting as scouts seemed ample, but their task had suddenly become more vital than ever and Alexander Elliot did not take unnecessary risks. He decided to send reinforcements to the three scouts. He knew that Big Jock would be difficult to locate, the old reiver knew all there was to know about keeping out of sight, but he sent a pair of riders anyway with orders to find the scouts and warn them of the new danger to Liddesdale from Bothwell and King Jamie. It was more important than ever to know when James rode back out of Dumfriesshire, and if he was heading for Liddesdale. Once the riders were satisfied that all was well with the scouts, one man was to return to the tower with the news and the other would remain with Big Jock and his sons.

The riders left and Alexander settled down to wait. He waited for two full days, which he felt was the minimum time the riders would require to find Big Jock, relay his orders, and for one of them to ride back. When a rider failed to return in this time, he still felt that he could wait a further day before becoming concerned. By the fourth morning, however, his anxiety was beginning to show. Then there was a shout from the tower. A rider was approaching. He dashed up to the roof. One of his riders was at last returning and Alexander heaved a sigh of relief.

His relief was short lived. His riders had searched east Dumfriesshire and even the the Debatable Land from end to end, but failed to find Big Jock and the heidsman's sons. The rider reported that they had heard stories of a lone rider crossing the dyke chased by a band of the English warden's men, and there had been a fight with some Hetheringtons. They had found the frozen bodies of two Hetherington riders, but they could find nothing to show who had killed them. One of them, however, had died from a pistol shot.

The only indication of what might have happened to Big Jock and the heidsman's sons were tracks in the snow leading first to the north and then turning west, but with a thaw setting in these were fast disappearing and were difficult to follow.

Chapter 12

The first vestiges of daylight began to appear over the Dumfriesshire hills. The wind now came from the warmer west. As the temperature rose and the cold became perceptibly less severe, the frost gave way to a fine mist, as Musgrave expected it would.

Nevertheless, the sound of the pistol shot carried clearly through the damp air and galvanised Sandy Elliot into action. He knew that there could be only one reason for that shot; his brother was in trouble and his immediate reaction was to ride to Rabbie's aid. Big Jock grabbed his rein in an attempt to restrain him, but he pulled free and galloped off in the direction of the shot. The big man had no option but to ride after him.

Musgrave felt an urge to follow but thought better of it and remained where he was. He did not have the same deep concern for Rabbie Elliot's welfare and was experienced enough to think his options through before acting. He clung to his usual practice of analysing the situation, assessing the possible dangers, and seeking out what advantages, if any, the situation held for him. The sound of hoofs receded and there were no further pistol shots. He heard shouting but it was too far away for him to make out the words, and following a period of silence, he felt certain that both of the Elliot brothers were by now either dead or taken as hostages by the Maxwells, although he very much doubted if the same fate had befallen Big Jock. Unlike the two youngsters, that old rogue was far too canny to ride into a trap. He would ride hard, but if he failed to catch up with Sandy before he ran into the Maxwell reiving party, he would stop, proceed with extreme caution, and then watch and wait from hiding.

If the two Elliots were dead, Big Jock would have little option but to take the news back to Liddesdale and hope that Alexander Elliot didn't hang him, or worse, for failing to save his sons. On the other hand, if one or the other still lived, he would watch and see how the situation developed. It was what Musgrave himself would have done. He felt that his own wisest course of action would be to simply ride away, forget all about Lochmaben, and rethink his options. He was sure that Big Jock would not have taken everything he told him about his flight over the dyke at face value, and if he had mentioned his suspicions to Alexander's sons, they might in turn pass it on to Maxwell. Providing, of course, that the reivers allowed them to live and took them to Lochmaben. Sandy might be wise enough not to say any more than he had to, but he feared that the unpredictable young Rabbie would not be able to resist telling Maxwell all about their suspicions regarding the Englishman – if only out of sheer bravado – and that would cause him problems when he rode in to try joining Maxwell's riders. The more he thought about it, however, the less likely that possibility became and, on reflection, he doubted if Big Jock had said anything much to his two charges. For one thing, the old reiver would not want to give Rabbie further cause to fuel his already boiling resentment, something that could be detrimental of the task that brought them into Dumfriesshire in the first place.

As he sat and pondered, a more positive thought came to him and he saw a possibility of turning this setback to his advantage.

A thaw was setting in and the snow was already beginning to melt. Musgrave was not exactly sure, but he thought that the year must have advanced almost into May. Spring was late this year, even for The Borders. Now that it had finally arrived, the tracks would disappear with the snow and all evidence of his dash over the Scots Dyke, and his ride to join Maxwell, would disappear. Assuming that Big Jock had not voiced his doubts about him, then young Rabbie would tell Maxwell the original story about him being an outlaw; having an Elliot vouch for him would provide all the proof he needed.

It all depended on there being at least one Elliot still alive, and there was only way of finding out. He gathered his reins and rode cautiously after Big Jock and Sandy.

***

By now, Alexander Elliot was, unusually for a reiver, an extremely worried man. He was completely at a loss to know what might have happened to his sons, and the fact that Big Jock was also missing meant that something quite serious must have occurred, something serious enough to cause the ultra-reliable Big Jock to abandon his post. The report regarding dead Hetheringtons and tracks in the snow leading westwards, served to reinforce that assessment and increase his sense of anxiety but, thankfully, his rider had not brought news of any dead Elliots and that gave him some cause for hope. He questioned his man again but learned nothing new. He had to accept that Big Jock and his sons were not where they were supposed to be, and his best guess was that, for whatever reason, they had ridden west, further into Dumfriesshire, probably into Johnstone land, or more worryingly, into Maxwell territory.

His every instinct urged him to gather a band of his best riders, follow the tracks in the snow and find his sons, but that was not possible. With Bothwell poised to attack at any minute he had to remain in Liddesdale with every rider he had. It was not easy, but he forced himself to accept that there was more at stake here than even the fate of his sons. The whole of Liddesdale was in danger. He sent the rider back to rejoin the other man on watch for King James, but they were also to carry out another search for any signs of Big Jock and ride back immediately they found anything. If they found nothing more, he knew what he had to do.

If his sons had not returned by the time Bothwell had been beaten off – as an Elliot he did not contemplate defeat – he would take as many men as could be spared and ride into Dumfriesshire, himself. By then, however, the task would have become more difficult. With the thaw, the tracks in the snow would have completely disappeared, but even so, he was determined to discover what had happened his sons.

***

The sound of hoof beats ahead reached Rabbie Elliot sooner than he expected. Something must have caused Musgrave to slow down. His heart raced. His quarry was almost in sight and he had him now! Overflowing with confidence, he drew his pistol, checked the load, and galloped forward. If he could kill a Hetherington from the back of a galloping horse, he could deal with the Englishman with equal efficiency. Too late, he realised that the hoof beats were not Musgrave's. They belonged to two men bringing up the rear of a band of riders, and before he had time to react, Rabbie was already in trouble.

The two Maxwell riders were fully alert. Acting as rearguards for the reiver band, they had heard his noisy approach and were ready for him. Seeing someone charging at them out of the early morning mist waving a pistol, meant only one thing to them; this could only be the leading rider of an attacking force with the rest following close behind. Their first duty as rearguards was to warn the rest of the band, and they yelled out a warning, "Johnstones", then turned their attention to Rabbie. They were wary of that wheel lock pistol but they were well-practised reivers and knew what to do. One man rode straight at the rider he thought was part of an attack by a group of Johnstones and thrust at him with his lance to draw his fire. Still confused, Rabbie raised the pistol and fired, but his aim was unsteady and the ball flew wide. Taking advantage of the diversion, the second Maxwell rider got behind Rabbie and delivered a smart blow to the side of his head from a stone-headed club. Out cold, young Elliot fell from his horse. Had he not been wearing his steel bonnet, the blow would have ended his life.

If the shouts of the rearguards had not alerted the rest of the reiver band, the pistol shot certainly had. A rider, clearly their leader, followed by several of his men, galloped out of the mist just as the man with the lance was about to finish the unconscious Rabbie off.

The newcomer quickly ordered the man with the lance to hold. "We'll use him for bait."

They led Rabbie's horse away and tethered him out of sight. The unconscious young reiver remained lying out in the open while they set an ambush for the Johnstone riders they thought would be arriving at any minute. When the Johnstones saw their fallen comrade they would stop and the Maxwell ambushers would attack. They had not long to wait. To their surprise, it was not a party of Johnstones who rode into their trap but the lone figure of Sandy Elliot.

Sandy was much too overcome with anxiety for his brother to notice anything amiss. He dismounted, ran to his brother's side and was relieved to find that Rabbie was still breathing. When he looked up, he found himself surrounded by a group of heavily armed riders. Two of them came at him with drawn swords in their hands and murder in their eyes, clearly intent on killing two men they thought were hated Johnstones. Their leader, however, had other ideas.

"We'll take them tae the laird. He's no' killed a single Johnstone since Jamie sent him tae Spain."

Sandy realised what was happening. "We're not Johnstones," he shouted in alarm. "We're Elliots from Liddesdale and we're looking for an English outlaw."

The leader of the Maxwell band thought for a minute, then burst out laughing. "That's a guid yin," he said, and the rest of the reivers joined in the laughter.

The laughter subsided and he grew serious. "I heard aboot this Englishman, but wha' wuid he be doing' here, and what wuid Elliots frae Liddesdale want wi' him? Ye're Johnstones right enough and we're takin' ye tae Laird Maxwell. He kens well what tae dae wi' Johnstones."

Rabbie was beginning to recover, but his brain had yet to register what was happening. Both Elliots were disarmed and had their hands tied firmly behind their backs. The leader inspected the two-wheel lock pistols. Like Alexander Elliot, he had little time for firearms but thought that these would fetch a good price at the market in Dumfries. Sandy continued to try convincing his captors that they were not Johnstones, but his protests continued to elicit nothing but laughter. They were set back on their horses and led away to where the remaining reivers were guarding the stolen cattle. The rest of the reiver band reset their ambush in case of a Johnstone attack, and when this failed to materialise, they rode off towards Lochmaben and Lord Maxwell, taking their captives with them.

From his hiding place in a clump of gorse, Big Jock watched the scene unfold. It was now full daylight and even through the fine, damp, mist that persistently still clung to the hills, he was able to see everything that happened, and he picked up enough of the conversation to realise that his heidsman's sons had managed to get themselves into deep trouble.

When Sandy had broken loose from his grip on the reins, Big Jock had little option but to follow him, but all those years of raiding and night riding had imbued him with a true reiver's instinct, and in spite of the temptation to hurry, he rode with his usual high level of caution. He had not gone far before the sound of gradually decreasing hoofbeats told him that if he continued at the same cautious rate, he would not catch up with Sandy before he made contact with the Maxwell reivers. Those same years of hard-earned experience, however, warned him to stick to the tactics he knew best; he could not help Sandy and Rabbie if he, too, fell foul of the Maxwell reivers. He searched around and found a spot where a clump of bushes had prevented the snow from collecting on the ground. Here, his tracks would not show and he turned off the path. He rode to the top of a nearby hill and assessed the available cover. In this part of the gorse-covered hills, stands of timber were few and far between, but he was confident that the acres of gorse combined with the clinging mist, would serve him just as well. He heard the shouts of the two Maxwell guards and felt a rare moment of panic. If the Maxwells mistook them for Johnstones, the two young Elliots were as good as dead, but his reiving experience continued to force him to be patient. He dismounted, tethered his horse, went forward on foot and found a concealed spot from where he could see most of what had befallen his two careless young kinsmen. Under different circumstances, he might have felt that it was no more than they deserved, but as he watched them being tied up and taken off to Lochmaben, he put such thoughts aside.

For the first time in his life, Big Jock Elliot experienced a feeling approaching helplessness. He was a man born for violent action and even in the midst of the most heated battle, he could make instant life or death decisions, and had never been known to get one wrong. When faced with a problem that could not be solved using a sword, lance, or established reiver tactics, however, he felt out out of his depth. He knew that he had to think clearly, but it took a supreme effort of will for him to resist riding recklessly after the Maxwells and their two hapless prisoners.

Slowly, he forced himself to assess the situation rationally. He realised that, for the moment at least, it would be futile to try to rescue the pair. The Maxwell reivers would still be wary of an attack by the Johnstones and be well prepared. He could follow them to Lochmaben and try to persuade

Maxwell that his captives were not Johnstones but Elliots; being one of the best known of all Border Reivers, he was confident that someone there would recognise him. But would they listen to what he had to say? The problem was that while the Maxwells had no active quarrel with the Elliots, in his current situation the laird could never allow Sandy and Rabbie to ride back to Liddesdale. They would have seen and heard far too much for him to contemplate letting them go. Worst of all for Big Jock was that riding back to Liddesdale for help was not a viable option. The valley was gearing up for an attack and would not have men to spare to ride into Dumfriesshire and take on Maxwell and, in any case, by that time it would probably be too late for Sandy and Rabbie. He thought about approaching the Johnstones for help but dismissed the idea. They would be preparing to join up with King James. For Laird Johnstone, the situation offered a perfect opportunity for him to strike a decisive blow against Maxwell and plunder his lands after James returned to Edinburgh. He would have no time to waste on two foolish young Elliots from Liddesdale.

Nevertheless, even though for once in his life Big Jock was at a loss to know what to do, his instincts did not completely desert him. His senses told him that there was someone behind him. He gripped his lance and turned slowly round to face an attack.

Chapter 13

Laird Maxwell was more than satisfied with the progress of his plans, but it was a satisfaction accompanied by a definite feeling of relief. His return from exile had been most opportune and he was sure that he could not have stayed away any longer. Had he done so, the Johnstones would have gained control of the whole of the Scottish West March, and that would have amounted to total disaster for him. In the event, his timely arrival had blunted Johnstone's ambitions to replace him as the dominant force in the March. And his audacious raid into Douglas territory had produced the desired effect. Men were flocking to join him, and not just Maxwells. He was recruiting riders from many other West of Scotland reiving families including Irvines, Bells, and Scottish Grahams, all drawn to him by the promise of seemingly unlimited plunder. It would not be long before he was strong enough to wipe the Johnstones from the face of the earth and become the undisputed strong man of the Scottish West March, if not the entire Border region.

King James would have no option but to reinstate him as March Warden, and from there he could plunder at will on both both sides of The Border. But that was not the limit of his ambition; thoughts of how he planned to deal with King James also made him smile quietly to himself. He still harboured a deep resentment against James Stewart for not attempting to free his beloved Mary Queen of Scots from Elizabeth's clutches. Mary was dead now, and while there was nothing he could do about that, he could still properly avenge her death, and he was determined to make James pay for having abandoned her.

Maxwell was aware that the king would already know of his return from Spain and be determined to do something about it. He would attack in force, a force that would certainly include the Johnstones, but in his view, it would do James little good. The king would have to overcome his three solid fortresses at Langholm to the east, Lochmaben north of Dumfries where he had set up his main headquarters, and Caerlaverock in the south, close to the Solway Firth. These strongholds were so spread out that even with the largest army he could muster, the king could not possibly attack all three at once, and Maxwell planned to use the fact to ride James, his army, and the Johnstones, ragged. He did not expect it to be easy – nothing in The Borders ever came easy – but he was confident that he would win through in the end. Especially as he had an ace up his sleeve that James knew nothing about: The Spanish!

He congratulated himself on the success of his ploy to persuade King Philip of the advantages of landing a force in Scotland to attack England from the north. Once the landing took place, James would have to abandon his attempt to arrest him, and divert his army to repel the Spaniards.

James had designs on the throne of England when Elizabeth died, and he might initially think that a Spanish conquest of England would help his cause. With Mary Queen of Scots dead, James would be Philip's obvious choice to become the new Catholic monarch. Maxwell, however, gambled that James was astute enough to know that under those circumstances, he would never be anything more than Philip's vassal, and as such, easily replaceable. No, Maxwell thought. James had more to gain from waiting for Elizabeth to die, and his stock would rise among the English Protestant nobles if he helped to defeat the feared and hated Catholic Spanish. Besides, any king worthy of the name would have to respond to the threat of an armed invasion of his country by a foreign power; no monarch on earth could do any different and hope to remain king for long. The more he thought about it, the more Maxwell was convinced that James would act to repel the Spaniards first, and then turn his attention to him. At that point, the laird intended to turn the situation to his advantage.

In Spain, Maxwell had promised Philip that he would raise an army to support the Solway landing, and the king gave him Spanish gold to help him achieve it, but it was a promise the Scotsman had no intention of keeping. He would keep the vast majority of his own forces intact until James was embroiled in a battle with the invaders, and then ride to his king's aid. For maximum effect, both the king and the Spaniards should arrive in Dumfriesshire at roughly the same moment, but Maxwell realised that this was highly unlikely. James had only to march from Edinburgh, while the Spanish had to undertake a long and dangerous sea voyage to reach the Solway. In all probabability, the king would arrive in Dumfriesshire first, but Maxwell had confidence in the strength of his three fortresses. They would hold James up until the Spanish landed and the king was obliged to turn away from him to deal with an invasion of his country.

The effort required would badly weaken James, and only when Maxwell judged that the king was in danger of receiving a severely bloody nose, would he ride to his aid. James could not possibly ignore such a demonstration of loyalty and would be obliged to reward his loyal laird. The badly weakened king would return to Edinburgh to regroup and squeeze as much political capital as possible out of his triumph over the Spanish, which would give Maxwell a breathing space long enough for him to consolidate his position as the undisputed top dog in the west of Scotland, and possibly the whole Border Region. And especially, to strike a decisive blow against the Johnstones.

That was the basic plan, but there was something else. He was confident that at least one of the three ships coming to land the invasion force would be carrying Spanish gold. Gold that would be necessary to consolidate their conquest of England.

In spite of his ambitions to rule over The Borders, and in spite of his resentment at King James for having abandoned Mary, Maxwell was still a reiver at heart, and he was determined to appropriate that Spanish gold for himself. He had not yet quite worked out exactly how to do it, but he was confident that he would find a way.

His only potential problem was Cortez, the Spanish spy foisted on him by de Recalde, but this he regarded as a mere annoying inconvenience. The Spaniard was nothing more than a foppish diplomat, and could be easily dealt with when the time came. In the meantime, his reiver army was growing. He knew his riders cared nothing for their laird's personal ambitions and had their minds set on plunder, which suited him very well.

The noisy arrival of one of his scouts brought his thoughts back to the present. A band of riders was approaching Lochmaben to join him. They were bringing stolen cattle and other plundered goods, but, more importantly, they had two prisoners who must be captured Johnstone riders. Maxwell smiled with satisfaction. Yet more men were coming to join his growing army, and bringing him the added bonus of Johnstone prisoners.

He would make a very public show of hanging these Johnstones in the marketplace at Dumfries to show his contempt for the current March Warden, and as a demonstration of what fate awaited anyone who dared to oppose him!

***

Big Jock turned to face whoever was behind him, holding his lance at the ready. He knew better than to move too quickly, in a clump of gorse it was all too easy to become caught up in the prickly spikes, thrown off balance, and find yourself at an immediate disadvantage against your attacker. His senses told him that only one man was watching him, but he was much too experienced to leave anything to chance, especially as he was still in danger of being captured, or killed, by the Maxwells; that was something he had to avoid at all costs.

To his relief, however, he had nothing to fear from the man striding out of the mist with his hands in the air, and a wide grin on his face. Musgrave!

Once the Englishman had made up his mind to follow up the possibile personal advantages he had discovered in the situation, he rode after Big Jock and soon found the most likely place for the big man to veer away from the tracks left by Sandy and Rabbie. He followed to where the old reiver had tethered his horse and dismounted. He could easily have ridden to where Big Jock was in hiding, but two men hiding in the gorse were in far greater danger of discovery than one.

From where he stood, he did not have a view of what was happening, but the sound of raised voices carried to him. Much of what they said was indistinct, but one word rang out clearly, and it was enough to give him cause for concern. The Maxwells had mistaken the two young Elliots for Johnstones and there was every chance that they would kill them on the spot, which could completely ruin his hastily revised plans. He knew that he should wait for Big Jock but decided to take a chance and move a little closer. From there, he could see a little of the action and pick up the last part of what was being said. It was enough to bring on a sigh of relief. The reivers were taking the Elliots to Maxwell as hostages, and that suited him fine. As he heard the reiver party set off for Lochmaben, he returned to where he and Big Jock had tethered their horses. Then he moved forward to find the old reiver.

Jock lowered his lance as the Englishman approached his hiding place. Together they walked back to where they had left the horses.

Musgrave was on the point of making some flippant remark at Big Jock's expense but the look on the big man's face forced him to think better of it. He quickly removed his broad grin and simply sought confirmation of what he had already guessed. "So the Maxwells have them both and think that they're Johnstones."

Big Jock didn't ask how Musgrave knew. He simply leaned despondently on his lance. "Aye."

Musgrave made a vain attempt to cheer the big man up. He knew it would be of little use but he said it anyway. "Well at least they're still alive."

"Aye," Big Jock replied. "But they might be better aff deed, an' me alang wi' 'em."

From his demeanour, coupled with his brief responses, Musgrave suspected that Big Jock would really prefer not to talk, but he continued to press on with the conversation. He had devised a scheme that he was anxious to set in motion before the big man snapped out of his current mood, which, in all likelihood, would be quite soon. It took a great deal to drive men like Big Jock Elliot to lose heart and even then, the effects were likely to be extremely short-lived.

"I know that this is a bad situation, but we can still do something about it, Jock." He decided to refer to 'we' rather than 'you' in order to give the big man the impression that he had an ally.

"I dinna ken whit we can dae, I canna ride hame tae Liddesdale for help, they'll be busy wi' Bothwell. Anyhow, it wuid tak too lang, an' I canna leave the hiedsman's bairns alane fae Maxwell tae hang."

Musgrave noted that Big Jock had not asked him why he should be concerned about Maxwell hanging a couple of Elliots, which meant that the big man was still totally absorbed in trying to find a solution to the problem. Hearing Big Jock refer to his two young kinsmen as 'bairns' was a measure of how hard he was taking their current plight.

The old reiver eventually came to a decision. "I hef tae ride tae Lochmaben. Somewan there is sure tae ken who I am an' I'll be able to tell Maxwell that they're Alexander Elliot's sons. He'll have tae believe me."

Musgrave had expected that sooner rather than later, Big Jock would have to resort to this. It was time to step in with a proposal of his own. He waited until he judged that Big Jock was about to mount and ride after the Maxwell reivers, before saying anything. Then he spoke urgently.

"That's no good, Jock, you know as well as I do, that even if you did manage to convince Maxwell that those two young fools are really Elliots, he still won't let any of you go. He might hold the three of you for hostages, but he won't think any more about killing Elliots than he would Johnstones. Either way, you won't be able to warn Liddesdale when King James rides into Dumfriesshire. And that's what you were doing here in the first place, wasn't it?"

"Aye," Jock reluctantly admitted.

"So you have to go back home soon; the weather is changing fast and the king will be on his way here before long," Musgrave argued. "You can't risk letting James ride into Liddesdale without warning them. And anyway," he added pointedly, "those two were bound to get themselves into trouble someday soon."

Big Jock found himself torn between completing the task his heidsman had sent him to do, and his urge to try to rescue Sandy and Rabbie from Maxwell or, at least, convince the laird that they were Elliots and not Johnstones. He had to admit that what Musgrave said about the pair eventually getting into trouble was right, they only had themselves to blame, but he doubted if their father would see it that way. And there was something else of vital importance to Big Jock: they were Elliots, his kinsmen, and whatever they did he would never abandon them. He was in an impossible situation, and much as it went against the grain, he said to the Englishman:

"What else can I dae?"

Musgrave had the opening he wanted. Now that he had managed to manoeuvre Big Jock into a position where he had to ask for advice, it was time for him to make his move. "Hold on a minute, Jock, there might be another way out of this."

Big Jock failed to keep the hopeful look from his eyes as he waited for the Englishman to explain what he meant by his remark. For his part, Musgrave stood and pretended to be mulling something over in his mind, as if he was still adding some details to a solution he had just thought of. In fact, he had already decided on his course of action, but was not about to let Big Jock know that.

Finally he explained: "I thought that I might ride back to watch for the king and warn Alexander for you, but I'd have to ride close to the Debatable Land and either Scrope or the Broken Men would have me before I could do anything. But seeing as I was going to try and join Maxwell anyway, why can't I be the one to tell him that the pair he captured are Liddesdale Elliots and not Johnstones? He'll see no reason for me to lie to him, and even if he doesn't let them go, he'll hold them for ransom instead of hanging them. They'll be no worse off than they would if you ride in there, and at least you'll be able to go back to watching out for King James."

Big Jock could see some logic in what Musgrave proposed, but the ease with which Scrope's riders had given up the chase had convinced him that the man was an English spy, and he was still highly suspicious of the Englishman's motives. He was well aware that whatever Musgrave did would be for personal gain, but that was only to be expected and he could accept it.

On the other hand, what Musgrave said did offer him a glimmer of hope, but he needed further proof before he could bring himself to trust the devious Englishman. "Why wuid ye bother yer heid aboot a pair o' Elliots. An' dinna try tae gi' me any stories aboot bein' an English outlaw. I ken well enough that ye're a spy for Scrope."

Musgrave had already guessed that Big Jock would see through his pretence before long, but was not in the least worried. He smiled inwardly to think of how Lord Scrope would react to him actually revealing the true purpose of his wild ride into Scotland to a well-known reiver, but that was what he fully intended to do. In spite of his long experience as a March Warden, there were things that Scrope still failed to understand about the reiver mentality, while Musgrave on the other hand, had been born to it. He knew that it mattered little to Big Jock Elliott whether he was a spy or not, as long as he confined his snooping to Maxwell. He also knew that if the old reiver suspected for one minute that he posed the slightest danger to Liddesdale, he would probably be dead by now, so he was confident that his secret was safe with Big Jock.

"You're a canny old fox Jock," he conceded. "I knew I couldn't fool you for long. But I want you to know that I don't care for the idea of being a spy. It was the price I had to pay for my life when Scrope found out what happened to the cattle you and Alexander reived from under his nose at Bewcastle."

Big Jock grunted; Musgrave's explanation carried a definite ring of truth, but he was still far from being satisfied. "That dis'na tell me why ye would want tae help the Elliots when wan of them wants tae kill ye."

Musgrave had a ready answer. "I told you that I'm not happy about spying for Scrope, and if Maxwell catches on to what I'm doing as easily as you did, I'll be leaving there quicker than I left England. But if I don't do what Scrope wants, I can't go back home, so I might as well take a chance to do a bit of riding for Maxwell and then get out quick. Anyway, if Alexander Elliot knows that I helped his sons, I'll have one friend this side of the border. It's my only way out."

Musgrave could see that Big Jock was thinking about this, so he laughed and added a rider. "Besides, I want to see the look on young Rabbie's face when he sees that it's me who came to help him."

Big Jock was still far from satisfied, but could see no better way out of his dilemma. "I suppose I have tae trust ye. But listen guid, Musgrave, if ye're playing games wi' me, ye'll be sorry ye ever met me."

It was the one major flaw in Musgrave's scheme. He knew that Big Jock meant every word, and if need be, he would certainly carry out his threat. He had lied to the big man about almost everything he had told him, and that would not help his cause if things went wrong, but like all men of The Borders, he lived by his wits and was determined to come out of this with something to show for his trouble. He doubted if Maxwell would catch him out as quickly as the old reiver had. Big Jock had witnessed his dash over the dyke at first hand and could read the situation accurately, but in The Borders, stories were usually enhanced with the telling and by the time the news reached Maxwell's ears, Musgrave was confident that he would be portrayed as a notorious English outlaw. And if young Rabbie Elliot told the laird everything, it would reinforce that impression. He still harboured hopes that he might be able to gain a share of the plunder he expected Maxwell to amass, and it remained his principle objective, but should that fail to materialise, his best course of action would be to try to gather some useful information to take back to Scrope. If the information proved to be of vital importance, it might just get him reinstated as Captain of Bewcastle and he could go back to using the position to hide his private reiving activities.

Better still, if he could somehow manage to return with a valuable hostage like one, or hopefully both, of Alexander Elliot's sons, he could claim a handsome reward as well. At least that was his hope, and all he had to do was to carry it off and, more importantly, remain alive while doing so.

He mounted. "I'll do what I can," he said to Big Jock, "but you know very well that I can't make any promises."

As he watched the Englishman mount and ride after the Maxwell raiders, Big Jock was not at all happy about placing his trust in Musgrave, but he was at a loss to think of what else he could do.

Chapter 14

Don Juan Cortez stood and gazed out over the loch from the ramparts of Maxwell's impressive stone fortress at Lochmaben. In the courtyard below, 'the laird' was holding court with a group of his closest allies, most of whom appeared to be Maxwell's kinsmen. To the Spaniard, there was nothing at all unusual about this. Appointing relatives as advisers was a generally accepted practice, and even more so here in Scotland where, as Cortez was beginning to learn, family ties ran deep. Such a scene would not have seemed out of place in any nobleman's castle courtyard, either in Spain or anywhere else in the world for that matter, and Maxwell himself would certainly have fitted in.

Now that the weather had improved, the laird had appeared this morning looking every inch a fashionable gentleman. He had discarded his rough reiver clothes and replaced them with a linen shirt with ruffs at the collar and cuffs, a woollen doublet, panelled trunk hose, and soft leather bucket-topped riding boots. This elegant ensemble, all of the highest quality, was finished off with a tall felt hat and a silver hatband. The entire wardrobe, Cortez suspected, had been acquired by Maxwell in Spain, and probably paid for by King Philip.

In spite of Maxwell's noble appearance, however, the Spaniard was becoming increasingly concerned about the prospects of success for the planned Spanish landing in Scotland. He was mindful of de Recalde's suspicions about Maxwell's real intentions, and current events seemed to be adding weight to those concerns. The former exile, now back in his home territory, had resumed his position as 'Laird' and was certainly acting the part. He was assembling a formidable force of obviously experienced fighting men, but Cortez was beginning to question whether its sole purpose was to support the Spanish landing. No preparations whatsoever seemed to be in hand to receive the landing force, and when questioned, none of Maxwell's men seemed to know anything at all about Spanish troops landing in Scotland. To a man, they seemed to have only one thing in mind: the plunder they expected to win from raiding with Laird Maxwell. Cortez demanded an explanation and Maxwell told him that for the moment, it was wiser to keep his real intentions hidden from his men. They had joined simply for the plunder they hoped to gain, and would have no interest whatsoever in either helping Spain or defeating England. If he told them that they had to wait for a Spanish landing before getting their first sight of any loot, many of them would become impatient and probably desert. This, Maxwell said, was the reason for his raid into Douglas territory; he needed to show his men that there was plunder aplenty to be had by joining him.

When the time came, Maxwell promised Cortez, he would show them some of the gold given him by King Philip and promise that it would be theirs once Spain had conquered England. That would be enough to make them fight alongside the Spanish.

Nevertheless, while this sounded logical enough, Cortez was not convinced. Any leader worth his salt would have discussed his plans with at least some of his senior men. Otherwise, how could they make any meaningful preparations? To add to his doubts, although he was clearly a foreigner and in league with their leader, none of Maxwell's senior lieutenants showed the slightest interest in Cortez's presence here and he could not help but wonder why. He reached the worrying conclusion that Maxwell must have concocted some, completely false, story about him.

Considering what he had seen and heard since his arrival in Scotland, Cortez was convinced that de Recalde was right. Maxwell was ideed playing a devious game.

His thoughts were interrupted when yet another group of armed horsemen came clattering into the courtyard. The newcomers were driving a small herd of cattle, and leading two men who were clearly their prisoners. Curious, Cortez descended from the ramparts and stood concealed in a doorway to see what was happening. Word went around that the prisoners were Johnstones, but Cortez heard them protesting loudly that they were not Johnstones, but Elliots.

Their protests, however, were completely wasted on Maxwell. He simply stood with a satisified smile on his face as the hapless pair were marched off down to the castle dungeon.

From snippets of conversation picked up from Maxwell's men, the Spaniard had a vague idea of who the Johnstones were, but he knew nothing at all about any Elliots. Soon after landing, he learned that the Johnstones were traditional enemies of the Maxwells, and he guessed that these Elliots must be friends. Otherwise, the two prisoners would not have claimed to be members of that particular family. For a moment, he thought that they might be English, but he soon realised that the idea did not stand up. Everything he had seen and heard made him doubt that two Englishmen would have ventured into Scotland alone, so they must be Scottish. The Johnstones, he knew, were Scots, and Maxwell seemed delighted to have two of them as his prisoners. He made no secret of the fact that he intended to make a public spectacle of hanging the hapless pair in the marketplace at Dumfries simply on the supposition that they might be Johnstones. The Spaniard approached Maxwell and asked why he would want to do such a thing to men not even suspected of a crime, and was told that it would serve as a warning to any who thought to oppose him, especially any other Johnstones. This last assertion by the laird added some disturbing weight to Cortez's suspicions; Maxwell was more intent on hanging two of his fellow countrymen than in defeating the English!

To the cultured Spaniard this was not only uncivilised, it was also a basic mistake. He had travelled the world in the service of Spain and had witnessed more than his share of barbaric behaviour, and he had learned by experience that actions such as the one Maxwell proposed, rarely frightened anyone. All they ever achieved was to invite retaliation. He could not imagine that Maxwell would not be aware of this, and he came to the worrying conclusion that it was exactly what the laird wanted.

So, was this what his erstwhile ally was really planning, provoking an attack by his traditional enemy now that he had gathered sufficient strength to ensure a decisive victory? Cortez had the worrying thought that it was, and that could only mean that Maxwell had no intention of supporting the planned Spanish landing in Scotland.

Then, to further convince Cortez that he was right, he heard something even more disturbing. The younger of the two protesting prisoners proclaimed loudly that they were in Johnstone land chasing after an English outlaw. The prisoner's assertion shocked Cortez to the core. The very idea of an Englishman, outlawed or not, being here in Scotland at this time could only mean one thing. He was one of Walsingham's spies! If Maxwell really did intend to keep his promise to King Philip and support the Spanish landing, then an English spy in the area was something that he could not possibly tolerate.

Cortez, however, hesitated before approaching Maxwell and demanding some straight answers. He was under no illusions that if the Scotsman finally admitted that it was all a sham then he, Cortez, would be in an invidious position. He would be of no further use to the devious laird. Nevertheless, the Spaniard doubted if Maxwell would kill him out of hand; whatever else he might think of this devious Scotsman, the laird was extremely astute when looking out for his own interests. To Cortez it seemed all too clear: Maxwell would keep him alive until the Spanish landed and then use him in some underhand way to help him steal the Spanish gold he must know would be on one of the ships. Only then would the Scotsman finally dispose of him. He decided that his wisest course of action was to keep his suspicions to himself. Letting Maxwell know that he was harbouring serious doubts about his true intentions would solve nothing, the Scotsman would simply deny everything and keep him under close supervision, too close to allow him the freedom he needed in order to do something to help his country.

The Spaniard had already made up his mind that Maxwell's promise to Philip had been nothing more than a ruse to help him escape from exile in Spain, when something happened to reinforce his fears.

A pair of Maxwell's scouts rode into the compound at Lochmaben with yet another prisoner. Cortez watched from a distance and was appalled by what he witnessed next. Maxwell walked across to see who this new prisoner was, no doubt hoping that it was another Johnstone, but much to the Spaniard's surprise, Maxwell appeared to greet the newcomer like an old friend. The Spaniard was learning that it was never prudent to take Maxwell's outer appearance and gestures as an accurate indication of what the Scotsman was really thinking, but it was obvious that he had met this new arrival before.

Maxwell looked the man up and down for a minute and laughed before he spoke. "Good day to ye, Mister Musgrave. I haven't seen you since that Truce Day when you accused me of stealing Lord Scrope's cattle."

"Good day to you, my lord," the newcomer replied, showing what he judged to be the appropriate level of deference, and then continued in a less formal manner. "But they weren't his lordship's cattle, they were mine."

Maxwell laughed. "Well what difference does it make? You reived them from someone else in the first place, you regarded it as a part of your payment as Captain of Bewcastle."

"Ah well, a lot of water has passed under the bridge since then," Musgrave said.

Cortez was amazed to find that, in spite of what they said, there seemed to be no malice between the two men. In his society, accusations of stealing would certainly have resulted in harsh words, which would invariably lead to a duel.

Maxwell shrugged. "That's true," he said. "But I don't suppose it'll happen again now that you had a falling out with the English warden."

Musgrave feigned surprise. "How did you know about that?"

This response seemed to please the laird, as Musgrave thought it would. He guessed that Maxwell would not pass up the opportunity to demonstrate his knowledge of everything that went on in The Borders. "Oh I know all about you, Mister Musgrave. Scrope caught you out and you had to ride for your life over the dyke. Now he has you posted as an outlaw."

Musgrave was silent. Maxwell laughed, shrugged his shoulders, and spoke from experience. "These things happen."

He dropped his affable guise and became deadly serious. He stared hard at the Englishman. "But why, I wonder, would you turn up here of all places?"

Musgrave knew that the significance of this remark lay, not in what Maxwell said, but in what he had pointedly not said. The laird was letting him know that he had his suspicions about his sudden appearance at

Lochmaben, but that was nothing more than Musgrave expected, and he had prepared for it.

"Well," he said, "I couldn't go to the Johnstones or the Grahams, they'd only sell me back to Scrope, and I wouldn't be all that welcome in Liddesdale or beyond. So, where else could I go except here? I was half hoping that I might be able to ride with you for a while."

Maxwell mulled this over in his mind. He knew about Musgrave's mad dash over the Scots Dyke and, while he dismissed most of the stories now in circulation about him, Maxwell, like Big Jock Elliot, readily accepted that the Englishman had been caught reiving by Lord Scrope. If that were true, it would certainly have warranted the warden posting him as an outlaw. He had also heard about Musgrave, as Captain of Bewcastle, having been involved in a hot trod against an Elliot raiding party, and knowing something of this Englishman's past history, it was not difficult to accept that he had reived some stolen cattle he was supposed to recover for their rightful owners.

Under those circumstances, Musgrave coming to join him made perfect sense, but Maxwell was a man who had survived by his wits and he was not about to break the habit of a lifetime. He decided to wait and see what else Musgrave had to say.

"I heard that you chased a band of Elliots out of England," he commented by way of prompting Musgrave to say more.

Musgrave had played this game before and knew better than say too much at once. Blurting out a long and detailed explanation would give the impression that it had been prepared in advance, and that would certainly raise Maxwell's suspicions. Besides, knowing Maxwell, he was sure that the laird would know more about his flight over the dyke than he was letting on. He took his time before answering, and if, as he assumed, the two young Elliots were now Maxwell's prisoners, young Rabbie at least could be relied on to back up his story.

Hoping to boost Maxwell's ego, he again feigned surprise. "That's true," he admitted. "And there's two Elliots after me now. I ran into Big Jock and two of Alexander's sons this side of the dyke and one of the young hotheads decided to try to make a name for himself by coming at me with a fancy new pistol. I held him off, but the two of them rode after me."

It had the desired effect. Maxwell's interest was aroused. "Elliots you say? And only three of them. What would they be doing in my part of the world?"

"I don't know, my lord." Musgrave managed to sound mystified. "I thought at first that the two brothers rode out on their own and Alexander sent Big Jock after them. But I'm thinking now that there's more to it than that."

Maxwell no longer tried to disguise his interest. "And what happened to Big Jock? Did he ride after you too?"

Musgrave felt somewhat relieved. He felt that he was beginning to gain the laird's confidence. "I don't think so, my lord," he answered. "If Big Jock Elliot came after me, I'd either be dead or a hostage in Liddesdale by now."

Maxwell nodded in agreement. He knew all about Big Jock Elliot. "That's true," he said.

There was a period of silence. Maxwell sauntered around the courtyard mulling things over in his mind, but never straying far from where he could watch Musgrave as the Englishman sat on his horse with his hands still tied in front of him. Musgrave showed no emotion as he waited for the laird to say something, but inside, his stomach was churning as he waited for the further questions he knew were coming, and which would require plausible answers. After leaving Big Jock, he did not attempt to evade Maxwell's scouts and was obliged to complete the last part of his journey to Lochmaben as a prisoner. During that ride, he had considered several possible ways of answering the questions Maxwell would inevitably have, but he could not possibly anticipate everything the laird would ask, and so he rejected them all. He had already lied to Maxwell once when he told the laird that he had not seen Big Jock following him, and he was aware that the more he lied, the more likely it was that he would be caught out. From now on, he thought, wherever possible it would be safer to tell the truth and hope for the best.

Maxwell eventually gave up wandering around the courtyard. He stopped and looked up at Musgrave.

"Two Liddesdale Elliots, you say. What would they be doing so far from home? My scouts haven't seen any Elliots, so what happened to them?"

It was a clever trap. Musgrave had expected to have to explain further about his encounter with the Elliots, but he had not anticipated having the question posed in this particular manner. Still, the fact that Maxwell had thought to lay such a trap seemed to indicate that Sandy and Rabbie Elliot actually were here at Lochmaben, and if Maxwell was going to lay snares for him he knew that he had been wise to decide that anything he told the laird would be substantially, if not completely, true.

He looked directly at Maxwell and smiled broadly. "I'd lay odds that they're either dead or you have them here," he said. "I let them get past me during the night and I saw where they ran into a group of riders, your riders I suppose."

Maxwell's eyebrows raised perceptibly, but his face showed no other emotion. "And what about Big Jock?" he asked.

"I haven't seen hide nor hair of him since I left the three of them this side of the Debatable Land."

Having lied once about Big Jock, Musgrave had no option but to continue on the course he had set. As he did so, he could only hope that the thaw had erased the tracks left at the spot where Big Jock had watched as the reivers took his young kinsmen as captives. He felt that it would be a good idea to expand on his last answer.

"But he'll be somewhere around here; he wouldn't let Alexander Elliot's sons ride into Dumfriesshire on their own." He paused before adding, "And if Big Jock doesn't want to be seen, he won't be seen."

It was the second time he had referred to Alexander by name, hoping that it might make Maxwell stop and think before hanging his two prisoners.

Maxwell considered this and failed to find fault. He changed the direction of his questioning.

"How did you know that I was home from Spain?" he asked.

"Young Elliot let it out; that lad never learned to keep his mouth shut. My guess is that Alexander heard a rumour and sent them here to find out if it was true."

Maxwell spoke casually, as if the answer was of little consequence. "I suppose Scrope already knows that I came home?"

Just in time, Musgrave realised that the laird was attempting to trap him into giving a direct answer. It would not matter whether he said 'yes' or 'no', it would mean that he had been briefed by Scrope.

He smiled ruefully and chose his words with care. "I'm afraid that his lordship hasn't seen fit to discuss things like that with me for a while now, but not much happens, even on this side of the dyke, that he doesn't hear about. And let's face it, nobody expected Laird Maxwell to stay in Spain for ever."

Maxwell's face displayed a satisfied smile. He was pleased with Musgrave's backhanded compliment and he warmed to the Englishman. "Be that as it may, what makes you think I might take you with me?"

So far, things had gone well for Musgrave but he was wary of overplaying his hand. He could still easily ruin everything and end up at the end of one of the ropes Maxwell seemed so keen to use. Again, he had to tread carefully.

"I'm afraid that I can't say, my lord, except that you know I've done my share of night riding. And as things stand, just about everybody on either side of the dyke is either after my blood or wants me for what Scrope would pay to get me back. The way I see it, I don't stand much of a chance on my own; someone is sure to catch me before long. The Elliots could have done it if their minds weren't set on something else, and I bet Johnstone would love to get his hands on me; it would get him well in with Scrope."

Musgrave hoped that by casually mentioning the idea that Johnstone would want to take him to Scrope, would increase his standing with Maxwell. He thought that at the very least, the laird would be determined to prevent his enemy gaining credit for capturing an English outlaw. He was confident that it would gain him a breathing space.

He gave Maxwell a moment to think it over before continuing. "To be honest," he said. "I didn't know what to do until young Elliot let slip that you were home and I got the idea that you might be looking for some good riders. In any case, if you throw me out I won't be any worse off than I am now."

Maxwell stood with his hands on his hips and looked the Englishman up and down. He laughed. "From here, you don't look very well equipped to be a rider."

"No," Musgrave conceded. "But I was hoping I might get a loan of some of the stuff that belonged to those two Elliots you're holding. I wouldn't mind getting my hands on one of those brand new wheel lock pistols."

Again Maxwell laughed, this time with obvious amusement. "Ever the reiver eh, Musgrave? What makes you so sure I have two Elliots here? My riders brought in a couple of Johnstones for me to hang, but no Elliots."

"I read the tracks in the snow," Musgrave replied. "They were Elliots all right, and they were brought here."

When Maxwell failed to comment, he took a deep breath and carried on. "You haven't done for them yet have you? Johnstone would love to hear that you strung up a pair of Elliots thinking that they were Johnstones. He'd make a hearty meal out of that."

Maxwell's face clouded. "What do you care whether I hang a couple of Elliots or not?"

"It makes no odds to me," Musgrave replied. "But if I'm going to ride for you it's something I thought I should mention."

The laird felt compelled to give this some thought. Musgrave had raised some points regarding Johnstone he had failed to consider, and although he did not like being reminded of them by the Englishman, he admitted to himself that they were worth taking into account. It prompted him to think that this former English officer might actually be of value to him; He knew everything there was to know about the English West March and that knowledge might prove useful.

Eventually, he looked the Englishman in the eye. "All right, Musgrave. I'll give you a chance. You can ride with me but only for a while; after that we'll see. And," he added pointedly, "you know what will happen if I get the slightest hint that you're playing games with me."

"Of course my lord," Musgrave replied.

He heaved a sigh of relief. He had managed to get himself into Maxwell's confidence. With someone like Maxwell, this could prove to be no more that a temporary arrangement, but for however long it lasted, he had the opportunity to learn something of the laird's plans. Whether or not he took what he learned back to Scrope would depend on circumstances, and as neither he nor Maxwell had once mentioned King James taking a hand, he still had plenty of options open. If Maxwell had taken his hint about Johnstone making capital out of hanging the Elliot brothers, he might hesitate to carry out his planned demonstration of power, and he might be able to help them escape from Maxwell and take them to England as hostages. In Carlisle, they would certainly attract a substantial reward. There was also the possibility of handing them over to King James, who would also regard them as valuable hostages in his attempts to subdue Liddesdale. And even if all that failed, he could help them get back to Liddesdale, which would go down well with Alexander Elliot.

He smiled as he imagined the look on Rabbie's face when he learned who had saved him from Maxwell's rope.

That, however, was all in the future. There could still be serious obstacles lying in wait for him. Apart from Maxwell, he would have to get around Big Jock Elliot. He must not get ahead of himself, but even if all else failed, riding with Maxwell might still prove to be well worth his while.

***

Completely unnoticed, Don Juan Cortez had listened to the exchange between Maxwell and Musgrave, and the longer he listened to, the more he was appalled by what he heard. The references to Lord Scrope were enough to confirm his worst suspicions. He knew that Scrope was what the English called a March Warden and this newly arrived Englishman had apparently been one of his officers. Yet Maxwell had seen fit to accept everything the man had told him, and had even agreed to enlist his services in his army!

Cortez dismissed all this talk of his being an outlaw. To his Spanish mind, as an Englishman, Musgrave was an enemy and not to be trusted. The man was an English spy, and yet here he was in Scotland and welcomed by Maxwell like an old friend!

He ought to talk to Maxwell and make him see sense, but he had a sinking feeling that the laird would refuse to listen. He would have to deal with this English spy himself.

Chapter 15

Big Jock matched Alexander Elliot in age, and more than matched him in build, yet in spite of his years of experience as a reiver, he acted like a repentant small boy in front of an irate father. He said nothing but stood and faced the fury of his heidsman's tongue.

Big Jock had set out to do as Musgrave suggested and gone back to pick up his task of watching for King James to come with his army to arrest Maxwell, but as he neared the western edge of the Debatable Land, he encountered one of the two riders sent by Alexander to look for him. The rider explained how, on hearing that all three of his scouts were not where they were supposed to be, the heidsman had sent two men to replace them. The rider also explained the new danger facing Liddesdale from a possible judicial raid by the king and, in spite of the increased danger to the valley the news gave Big Jock some unexpected freedom of movement. The rider prepared to locate the second scout and then ride to Liddesdale to report that he had found Big Jock, but the old reiver told him to wait. He was concious that he was the one responsible for what had happened by committing the basic error of allowing young Rabbie to chase after Musgrave. With hindsight, he realised that he should have instructed the young hothead to ride east after the fracas with the Hethringtons, and ridden west himself. That simple lapse of judgement had led to his failure to complete the task given him by his heidsman. On top of that, he should have known that exposing their presence to Musgrave, and attempting to find out what the Englishman was up to, was bound to lead to trouble involving his volatile young kinsman.

There was no doubt in the old reiver's mind that he must be the one to go and tell Alexander why he and the heidsman's sons had left their post. Besides, it was a complicated story and it would be dangerous to give Alexander Elliot a watered-down second-hand account.

Although the thaw had obliterated the covering of snow, and consequently reduced the visibility, when he came into sight the lookouts on the tower roof recognised him instantly. As he rode through the gap in the barmekin, Alexander came rushing out, and Big Jock was surprised to see Martin Elliot of Braidley following close behind. They had been discussing progress with the plan to ambush Bothwell, and before Alexander could get over his surprise at Big Jock's timely arrival, Braidley demanded some vital information.

"Is Jamie on the move already, Jock?"

"No' yet," Big Jock replied.

Martin of Braidley cast him a questioning look, clearly wondering why he had ridden back to Liddesdale instead of waiting for the king to attack Maxwell, but Big Jock pre-empted the question.

"We ran intae some Hetheringtons, an' we had tae fight them. We kilt two an' wounded wan. I came back tae tell the heidsman aboot it."

Before Martin could ask anything further, Alexander chipped in, "We still have riders watching for Jamie," he assured Braidley.

Big Jock confirmed his heidsman's statement. "We have, aye."

Alexander had intervened to reassure Martin of Braidley that he had nothing to worry about regarding the watch he had set for the king, but he also wanted to prevent him asking too many further questions. He was anxious to hear what Big Jock had to say about his sons before saying anything to Martin about the three original scouts having gone missing, and he was relieved that Braidley seemed satisfied. He took his leave of Alexander, and rode off to visit the other heidsmen involved in his plan for the defence of Liddesdale.

Alexander was both relieved and worried by Big Jock's timely arrival. Seeing the big man ride in out of nowhere alive and well, gave him hope that his sons were also safe, but knowing the old reiver as he did, he was worried about the apprehensive glances Big Jock was casting in his direction. Seeing the big man display such unusual signs of nervousness gave him real cause for concern.

He turned on Big Jock and demanded to know the full story. The old reiver held nothing back, apart from the part played by Alexander's son, Robert. Alexander was stunned. One of the greatest insults to direct at an Elliot, or any other reiver for that matter, was to take him for a member of another family. He could imagine nothing worse than having his sons mistaken for Johnstones and captured by Maxwell of all people. From the way that the Maxwells and Johnstones conducted their feud, he could see his sons dying extremely painful deaths. Better for them if they were dead already. And to hear that their only hope of survival lay with an English outlaw, the former Captain of Bewcastle no less, was the last straw! He looked at Big Jock as if hoping that the big man would burst out laughing and admit that the whole thing was really a sick joke, but not once in his entire life could he remember a single occasion when he had heard Big Jock Elliot make anything approaching a joke.

As the awful truth sank in, his temper began to rise but he kept it under control and managed to refrain from shouting. Big Jock would have preferred it if the heidsman had screamed at him, but as it was, Alexander's words still held a deadly menace. He made his feelings clear to the big man in coldly calculated terms that held far more menace than any amount of shouting could convey. To drive home his point, he picked up a lance. He had not thought to use it, but once it was in his hand it required a supreme effort on his part to prevent himself running the old reiver through. The fact that Big Jock just stood there without making a move to defend himself was the only thing that made him stay his hand. After a long pause, he threw the lance away in disgust, a disgust directed mainly at himself for his failure to use it.

He calmed down and began to question Big Jock more closely in the hope of finding something, anything that would give him cause for hope. He found nothing, and in his frustration, he grabbed another lance from one of the men guarding the tower, but once again Big Jock stood his ground and Alexander sensed that he would once again do nothing to defend himself. It had the same effect as on the previous occasion but this time he just dropped the weapon instead of throwing it away in frustration. The worst of his anger subsided, his mind began to clear and he was able to think more rationally. Big Jock had said nothing about how Malcolm and Robert had reacted to the situation but he was confident that they would have acquitted themselves well in the fight with the Hetheringtons. They had already proved themselves in battle but he suspected that the encounter with the former Captain of Bewcastle might well have caused them, young Robert in particular, to rush into doing something without thinking. However, it would be useless trying to prise the truth out of Big Jock. The old reiver would never try to shift the blame he clearly considered was his alone to bear.

Alexander's frustration was still evident but he changed the focus of his anger away from Big Jock and directed it at Bothwell. He blamed the Keeper of Liddesdale for preventing him from gathering every man he had and riding into Dumfriesshire to wrest his sons from Maxwell's grasp.

But he simply had to do something to help them and, apart from himself, there was only one man who stood any chance at all of rescuing them.

He took the big man aside to discuss the possibilities. Alexander did not apologise for threatening Big Jock with a lance, heidsmen did not say 'sorry' however badly they might feel about their rash actions. He thought of sending Big Jock back into Dumfriesshire with as many men as he could spare, but almost as soon as the idea came into his mind, he knew it was not a practical solution. King Jamie was on the march and if he came across a band of Liddesdale reivers, he would turn his entire army on them.

Again, he questioned Big Jock. "How far can we trust Musgrave?"

Big Jock expected the question. "Weel," he answered, "I think that he's a spy for Scrope, an' I widna trust him wan bit if it wisna for that. He'll have tae get oot o' Lochmaben an' he reckons that if he brings yon two wi' him, ye'll help him get back tae England. An' tae dae that, he'll have tae tell Maxwell that they're Elliots and no' Johnstones."

Alexander considered this. It gave him no more than a painfully slim hope for his sons, but it provided a glimmer of hope, perhaps his only hope, of saving his sons. He could not contemplate taking the risk of leaving their fate in Musgrave's hands alone. At the first sign of trouble, the Englishman would simply abandon them and save himself. He had to have someone he completely trusted on the scene.

After a hasty meal and a short rest, Big Jock rode back to Dumfriesshire on a fresh horse and with an ample supply of provisions. As well as food, Alexander, in an effort to give himself some fraction of comfort, insisted that he carry a small amount of powder and shot for the wheel lock pistols.

***

Juan Martinez de Recalde had done all he possibly could. The great armada was ready for sea. Now, everything was in the hands of God and, he hesitated to say, the Duke of Medina Sidonia. The closer they got to the departure date, the more concerned he became about their chances of success.

Sailing from Spain to England was not as straightforward as both King Philip and Medina Sidonia seemed to think. In truth, it was fraught with danger. The main danger came from the elements, and de Recalde knew all about the perils presented by the wild storms that regularly blew up in the great Western Ocean. Violent gales charged across the ocean from the New World and whipped up the already turbulent seas into a veritable maelstrom; and they could spring up at any season of year. Many years at sea had taught him to read the signs, and while at present they seemed favourable, he knew from painful experience that the portents often lied. One of these storms could arrive completely unannounced, and in spring, they were particularly unpredictable.

De Recalde knew that Medina Sidonia would insist on putting to sea on the designated date without giving the weather a single thought. King Philip had decreed that they sail immediately following the sacred season of Easter in the last week in April, and as far as the senior commander was concerned, that was when he would weigh anchor, and not a single day later. As second-in-command, de Recalde had already raised the question of adopting a more flexible approach, only to have his arguments summarily dismissed. Medina Sidonia would not countenance a delay for any reason whatsoever. He agreed with the king; any delay would give the English more time to prepare. To de Recalde this was nonsense, he was certain that the English already knew all about the armada. Elizabeth's spy network, organised and operated by Francis Walsingham, was the best the world had ever seen, and it was fanciful to think that you could keep such a massive fleet a secret from them. The English were already prepared, and in de Recalde's opinion, it was better to arrive in English waters late than not at all. In fact, it would do no harm to keep Elizabeth and her navy on tenterhooks, waiting for the armada for as long as possible. The enemy might even relax, thinking that reports of a Spanish invasion were, after all, unfounded.

Not that it mattered much. He had made his opinion clear to his commander and had it rejected. All he could do now was follow his orders.

***

Big Jock rode back across the Debatable Land into Dumfriesshire. The snow had thawed, taking with it all evidence of what had recently occurred there. The coming of the thaw seemed to have stirred the region into life and people were beginning to emerge from their winter boltholes to resume their farming activities; presumably to fall victim to the bands of broken men who plagued the area. Big Jock, however, felt no need for caution; if there was one man in The Borders the Broken Men would not dare to molest, it was Big Jock Elliott.

He rode to where he hoped to encounter the two men sent to replace him and the Elliot brothers. They would have gone north, as Big Jock himself had intended to do, in order to make sure of intercepting King James on his way to attack Maxwell and, as experienced reivers, they were well versed in the art of seeing without being seen. They spotted Big Jock long before he saw them, but all they could tell him was that a large body of riders had crossed the Scots Dyke, clearly searching for something or someone. Hetheringtons, Big Jock thought, looking for the Elliots who had killed two of their kinsmen. They would have found nothing except the two bodies to take back over the dyke with them. To his immense disappointment, however, the riders could offer him nothing about what was happening in Dumfriesshire, so all Big Jock could do was to retrace his steps of a few days ago and ride west. He did not dwell on his visit to Liddesdale and his uncomfortable encounter with his heidsman, but concentrated his thoughts on the task in hand.

He was determined to rescue Alexander Elliot's sons, assuming they were still alive, or lose his own life in the attempt.

Chapter 16

The door of the cell creaked slowly open. Two of Maxwell's castle guards entered and hauled Sandy and Rabbie to their feet. The guards manhandled them roughly out of the bare damp cell they had occupied since their arrival as captives at Lochmaben. By now, they were thoroughly confused and found it difficult to fathom what was happening as they were ushered up the stone steps and out into the daylight. The dungeon was located in the bowels of the castle where there were no windows, and the brothers had not seen daylight since their incarceration in the gloomy cell. They had to shade their eyes from the unaccustomed glare of the sunlight, but they gratefully breathed in fresh clean air, the first they had enjoyed for several days.

In the cell, they had again protested that they were Elliots and not Johnstones, but nobody was prepared to listen. Least of all Maxwell, who had come down to inspect his two prize captives and did nothing more than laugh at their protests. He promptly announced that he knew they were Johnstones and he would enjoy hanging them for all to see on market day in Dumfries.

***

When they were first taken down to the dungeon, Sandy, knowing that it would be futile to resist, had done his best to maintain some semblance of Elliot dignity as he was marched down the cold stone steps by the castle guards. Not so Rabbie. He fought his captors every step of the way down to the cells, and once inside, his frustration boiled over. His head still hurt from the blow that had knocked him off his horse and it did nothing to improve his mood. In spite of his predicament, he swore savage revenge first on Musgrave, for leading him into the reiver trap, then on Maxwell, and finally on Big Jock for not coming to their aid.

"Where was Big Jock when he should have been there to help us?" he wanted to know. "The bastard ran out on us, Sandy."

That was too much for Sandy. In a rare moment of temper, he grabbed his brother by the front of his jack and threw him into the pile of evil smelling straw in the corner of the cell that was to serve as their bedding.

"Big Jock never ran out on anyone in his whole life!" Sandy yelled. "He was there behind me looking for you. But just because he was canny enough not to go charging into a band of riders out on a raid like we were stupid enough to do, it doesn't mean that he rode off and left us. He knew that he couldn't help us by getting killed himself and he was right. But he'll be around here somewhere and he's our only hope of getting out of this alive. Remember that, Rabbie!"

Such an unusual demonstration of anger and rough treatment of him by Sandy, was sufficient to make Rabbie stop and think. He rose shakily to his feet and stood for a while collecting his thoughts. Finally, he looked sheepishly at his brother. "I should have been more careful when I went after Musgrave. I let the bastard trick me, and that's why I got caught by the Maxwells. It was my own fault, Sandy."

"It was that," his brother agreed angrily. "And it wasn't a question of being careful either. You shouldn't have gone riding after Musgrave on your own in the first place."

Deep down, Rabbie knew that it had been foolish of him to chase after the Englishman without thinking. Now he had landed not only himself, but also his brother in trouble. It went against the grain, but he knew that Sandy was right.

He looked suitably chastened and took a deep breath. "You're right, Sandy."

Sandy was relieved to see that his words had sunk in. He knew how difficult it must have been for Rabbie to admit that he had been in the wrong, and he could not recall a single previous occasion when he had heard his brother own up to having made a bad mistake. He decided that he had chastised Rabbie enough, and besides, he felt that he, too, must shoulder a portion of the blame.

"Anyway," he said ruefully. "It's my fault as well. When I heard that shot, I went charging off like some young dunderhied. Big Jock tried to stop me but I broke away from him."

As their eyes grew accustomed to the gloom, they found what seemed to be the least filthy corner of the cell and sat in silence with their thoughts.

Rabbie was the first to resume the conversation. "What do you think Big Jock will do now?"

Much as Sandy wanted to spare his brother any further distress, he decided that he could not hold anything back and had to tell Rabbie the stark truth. "Big Jock is in a worse position than we are," he said. "He won't know whether to come here to try and get us out, or to go back to watch for Jamie's army like we were supposed to be doing."

His honest assessment had a profound effect on Rabbie. The unpalatable truth sank in. He had not only led his brother into trouble, but might also have helped to put the whole of Liddesdale in danger.

His shoulders slumped. "He'll have to go back and watch for Jamie, won't he Sandy?"

The note of despair in his voice prompted Sandy to try to give him at least some cause for hope. "I'm afraid that he will, Rabbie," he admitted. "But you can be sure that he'll work out a way to help us as well."

"I hope to God that he does," Rabbie replied. The thought that there might be at least some slight ray of hope, helped to dispel the worst of his despair and it brought back a little of his natural belligerence.

"I'll tell you this Sandy, if we do get out of here without being hung, I'll still find that bastard Musgrave; the next time, I'll be a lot more canny about it and make sure that I get the bastard."

Sandy was glad to see the old spark return; it would help his brother to get through whatever was in store for them.

"Aye, and I'll help you, Rabbie. But we have to think of a way of helping ourselves. We can't leave it all to Big Jock."

"But what can we do, Sandy?"

Sandy gave him a playful dig in the ribs. "Maybe we should try and say a few of those prayers our mother tried to teach us."

They lapsed into silence but that left them prey to their own worst fears. Sandy was first to snap himself out of what was quickly developing into a mood of abject despair. He set his mind to generating ideas for effecting an escape and, in an attempt to raise Rabbie's spirits, he began to think aloud and put his ideas to his brother. Eventually, Rabbie joined in and they enthusiastically discussed the most improbable schemes. All had to be rejected but it helped to pass the time. The only workable solution was to overpower one of the men guarding them, steal a weapon and fight their way out, but the opportunity never presented itself. The guards expected such an attempt and were well prepared. They always arrived in pairs, but only one ever entered the cell, and always unarmed, and there was no possibility of acquiring a weapon by attacking him. The second man waited outside with a drawn sword. Even so, Rabbie was all for trying to overpower the guard, but Sandy knew that it would be a futile gesture. At least one of them would certainly die before they could acquire a weapon and make a break for freedom.

What they didn't know, but should have guessed, was that the guards were under strict orders not to kill or severely wound the prisoners. That would deprive Maxwell of the pleasure of serving notice to Laird Johnstone by publicly hanging two of his riders in Dumfries.

In the gloom of the cell, it was difficult to distinguish between night and day and they completely lost track of time. Their only method of calculating how long it was since their incarceration, was provided by the guards bringing them stale bread and tepid water once a day. At first, they refused to eat the unpalatable fare but hunger eventually got the better of them. On one memorable occasion, the guards brought them some hot broth, which they gratefully wolfed down, only to have their enjoyment ruined when the guard smilingly informed them that it was simply because the laird wanted them looking fit and well for their imminent hanging.

They eventually gave up trying to think of ways to escape and optimism gave way to lethargy. They had almost reached the point where they would do nothing but simply sit and await their fate when the cell door creaked open and the guards came to haul them outside.

Out of the darkness of the dungeon, they blinked as the bright sunlight suddenly hit their eyes and it took several minutes for them to become accustomed to the glare but, gradually, they recovered enough to take note of their surroundings. They stood in the castle courtyard and, as their eyes cleared, they found themselves in the presence of a very elegant looking Laird Maxwell. It was not the nobly attired laird, however, who immediately attracted their attention; it was the man standing beside him with a broad grin on his face: Musgrave!

If the appearance of his mortal enemy was not enough to fuel Rabbie's resentment, then the sight of the two new wheel lock pistols stuck in the Englishman's belt certainly was. The blow he received to his head, the time he spent in the filthy dungeon, the rough treatment meted out by Maxwell's men, all built up inside him and boiled over. He flew at Musgrave but was hauled back by the guards and thrown to the ground before he got halfway to where the Englishman stood laughing at him.

Sandy helped him up and held him back but could not keep him quiet. "You bastard, Musgrave," Rabbie yelled. "It was you who told these Maxwells that we were Johnstones. And what are you doing with our pistols?"

Musgrave managed not to let his anger show. He did not like young Elliot shouting at him in front of Maxwell, and if Rabbie persisted in calling him a bastard, he would have to do something about it or lose face in front of the laird and his men. Given the importance of family in the culture of the borders, 'bastard' was a term that had led to more than one inter-family blood feud. He drew one of the pistols and waved it in Rabbie's face just as young Elliot had once done with him.

"Tell your brother to keep quiet, Sandy," the Englishman said menacingly. "Or I'll shoot him with his own pistol."

For once, however, an outburst by Rabbie had a positive effect. It was sufficient to make Maxwell believe, albeit reluctantly, that they might after all be telling the truth, and they really were Elliots rather than Johnstones. He had reluctantly considered whether they might be the two Elliots Musgrave had spoken about, but he had put the thought to the back of his mind. It was much more pleasurable to regard them as Johnstones and treat them accordingly. Many of his riders were looking on and the story would soon spread that the two prisoners were Elliots and not Johnstones. It was disappointing, but he would have to call off the hanging. He had no personal qualms about hanging Elliots, but he remembered what Musgrave had said about the capital Johnstone would make out of him hanging two of them by mistake.

He turned to Musgrave in the hope that he was still angry enough at young Elliot to change his mind and assert that they were Johnstones. "Are ye sure that these two are who they say they are? They don't look much like Elliots to me, Musgrave."

He would never know how close he had come to getting his wish. Musgrave was still angry, and the thought of telling Maxwell that he was right about them not being Elliots actually crossed his mind, but he remembered his reason for telling Big Jock that he would try to help them in the first place. If things worked out as well for him as he hoped, the pair would provide him with a safe passage back into England, and he might still receive a nice reward from Scrope for capturing them. He looked closely at the two hapless prisoners as if to make certain. Their time in the cell had done nothing to improve their dishevelled appearance, but not to the point where he could argue that they were completely unrecognisable.

Eventually, and with obvious reluctance, he confirmed their true identity. "They don't look like anything much, but I'm sorry to say that they're the two who were with Big Jock."

The laird was on the point of pressing Musgrave in the hope that he would change his mind, but thought better of it. It would only demonstrate his disappointment to his watching riders. His two prisoners were not Johnstones and he simply had to make the best of it. The fact that they were Elliots was immaterial to him, but they did pose a problem. He definitely did not want them at Lochmaben but neither could he allow them to ride away; they had already seen too much, and it would be foolish in the extreme to trust them not to tell anyone about it. He had to do something with them and he needed time to think of what.

He glared at Sandy and Rabbie. "You can count yourselves lucky that this Englishman is prepared to vouch for you, although I don't really understand why he should. I never heard of the Captain of Bewcastle being particularly concerned about anybody but himself."

He was still angry that Musgrave had chosen to stand up for the Elliot brothers, and not knowing the Englishman's reason for doing so, was giving him cause for thought. He was intrigued, but he was not about to afford Musgrave the satisfaction of hearing him ask for an explanation. He could easily force Musgrave to tell him under torture and then dispose of him, but he still thought that the former Captain's knowledge of the English West March and its March Warden would prove useful in furthering his plans for the future. He reached the conclusion that if he had to keep Musgrave and the two Elliots at Lochmaben, he might as well keep them together.

"All right, Mr Musgrave," he said. "Seeing as you're so concerned about their welfare, you can have them. I'm going to make you responsible for them. You can do what you like with them, but make certain that they don't leave here or you'll swing in their place. And nobody will worry too much about me hanging an English outlaw."

He turned and stalked off, but had not gone far before he seemed to have second thoughts and came back. He walked up to Musgrave and held out his hands. The Englishman realised what he wanted and with the greatest reluctance, removed the two-wheel lock pistols from his belt and handed them over. He had hoped that the laird would let him keep them when he asked to use them as bait for young Rabbie, but now that he had angered Maxwell by standing up for the Elliots, he was obliged to hand them back.

In the meantime, Rabbie Elliot's mind was in turmoil, so much so that he failed to react to Musgrave handing his pistol over to Maxwell. He was having difficulty coming to terms with the idea that the reviled Englishman had saved him from the fate that Maxwell had planned for him and his brother, but he knew that they would continue to be prisoners at Lochmaben.

He turned to his brother. "We can't stay here, Sandy, we have to go back to help Big Jock watch for King Jamie. He'll be here any day now and Bothwell will be riding on the tower."

Sandy looked anxiously at Musgrave and Maxwell, hoping against hope that they had not overheard Rabbie. It had occurred to him that they might be able to strike a deal with Maxwell using the information that the king would soon be riding in here with his army to arrest him. The laird, however, had heard, and grasped the significance. Young Elliot's chance remark carried the ring of truth, but he still sought confirmation.

He walked over to Rabbie. "Are you saying that King James is on his way here now, without waiting for the weather?"

Rabbie realised that, once again, he had allowed his tongue to run away with him and that he had made a serious mistake. He said nothing, and that in itself was enough to convince Maxwell that what he said was true. The laird was well aware that the king would have to come against him at some point; James simply could not afford to let his return from exile go unchallenged, but he had been banking on the king's attack coming much closer to the date of the Spanish landing, which was scheduled for June. Maxwell had made his plans accordingly, but should James decide to attack well before the Spanish arrived, it could spell serious trouble. He had been confident that his fortresses could hold out until James had to break off his attack to go and repel the Spanish invasion, but if the king struck now, Maxwell was not at all certain that they could withstand such a lengthy siege.

He turned to Musgrave. "Did you know that James could be on his way here soon?" he demanded.

Musgrave did indeed know. Big Jock had told him, but he dare not tell Maxwell that or he would face the laird's wrath for not informing him as soon as he arrived at Lochmaben. He had to tread carefully. "Everyone knows that the king will have to ride in here after you sometime," he said with a confidence he certainly did not feel. "But if I thought that he was already on his way, I wouldn't have come anywhere near here."

This made sense to Maxwell. He accepted it as the truth and realised that he had to revise his plans. In the meantime, he had to solve the problem of what to do about Musgrave and the Elliots. Now that the English outlaw knew that the king's army was on its way, he might decide to ride off at the first opportunity, and the laird was certain about where he would go. Musgrave would ride to the king and tell him everything he had seen and heard at Lochmaben. Likewise the Elliots. He would have to deal drastically with all three, but knew that he would have to step carefully.

He did not believe that Big Jock Elliot would have abandoned his heidsman's sons and stayed in east Dumfriesshire waiting for the king to ride past. He would be somewhere nearby. If he found that the laird had killed the Elliot brothers, Big Jock would immediately ride back to

Liddesdale and God only knew how Alexander Elliot would react. Getting into a feud with Liddesdale would give Maxwell yet another problem on top of those he already faced. Knowing Big Jock, he realised that the old reiver would be difficult to find, and in any case, he couldn't spare the men to go searching for him.

Time was short. He called the men who were guarding the Elliots. "Take these two back down to the dungeon," he ordered. "And take this Englishman with them while I think of what to do with them!"

Chapter 17

Big Jock Elliot rode around in circles, not because he was lost, but because it was the only way of keeping track of all the many comings and goings in and out of Lochmaben castle. The position of the castle meant that it was approachable from too many different directions for him to be able to see everything that happened from one hiding place, so he was obliged to keep circling around the fortress. Being just one man, he realised that trying to cover every possibility was an impossible task. If he rode too far out, it would take so long to complete a circuit that he could easily miss people coming or going on the opposite side; if he rode too close, he stood a good chance of running into Maxwell's guards. But it was the best he could do.

Alexander had offered to send a few men to help him but he had declined. Too many watchers would increase the chances of discovery. Big Jock was the man the Elliots invariably relied on to act as scout on reiving raids, so he was accustomed to riding on his own, and besides, after recent events he preferred it that way. He still blamed himself for what had happened and it was up to him alone to put things right.

Lochmaben Castle stood at the northeastern corner of a small loch, and with the trees not yet in full leaf, he had an adequate view of the fortress from the far side of the loch. He used that to set his mean distance from the castle but, while it formed a basis for Big Jock's plan, it was, of course, an oversimplification. A reiver of his experience would never dream of setting such an obvious pattern, and so he varied his tactics while ensuring that he still kept an adequate watch. He rode carefully and for most of the time, the speed of his progress was subject to the presence of Maxwell's sentries, but he soon discovered that these generally tended to remain in set positions.

Most of them were on foot and stationed inside his chosen circular route, but he guessed that there would be several more mounted men keeping guard much further out. The laird presumably did not expect to find trouble close to his seat of power, and this afforded Big Jock some unexpected freedom of movement. Even so, he had to keep his wits about him as, on occasion, he was obliged to take some chances and ride closer to the fortress in order to give himself a better opportunity of finding out what was happening there. If Sandy and Rabbie were alive and held captive, to have any chance of rescuing them it was vitally important to know what was happening at Lochmaben.

He realised that the brothers might already be dead, left swinging from a beam in Dumfries marketplace, hanged by Maxwell believing them to be Johnstones. He was tempted to ride directly to Dumfries to find out, but he dismissed the idea. If they were already dead then he could do absolutely nothing about it. Better to stay here at Lochmaben in the hope that Musgrave might just have been as good as his word and convinced Maxwell that Sandy and Rabbie really were Elliots.

Trying to absorb and analyse every single possibility was proving extremely difficult for the big man, so he gave up speculating and concentrated on the task in hand.

For the first few days of his watch, the comings and goings from the castle consisted almost entirely of small groups of riders going out on raids, and then returning with their spoils. From what Big Jock knew about Maxwell, this was most unusual; the laird had always preferred to raid with large numbers of riders as he had recently done in Douglas lands. The direction the reiving parties took was always either south or east, which told Big Jock that Maxwell was concentrating on raiding Johnstone lands, and he was using small parties of reivers to cause as much disruption as possible while keeping his real strength a secret. Unknown to Maxwell, his tactics actually helped Big Jock; as the groups came and went, they felt no need for caution and he had no trouble avoiding them.

Then things changed dramatically. Several single riders left in a hurry, galloping off in all directions. Such was their urgency that one of them actually spotted Big Jock and completely ignored him.

No more groups of riders left the castle but the numbers coming in increased. Most of these were not loaded with plunder and had clearly not been raiding. The number of riders arriving increased to such an extent that the castle could no longer accommodate them all, and a haphazard encampment spread along the shores of the loch. To Jock, it seemed clear that something had prompted Maxwell to concentrate his forces at Lochmaben, and the only possible reason he could have for doing that was that he had learned the king was about to attack. The realisation caused a shiver to run down the old reiver's spine. The one most likely to have told Maxwell that Jamie was going to attack sooner than he expected was young Rabbie, and the old reiver desperately hoped that the hiedsman's son had not been compelled to divulge that information under torture.

He decided to try to infiltrate this seemingly disorganised body of reivers on the loch shore at night and risk being recognised, but before he could put his plan into action, the whole group stirred into action. Something important was happening and it presented Big Jock with something of a dilemma.

***

Rabbie Elliot sat in morose silence in a corner of the dungeon, aware of the accusing looks cast in his direction by both his brother and Musgrave. Both clearly blamed him for their incarceration in the Lochmaben dungeon, but neither said anything. Each, in his own way, felt that he too, must shoulder some portion of the blame.

Musgrave knew that he had badly miscalculated when he decided to keep what he knew about the king's intentions from Maxwell. Young Rabbie had blabbed the whole story to the laird at exactly the wrong time for Musgarave, and in the process ruined the Englishman's plans. He was certainly feeling bitterly frustrated about being thrown into the dungeon just when everything seemed to be going so well, but it would serve no useful purpose to take it out on young Elliot. On the contrary, he feared that if he said anything about what had happened, and Rabbie retaliated in his usual hot-headed way, he might not be able to hold back. He would dearly love to give the young idiot the beating of his life, but if he did, he knew that he would have to deal with his brother as well. He had already seen how Sandy reacted when he thought that Rabbie was in danger, even Big Jock had failed to restrain him, and he knew that he would react in similar fashion again. Musgrave had no doubt that he could deal with both Elliots at the same time, the confines of the dungeon cell would give him an advantage, not that he felt he needed one. However, beating the daylights out of the brothers would serve no useful purpose and do nothing to help him get out of his current predicament. He also felt that Maxwell might just decide to spare the two Elliots, their deaths would not go down well in Liddesdale, and trouble with that particular valley was something the laird would not want to add to his other problems. But he doubted that Maxwell would be equally lenient when it came to dealing with him. The laird had already made it clear that hanging someone who by his own admission was an English outlaw, would not invite any repercussions whatsoever. The Englishman realised that unless he could think of a way out of the trouble he was in, he was already standing on the gallows. He needed the two young Elliots as allies, so he held his temper and set his mind to thinking of how best to use them.

In his own way, Sandy had reached a similar conclusion. He, too, was angry with Rabbie, but like Musgrave, he could not honestly say that he himself was blameless. He should have known his brother well enough to anticipate some form of outburst, and he blamed himself for not warning Rabbie not to say anything at all before discussing it with him. He realised that was a lot to ask of Rabbie, but he still blamed himself for not trying. Like the Englishman, albeit for different reasons, Sandy knew that if they were to have any chance of escape from Maxwell they had to stick together. Their only real hope was Big Jock, but they could not simply leave everything up to him. For the big man to have any chance of helping them, they must first do something to help themselves, and that meant all three of them working to the same plan. He might not like it, and he knew that Rabbie would certainly not be happy about trusting Musgrave, but they had no option but to work closely with a man he was now convinced was an English spy.

For his part, Rabbie would have much preferred his cellmates to vent the anger they must surely be feeling towards him, if only to give him some relief from the guilt he was feeling. He knew that he was to blame for them being back in the Lochmaben dungeon, and to add to his feeling of guilt, he was once again feeling decidedly foolish. His impetuous reaction to the sight of Musgrave carrying 'his' precious pistol was an extremely foolish thing to do, and letting slip to Maxwell and his men that King Jamie was already on his way with an army, had been even more stupid. It went against every lesson his father had tried to drum into him about how to act when dealing with strangers. As he sat and brooded, he began to realise exactly how big a fool he had been. When, to his complete amazement, Musgrave vouched for him and Sandy, it gave him an uneasy feeling that he may have got things very wrong, and Maxwell taking the pistols away from the Englishman seemed to confirm it. Too late, he realised that the incident with the pistols had been a deliberate ruse by Maxwell. The laird had guessed how he would react and had set a trap for him. To his shame, he had walked right into it!

No wonder Sandy had nothing to say to him; his brother was clearly fed up with him constantly giving way to his feelings and acting without thinking, and worse still, if his father ever learned how utterly stupid he had been he, too, would be ashamed of him. Rabbie knew that he had definitely not conducted himself as a Liddesdale Elliot should, and if Martin of Braidley found out how he had ruined his carefully laid plans, the consequences would be much more painful.

He realised that none of that mattered while they remained locked up in the Lochmaben dungeon, and he failed to see how they could possibly escape. Their fate was in Maxwell's hands, and there was not a thing they could do about it.

Chapter 18

Cortez was surprised, but nonetheless a little relieved, when Maxwell threw the English spy into the castle dungeon, but he was not altogether reassured. He had witnessed the incident in the courtyard and heard every word that had passed between the 'laird' and the three strangers, and it did not give him cause for optimism. It worried Cortez that Maxwell still believed that the Englishman was nothing more than a common outlaw and no danger to their plans. But that was far from being his greatest concern.

It appeared that James of Scotland was on his way with an army to arrest Maxwell and, much as he disliked and distrusted the Scotsman, Cortez feared that his capture would place King Philip of Spain's great crusade in jeopardy.

In Spain, the devious Scotsman had said nothing about the possibility of King James sending an army to arrest him as soon as he landed on Scottish soil. On the contrary, when questioned about how James would react to him helping Spanish soldiers to land in his country, he had implied that the Scottish king would welcome a Spanish landing. According to Maxwell, now that the Protestant Queen Elizabeth had murdered the Catholic Queen Mary, James would see himself as the natural choice to rule England once Elizabeth was defeated. This may well have sounded like music to King Philip's Catholic ears, but Cortez now realised that his king had been subtly deceived, and in reality, it had not been difficult. Even before the plan for the invasion of England had been finalised, there had been strong rumours that James of Scotland would be first in line for the English throne when the childless Elizabeth died. That alone should have been sufficient to ensure that England returned to the Church of Rome. But

Philip, as usual, ignored his advisors. Instead, he placed his faith in his mighty armada to bring England back to the Catholic fold.

None of that, Cortez realised, mattered now. If James captured and executed Maxwell, or even simply held him prisoner, the Spanish landing in Scotland was doomed. He could wait no longer. He sought out the 'laird' and reiterated his earlier opinion that the Englishman he was holding was much more dangerous than the mere outlaw Maxwell thought he was. This man, Musgrave, was a spy and the fact that he was one of Lord Scrope's officers, proved the point beyond doubt. Much to Cortez's dismay, Maxwell would have none of it; the more Cortez protested, the more Maxwell dug his heels in, and the Spaniard was at a loss to understand why.

The truth was that Maxwell, now back in his home territory and in complete control, was asserting his authority over the Spaniard. While, privately, he might have his doubts about Musgrave's story, he was not about to be told who was, or was not, to be trusted, and especially by somebody he himself regarded as a spy. There was also the fact that, regardless of what else he might be, Maxwell was at heart a reiver, and he was instinctively disposed to accept the word of a fellow reiver, English or Scottish, before that of a Spanish diplomat. No one, least of all Maxwell, thought to explain this to the Spaniard, and even if they had, Cortez would never have been able to accept that there was a culture in this backward country where family counted for more than nationality.

In spite of his misgivings, however, Cortez decided that he could not afford to waste any more time on Musgrave. Maxwell, in spite of what he said, had locked the spy up where he could at least do no immediate harm, and in the meantime, Cortez had a much more important matter to raise with this self-styled 'laird'. He angrily demanded to know why Maxwell had not informed King Philip that James of Scotland would take a hand and come to arrest the man who was supposed to be helping the Spanish landing. What exactly, he asked, did 'Laird' Maxwell intend to do about an imminent attack by King James?

The Spaniard's aggressive attitude incensed Maxwell even more. How dare this pompous diplomat question him about his plans for dealing with James? Cortez, as far as the laird was concerned, was here on sufferance and, while in Scotland, was subject to his orders. Here in his country, this, or any other Spaniard, had no right to even approach him without his permission, let alone question his competence to deal with an unexpected hitch to his plan. Did Cortez think that the man who was responsible for planning the Spanish landing would not have made provision for such a minor setback? Yet here he was talking to a laird as if he had a right to know his every thought. This Cortez was getting too big for his fancy Spanish boots. The Spaniard was getting under the Scotsman's skin and Maxwell's first thought was to throw Cortez into the dungeon with his other prisoners, or even get rid of him permanently. But he realised that would do nothing to help the situation. When the Spanish ships arrived, their leader would expect to meet Maxwell to discuss his next move, and it occurred to the laird that a meeting with Philip's representative would serve just as well, but he would ensure that the meeting did not take place until after the troops had actually landed. He could not run the risk of having the Spanish learning that they would have to face a Scottish army before they engaged an English one. And if they heard it while they were still at sea, they would simply turn tail and sail away. On considering the situation, he decided that it would be best to keep Cortez alive until then, but only until then.

In the meantime, he was not prepared to put up with the further complaints the Spaniard was bound to make, and keep on making, regarding every aspect of his plans. He had to do something to keep the interfering diplomat reasonably happy until he needed him, and that meant getting him away from Lochmaben.

In spite of the need for haste in preparing to face the king, Maxwell forced himself to set aside some time to work out solutions to the problems posed by the presence of Cortez, Musgrave and the two Elliots. Thinking about the various elements as forming parts of a single problem, soon led him to a workable solution; he could kill not only two, but possibly four, birds with one stone.

He decided to give Cortez a highly edited version of what he planned to do, not because he had changed his mind about the annoying diplomat, but because the Spaniard would have to know some elements of the plan in order to be of any practical use. Maxwell did not, of course, tell the Spaniard the whole truth, or anything like the whole truth, that would have been tantamount to admitting that he intended to betray King Philip, but hoped that he revealed enough to keep Cortez quiet until the time came to make use of him. Cortez listened and his worries were somewhat relieved. He guessed that not everything Maxwell told him was true, but he did glean enough in what the 'laird' said to give him at least some hope for the future. In the meantime, among other things, it presented him with an unexpected opportunity. Maxwell had not said anything specific on the subject, but Cortez believed that he had given him his blessing to silence the English spy. Irrespective of whether Maxwell had meant exactly that or not, Cortez simply had to prevent the Englishman from learning about the Spanish plan to land troops in Scotland.

To achieve that, he had to kill the English spy before he could report to his superior in England, who would undoubtedly be the reviled Sir Francis Walsingham. The armada was due to sail and he could not allow anything to interfere with its ultimate success.

***

The ships of the armada weighed anchor and set sail. Juan Martinez de Recalde stood on the deck of his own ship, the *San Juan de Portugal*, and watched his sailors get the ship under way with practised ease. De Recalde was second-in-command, and as such, the Duke of Medina Sidonia had suggested that he sail on board his flagship, the *Santa Ana*; but as it was a request rather than an order, de Recalde felt at liberty to decline.

His 'official' reason for not accepting the invitation was that he felt that he and the commander should sail separately to minimise the risk of both senior officers being killed or wounded in the same action. In reality, on board the *Santa Ana,* he would be constrained by Sedonia's stubborn refusal to contemplate the slightest deviation from King Philip's orders and he feared that sailing with his dogmatic commander would lead to friction. He did not wish to become embroiled in arguments he could not hope to win, and besides, as a seasoned seaman who had seen action in all the oceans of the world, he wanted to command his own ship. He believed that on board the *San Juan de Portugal,* he could contribute far more to the great enterprise than he could cooped up with the fleet commander. For one thing, his own ship boasted fifty guns, while the *Santa Ana* carried only thirty.

To begin with, everything went to plan. De Recalde joined the vessels from Spain's southern ports and waited off Cadiz for the ships based in the Mediterranean to arrive. The sheer number and variety of ships: galleons, galleys, galleasses and hulks, meant that it took quite some time to assemble the armada and form it up into the pre-arranged order. The speedy and manoeuvrable little pinnaces darted around and shepherded the large ships into position, and de Recalde led what was already a formidable fleet north to the rendezvous with Medina Sidonia. At exactly the appointed spot on the limitless ocean, he joined forces with the rest of the great armada.

Once the ships of the armada were finally shepherded into their predetermined order, Medina Sidonia called a conference of his senior commanders aboard his flagship. Sidonia reiterated the king's orders and, by way of boosting morale, he reminded everyone that this great enterprise had the blessing of Pope Sixtus V. His Holiness, he stressed, was most anxious to see England returned to the true faith, and Sidonia ordered all of his captains to ensure that their crews and the soldiers they were transporting, were aware of the fact. Much to de Recalde's consternation, however, he learned that the three ships carrying the force to land in Scotland had already been despatched by Sidonia without his knowledge in line with Philip's orders.

Once at sea, and away from Philip's influence, he had hoped that the commander would see sense and abandon that element of the plan. De Recalde hoped that, even though the three ships had already sailed, it might still not be too late to call them back, and he felt that he had to make one last try. Sidonia clearly had no idea of what was involved in sending ships far out into the Western Ocean to avoid Elizabeth's navy, then navigate the dangerous seas off the north coast of Ireland and into the narrow waters of the Irish Sea with its treacherous tides and currents, to land troops in southern Scotland. He relied on the fact that among the seasoned captains, there would at least be some who were prepared to support him in making the commander aware of the dangers such a voyage presented, but to his immense annoyance, he found that his was a lone voice. At this early stage in the enterprise, not one of the captains was disposed to argue with either their commander, their king, or especially, their pope. The captains returned to their ships and, in a mood of supreme optimism, the great armada set sail for England and glory.

There was nothing more de Recalde could do except say a silent prayer for Don Juan Cortez.

Chapter 19

Musgrave's control finally snapped: "Shut up, Elliot, haven't you got us into enough trouble already? If you had the sense to keep your stupid mouth shut, I could still be out there trying to get a message to Big Jock. I'll sort this out with your brother and we don't need any more nonsense from you."

Sandy felt the tension of the moment and fully expected an immediate retaliation from Rabbie. He had to admit that his brother deserved to have his head bitten off and on several occasions he had been on the point of doing it himself, but should things come to a head, he knew he would spring to Rabbie's aid. He was well aware, and had been for some time, that by constantly helping Rabbie out of difficulties of his own making, he was not really doing anything to help his brother learn fom his mistakes, and the more he continued to get him out of trouble, the more the hothead would keep getting into it. He knew that he would soon have to let his brother stand on his own two feet, but on this occasion, while Rabbie may well need to have some common sense knocked into him, that was for an Elliot to do. Sandy would never stand by and allow this Englishman to do it.

He knew what was getting under Musgrave's skin. While he and the Englishman sat and rationally discussed ways out of their current plight and tried to come up with viable solutions, Rabbie kept butting in with the most outlandishly impossible schemes, most of which involved ways of overpowering the guards and fighting their way out of Lochmaben. Sandy could well understand the Englishman's frustration. He, too, was getting sick and tired of constantly having to explain to his brother why his latest scheme was not workable, when on every occasion it seemed to be for the same reason. Taking up any one of Rabbie's outlandish suggestions, would only present Maxwell with a valid excuse for killing them and claiming that it was their own fault. In the event of his ever having to answer for their deaths, the laird would claim that they had been in league with an English spy.

To begin with, Musgrave held his temper, but that could not possibly last and his patience eventually ran out. He spoke his mind and, as a result, Rabbie and the Englishman stood and glared at each other. Sandy thanked his lucky stars that there was nothing to hand they could use as weapons. All three of them were tired, dirty and hungry, which he knew was a recipe for shortened tempers, but he made a last ditch attempt to take the heat out of the situation.

"Let it go, both of you. Fighting between ourselves will get us nowhere. If we ever do get out of this, you'll have plenty of time to settle your differences then."

Rabbie's every instinct was to fly at Musgrave and break every bone in his body but, and somewhat to his own amazement, he held off. It occurred to him that in spite of Sandy's plea for peace, his brother would back him up as he had always done, and that could result in all three of them being hurt, or worse. Even in his present belligerent mood, Rabbie knew that once these things started, they were impossible to stop, and some small voice at the back of his mind told him that attacking Musgrave would only lead to disaster. There could be no escaping the fact that Sandy was right. Unpalatable as he found it, to have any chance of escape they must work together. And, although it was equally difficult for Rabbie to accept, the same small voice reminded him that he owed Musgrave a debt, which, as an Elliot, he was bound to repay. Spy or not, if the Englishman had not vouched for them, both he and Sandy would now be dead, and to make matters worse, Musgrave was right in telling him that were it not for his ill-advised outburst, the Englishman might still be free. Much as he hated backing down to anybody, and particularly Musgrave, he knew that he had to. He took a deep breath, relaxed and sat down.

Sandy heaved a huge sigh of relief. He nodded approvingly at his brother and turned his attention to Musgrave. "All right?" he asked.

Musgrave hesitated, thought about it, then nodded his agreement and he too sat back down.

They resumed their discussion. Sandy and Musgrave agreed that Big Jock was their best, in fact their only, chance of getting away from Lochmaben. Big Jock, Musgrave said, would not remain on watch for the king for any longer than he had to, and as soon as he knew that James was on the march, and he had warned Liddesdale, he would be back. Sandy had never doubted it for a minute, and he knew that if Rabbie took the time to think, he would realise it too. Nevertheless, they still had to work out exactly how to help the big man when he did eventually come to rescue them. They knew that their first objective must be to remain alive, so Musgrave and Sandy turned their minds to finding ways of ensuring that they did.

Had they known that Big Jock had already arrived at Lochmaben and was keeping watch on the events unfolding around the castle, it might have given them at least a little more hope for the future. But they did not know, and so they continued to discuss the problem.

Rabbie sat in silence. He was still trying to come to terms with being obliged to rethink his approach to their predicament and particularly his attitude towards Musgrave. He realised, albeit belatedly, that he had yet again been making a complete fool of himself. What he had been arguing for, and what had caused the spat between them, would achieve nothing except to get them all killed. With his thoughts elsewhere, he hadn't been listening to what the others were saying but, eventually, he found himself taking an interest and he began to think rationally. He noted what Sandy and Musgrave were saying about the importance of their still being alive when Big Jock finally arrived, and it occurred to him that they had forgotten something of importance they ought to have considered. It occurred to him that there must be some reason why they were not already dead.

"Maybe Maxwell doesn't want to kill us; if he did, we'd already be dead," he said. "He was keeping us alive to hang us, but he hasn't done it yet. So what's he waiting for?"

Initially, the others took no notice of him. He didn't like being ignored, but realised that it was his own fault, so he persisted and evenually made them listen.

Sandy turned to Musgrave. "Rabbie has a point. Maxwell has had plenty of chances to hang us but he hasn't, so what's holding him back?"

Musgrave had to admit that it was something he had failed to consider, especially as it had been staring them in the face all along. It was annoying to find that it had taken Rabbie to think of it, but young Elliot was right. He thought hard before coming up with the only answer that seemed to make any sense.

"He's keeping us as a present for the king. If James gets the better of him, he'll use you to bargain his way out of trouble. James would give a lot to get his hands on a couple of Elliots, so Maxwell will hold you two as hostages to bring your father into line, and he'll exchange me for some of his friends that Scrope has locked up in Carlisle."

"So we might have more time than we thought to wait for Big Jock," Sandy said excitedly. "Well done, Rabbie."

Once Rabbie had changed the direction of their thinking, another thought came to Musgrave. "Maybe James is doing us a favour. Maxwell must know that the king will come after him sometime and I bet the canny bastard has a plan in mind for when the king attacks. I don't know what his plan is, but James coming early might make him have to change it."

"But how does that help us?" Sandy wanted to know. "Maxwell might still hang the three of us together and say that we're all English spies."

Rabbie was again the one to spot the significance. "He won't want to hang us here and, with Jamie around, he can't go anywhere else without taking a whole army to protect him."

Musgrave had to admit that the younger Elliot was at last beginning to think rationally. "That's right, and whatever he has in mind for us, he wants to deal with the king first. The bastard is up to something, and I have a feeling that King James might be in for a big surprise."

***

Without knowing it, Musgrave had stumbled on the truth. Maxwell did indeed have a plan for dealing with the king's unexpectedly early arrival. The laird was, at that very moment, preparing to ride out from Lochmaben to meet James at Langholm. He was leaving his brother, David Maxwell, in command of the garrison at Lochmaben, but before leaving, Maxwell had made a decision about what he would do with his three captives.

Had they known what Maxwell planned for them, it would have dashed the prisoners' newfound sense of optimism, but there was no getting away from one simple fact: there was still nothing they could do except sit and wait for something to happen. For men of The Borders who were used to being constantly in some form of, invariably deadly, action, this kind of situation was difficult to cope with and could easily set their reivers' nerves on edge, and especially Rabbie's. But to Sandy's relief, and Musgrave's amazement, there were no more sudden ill-advised outbursts. Rabbie was managing to hold his emotions in check. Perhaps, Sandy thought, his brother was at last learning some much-needed lessons and the fact that he had thought of something with the potential to help them in their current predicament, seemed to prove it.

As far as he and Musgrave could work out, the year must now have advanced into late April or early May bringing with it a spell of pleasant spring weather. Conditions in the cramped confines of the tiny cell were rapidly deteriorating, and for men who lived their lives almost entirely out of doors, the stuffiness generated by the warmer weather was becoming almost unbearable, and the accompanying smell from the filth was nauseating. In these conditions, the three prisoners were feeling tired, dirty and extremely uncomfortable, and they were in danger of succumbing to drowsiness. The only relief seemed to be to give up and accept their fate, but the Englishman, following his experience of the dungeon in Carlisle, realised that there were ways of coping with the advancing lethargy. Very little light penetrated the dungeon, and with the improved weather, it became difficult to distinguish between moonlit nights and daylight. The nights, however, were noticeably cooler and Musgrave suggested that they sleep during the day and stay awake at night. This was, after all, something that reivers were accustomed to doing. Seeing them sleeping, the guards might think that they had finally been overcome by the conditions and no longer posed a threat, but they would continue to wake them during the day when delivering what passed for food. Food which at Musgrave's insistence, they ate, and drank the tepid water. Three skeletons, he asserted, would be no use to anybody when the time came to take action.

The Elliot brothers accepted Musgrave's suggestion but never had an opportunity to test it. Early next morning, there was a flurry of activity in the castle courtyard, and even in the depths of the dungeon, the sound of men and horses was clearly audible. They quickly realised that there were many more men and horses than had previously been at Lochmaben.

Musgrave looked at the Elliots. "Something is up. Get ready, and this time don't do anything stupid." The last remark clearly directed at Rabbie.

There was a clatter of booted feet on the stone steps leading down to the dungeon. They were ushered out of the cell one at a time and had their hands tied in front of them, not by the usual castle guards but by a band of heavily armed reivers. The men looked familiar but, in the confusion of the moment, neither Musgrave nor the others could place them. Out into the open, all three took deep breaths of the sweetest fresh air they had ever savoured, and all signs of lethargy slowly disappeared as anticipation dispelled all thoughts of sleep. It was not yet full daylight and the light was not sufficiently strong to blind them, but it was bright enough for them to see that something important was happening. All around them, the castle courtyard was crowded with heavily armed men on horseback. To Musgrave, the activity bore all the signs of an army preparing for battle. Through the open gates, yet more mounted men were visible outside the castle, all clearly prepared to ride. The Englishman instantly knew what was happening. Maxwell was riding to confront the king. He was not going to wait for James, but planned to surprise him before he was fully prepared.

"What's happening, Sandy?" As soon as he asked it, Rabbie knew that it was an unnecessary question. He had seen enough large bands of men riding out on raids to know the answer.

Sandy looked at his brother and noted the ravages that two terms in the Lochmaben dungeon had wrought; Rabbie looked more like a scarecrow than a reiver. He had lost his steel bonnet and his hair was dirty and knotted, his dark beard had grown, and was similarly unkept, and his clothing was filthy and hung loose, a legacy of the sparse prison diet. Sandy knew that he must be in a similar state himself, and as his brother's spirit seemed to have survived the ordeal, he let the remark pass without comment. He was more concerned about what Maxwell had in store for them than in what the laird was planning to do about King Jamie. He looked questioningly at Musgrave. The Englishman, understanding what was on Sandy's mind, shrugged his shoulders.

Musgrave, however, had at least one suggestion. He held up his tied hands. "Whatever they have in mind, we'll be riding first."

Sandy saw the significance of the gesture. The reivers had tied their hands in front of them so that they could control a horse, and probably for a long ride.

There was a surge of activity around the castle entrance and Maxwell emerged. The laird had abandoned the nobleman's apparel he had been sporting of late, and was dressed and equipped for reiving. He mounted and rode over to where his three prisoners stood surrounded by a group of heavily armed men.

"This is where I must take my leave of you gentlemen," Maxwell announced jovially. "I have an urgent appointment with His Majesty the King."

Musgrave decided that he had nothing to lose from playing along. "Well, be sure to give James my regards," he said.

Maxwell laughed. "Oh I'll do better than that, Captain," he replied. "I'll bring him to meet you and you can give him your regards in person."

"In that case, I'll get someone to prepare suitable rooms for His Majesty. My present quarters aren't exactly fit for a king."

"Oh, I wouldn't dream of bringing him here," Maxwell replied, relishing this little by-play.

"So where am I to meet him?" Musgrave was the picture of innocence. "I'll have to get everything ready to receive him properly."

"Well then, I hope that Caerlaverock will suit your purposes."

"Caerlaverock?" Musgrave held up his bound hands. "I don't think that at the moment I would be quite up to such a ride, my lord, and I haven't had my breakfast yet."

Maxwell laughed. "Och, I'm sure you will survive, Mr Musgrave. Anyway, His Majesty will see that you are royally entertained."

With that, the laird took his leave. Outwardly, he was the picture of calm but inwardly he was angry with himself. He had not planned to get into a frivolous conversation with Musgrave, or to tell the trio what he planned for them, but the Englishman had tricked him into it. Still, he consoled himself with the thought that a meeting between Musgrave and the king would never take place, at least not in this life. If his plans came to fruition, both James and the Englishman would soon be dead, along with his other two prisoners. Maxwell did not intend to allow any of them to survive for very long once they reached Caerlaverock. It was, in the laird's opinion, a flawless plan. He had relegated the problem of what to do with his prisoners to the back of his mind, but when young Elliot let slip that the king was due to ride into Dumfriesshire sooner than expected, it suddenly assumed a measure of urgency. Knowing what they did about his plans, he could not allow any of the three to live, but the old problem involved in killing the Elliots while they were under his roof at Lochmaben, had not gone away. He would be storing up trouble for the future and so, they had to die somewhere else. He had briefly considered doing what Musgrave thought he would do, and hold them as a bargaining tool against the king, but he decided against it. Once the king had been defeated, Laird Maxwell would be the man people would have to make bargains with, not James Stewart.

Maxwell had also decided to send Cortez to Caerlaverock with them. He intended to keep the Spaniard alive until after the Spanish force landed, but could not have the interfering diplomat anywhere around while he dealt with with James. If the king learned of a Spaniard at Lochmaben, he would become curious and look closely into what was happening in his West March, and might even suspect that the Spanish were involved in whatever his errant laird was really planning to do. He lied to the Spaniard and told him that the time was now ripe for him to inspect the area where the invading force would land, and the best place to begin was the fortress where he intended to base the Spanish troops while they prepared to invade England. On a rough map, he pointed out to Cortez how close his fortress was to both England and the site of the landings, and as an added bonus, he told Cortez that he was sending the Englishman with him, escorted by a group of his riders, to Caerlaverock. The riders would act as an escort for the prisoners and, if Cortez wanted to make sure that Musgrave never arrived at the fortress alive, they would do nothing to stop him.

Cortez was delighted. It seemed as if Maxwell had seen sense at last and finally accepted that the Englishman was a spy and as a loyal Spaniard, he would be more than happy to put a permanent end to his spying. By killing an English spy, he would be performing an invaluable service for both his country and the Catholic faith and, more importantly, Maxwell finally seemed to have grasped the urgency of making proper preparations to meet the Spanish ships.

For his part, Maxwell doubted if this soft Spanish diplomat was up to the task of killing even an unarmed reiver like Musgrave and, consequently, his men had instructions to kill the Englishman along with the Elliots when they neared Caerlaverock. There would be no repercussions attached to the death of an English spy, and Caerlaverock was as good as anywhere, and better than most, to get rid of the two Elliots. His men had instructions to throw their bodies into the sea and the Solway tides would do the rest. If Alexander Elliot ever questioned the death of his sons, Maxwell would point the finger at either King James or the Spanish. Once he found out who they were, he would argue, he had sent them to Caerlaverock for their own safety, but either the king or the invaders had caught up with them. If the Elliots were not satisfied, they would have to take it up with either Jamie or Philip of Spain.

As he watched Maxwell ride away at the head of his reiver army, Musgrave was certain that the laird's jovial nature hid the disturbing fact that neither he nor the Elliots were destined to reach Caerlaverock alive. He looked across at his fellow prisoners and saw that they, too, understood. He recognised the riders forming the escort as members of the reiver band who had captured the two Elliots, and he was under no illusions that they would turn out to be more execution party than escort. Three saddled horses stood ready and the prisoners mounted.

The party was about to ride out when a man, who definitely did not fit the description of a Border Reiver, came out of the castle to join them. Wearing doublet and hose, and sporting a feathered felt hat, Cortez was still dressed as a man of high standing. Musgrave had seen him around Lochmaben Castle and assumed that he was some sort of clerk or secretary employed by Maxwell as part of his determination to play the part of a nobleman. He still looked the part, but Musgrave noticed that the man now wore a pair of expensive, but well-worn, riding boots and sat on his horse like an experienced rider. He wore a rapier in an ornate scabbard, and attached to his saddle, were a pair of holsters housing two familiar-looking pistols. Musgrave sensed that the stranger was much more than a simple clerk, and would bear watching.

Rabbie could not take his eyes off the newcomer and particularly the weapons. Unknown to him, the pistols had been presented to Cortez by Maxwell to further convince the Spaniard that he had nothing to fear regarding the expected invasion. The laird, however, had explained that, unfortunately, he did not have any ammunition for the weapons. That too, was a lie; he had left some with the leader of the escort. The control that Rabbie had shown over the last few days almost left him, but he remembered how Maxwell had used those same pistols to bait him, and he managed to hold his temper.

He turned to his brother and pointed at the leader of the escort. "I know him, Sandy, he's the bastard that ambushed us and took us to Maxwell." He turned to Cortez, "but who in God's name is that, and what is he doing with our pistols?"

Sandy, just as mystified as Rabbie, shook his head, but the leader of the escort, soon to be execution party, overheard and laughed. "Och, he's a friend o' the laird's frae Spain."

He rode off still laughing, but a sudden further realisation hit Musgrave like a blow from a war club. This stranger was a Spaniard and a friend of Maxwell's! He suddenly realised that Maxwell had not planned his own escape from Spain, as he would have people believe, but had Spanish help. The presence of a Spaniard at Lochmaben proved that beyond doubt, but why had a lone Spaniard come to Scotland with the escaping laird? Only the Spaniard could tell him that, and that particular piece of information would be useful not only to him, it would be especially valuable to Lord Scrope. He was convinced that Maxwell did not intend that any of his prisoners would reach Caerlaverock alive, but he was confident that, in his own case at least, he could prevent that happening. He had one small advantage nobody, not even his fellow prisoners, were aware of; before he reached Lochmaben, he had hidden the small ballock dagger in his boot. Under this new set of circumstances, he abandoned the idea of returning to Carlisle and taking the two Elliots as a present for the English Warden. That would be impossible if Maxwell had them killed, but the unexpected appearance of the Spaniard had opened up new and interesting possibilities.

If he could take a real live Spanish prisoner back to Scrope and Walsingham, he would be set up for life! He had, of course, to keep himself and the Spaniard alive in order to do so, and even with the dagger, that would not be easy, but if he lost the two young Elliots in the process, it would matter little.

The arrival of the Spaniard had rekindled his determination. He did not yet know exactly how, but somehow he would get back to Carlisle and take this Spaniard with him. There would be risks involved, but they were worth taking.

Chapter 20

Big Jock watched as Maxwell rode out from Lochmaben Castle to where his men, already mounted, waited on the northern shore of the loch. The laird led his reiver army east and Big Jock guessed that he planned to do battle with King James at Langholm, his most easterly fortress. There was, however, a flaw in that theory. Maxwell's force, although impressive by reivers' standards, did not match anything like the number of men the king could put in the field, and even with the advantage of surprise, he could not hope to win a decisive victory over the royal army.

"The canny bastard," Big Jock muttered quietly to himself. To the old reiver's mind, there could be only one explanation for Maxwell's tactics. As soon as he sensed defeat at Langholm, a defeat he must know he was bound to face, he would fall back to Lochmaben, and then, if necessary, move further and further west. He intended to lure the king as far as possible into the Galloway Hills, where he would have the advantage of knowing the ground. There, he could harass the king's army and cause James a great deal of trouble. But for how long? Maxwell's own men would follow him to the death, but those from other families, reivers all, would support him only as long as there was plunder available. At some point, there had to be a definite resolution to the dispute between Maxwell and his king, and in the end, the sheer size of Jamies's force would tell.

Big Jock, however, did not have time to dwell on what might happen in the future. He had too many other more important matters on his mind.

He considered taking news of Maxwell's plans back to Liddesdale where Martin Elliot of Braidley might be able to use it to gain an advantage over Bothwell, but that would mean abandoning his watch on Lochmaben Castle and possibly losing any chance of rescuing his heidsman's sons. He had little time to plan his next move, but in reality, there was only one thing he could do. He decided that he had to trust the watchers sent by Alexander to replace him, both of whom he knew to be reliable riders. The sight of

Maxwell riding east, when they were expecting to see the king heading west for Dumfriesshire, would confuse them, but Big Jock believed that once they spotted the size of Maxwell's force, they would know what to do. They would ride to warn Liddesdale. He would dearly love to fight beside his heidsman when the Keeper of Liddesdale rode to attack the tower. He had some personal scores to settle with several of Bothwell's men, but until the current dangerous situation was resolved, he represented Sandy and Rabbie Elliot's only hope of survival. He had to stick to his chosen course of action and there was no time for further delay. His immediate task was to determine whether Maxwell was taking the heidsman's sons with him to use as hostages.

He rode as close to the laird's column as he dared and, to his immense relief, there was no sign of them among the riders. Satisfied that they were not with Maxwell, he decided that they must still be at Lochmaben. Providing, of course, that they were still alive. King Jamie's early arrival might well have prompted Maxwell to dispose of all his prisoners.

With his heart in his mouth, Big Jock turned his attention back to the castle. He set out on yet another circuit of the fortress and came in sight of the main gates just in time to see the small group of riders leaving and heading south. Sandy and Rabbie were with them and, thankfully, alive and well, as was the Englishman, Musgrave.

They were clearly closely guarded prisoners, but the fact that they were alive, gave Big Jock reason for hope.

***

On the northern edge of the Debatable Land, Alexander's riders sighted the large band of riders heading east, and from a distance, the scouts could not be sure of who they were. Coming from the west, they could not be part of Jamie's army, which would have come from Edinburgh in the east, but as the band drew nearer, they recognised the leader as Laird Maxwell, and although confused about what it might be, they realised that something important must be happening. One man rode back to Liddesdale to inform the heidsman.

Like Big Jock, Alexander immediately suspected what Maxwell planned to do. The laird had somehow learned of the king's intention to attack as soon as possible after the snow cleared, and for a reiver like Alexander, it was easy to guess how he would deal with the situation. Maxwell's tactics were clear. Rather than allow Jamie to ride into Dumfriesshire unhindered, and was going to confront the king at Langholm. He would allow Jamie to besiege his castle and then attack him from the rear. It was nothing more than a version of the tried and trusted reiver ambush, and not very different from the tactics Martin of Braidley intended to employ against Bothwell. But, although Maxwell's intentions were clear enough, they gave Alexander cause for concern; they held a significant danger for Liddesdale.

It was widely believed that following Maxwell's capture and exile to Spain, he had left his fortress at Langholm lightly defended, and both Alexander and Martin of Braidley assumed that Jamie would simply bypass it on his way to Dumfriesshire. What happened between Maxwell and the king would normally have been of little consequence to the reivers of Liddesdale, but a major encounter between the two at Langholm could have serious consequences. Situated just to the west, Langholm was uncomfortably close to Liddesdale and if Jamie won a resounding victory over Maxwell there, he could easily turn his attention to them and ride to support Bothwell. He despatched a rider to warn Martin of Braidley of the latest disturbing development and sent the scout back to keep watch on Maxwell.

He had done everything he could do for the defence of his tower in the event of Bothwell breaking through Braidley's ambush. Although not as strong as he would have liked, his garrison was comprised of experienced men from all the families of Liddesdale, men he knew he could rely on to fight to the last. He had ensured that they were well armed and provisioned, but the sudden turn of events at Langholm, prompted him to add a further precaution. The king might have brought up siege artillery, which he could turn on his tower once he was finished with Langholm, so he ordered a supply of peat to be stacked in the lower floors. If the defences of the tower were breached, the peat would be set to smoulder to prevent the enemy destroying it with gunpowder.

The difficulties caused by King James, Maxwell and Bothwell, had already subjected the reiver families of Liddesdale to a large measure of inconvenience. The best of the reiving season was past; their opportunities for raiding were severely limited, and deprived of the opportunity to raid left them in a vulnerable position. For families outside the valley, the Scotts, the Grahams, the Kerrs and the rest, it was business as usual, and the English reivers: the Hetheringtons, the Fenwicks, the Charltons and all the others, were as active as ever. Due to the level of activity and the numbers of armed riders evident in the valley, raiders steered clear of Liddesdale, but Alexander knew that it would only take one English warden, Sir John Foster, Warden of the English Middle March in particular, to spot an opportunity. Foster, as much reiver as March Warden, might just decide to take a hand and mount a large raid into Liddesdale on the pretext of apprehending the reivers, but in reality seeking plunder. So the sooner the problems involving Bothwell and James were resolved, the sooner things would get back to normal.

With nothing much else to do but wait, Alexander found his thoughts turning inexorably back to the plight of his two sons. Not that they had been very far from his mind since he first heard that they were missing, but the news that Maxwell was riding out from his Dumfriesshire stronghold, added to his concern. The laird had obviously learned that Jamie intended to come and arrest him sooner than he expected, and there was only one possible way he could have come upon that particular piece of information. He must have got it from either Big Jock, Malcolm or Robert, and, although he was loath to admit it, by far the most likely source was young Robert. The possibility that his son was tortured in order to divulge this information, was almost too much to bear, but if that proved to be the case, Alexander vowed that Maxwell would pay dearly for it, irrespective of what the king might do.

A calmer voice reminded him that his youngest son was prone to say too much at inappropriate moments and might well have simply let his tongue run away with him. But if Robert had been tortured, he would hunt Maxwell down in the furthest parts of Dumfriesshire or the deepest dungeon in Edinburgh, and even if Jamie sent the laird into exile again, Alexander was prepared to follow him to Spain to exact revenge.

Chapter 21

Maxwell rode at the head of the largest reiver band he had ever assembled. He had complete confidence in his chosen plan, as did the men, reivers all, who rode with him. Had the laird known that as soon as both Alexander and Big Jock learned that he was riding east they had instantly realised how he intended to counter the threat to his freedom posed by King James, it would not have surprised him. It took a reiver to know how a reiver would react, while the king, for all his authority and resources, would never suspect what tactics his errant laird was most likely to employ.

James VI was no reiver but he was a competent enough soldier, and wise enough to surround himself with some old military heads who knew their business well, but these men, skilled in the art of soldiering as they undoubetedly were, had learned their trade in conventional warfare. Although they had fought the reivers in many bitter encounters, they had never thought to study the reiver's tactics, and even with their depth of military experience, they never stopped to consider how Maxwell would react to the king's moves to arrest him. As fellow reivers, however, Alexander and Big Jock had no doubts whatsoever what Maxwell would do. He would ambush the king. The watchers sent out to replace the three original scouts, not used to seeing reiver bands as large as Maxwell's, had not reported on numbers, and only Big Jock knew their true strength, but that mattered little. Like Big Jock, Alexander knew that Maxwell could never assemble a force strong enough to defeat King James's army in a pitched battle, but neither would he risk suffering a heavy defeat. Hence his reliance on proven reiver tactics.

Big Jock had guessed, and Alexander was certain, that Maxwell was trying to lure the king into the Galloway Hills, and he could understand why. The laird would still not be able to match the king in open battle but once in those familiar hills, he would resort to the ever-reliable reiver ambush and try to wear the king's army down. The reivers had been successfully using such tactics against both English and Scottish armies for centuries but, while Alexander was confident in his assessment of Maxwell's basic scheme, he knew nothing about the laird's ultimate objective.

Maxwell's strategy was indeed to let James besiege Langholm and then launch an attack when the king's forces were fully committed, inflicting as much damage to the royal army as he could. Once he sensed that the enemy was gaining the upper hand, he would retreat and let James chase him into the Galloway Hills. He would bypass Lochmaben, leaving the garrison there to defend the castle as best they could while he harassed James with well-placed ambushes to keep the king busy until the Spanish landed. It would take longer than he originally anticipated, but he would eventually set his original plan in motion. James would have to abandon chasing Maxwell to deal with the Spanish invasion, and when the king was fully committed in the battle with the Spaniards, Maxwell planned to ride to his aid on the pretext of helping him defend his country.

If Maxwell's ambitious scheme went as planned, King James VI would not survive the battle with the Spanish. Among the laird's reiver band were men whom he knew would be ready and willing to kill the king for a price, and should the opportunity arise, he fully intended to use them.

In the heat of battle, however, nothing was certain and there was no guarantee that the king would die, but even if James survived, Maxwell could still legitimately claim that he considered it far more important to defend his king and his country rather than pursue his personal ambitions. If James survived, he could not very well imprison his loyal laird or send him back into exile after that; and if James died as planned, his successor would face the same dilemma. Either way, Maxwell would be free to resume causing havoc throughout The Borders and especially against the Johnstones. He cared little for what happened in England, but if the main Spanish invasion succeeded and Elizabeth was dethroned, it would be an added bonus. James or his successor would be king of two countries and have little time to address the problem of his lawless Border Region.

As for the Spaniish, they would have to defeat the English without the help of the troops landing in Scotland, and in the meantime, Maxwell did not intend to let all that Spanish gold slip through his fingers.

***

From his vantage point on the roof, Alexander watched the battle develop as Bothwell's army attacked his tower house. The besiegers, however, did not seem to be pressing home their attacks with their usual determination and he had little doubt that he could hold out indefinitely. As his men beat off attempt after attempt to take the tower with relative ease, he knew very well what Bothwell's intentions were. The attack on the tower was no more than a diversion to tie Alexander down until the king arrived, possibly with artillery. The Keeper of Liddesdale was clearly attempting to isolate as many of the reivers as possible prior to annihilating them, with the king's help, in a pitched battle.

That, Alexander hoped, would eventually prove to be no more than wishful thinking on Bothwell's part, and the Keeper really ought to have known that reivers did not engage in conventional warfare. Centuries of being confronted by far superior enemy forces had taught them not to fall into such traps. They would never make the mistake of exposing part of their force by riding to relieve the siege of Alexander's tower, and neither would they engage in a conventional battle. If Bothwell was aware of the reiver's favourite tactics, he had chosen to ignore them and was relying on the hope that the Liddesdale reivers were still unaware that King James was riding against Maxwell. They would soon learn that James was besieging Langholm and be both surprised and confused. Then, as Martin Elliot of Braidley had predicted, he would lead his main force into Liddesdale. In the meantime, he continued on his set course and continued with the half-hearted attacks on Alexander Elliot's tower house.

This situation could not possibly last, and events inevitably came to a head. The whole of Liddesdale erupted in an explosion of blood and violence as two bitter battles broke out within a scant few miles of each other. In both cases, the action opened with an attack by the authorities, but the reivers dictated the tactics.

King James had assembled a force as strong as any army that had ever marched into battle in The Borders and the fact that he was going to arrest Maxwell, was reason enough for men to join him. Lairds Douglas, Johnsone and several others had good reason to see the man who had plundered their lands returned to Spain or, preferably, hanging from the ramparts of Edinburgh Castle, and they sent strong contingents to Edinburgh to join their king. Other reivers from a variety of families, while not having any great personal interest at stake, saw an opportunity for easy plunder and joined James on the march.

The king attacked Maxwell's castle at Langholm according to the established principles of siege warfare. He gave the defenders the traditional opportunity to surrender and when his offer was, as expected, declined, he began a siege, and he did not anticipate it taking long to crack this particular nut. Like the leaders of Liddesdale, he believed that Maxwell had abandoned Langholm and left only a token garrison behind, and it would not require much expenditure of time or effort to subdue them. Consequently, he had chosen not to include cumbersome siege artillery in his force. He did not expect Maxwell to be in the castle in person, which meant that he could expect no more than a token resistance mounted by the men stationed there. He would not need to deploy his full strength to subdue Langholm, so he could spare a strong force to help Earl Bothwell put paid to Liddesdale once and for all. The extremely confident James considered both Langholm and Liddesdale to be mere diversions from his principle objective, Maxwell. He would get these irritations over with quickly and move on to Lochmaben, where he could expect to meet much tougher opposition.

It came as a surprise, therefore, when his scouts informed him that Maxwell was riding with a sizeable force to relieve Langholm, which James and his advisers considered was a grave error of judgement on Maxwell's part. The laird could not hope to succeed against such overwhelming odds and had left himself vulnerable to capture. James jumped at this unexpected chance to apprehend Maxwell here and now and redeployed the force allocated to help Bothwell. Leaving an ample force to take Langholm, he personally led them to face the laird's attack. Liddesdale would have to wait – but not for long.

The engagement was short, sharp, and extremely vicious. Maxwell's men charged into the royal army with bloodthirsty abandon and initially set the king's forces back on their heels. The laird was perfectly aware that he could not sustain this level of success for very long, but that was not the essence of his plan. He had set out to give James a sufficiently bloody nose to entice the king to chase him into the far reaches of the Galloway Hills, where he could harass the royal army at will. His plan was a good one but it very nearly ended in disaster. His riders' blood was up. They had little thought for anything other than plundering the king's men and Maxwell feared that he might not be able to extricate them when the time came. James's men had little choice but to fight back with equal ferocity and, after just thirty minutes of deadly action, swords, lances and daggers were red with blood, and the field was strewn with dead and dying. Eventually, however, Maxwell managed to break off and lead his men away. He was satisfied that James would now have to follow him or lose credibility in front of his army.

Maxwell had suffered higher than expected losses, but he had achieved his main objective. James's original annoyance with the laird now turned to outright hatred. How dare the man he had exiled to Spain return home and ride out from Dumfriesshire to attack him? He viewed the bloodstained battlefield and his own blood boiled. Taking only enough time to overwhelm the meagre garrison at Langholm, he set off in pursuit of Maxwell and, in the process, all thoughts of Bothwell and Liddesdale vanished from his mind.

***

Unknown to Liddesdale, Maxwell had done them an immense service. He had drawn James off into Dumfriesshire and away from them. Bothwell could no longer rely on his king's support and it was the Keeper's turn to receive an unpleasant surprise. He waited for news from James, but none was forthcoming. He sent a rider to find out what was happening and when he finally learned the truth, he found himself saddled with an unwelcome dilemma. He must either attack Liddesdale on his own, or retire to Hermitage Castle and abandon the whole enterprise, but, in the meantime, he still had part of his force besieging Alexander Elliot's tower. He had never entertained any real hopes of taking the tower with this particular siege, but once, with the king's help, he had quashed the reivers of Liddesdale, Elliot's tower, along with several others, would fall easily into his hands. Consequently, he had not committed a strong force to the siege. Now, however, with the king's artillery no longer available to him, he was the one who had men tied down, men he would need in order to mount a major effort to conquer Liddesdale. The reivers were clearly not going to try breaking the siege, but that was no longer of major importance.

Bothwell gave the matter some careful thought, but he knew that, in the end, there was only one decision he could possibly make.

It did not matter whether you were a reiver, or held a position of high authority, in The Borders you simply did not walk away from a fight. Especially if, as in his case, he still held a sizeable numerical advantage over his enemy. Bothwell was uncomfortably aware that if he failed to continue with his attempt to subdue Liddesdale, he would lose face completely, not only with his own men but also with the king, who would never again have reason to treat him with anything other than abject contempt. He might as well give up his office as Keeper of Liddesdale and hand over the keys to Hermitage Castle. Moreover, he would have to abandon any hope of personal advancement when James eventually came to sit on two thrones.

Bothwell was not someone who easily accepted counselling from men who held offices inferior to his own and, no longer able to rely on any help and advice from his king, he wrestled with the problem of how to salvage something from the wreckage on his own. Eventually, he devised a plan, which would, he hoped, allow him to retrieve the situation. He called off the siege and made a show of leading the besieging force back to Hermitage Castle to give the impression that he had given up the entire enterprise. The reivers, he reasoned, must know that the king no longer posed an immediate threat to them, and his seeming retreat would throw them off guard. Once he reached Hermitage, however, he quickly regrouped, turned around, and led his forces back down into Liddesdale.

Martin Elliot of Braidley was not about to be taken in by Bothwell's ruse. He allowed the Keeper to advance well into the reivers' valley before showing his hand.

Alexander, relieved of the responsibility of having to defend his tower, took the men who had formed the defence, collected several more riders from all of the Liddesdale families and led them to attack Bothwell's column head on. The Elliots, Armstrongs, Nixons and Crosiers fought with typical bloodthirsty ferocity. Alexander's skill with his lance accounted for three of Bothwell's men in quick succession. His riders were equally successful with their lances, basket-hilted swords and daggers. The clash of swords was interspersed with the occasional pistol shot, but each pistol could fire only once and, in the close hand-to-hand killing, there was not time to carry out the cumbersome task of reloading. The giving and receiving of quarter was not a concept that featured largely in encounters between the reivers and the authorities, and combat was to the death. Over the noise of battle and the screams of dying men and horses, the wild yells of the reivers were clearly audible. Initially, Alexander's reivers drove Bothwell's men back in some confusion but in spite of spilling copious amounts of blood, they were never going to overcome such a vastly superior force. Bothwell rallied his men. Alexander withdrew his riders and retreated. Bothwell might have suspected that he was probably falling into a trap, but he could not possibly give up now. He followed Alexander up the valley and Martin of Braidley sprang his ambush.

The fighting was again deadly. The reivers fought not only for their homes and families, but also for their entire way of life. The Keeper of Liddesdale urged his men on, but in The Borders and particularly in Liddesdale, even the finest army the authorities could muster was never strong enough to counter a reiver ambush. The outcome was inevitable, but it required a great deal more bloodshed before the forces of law were compelled to withdraw from the valley.

Earl Bothwell retired to Hermitage Castle and prepared to defend the fortress in case the reivers decided to attack it and complete their triumph, and he certainly could not allow that to happen. He had suffered an ignominious defeat in battle, but if anyone questioned his tactics or fighting nous, he had a ready answer. He could blame King James for not supporting him as originally agreed, which, he reasoned, would be sufficient excuse. Although kings did not have to account for their actions, James would not want it known that he had abandoned an ally in order to follow his own personal grudge against Maxwell. On the other hand, if Bothwell were to lose Hermitage as well, then no excuse on earth would hold water.

Reivers, however, were not adept at attacking heavily fortified positions from the outside. They knew that with Bothwell occupying it with a large force, the taking of Hermitage would require a long siege and heavy artillery. To them, it was simply not worth it. They buried their dead, tended their wounded, returned to their homes, and prepared to go reiving.

Alexander cleared out the peat from his tower-house and prepared it for the return of his wife and daughter. He would somehow have to explain to Margaret why Malcolm and Robert were not there to welcome her home but he would lie and stress that they were safe. His every instinct urged him to gather his men – even after a hard battle with the Keeper of Liddesdale they would not hesitate to follow their heidsman – and ride into Dumfriesshire to ensure that his sons were indeed safe, but with both the king and Maxwell riding roughshod through the Scottish West March, that was impossible.

He could do nothing but place his faith, and the lives of his sons, in the capable hands of Big Jock Elliot, assuming that Big Jock himself was still alive.

Chapter 22

Eight of Maxwell's reivers, with their three prisoners, filed out of Lochmaben Castle and rode in silence for some miles. The Spaniard, Don Juan Cortez, pointedly ignored by both prisoners and escort, rode alone at the rear of the little column but he did not mind in the least. He revelled in the thought of having an opportunity to deal with this English spy, but after over an hour of silence, his sense of anticipation overcame his diplomatic caution and boiled over. He simply could not wait for a minute longer. In his opinion, they were now far enough away from the so-called 'Laird' and his overbearing attitude for him to take a hand. In spite of what Maxwell had told him about waiting until they reached Caerlaverock, he considered it his duty to deal with the spy as soon as possible. Besides, he suspected that the 'laird' had not told him everything and had some other devious scheme in mind.

He rode close to Musgrave, and in an effort to provoke the Englishman into retaliating, spat at him. "I know who you are and what you are, Englishman," he said. "You are a spy for the heretic Elizabeth of England. But your spying days are about to come to an end."

Musgrave seethed inside at the insult but somehow managed to appear as if he ignored it. His captors had bound his hands in front of him rather than behind his back to allow him to guide his horse, and he managed to raise them to wipe the spittle from his face. Dressed in doublet and hose, Cortez stood out like a sore thumb among the roughly clad reivers and Musgrave made a show of looking him over carefully and feigned surprise.

"Oh, so you speak the Queen's English do you? So tell me, who are you, and what's a Spanish popinjay like you doing with a reiving bastard like Maxwell?"

'Popinjay' was not a term Cortez was familiar with, but he knew it had to be derogatory, and his loathing of the Englishman rose perceptibly. He was about to respond angrily but realised that Musgrave was paying him back in kind and now he was the one being provoked. It was important that he regain some of his diplomatic composure so he took a moment to think before deciding to continue on his original path. His voice remained calm, but his words held every bit of menace he could possibly muster.

"I am Don Juan Cortez, a loyal subject of King Philip, not that it will do you any good to know that, Englishman. Nor will you ever know my mission here in Scotland. Your spying days are over and you will taste Spanish steel before you can inform your heretic queen of my presence here."

Outwardly, the Englishman remained a picture of calm, but he knew that he was riding on dangerous ground and needed to find a safe path out of it. If Maxwell's riders had instructions to kill them, and he was sure that they did, he thought they were unlikely do it before reaching Caerlaverock Castle. With the bodies dumped in the Solway Firth and carried away on the tide, Alexander Elliot would never find out what had happened to his sons when he rode into Dumfriesshire looking for them, as he surely would. This Spaniard, however, clearly did not intend to wait, but was primed to kill him now. His years of experience told him that his best, and perhaps only, chance of survival was to take the initiative and act now; the nearer they got to Caerlaverock, the more difficult it would become. Maxwell might hesitate before disposing of the two Elliots, but nobody, including Lord Scrope, would worry much about what had happened to him. Unless he did something quickly, or was extremely lucky, he was unlikely to survive the journey.

It was clear that Cortez was a man of high status, but Musgrave guessed that if pushed far enough, the Spaniard would have difficulty holding his temper, and consequently, become careless. That might give him the opportunity to use his secret, and only, weapon, the ballock dagger in his boot. But in order to retrieve it, he would somehow have to get his hands free. He knew that he could not hope to take on all of Maxwell's men, but for the moment, Cortez represented his most immediate danger. The Spaniard had already confirmed his initial suspicion that Maxwell did not intend to allow any of them to live once they reached Caerlaverock, but Cortez was obviously not going to wait until then. It occurred to the Englishman that the Spaniard would be anxious to gloat before killing him, and he might be able to use that as a weapon against him. In any case, he had nothing to lose by goading Cortez further.

He laughed in the Spaniard's face. "So you're going to do Maxwell's dirty work for him are you? You must be out of your mind to trust that bastard. Can't you see that if he has his way, none of us will reach Caerlaverock alive?"

Cortez had already reached the conclusion that, once he had served the 'laird's purposes, Maxwell planned to kill him too. He had every confidence that he could outwit the rabble who were supposed to be escorting him, but in case something, anything, went wrong, he had to ensure that he carried out his duty to both his king and his faith, and eliminate the English spy. He did not like the Englishman laughing at him in front of a band of common thieves and he decided to let the spy know just how serious he was.

"What happens to me is not of any great importance. All that matters is that you die, Englishman."

Musgrave felt that his predicament was becoming desperate. He simply had to get his hands free and the Spaniard was the only one in a position to do it. His only other allies were the Elliot brothers but they also had their hands tied. It occurred to him that, as a Spanish gentleman, Cortez lived by a code of honour, and he set out to try to hurt the Spaniard's pride.

"And you think that you're man enough to do it, do you? If you were to face me man to man, you'd soon find out that you're not, but I don't suppose a Spanish popinjay like you ever had the courage to fight a real man. You'll do what all Spaniards do, you'll shoot me with one of those fancy pistols you stole, or stick that toy sword in my back while I have my hands tied."

Don Juan Cortez showed the first signs of losing his composure. He could not allow his own, and his country's, honour to be ridiculed by an

Englishman, and a despicable spy at that. His anger rose and he was on the point of challenging Musgrave there and then, but his years of experience as a diplomat, coupled with his sense of duty and the importance of his mission, helped him to hold his temper in check.

He took a deep breath. "I know that you are trying to provoke me, Englishman, but you are wasting your time. As an English spy, you do not have the right to expect an honourable death, and neither does your heretic queen. When King Philip takes her throne, he will be honourable about it and take off her head quickly with good Toledo steel instead of burning her at the stake for the heretic she is. But even hanging is much too good for vermin like you."

Musgrave's confidence rose. He sensed that he was on the verge of pushing Cortez into making what he hoped would be a fatal mistake. His main objective was still to escape from Maxwell's men and get back to Lord Scrope with news of the Spaniard's presence in Scotland and, although he still had no idea of what Cortez was doing with Maxwell, he could leave that for Scrope and Walsingham to work out. It would be nice if he could take the Spaniard with him, alive if possible, as evidence, but there seemed little chance of that. Still, if he could return with some proof of a Spaniard's association with Maxwell, and convince Scrope that he had killed the Spaniard, it should be enough to get him reinstated as Captain of Bewcastle.

He sensed that if he could provoke Cortez just a little more, he might be able to goad the Spaniard into cutting him free before trying to run him through with that fancy rapier. Then, he would have a chance. He was counting on Cortez's sense of honour prompting him to cut his bonds so that he could roll off his horse and force the Spaniard to dismount in order to finish him off. At that stage, he would pull the ballock dagger from his boot, overpower the foppish Spaniard, and hold him as a hostage. It was risky but he reckoned that it was his only chance. The Elliots would recognise his action as much the same ruse used by Big Jock's father, Little Jock, to outwit the 4th Earl Bothwell, and it would help if he could enlist their help in his plan, but he doubted if that was possible. If successful, his best option was to ride as far away as he could get, and the Elliots would simply have to take their chances until Big Jock, who was certainly somewhere around, came to their aid.

He continued to goad Cortez. "So you're going to kill me, and your cowardly king is going to kill Queen Elizabeth. No doubt we'll both have out hands tied when you do it."

The Spaniard was by now almost speechless with rage, and before he could react, Musgrave pressed home his advantage. "And your cowardly king needs Maxwell's help before he dares to invade England. He must be out of his mind to trust that old reiver. I knew that you weren't a very bright Spaniard, but now I see that the pious old idiot you call Philip of Spain is just as stupid as you are."

This was too much for Cortez. He reacted just as Musgrave hoped he would. He reached for his sword. "That is enough of your insolence, Englishman! Now you die!"

Musgrave's heart missed a beat. He had gone too far. The Spaniard intended to run him through without releasing his hands. He prepared to roll off his horse to avoid the sword thrust.

Cortez, however, had more to say. "But before you die, I'm going to cut you free so that you can get on your knees and beg forgiveness for speaking of King Philip like that. Then you will blaspheme no further." Exhibiting a skill born of years of practice, the Spaniard drew his rapier.

***

Big Jock Elliot watched as the reiver band filed out of Lochmaben Castle with their three captives, and he recognised the riders guarding the three prisoners as some of the reivers who had originally taken Sandy and Rabbie prisoner. Confirmation that the heidsman's sons were alive, removed the last vestiges of worry from his mind and allowed him to concentrate fully on how to get them away from Maxwell's riders. Had they still been prisoners in the castle, getting them out would have involved some kind of negotiation with Maxwell, a skill that Big Jock was not competent in, but now that they were out of the castle, and heading away from Lochmaben, his confidence returned. This was where he was in his element and now he knew that he stood a real chance of rescuing his hiedsman's sons. He was not at all surprised to see that Musgrave, also a prisoner, had managed to survive. The Englishman had obviously been as good as his word and convinced Maxwell that Sandy and Rabbie were Elliots and not Johnstones, but Big Jock knew the Captain of Bewcastle of old and was well aware that whatever Musgrave did was always for personal gain. In The Borders, however, that was nothing out of the ordinary and Big Jock accepted it as such. The Englishman must have fallen out with Maxwell and got himself taken prisoner as well, and that puzzled Big Jock. It would be more in keeping with the laird's usual practice to have swiftly eliminated Musgrave rather than going to the trouble of keeping him prisoner, which meant that he had some further use for the Englishman. What use that might be mattered little to Big Jock, but, as a prisoner, the Englishman would certainly want to escape, and so could be enlisted to help in rescuing the two Elliots.

Having a much clearer grasp of the situation convinced Big Jock that he would find a way of rescuing Sandy and Rabbie, but one thing still puzzled the big man. The rider bringing up the rear of the column was certainly not one of Maxwell's men. Dressed in doublet and hose and armed with a stylish rapier, he was clearly not a reiver, but neither was he a prisoner. Yet, in spite of his courtly appearance, Jock recognised him as a competent rider and suspected that he might be equally efficient with that fancy sword. Who he might be, or what he was doing with a band of reivers, was a mystery, and Big Jock did not care much for unknowns. This stranger would bear watching.

The old reiver knew that getting too close to Maxwell's riders would increase the risk of discovery. Although he had yet to locate him, even here in their own domain, these reivers were sure to have a rider somewhere watching their backs.

He rode warily and followed at a distance until he was sure that they were making for Maxwell's base at Caerlaverock, and that gave him further cause for hope. The country between Lochmaben and Caerlaverock was solid Maxwell territory and, in such familiar surroundings, the riders guarding the prisoners would inevitably become less vigilant. Knowing where they were going also allowed him to keep in touch with them without risking revealing his presence. He could circle around to the west and watch them from the cover of the Galloway Hills, which stretched off to the west, and meant that he would not have to stray too far away from their route to Caerlaverock.

***

Sandy and Rabbie Elliot, in common with the reivers guarding them, could hardly fail to hear the raised voices, and everyone stopped to watch the confrontation between Musgrave and the Spaniard.

Rabbie rode close to his brother. "What's going on between Musgrave and that foreigner?"

Sandy expressed some concern. "I'm not sure, Rabbie, but as far as I can make out, the man is Spanish, and he thinks that Musgrave is an English spy. It looks like he's all set to do for him."

"We know for sure that Musgrave is a spy," Rabbie replied. "But if it wasn't for him, Maxwell would have us hanging high in Dumfries. We should try to help him."

Sandy knew what his brother was getting at. They owed their lives to the Englishman, but he was at a loss to see what they could do to repay their debt. He held up his bound hands. "You're right, Rabbie, but we can't do much tied up like this."

Rabbie had to accept that his brother was right and his frustration, which had been steadily rising since they left Lochmaben, was beginning to get the better of him. Sandy sensed that his brother would say or do something that would only serve to get them into deeper trouble and he got ready to intervene, but to his surprise, not to mention relief, that was not necessary. His brother seemed to be learning to keep his emotions under control.

By now, the fracas between the Englishman and the Spaniard had grabbed everyone's attention. The reivers, including their leader, were viewing the scene with great amusement and some were even making bets on who would come out on top. With the escort's attention distracted, Sandy sensed an opportunity. Riding immediately behind Musgrave, he reined his horse gently backwards and motioned Rabbie to do the same.

"I know we should help Musgrave, but we'll never have a better chance than this to make a run for it. If we go in different directions like we did when we met the Hetheringtons, one of us could ride back and find Big Jock. He's bound to be following us."

Rabbie looked around and agreed that what his brother said was right. The disturbance gave them at least a reasonable chance of escape.

"You're right Sandy, but Big Jock won't be behind us. He'll know that these riders will have someone watching their backs. If he's anywhere around, he'll be watching us from those hills. I'll go that way and you ride east to draw them off. They're going to kill us anyway when we get to Caerlaverock so we have to try something, and we'll never get a better chance. Get ready!"

Sandy nodded, it was his brother's idea, so he allowed him to dictate how it should be done. "We'll do it."

Rabbie checked that the reivers were still distracted. They were. "Ride, Sandy!"

He wheeled his horse and galloped off towards the hills. Sandy was about to ride in the opposite direction when out of the corner of his eye he saw Cortez draw his sword, and immediately changed his mind. He kicked his horse into motion, galloped forward and barged into the Spaniard's horse. Taken by surprise, Cortez dropped the rapier. His horse reared and it was all he could do to stay in the saddle. Musgrave, although also taken by surprise, was quick-witted enough to change his mind about dismounting. He decided to take advantage of the situation and make a break for freedom, but he never had stood a chance. The leader of the band had been watching Cortez and the Englishman in great amusement when Sandy's violent intervention jolted him back into reality. He immediately sprang into action and yelled to his men to look to the prisoners. Sandy and Musgrave found themselves surrounded by reivers with lances at the ready.

It was only then that the reivers realised one of their captives was missing.

The leader rode up to Cortez and grabbed one of the wheel lock pistols. He held it to Sandy's head and demanded, "Where did yer brither gang tae?"

Sandy looked around and pretended to be surprised not to find Rabbie behind him. He looked at the reiver and shrugged his shoulders. "How would I know? I wasn't watching him. Why don't you ask the men that were supposed to be?"

The reiver bristled with rage. He came within an inch of pulling the trigger but realised that the gun was not loaded and he pulled himself together. It was more important that he find the missing prisoner before he got clean away and he could ill afford the time it would take to force an answer out of this Elliot – even if he actually knew where his brother had gone. He glared at his men and demanded to know who had been responsible for allowing the prisoner to escape, and looking at a number of sheepishly blank faces did nothing to improve his temper. He didn't think that with his hands tied, the runaway could get far, and besides, he doubted if an Elliot would desert his brother. Reiver families simply did not do that. All he could do was despatch all the men he felt he could spare to bring the runaway back. Two riders went east and two west; if the fugitive went back towards Lochmaben, he would run into the rider following behind.

As the riders left, he made his feelings plain. "Bring him back. Alive or deed, it's all wan tae me. We'll wait here, but if ye canna find him, dinna come back yersens. D'ye hear me!"

"Aye, Tam," one said nervously as he rode off.

Sandy and Musgrave sat and watched but could do nothing. The reiver, who they now knew was called 'Tam', and whose foul mood was patently evident, personally checked his prisoner's bonds none too gently to make sure he was not going to lose another prisoner,

Cortez had dismounted and retrieved his rapier. He remounted, but he was having difficulty holding his temper at young Elliot for denying him the opportunity to cut the Englishman loose and kill him. He resolved to finish off Elliot along with the spy, before anything else went wrong. Before that, however, he confronted Tam.

"*Madre de Dios!* How could so many guards let a single prisoner escape? I have never before had the misfortune to see such incompetent fools." He brandished his sword and continued to shout at Tam. "I'm going to put an end to that Englishman's spying here and now, before you let him escape too."

The reiver was still seething over Rabbie's escape. He suspected that the prisoners had tricked him, and the affair involving Musgrave, Cortez and Sandy Elliot had been a carefully staged diversion. He was looking for someone to take his frustration out on, and besides, he had to do something to regain control of the situation.

He turned angrily on the Spaniard. "Ye shut yer mooth! Ye'll no' kill anybody till I say ye can. An' put yon daft wee sword away before I stick it up yer arse."

Cortez's temper flared. Twice now, he had been grievously insulted, first by the English spy and now by this ignorant Scottish ruffian. A man of his standing and background could not possibly stand by and permit these people to subject him to any more such treatment.

"You insolent Scottish pig! How dare you address King Philip's representative in such a manner? I will deal with this Englishman now, and you will answer to me when His Majesty's ships arrive."

Tam knew nothing about Spanish ships and, had he known, he would not have cared. All he knew was that he had to do something about the Spaniard or lose face in front of his riders and with it their respect for him as a leader. The laird had told him to get Cortez to Caerlaverock alive but had said nothing about how, and he decided that it would be easier to accomplish the task with the arrogant Spaniard as a prisoner. He deftly knocked the rapier from the Spaniard's hand, then held it to Cortez's throat while he removed the second pistol and shoved it in his belt.

He motioned to his men. "Tie him up wi' the ither twa. An' tie yon horses together before wan mare tries his luck. We'll wait for the ither wan tae be caught an' then gang tae Caerlaverock."

Cortez struggled fiercely but to no avail. The reivers tied his hands as they had done with their other prisoners, and roped their horses together. There would be no more escapes. All the prisoners could do was sit and wait for a fate that now seemed inevitable.

To make a bad situation even worse, the weather broke and it began to rain a persistent Border rain.

Chapter 23

The great armada's first attempt to invade England, depose the Protestant Queen Elizabeth, and replace her with a Catholic monarch, ended in abject failure. The ships assembled and formed up into their proper positions without incident. Their crews had complete confidence in their ability to defeat England's Royal Navy, but found that they were no match for the unpredictable, and unforgiving, weather of the Western Ocean. A mere few days into their great voyage to change the course of history, the storms struck and such a close formation proved impossible to maintain. Soon, the ships were scattered all over the ocean. Several suffered damage from various mishaps, and from colliding with each other, and had no choice but to make for the nearest port. With his armada in complete disarray, the Duke of Medina Sidonia had no option but to return to Cadiz, report to the king, and leave de Recalde to round up the stragglers.

Eventually, following weeks of feverish activity, the ships had refitted and reprovisioned. They reassembled and set sail again. Weather conditions had significantly improved since the first attempt and confidence throughout the fleet was once again running high.

De Recalde, while relieved to have succeeded in finally getting the mighty armada to sea, was still extremely worried about the fate of the three ships bound for Scotland. He understood the perils they faced in the unwelcoming Western Ocean far better than the inexperienced Medina Sidonia and once again took his concerns to the fleet commander. Yet again, Medina Sidonia blindly refused to listen to reason. In his opinion, three ships could weather the storms better than a vast armada, and they were well on their way to Scotland. Moreover, like the rest of the great crusade to restore England to the Catholic faith, they had the prayers of the king and the blessing of the Pope to see them safely through. It was on the tip of de Recalde's tongue to remind his commander that neither the king's prayers nor the Pope's blessing had prevented their first attempt from failure, but he thought better of it. All that would achieve would be to evoke an accusation of blasphemy, a crime for which he could lose his lands and titles, if not his head. He tried to argue that, even if the force did reach Scotland, they would have to wait until the delayed armada arrived. That meant they would have to keep their presence secret and rely on the outlaw, Maxwell, to help them, and that particular Scotsman was not, in his opinion, to be trusted, Still Medina Sidonia would not budge but continued to insist that Lord Maxwell had the king's total confidence, and that was that.

De Recalde suspected that, as usual, none of the other captains would support him, even when the most junior among them knew that he was right. In the end, all he could do was return to his ship, keep his misgivings to himself, and ensure that his sense of pessimism did not show. After the recent setback, it was vitally important that he maintain an air of confidence in front of his crew.

Once they were in the English Channel, he resolved to make one last attempt to get Medina Sidonia to see sense and mount an invasion of The Isle of Wight.

In spite of all his misgivings, however, he still believed in the righteousness of their Holy Cause, and he was resolved to do his duty.

***

As the great Spanish fleet sailed towards her Western Approaches, Queen Elizabeth was exhorting Walsingham and her other senior advisers to find ways of saving her country from invasion and her crown from being ripped from her head. These men were hesitant to tell the queen that, without a standing army worthy of the name, England would have to rely on poorly trained, and even more poorly equipped, local militia bands to repel the Spanish. What forces were available were deployed at the most vulnerable points on England's south coast, but no one, except perhaps Elizabeth herself, placed much faith in them.

Sir Francis Walsingham's ultra-efficient spy network had already discovered that the armada intended to sail up the channel, link up with the Duke of Palma in The Netherlands, and escort a Spanish army across that narrow stretch of water to land on England's east coast. Against Palma's battle-hardened troops, the English militia bands would not stand a chance, and there would be nothing to stop the Spanish from forcing their way up the Thames and into the heart of London. Walsingham also feared that the Spanish would capture the Isle of Wight to support the main invasion from The Netherlands. Should that happen, England would certainly fall.

Their only hope lay in England's Royal Navy. Under the Lord High Admiral, Lord Charles Howard of Effingham, and including such experienced seamen as Lord Henry Seymour, Sir Francis Drake and Sir John Hawkins, the Royal Navy was England's most efficient, and indeed only effective, fighting force. As such, it represented England's, and the Protestant Faith's, only hope of survival. As preparations to defend their country gained pace, everyone clamoured for more resources, more ships, more men, more arms, more powder and shot, more of everything. Their pleas went unheeded. Everything they needed was in short supply, but even if it had been readily available, Elizabeth would demur and deny all requests for its release.

In the midst of all the uncertainty, Walsingham had little time to worry about events in Scotland. Nothing north of the border must interfere with the defence of England.

***

In Carlisle, the Warden of the English West Warch, Lord Scrope, viewed things differently. Unlike Walsingham, he was extremely worried about events north of the border.

King James's reaction to Maxwell's return from Spain did not surprise him in the least, but he had not anticipated the nature of Maxwell's response to the king's march on Dumfriesshire. According to the patchy information coming from across the border, the former exile had reportedly gathered an impressive force and was riding to confront James at Langholm. If he heard that anyone other than Maxwell had been bold enough to attempt anything even remotely similar, Scrope would have said that it was the action of a lunatic, but he knew enough about Maxwell to be certain that the man was anything but an idiot. No, Maxwell had something up his sleeve and Scrope had a nasty feeling that it might well mean trouble for him and his March.

Maxwell's return from Spain had prompted Scrope – at Walsingham's instigation – to send Musgrave on his spying mission into Dumfriesshire, but since then he had heard nothing from his erstwhile spy. There was always the possibility that the reiver turned spy might be dead, but Scrope somehow doubted it. Musgrave was a born survivor; he was also extremely resourceful and could even now be looking for a way to grab a nice profit for himself from the situation. In any case, he deemed it unlikely that he would ever hear from his former Captain again. Sending a reiver to spy on a reiver had seemed like a good idea, but the longer he waited for news from Musgrave, the more he had to accept that in all probability, his attempt to gain definite information regarding Maxwell's plans had failed. Nevertheless, that was not the most pressing of his current worries.

He had contacted Walsingham and informed him of the latest happenings across the border, and the danger it posed for the English West March. The Queen's Spymaster, however, was much too preoccupied with the imminent approach of the Spanish armada to worry about what was happening in the north, and his reply to Scrope did nothing to ease the March Warden's mind. Walsingham stressed that England was facing the greatest danger in her entire history. She was preparing to defend herself against a Spanish invasion and the fate of not only the country, but also that of the Queen and the Protestant faith, were in jeopardy. He also informed Lord Scrope that if the Spanish managed to land on English soil, the ill-equipped militia groups in the south would not be able to stop them. Without substantial reinforcements, England would be lost but, thanks to the constant unrest in The Borders, the soldiers serving in the English Marches, including his March, were the only men available with real battle experience. So, all of the March wardens were ordered to be prepared, should the necessity arise, to send every available man south.

Scrope recognised the danger posed by the Spanish, but he feared that stripping the Marches of their best men would simply be replacing one problem with another. The March wardens had never been able to gain complete control over either the English or the Scottish reiver families, but they had enjoyed some success. Deprived of their most experienced riders, however, they would become totally ineffective, and The Borders would descend deeper into anarchy than they already had.

He shuddered to think of what mischief a man like Maxwell could cause if given what amounted to a free hand.

***

Following the battle with Bothwell, the Liddesdale families returned to their homes, buried their dead and prepared to resume reiving. It was now late in the raiding season and time to look to what had, over the years, developed into a secondary, but necessary, occupation. Farming. The weather, however, as it had done for several years now, intervened. The fine spell, as if by prior arrangement, ended as soon as the valley was, temporarily at least, secure from attack, and the incessant Border rain returned to make the growing of crops virtually impossible. What crops as could be grown were, as always, in danger of being reived or burned in a raid, and the families' best hope of survival lay with their animals; but the cattle and sheep in the valley had been scattered far and wide by the fighting, and much of the stock had been lost or reived.

An immediate return to reiving was the only viable option and Alexander Elliot assembled his men and prepared to ride. His mind, however, was elsewhere.

He would have much preferred to be gathering men to ride into Dumfriesshire to search for his sons, but with both Maxwell's riders and the king's army in the area and unhesitatingly riding down anyone who got in their way, riding in there with armed men was out of the question. In their efforts to achieve their own ends, the two principal protagonists would be in no mood to tolerate any interference from a third party. In the current situation, riding into Dumfriesshire at the head of a Liddesdale reiver band would simply mean leading his men to their deaths, and possibly facilitating the deaths of his sons as well. Assuming they were still alive. He briefly considered riding into the region alone to find out for himself if Malcolm and Robert were alive, and if so, bring them home. But he knew that was not possible. His men would expect their heidsman to be riding with them and if he were to be seen puting the fate of his own sons before his responsibility to the Elliot family, he would lose their respect. He might as well retire to the Debatable Land and join the Broken Men.

His sons' only hope now lay with Big Jock. Alexander came as close as he ever had to praying that the big man was also still living, but in the end, he decided that a prayer offered by his wife would be more acceptable to the Warden of the Heavenly Marches.

Chapter 24

All over the Border Region, a persistent light rain was falling. In intensity, it reached a point somewhere between a heavy mist and a steady shower, but in The Borders such weather might go on for weeks. Driven by the wind, it had the capacity to soak everyone and everything unfortunate enough to be out in it, and once it fell, even in daytime visibility could drop from several miles to a matter of a few yards within minutes.

Rabbie Elliot was soaked to his skin but did not mind in the least. Following his imprisonment in the filthy, stuffy Lochmaben dungeon, the refreshing effect of the rain on his face came as a welcome relief. It washed off much of the grime from his clothes and removed some of the prison stench which still clung to him. Nevertheless, it slowed down the progress of his escape. In order to get away as far and as fast as possible, he had given his horse its head and, consequently, he had little idea of exactly where he was, other than that it must be somewhere in the Galloway Hills. He had not ridden this particular horse before, but he had every confidence in the sure-footed Galloway Nag, and as long as he kept heading roughly west, Rabbie was satisfied. He knew that there would be a pursuit and he hoped that the conditions would hinder the pursuers as badly as they did him; but they were Dumfriesshire reivers and they had the advantage of knowing the country well.

The rain meant that it would take a little longer, but Rabbie knew that unless he could do something soon, his pursuers were going to catch him. With their hands free, they could ride considerably faster than he could.

Added to his immediate personal problems, he was desperately worried about his brother. He had seen Sandy turn his horse, probably to ride to

Musgrave's aid and he had been severely tempted to turn and help him, but his instinct told him that he must keep on and try to find Big Jock. Now that he had managed to get this far, the urge to go back to his brother's aid returned stronger than ever, but the experiences of the previous weeks had taught Rabbie Elliot some hard lessons. He was learning to control his emotions.

He knew that his, and Sandy's, best chance for survival lay with Big Jock. He was confident that the old reiver was somewhere out there in the mist and ready to help, if only he could find him. Much as he hated to delay his search for the big man, he decided he must try to cut himself free, and he thought that he could do it by wearing his bonds through with a sharp stone. He rode on a little way and spotted a pile of rocks where one small boulder with a suitably jagged edge jutted out from the rest. He knew that his horse, bred for reiving, would not move, so he dismounted and set about trying to cut through the now sodden rope. After what seemed to be an age of frantic sawing, the first strands parted. It gave him heart to carry on but he worried about the time it was taking. Eventually, the last strands parted and his hands were free. He knew that his pursuers must be close and hoped that the mist would hide him for a while longer, but as he remounted, he heard them.

Two of Tam's riders were fast approaching and they were almost on him. He knew that he could not expect the mist to hide him for much longer and he prepared to ride for his life. Once again, however, the lessons learned by recent experience forced him to consider his position. It was not promising. He had nothing to defend himself with, but if he moved, they would hear him. It seemed that his only option actually was flight into the mist, but the minute he kicked the horse into action, there was a yell from close by. Now they knew where he was. He rode as fast as he could but he had not gone far before the first man caught up to him.

Mindful of what his leader had said about bringing the fugitive back dead or alive, the reiver decided not to take any chances. He charged at Rabbie with his lance poised to finish him off before he could run any further.

Chapter 25

Don Juan Cortez had been yelling at Tam, the leader of Maxwell's riders, until his throat was sore. He was the personal representative of the King of Spain and how dare a mere thieving ruffian treat him with such blatant disrespect. He protested long and extremely loudly at being tied up like a common criminal, and he threatened to report the reiver first to Lord Maxwell and then to King James. Spanish ships would soon be landing troops in Scotland to support the invasion of England and when they were ashore, he would have the insolent dog who insulted him whipped. When he ran out of suitably disparaging terms in English, he repeated the entire litany of abuse in Spanish. What seemed to upset him most was having his horse tethered to that of an English spy, and the very mention of it, served to increase his sense of outrage. The one thing he did not resort to was pleading; Don Juan Cotez could never bring himself to do that.

Tam simply ignored him. The reiver knew nothing about a Spanish invasion and consequently dismissed it as a ruse by Cortez. All that currently concerned him was getting his escaped prisoner back, and unburdening himself by killing the Englishman and the two Elliots here and now. That would provide him the opportunity of indulging in a little personal reiving on the way to Caerlaverock. With that in mind, he decided that he might as well get rid of the Spaniard as well. Maxwell might not like it but Tam thought that for the moment at least, the laird would be too busy with the king to bother about him. In the meantime, he amused himself by closely inspecting Cortez's rapier, which he had added to the two-wheel lock pistols to make up an impressive armoury, one fit for a reiver chieftain.

Adding to Cortez's frustration was the reaction of his fellow prisoners. Musgrave, who had been listening to his tirade, simply sat there with a most annoyingly broad grin on his face. The other captive, Elliot, simply sat quietly, clearly more concerned about the fate of his brother than the Spaniard's complaints. Cortez finally accepted that taking his frustration out on any of them was a complete waste of time, so he eventually gave up and lapsed into a surly silence

When all was finally quiet, Musgrave turned to the Spaniard. "I told you that bastard Maxwell was not to be trusted. He gave these riders orders to kill us all as soon as we reach Caerlaverock."

Cortez said nothing. Inside, he was still seething about Tam taking him prisoner. He feared that the Englishman was right about Maxwell disposing of him with the others, but in spite of his desperate situation, his dignity would never allow him to give the spy the satisfaction of hearing him admit to allowing the Scottish 'laird' to dupe him.

Musgrave ignored the Spaniard's silence and carried on with what he had to say. "And that includes you, Mister Spanish King's Personal Representative, but it looks as if they might have changed their minds about Caerlaverock and they're all set to do for us here. We're all in the same boat now, you, me and a Liddesdale reiver's son, and we'll all die together unless we can do something about it, and do it soon."

Once again, Cortez sensed that what the Englishman said made sense, and infuriating as it was, he actually was in the 'same boat' as Musgrave termed it, with an English spy and a Scottish bandit's son, if that was who this Elliot actually was. These two brothers had begun to intrigue him. The more he saw of them, the more they seemed to be in league with the English spy, and as he thought it over, he felt that it was unlikely that the English would have sent Musgrave into Scotland to spy on Maxwell on his own. Francis Walsingham, whose scheme this undoubtedly was, would surely have some other spies already in place. He remembered how quickly the Englishman had vouched for the pair following their capture by Maxwell, and unless he learned otherwise, he decided that he would treat all three as English spies.

Then the Spaniard's resolve finally cracked and he could no longer resist making a riposte: "That may be so, but I swear that before I die I will kill you, Englishman."

Musgrave simply laughed. "You're not in much of a position to kill anybody, and you won't be unless we can get away from Tam and his riders. We should be thinking about how we're going to do that instead of talking about killing each other."

The rain continued unabated, but that was nothing new in The Borders. Like Rabbie, Musgrave and Sandy welcomed its refreshing effects, while Cortez, who had not suffered imprisonment in the dungeon and was definitely not dressed for such conditions, cursed it.

Musgrave looked around to see what Tam's men were doing. Two had dismounted and were answering the call of nature while the others sat patiently eating. They appeared unconcerned about the prisoners, but Musgrave knew that they would be watching. Tam, for one, would certainly be on the alert. He might seem to be absorbed in his newly acquired weaponry, but Musgrave knew that he would not repeat his original mistake and allow another prisoner to escape. The reiver noticed Musgrave watching him and, as if to drive home the point, he raised his hand to show that he was holding the rope attached to the three horses. Getting away from him and his men, would not be as easy for them as it had been for Rabbie.

Sandy had also been thinking about trying to get away, but he saw the reiver's gesture to Musgrave and it was obvious that escape would now be virtually impossible. He had heard what Musgrave told Cortez about Tam killing them before they reached Caerlaverock, and it added an urgency to his thinking. He was, however, relieved that the Englishman had not mentioned Rabbie. He could easily have blamed his brother's flight for their present predicament and Sandy was sure that the thought must have crossed Musgrave's mind, but the Englishman had not said anything. He considered bringing up the subject himself just to clear the air, but decided that it would serve no useful purpose. His time would be better spent thinking about how he might get away to help his brother but, while he could not see a way of escaping from the reivers, one slim ray of hope remained.

He rode up to be closer to Musgrave and spoke for the first time. "Do you think Rabbie will find Big Jock?" he asked. "He rode that way because we thought that's where Big Jock is most likely to be."

"Well, he went the right way all right, but I don't know about him finding Big Jock, not in this weather," Musgrave replied. "But I think there might be a good chance of Big Jock finding him. If those two riders don't catch him first."

Sandy refused to let that put him off; he was desperately worried about his brother, and he almost regretted having suggested that they try to escape. He needed something to give him hope. "But if Rabbie does find Big Jock, we might have a chance."

It sounded more like a question than a statement, so Musgrave decided to try to put Sandy's mind at ease. "We might at that," he said.

In reality, Musgrave knew that it was not as simple as that. If Big Jock was somewhere close, and if by some chance he found young Rabbie before the reivers caught him, then yes, they had a chance. If anyone could think of a plan to rescue them, Big Jock Elliot could, and if they were still alive when he put that plan into action, they had a chance – a slim chance, but probably their only chance. Musgrave knew that they needed to do what they could to help the big man, but what, he asked himself, in their present condition, could they possibly do? Escape was out of the question so it had to be something else. It occurred to him that the first thing they had to do, was find a way of ensuring that the reivers didn't kill them before Big Jock could act, and the beginnings of an idea began to take shape in his mind.

He turned as if to survey the lie of the land. None of the reivers seemed to notice. He glanced at Sandy, caught his eye and silently mouthed 'back me up'. Sandy nodded. He waited until he was sure that none of the reivers had noticed the silent exchange then raised his voice enough for everyone to hear.

"How sure are you, Sandy, that Big Jock is around, and that your brother knows where to find him?"

Sandy responded. "Big Jock'll be there all right, and he won't be alone, so Rabbie is sure to run into one of them."

Maxwell's man, Tam, overheard, as Musgrave intended him to, and the mention of a name he recognised immediately grabbed his attention. Even in the depths of Dumfriesshire, the name of Big Jock Elliot was well known. Tam knew that he was a man to be wary of, and the mention of the old reiver's name, caused him to take notice. It occurred to him that the Elliots were bound to have sent someone to find Alexander's sons and Big Jock would be an obvious choice. Tam knew enough about the Elliots to know that falling foul of them was a dangerous game to play, and he knew that he could not ignore the possibility that Big Jock might be somewhere around. Had he been riding as part of Maxwell's reiver army, he would not have been concerned, but here, with just a few of his men to back him up, he could not afford to take chances. He could torture young Elliot to find out if Big Jock was actually in the area but from the looks of this particular Elliot, wringing the truth out of him would take time, too much time. As a result, he decided to alter his plans and postpone killing his remaining prisoners until he reached the safety of Caerlaverock, as originally planned. If Big Jock Elliot was somewhere around, and it was prudent to assume that he was, it would be wise to keep at least one Elliot alive to use as a hostage.

An experienced reiver, Tam could also make a good guess at where Big Jock was likely to be. He dispatched another rider after the first two to warn them to look out for the big man, and to make sure that if they killed young Elliot, to bring the body back and not leave it for Big Jock to find. It would be safer to take it to Caerlaverock and dump it in the sea with the others as Maxwell had ordered and, in the meantime, he thought it best to move on to the fortress by the Solway Firth as quickly as possible

Cortez, too, had heard the conversation between Musgrave and Sandy. He had no idea of who this 'Big Jock' was, but it seemed to confirm his earlier suspicion; the English did indeed have a whole spy network in the area, and it made his task of preventing the enemy from interfering with the imminent Spanish invasion of Scotland that much harder. To make matters worse, English spies were not his only concern. It was now patently obvious that he could no longer trust his erstwhile Scottish ally, Maxwell. The 'laird' was playing some devious game of his own. Cortez could not guess what that game was, but he suspected that the Scotsman had no intention of supporting the Spanish landing, and knowing that there was nothing he could do about it, was again driving him to distraction.

The two riders who had gone east to find the escaped prisoner returned having found nothing. Tam's band was still three men short, but he knew that the riders sent after the escapee would soon be back and they would know that he had resumed his journey to Maxwell's southern fortress. With his prisoners now securely roped together, he still had ample men to take them to their deaths at Caerlaverock. The reivers' leader ordered his men to prepare to ride.

As they moved off, Musgrave knew that he had managed to worry the reiver enough to force him into changing his plans. He had hoped that the mere mention of Big Jock Elliot would cause Tam to rethink, but he was surprised at how successful his ruse had proved to be. It had gained the prisoners a stay of execution and that meant that he could now turn his mind to other things. Self-preservation was still foremost in the Englishman's mind, but simply escaping from Maxwell's men was no longer enough. What if he could get back to Carlisle, and report everything he had learned from Cortez to Lord Scrope? Assuming that what Cortez had said about a Spanish invasion of Scotland was true, and he had no reason to think that it was anything other than the truth, it was information Scrope and Walsingham would pay handsomely for. Enough to set him up for life.

He looked at Tam and knew that he had struck a nerve. He pressed home the point.

"If you're going to Caerlaverock, Tam, you'd do well not to take too long about it or you'll have Big Jock Elliot on your arse."

Tam was not to be drawn. "Yon Elliot canna dae anythin' while I have wan o' Alexander's sons wi' me."

Musgrave knew that the reiver was right. As long as Tam held Sandy, there was little Big Jock could do, if indeed, the big man actually was in the vicinity, and that was yet to be proved. Still, he was pleased to have achieved one objective: Tam was now a worried man. The reiver couldn't safely dismiss the idea that Big Jock might be out there somewhere in the rain, and the thought clearly disturbed him. It rattled him enough to make him put off killing Sandy, and instead, hold him as a hostage until they reached Caerlaverock. In the process, Musgrave seemed to have gained a reprieve for both himself and Cortez as well, although he doubted if the Spaniard would thank him for it.

It was time to keep up the pressure. "I wouldn't be too sure about that if I were you, Tam," he said. "Big Jock Elliot won't be put off as easily as that."

He looked around to make sure everyone could hear. "And, anyway, you have more to worry about than Big Jock. What are you going to do when King James comes riding through here chasing after Maxwell? He won't be in the mood for taking hostages. He'll hang us all and he won't even bother to find out who we were."

That was something Tam had not thought of. He knew that Maxwell was riding to surprise James at Langholm, but the laird had said nothing about the king attacking Caerlaverock. While he had every faith in his laird, to his confused mind, what the Englishman said carried a ring of truth. But he decided to brave it out.

"Dinna worry aboot Jamie. The laird'll soon put a stop tae his wee game."

Musgrave detected a definite note of something less than confidence in Tam's voice. The reiver was no longer as sure of his ground as he would have his prisoners, and his riders, believe. It was time to pile on the agony.

He pretended to be choking with laughter as he turned to Sandy. He pointed to Tam. "Can you believe that, Sandy? He actually thinks that Maxwell can beat King James and his whole army at Langholm and send them all running home to Edinburgh."

Sandy took his cue; he shook his head as if he couldn't believe what he had just heard and then joined in the laughter. "Someone will go running home all right, only it won't be King Jamie."

Musgrave grew more serious and addressed himself directly to Tam. "Come on, Tam, you know as well as I do that Maxwell has no chance of stopping the whole Scottish army at Langholm; and the thing is, Maxwell himself knows it too. You can bet that the canny bastard has something else in mind and I'd say that he wants to lead James into this part of the world so that he can fight him on his own ground."

It was a shot in the dark by the Englishman. He didn't know if any of what he said was true, but it made Tam stop and reassess his position once again. To a reiver like Tam, Musgrave's assessment of what Maxwell would do made perfect sense, and if anyone was adept at using reiver tactics, it was the laird. He was also well aware that Musgrave was right about the king. If Jamie came riding through chasing Maxwell, he would let nothing stand in his way, and that would include him, his men and his prisoners. He thought about changing his mind and unburdening himself by killing the prisoners here and then riding to Caerlaverock as quickly as possible, but that was no good. He realised that the castle was the first place the king would look for the laird, and James would probably sack the fortress in his efforts to find him. Worse still, his confused mind told him, the king might already have some of his men on their way there!

He decided that his best bet was to ride west, wait for Maxwell in the Galloway Hills, and join up with his laird. He decided against killing the prisoners, although he was sure that one of them was already dead. Holding one Elliot hostage would be enough to keep Big Jock at bay until he teamed up with the laird. As far as the Englishman was concerned, he seemed to be in league with the Elliots and he, too, might prove to be a valuable hostage. If Maxwell wanted them dead, he could kill them himself. As for the Spanish invasion Cortez had been blethering about, Tam had more than enough on his mind already without worrying about that, so he decided to forget all about it.

As he listened to the exchange between the Scottish bandit and the English spies, Cortez was dismayed to learn of a frightening new danger to the approaching Spanish ships. King James would soon be arriving on the scene with a large army and, in spite of his friendship with Spain, firmly based on a shared religion, if the Scottish king discovered that a Spanish invasion force was landing on his shores without any form of prior agreement, James would have to act. Even if he learned that the Spanish force formed part of a plan to invade England and posed no danger to his own kingdom, he would have no option but to throw them back into the sea. Cortez knew that the Spanish landing force could no longer rely on the help of the man who had suggested the scheme to King Philip in the first place, and it was now clear that Maxwell had failed to mention that King James would come to arrest him as soon as he landed in Scotland. Had persuading King Philip to accept his invasion plan simply been a ruse to facilitate his return from exile? Cortez thought not. Maxwell must have had something more in mind, but for the moment, he had to put that to one side. The

Spaniard had a much more dangerous problem to deal with. He had to warn the Spanish ships that they were sailing into what amounted to a trap.

Whether it was a trap laid by Maxwell was not important. If Spanish troops landed in Scotland, they faced annihilation. Cortez knew that he was the only one in a position to warn them of the danger, but in order to do so he had first to escape from Maxwell's thieves.

He realised that escape on his own was not possible, and he simply had to accept that he needed help. Galling as it was, that meant cooperating with these despicable English spies.

Chapter 26

Rabbie felt a moment of panic as he heard the shout from behind him. He glanced round in time to see the rider coming at him out of the mist with a lance held at the ready and clearly intent on killing him. Even with his hands now freed, he knew that it would be impossible to outrun his assailant. The rider was coming on at full tilt, while he would have to kick his horse into motion and gather momentum. There was not enough time for that, and evasive action was his only hope. He managed to hold his nerve and remembered an old reiver trick. He prepared to jump off his horse; on foot, he could keep dodging around, behind and underneath both animals, and his assailant would have to dismount in order to catch him. Even the most experienced rider was vulnerable during the few seconds it took him to get off his horse. But he never had the opportunity to put his plan into action.

Without a hint of warning, events suddenly turned in his favour. Tam's rider gave a strangled cry and fell heavily to the ground, accompanied by the rattle of a reiver's metal accoutrements. Rabbie's attacker had been suddenly and expertly unhorsed and now lay on his back with blood spurting from a fatal sword slash across his throat.

In the heat of the moment, neither of them had heard the approach of Big Jock. The canny old warrior had galloped up and accounted for the reiver with a deftly administered 'Lockerbie lick' – a vicious backward sword slash.

Big Jock reined in his horse and spoke with some urgency. "There's anither wan behind. Get this wan's sword and lance an' we'll ambush the bastard."

Over the last several weeks, Rabbie had learned enough about what it took to become a reiver, and especially an Elliot reiver, to make further instructions from Big Jock unnecessary. Without any hesitation, he picked up the dead man's weapons and remounted. They left the reiver's body and horse where they were and rode into the mist, one on either side. The second rider sent by Tam to find Rabbie, stood no more of a chance than the first. He had heard his friend shout and ridden after him. In the failing visibility, all he saw was a riderless horse grazing peacefully and he almost rode over the body before he recognised the dead man and started in alarm. Big Jock yelled, the reiver turned his horse to run from the sound and ran straight onto his dead friend's lance wielded by Rabbie.

They left the bodies where they lay but took the two riderless horses. Big Jock led them off a short way to where a small burn bordered by thick bushes ran through a gully deep enough to hide a man on horseback. The misty rain had forced him to move closer to Maxwell's riders than he had originally planned, and the burn was where he had been sheltering while he waited for total darkness. When he heard the sound of the horses and the shout from Maxwell's reiver, it had taken him no more than a few seconds to assess the situation. He guessed what was happening and it immediately spurred him into action. He gave Rabbie some oatcakes to eat from his still adequate supply, and some peaty water to drink from a leather flask filled from the burn. The young reiver quickly recovered from his ordeal.

"Sandy said you'd be around here somewhere, Jock. We knew that you wouldn't ride off and leave us. Even after I buggered everything up," he added ruefully.

"No," Big Jock answered. "Yer faither wuid have my heed aff if I did that. He'd be here himself if it wisna for Bothwell an' Jamie."

Rabbie understood, but he was still desperately worried. He was worried not only about his brother, who as far as he knew was still a prisoner with Maxwell's men, but also about his father in Liddesdale. He was deeply conscious that his rash action had prevented them from riding to warn the valley about Maxwell and King James and, although he knew that Big Jock would be more concerned about rescuing Sandy, he felt that he had to raise the subject of the attack on Liddesdale first.

"Did they get a warning about the king in time to get ready for him?"

To his immense relief, Big Jock put his mind, partially at least, at rest. "Aye, they did," the old reiver answered. "But I dinna ken whit happened since, an' anyway we canna dae anything aboot it frae here."

Although relieved that his impetuous actions did not seem to have resulted in complete disaster, Rabbie was still worried about what might have happened in Liddesdale. He told himself that no matter how bad things were, his father would survive and come looking for him and Sandy, and he drew some confidence from the one development he hoped would have helped his father's cause.

"Maxwell has gone to stop Jamie at Langholm," he said. "He's making Jamie chase him here. So they'll only have Bothwell to worry about and Da will be be riding in here as soon as they beat him."

Big Jock lapsed into careful thought. He had already concluded that Maxwell did not contemplate defeating the king at Langholm, but was planning to lure James onto his home turf of Dumfriesshire. That being the case, both the laird and the king, each with hundreds of riders at his disposal, would soon be running loose in the area and that would prevent Alexander Elliot from riding in at the head of a band of Liddesdale riders. Knowing the heidsman as he did, he would not be at all surprised if Alexander hadn't considered coming to look for his sons on his own, but that would make little difference to their immediate predicament.

Big Jock turned his mind back to Sandy. It was extremely unlikely that he had managed to escape and even if he had, he might be in even greater danger than before. He knew that the only way to ensure his safety was to rescue him, and do it before Tam and his riders reached Caerlaverock, or before Jamie arrived in the area chasing after Maxwell. Either way, it was going to be no easy task. Young Rabbie seemed to have matured since his reckless ride off after Musgrave, and he had somehow managed to escape from Maxwell's riders, which said a lot about how much he had learned. He also had the presence of mind to take the time to cut the ropes that bound his hands and he had not wasted time asking questions when told how to deal with the second of Tam's riders. Rabbie had not been at a loss to know what to do without his pistol but had killed the man with a lance, and without the slightest hesitation. Big Jock felt confident that he could now rely on the lad to do what he asked of him, and do it well. Provided this newfound maturity lasted, Rabbie would prove to be a valuable ally.

His only reaction to what Rabbie had said, however, was to comment that: "Maxwell'll be stopping nae wan at Langholm. The bastard'll be riding through here any time noo wi' Jamie up his arse."

Before deciding what to do next, Big Jock needed to know more about Tam's men and their prisoners, and how Rabbie had managed to escape from them. He listened intently while the heidsman's son carefully explained how he and his brother had grabbed the chance to escape, and what had happened as he was making a break for freedom when Sandy had intervened to prevent Cortez killing Musgrave rather than ride off and, as a result, was still a prisoner.

Telling his story served to increase Rabbie's concern for his brother. "Do you think that Tam will change his mind and kill Sandy and the other two before they get to Caerlaverock?"

It was certainly something that had crossed Big Jock's mind but, on balance, he thought that it was unlikely. This Tam seemed to be an experienced reiver and would probably do what he himself would have done under similar circumstances.

"No," he said. "I think he'll hold yer brither for a hostage. It will no' be easy but we'll need tae be awa' wi' Sandy before Maxwell and Jamie ride in here."

Something else suddenly occurred to him. "Did ye say that yon fancy rider was frae Spain? Whit wuid the likes o' him be daein' here?"

"He was blethering on about how the Spanish were going to land soldiers in Scotland, but I can't see how that would mean anything to us."

Rabbie may not have seen any significance in the Spaniard's presence, but it really grabbed Big Jock's attention. Like everyone else in The Borders, except for those directly involved, a Spanish landing on Scottish soil meant little to him, but he realised that it had ramifications for their current tricky situation. It confirmed his earlier suspicion about what a former Captain of Bewcastle was doing in this part of Scotland; he was spying for the English March Warden, Scrope. More importantly, having found out about some Spanish plan to land troops in Scotland, seemingly behind King Jamie's back, he would be anxious to take the news back to

England, and that meant that he would first have to escape from Maxwell's reivers. Big Jock was under no illusions about Musgrave. The Englishman would not help Sandy simply because the lad had once helped him, but because he had to get away himself. They could rely on his cooperation, at least until after he had escaped from Maxwell's riders. Whatever happened to the Englishman and the Spaniard after that, would happen. It was of no concern to Big Jock Elliot.

He passed these thoughts on to Rabbie, but before his young kinsman had time to comment, he held his finger to his lips in the universal sign for silence. By now, darkness had fallen but his sharp reiver's ears had picked up the sound of yet another rider somewhere out there in the gloom and, almost immediately, Rabbie heard him as well.

"He must be another of Tam's riders looking for me," Rabbie whispered. "Maxwell or the king wouldn't send out one man on his own in this weather. If we can do for him, Tam will be three men down."

Big Jock nodded in approval. The lad was learning. There was no way of knowing who the lone rider actually was, but in the current circumstances, he could only be an enemy, and Rabbie's assessment made perfect sense. He listened intently for a few minutes more and decided that the man, whoever he might be, was not riding in a straight line but weaving around. He was clearly looking for someone, presumably the escaped Rabbie, and the other two riders sent to look for him. Big Jock was about to outline a way of trapping the newcomer and killing him, but decided to give Rabbie an opportunity to suggest a plan of his own. The more interested and involved he kept the lad, the more help he was likely to be, and he definitely did not want to give Rabbie an excuse to revert to his old mindless ways.

"Whit d'ye think?" he whispered.

Rabbie was surprised. After all that had happened, Big Jock inviting him to voice an opinion was the last thing he expected. He realised, however, that it was now up to him to respond, so he paused to give the matter some thought. He realised that time was short and he could not afford to take too long, so he quickly reached a conclusion.

"We can't try to ride him down, he'd hear us before we saw him and he'd make a run for it. In this weather, he'd be back to warn Tam before we caught him, and they'd be ready for us when we go to get Sandy."

Jock nodded his agreement. "Aye, they wuid be." He waited to see if the youngster had thought of a way out of the dilemma.

Rabbie realised that Big Jock was still waiting for him to say more but the rider, while still following a zigzag course, was coming ever closer. For a moment, the urgency of the situation almost threw him off balance. Not long ago, he might have charged off to confront the oncoming rider but he had learned the value of keeping calm and thinking clearly.

"He'll hear us if we make any noise at all, so we might as well let him. The only thing we can do is make him think we're the other two who came after me. If I take these spare horses back to where his friends are, he might think the sound is coming from them and you can get behind him."

It wasn't quite what Big Jock had originally thought of but it was as good an idea as any, and he decided to go along with it.

He had just one point to add. "Make enough noise tae cover mine."

Rabbie understood what was required. He took up the reins of the two riderless horses and led them a little way along the burn without bothering to disguise the noise they made. He rode out of the hollow, and when he reached the level ground, he called out, "Over here."

Tam's rider heard. He stopped and hesitated before reacting. Rabbie knew that the mist had a knack of distorting sounds and that the rider would not recognise his voice, so he shouted again: "Over here, Tam."

This time the rider took the bait. The sound of his hoofbeats increased as he rode directly towards the source of the call. He never even had time to discover that he had ridden into a trap. Big Jock Elliot rode out of the dark and struck him down with his lance.

Rabbie eyed the body on the ground and instantly recognised him. "He was one of Tam's men all right. That makes three so there are only five left. That'll make it a bit easier to get Sandy away."

"They have wan mair ridin' behind," Big Jock answered. "An' dinna forget they'll be holding yer brether as a hostage."

He didn't need to say more. Rescuing Sandy would not be quite as straightforward as Rabbie hoped and they would have to proceed extremely carefully. Having Big Jock so unexpectedly agree with his plan for dealing with the last rider, and the fact that it had proved successful, worked wonders for his confidence and he set about trying to think of a plan to rescue his brother. Because of what had happened in the past, however, when an idea did come to mind, he thought it through before voicing it.

"Did this one ride out here to help the first two to look for me, or did Tam send him out to call them back?" He was asking the question of himself as much as of Big Jock. "If he was calling them back, it must mean that something has got him worried and he wants to keep all his riders together, so he'll have to wait for them to come back. We could pretend to be Tam's riders again and surprise him."

Big Jock was again glad to see that the youngster was learning to think before acting. He had been thinking along similar lines himself, but had spotted a potential flaw. He was worried that the reivers might have a prearranged signal to identify members of their own band. However, he was careful not to put Rabbie down and decided to adopt a different approach.

"Aye, we cuid laddie," he said. Then, after a moment, he added as if the thought had just occurred to him, "D'ye ken if they had any way tae let on tae Tam that they're his riders?"

Rabbie was annoyed with himself for not remembering that reiver bands invariably had a sign or signal, a word or whistle perhaps, to help distinguish between friend and foe when riding at night, but he was determined not to act as he had in the past and argue, or sulk, every time he got things wrong. He recognised that the most important thing was getting Sandy away from Tam and his men, and now was not the time for worrying about his personal vanity.

"I didn't see any sign of them using a signal, but all the time I was with them, they had no need for it. So they might well have one, and we can't take chances."

Yet another positive reaction by Rabbie left Big Jock feeling even more confident that he could continue to rely on him. "D'ye think that we cuid use these spare horses tae make them think we're anither band o' Maxwell's riders?" he asked.

Rabbie was quick to catch on. "We could," he answered, and as an afterthought, he added, "or a troop of King Jamie's men, that would really make Tam shit himself."

"Aye, that it wuid," Big Jock agreed. "An' if he thinks that it's Jamie, he might no' kill his hostages just yet. He'll keep them alive tae bargain his ain way oot. It's as guid a chance as any."

Rabbie was finding that having a say in what they did next to be a liberating experience, but he was careful not to overplay his hand. He had no wish to be the instrument of his brother's death by wasting time arguing with Big Jock, and he was conscious of the need to work out the best way possible for Sandy's sake, so he made only an occasional comment, and then mostly to agree with what the big man said.

"Did ye say that Tam and the others were stopped when ye rode aff?"

Rabbie had left in such a hurry that there was not even time to think about whether Tam was planning to stay where he was or to keep on riding towards Caerlaverock. They assumed, wrongly as it turned out, that he and his remaining reivers were waiting for the third rider to return with the first two. Big Jock Elliot, however, was not one to take unnecessary chances. He left his companion to hold the spare horses while he rode off into the gloom to try to establish if the reivers were still where they were when Rabbie escaped.

He was back within a matter of minutes, and showing, for Big Jock, unusual signs of urgency. "They're ridin' this way."

He was not aware that Musgrave had spooked the reiver into believing that the king's army was likely to reach Caerlaverock before he did, and that Tam had decided to take his men and his hostages to the west to join up with Maxwell. Reivers all, there was never any doubt that they would find each other, even on this, the darkest and dirtiest of nights.

Anyone less vigilant than Big Jock Elliot would have ridden straight into them but there was little time to spare. "Move them bodies, or they'll see them," he said urgently.

They dismounted and threw the dead reivers into the hollow as quickly as they could and just had time to scramble down after them before the reivers arrived. To their immense relief, they saw that Sandy, although a prisoner, was still alive. The fact that his horse was roped to those ridden by Musgrave and the Spaniard, now also a prisoner, would not make the task of rescuing him any easier.

Rabbie realised that there was no time for yet another conference and deferred to the big man's greater experience. "What now, Jock?"

"We'll follow them for a wee while," Jock replied.

They remounted, but before they could follow Tam, they again heard the sound of hoofbeats. This time it was a single rider in a hurry. He was clearly the man Tam had set as his rearguard, and having reached the place where the rest of the reivers had left the route to Caerlaverock, he was hurrying after his friends to find out what was happening. Rabbie prepared to ambush him as they had done the others, but Big Jock shook his head.

"Leave him be. Tam will be expectin' him. He'll be lookin' for yon ither three too, but we canna do aythin' aboot that."

Tam, with his remaining reivers and his prisoners, continued to ride west and they fell in behind, close enough to keep contact but far enough back to avoid detection.

Having ridden for a few miles, Rabbie became concerned.

"They're making for Dumfries, Jock," he said. "We'll have to do something before they get any closer to it."

Big Jock shook his head. He was now certain that Tam was heading deeper into the Galloway Hills to join up with Maxwell, and his sparse knowledge of the geography told him that they would soon have to cross the River Nith. He explained this to Rabbie and told him that, once over the river, Tam would feel safe from attack and relax, and he outlined what he thought they needed to do once they had crossed. He looked closely at Rabbie to make sure that he fully understood his part, but first asked him if he agreed. Rabbie, again pleased to be consulted, nodded in agreement. They reached the river and found that it had not yet been swollen by the rain. Tam and his men, with their prisoners, forded it with ease and, when they were clear, Big Jock and Robbie, still undetected, followed behind. They rode on a little further and then slowed down. Big Jock decided that it was time to put his rescue plan into action.

They split up. Big Jock circled around to get ahead of the reivers. As he waited to carry out his part of the scheme, Rabbie experienced a brief moment of doubt but quickly suppressed it; Sandy's life depended on what happened next.

Chapter 27

Having struggled against mostly unfavourable winds all the way from Spain, the great armada was almost in sight of its goal. There was no sign of an English fleet prepared for battle and the supreme commander, the Duke of Medina Sedonia, called a conference of his captains on board his flagship, the *Santa Ana.* He was in jubilant mood as he expressed the opinion that they had caught the English unawares. In his view, Elizabeth and her commanders, in spite of Walsingham and his spies, had not learned that a great Spanish armada was coming to depose her and return England to the Catholic faith. Sedonia assured his captains that their holy mission was going exactly to plan.

Don Martinez de Recalde, his second in command, who held very different views, was yet again dismayed by his superior's naivety. The English, and particularly Walsingham, could not possibly be so blind. After everything that had happened: the initial assembling of the great armada, its scattering in the Atlantic storms, and the second sailing, the existence of such a massive fleet must surely have come to their notice. Even without a single spy in Spain, the enemy could not possibly have failed to read the abundance of signs pointing unerringly towards a Spanish invasion of England.Yet again, de Recalde tried to convince his superior of the dangers involved of sailing up the entire length of the English Channel with its varying winds and currents. Yet again, he stressed the advantages of attacking and taking one of England's great southern harbours, and especially invading the Isle of Wight. If they had caught the English sleeping, as the Duke seemed to think, it would be relatively easy to do. And once they had gained a foothold, all of England's forces, both land and sea, would be tied down trying to dislodge them. In the meantime, the Duke of Palma's army could cross from The Netherlands virtually unopposed. Palma would take London, depose Elizabeth, and Protestant England would fall as planned. For a moment, de Recalde noted that Sidonia seemed to be wavering, and he thought that his commander might at last see sense. His hopes momenterally rose, but were once again cruelly dashed. Having his own argument about the state of England's readiness used against him had angered Sidonia, and he stubbornly reverted to his original position. They would carry out King Philip's strategy to the letter and there would be no further argument.

As far as the diversionary landing in Scotland was concerned, Sidonia was equally intransigent. He argued that not hearing anything about the fate of the three ships did not mean that they had been lost, and even if they had, it would make little difference to the eventual outcome of their Holy enterprise. There was no cause for alarm, they had the blessing of both the king and the Pope and all would be well. De Recalde could see that several of his fellow captains agreed with his assessment but, as usual, they were not prepared to quarrel with their commander, their king or their Pope. All he could do was accept the situation for what it was, and return to his ship.

On his way back from the flagship, he took the opportunity to inspect the state of the armada, and what he saw helped to dispel many of his fears. After all their recent traumas, the great ships appeared to be in every respect ready for battle. Surely, no power on earth could stand against such a force.

Back on board his own ship, the *San Juan de Portugal,* and with time to reflect, he found that he agreed with Sidonia on one point. Irrespective of whether it was successful or not, the landing in Scotland would make little or no difference to the eventual outcome of the invasion of England. He had never regarded it as anything more than a scheme cooked up by the Scotsman, Maxwell, to help him escape from exile in Spain, but that did nothing to ease his mind about the fate of the man sent to liaise with Maxwell, Don Juan Cortez. He consoled himself with the thought that Cortez was a brave and resourceful soldier who would somehow manage to survive.

***

Had de Recalde seen his trusted emissary at that precise moment, his confidence would have suffered a severe setback. Cortez was riding through the mist and rain of Dumfriesshire with his hands tightly bound, held prisoner by a group of the same Lord Maxwell's men. Worse still, his horse was roped to the mounts of two other prisoners, at least one of whom he knew to be an English spy!

Cortez had spent the last hours frantically trying to think of a way to escape. It was imperative that he warn the Spanish ships that the Scottish king, James VI, was in the area with his entire army. Fellow Catholic and friend of Spain he may be, but James could not stand idly by while Spanish troops landed in his country totally unannounced. He wondered if any of King Philip's advisers had mentioned that if the king wanted Scottish help, all he had to do was follow proper diplomatic procedures, but Cortez was convinced that no one would have dared to say anything of the sort to Philip, and Maxwell certainly had not. That would not have suited the devious Scotman's purpose at all. The Spaniard had long given up thinking of Maxwell as an ally of Spain, and he prayed that the Scotsman would soon receive his just deserts.

Cortez was also harbouring serious doubts about the accuracy of the details Maxwell had given him about where exactly his compatriots were going to land. The Scotsman had shown him a rough map with the location of the landing site marked, and told him that it was near a place called Caerlaverock. He boasted about having another of his fortresses there and so it seemed logical enough that the landing should take place as close as possible to it. But, as Musgrave had pointed out to their captor, this ruffian called Tam, that was the first place King James would come looking for his wayward laird, and if that were to happen, a landing there would end in total disaster. Another worrying thought also occurred to him: if that particular part of the Scottish coast was a suitable landing place for sea-going vessels, why had Maxwell not landed so close to his castle on his return from Spain? While Cortez knew little about Scotland itself, he knew something about the waters surrounding these islands, and the treacherous nature of the tides. A chill ran up his spine as he realised that the waters near Maxwell's fortress being tidal, were shallow for much of the time. That would spell danger for large ships, and not only that, James would by then be in control of the nearby fortress! Maxwell was leading the Spanish into a trap!

He had to warn them of the twin perils awaiting them: King James's army and the Solway tides.

He could not begin to remember the name of the place where he and Maxwell had landed on their arrival from Spain, but he knew roughly where it was and would recognise it if he saw it again. That, his instinct told him, was where he must go. He had seen fishing boats there and he could use one to sail out, meet the Spanish ships while they were still at sea, and warn them that they were sailing into danger.

Because of Musgrave's goading, Tam was now leading them west instead of south and for the moment Cortez could be content with that. He still had to escape from Maxwell's men and he had not yet worked out precisely how, but he thought that he still had time to form a viable plan. Assuming that they continued to ride west, and assuming that Tam kept up their present rate of travel, he estimated that he could afford to wait until dawn. By then, even these Scottish bandits must begin to tire. His horse was the last of the prisoner's mounts in line, and he felt that it gave him a slight advantage; he only had to free himself from one other horse, a horse ridden by, of all people, Musgrave. Tam was keeping Elliot, his most useful hostage, close to him. Cortez doubted that he would get any help from the spy but he decided that was something he did not need. He could break free on his own and then lose himself in this diabolical Scottish rain. A more than competent horseman, he could rest in the saddle while his captors would have to remain on the alert. He could not afford to doze off completely in case Tam changed direction, but whatever rest he could get would serve him well when he made his break for freedom.

It would be even more satisfying to find a way of killing the English spy before he left, but warning the Spanish ships must take precedence. In any case, once the ships had turned back to join the main armada, it would be too late for Musgrave; anything he had learned on his spying mission into Scotland would, by then, be worthless.

***

Alexander Elliot was riding back to Liddesdale following a reiving foray into England. He halted his Galloway Nag and looked back to survey the devastation he and his riders had caused. Even through the misty rain, the flames from several burning farmsteads were visible for miles. The wet thatch had taken some time to catch but was now blazing fiercely. They had reived a goodly sized herd of cattle and their packhorses were loaded with plundered goods. In that respect, he could be quite satisfied with his night's work and all that remained now was to lead his men safely home.

The reiving season was over and the reivers of Liddesdale would soon be obliged to revert to being farmers. Their first task was to recover what animals they could from those scattered far and wide by the fighting, but much of their stock had inevitably been lost or reived and urgently needed replacing. The weather for the last several years had been the worst in living memory and not conducive to growing crops. They still tried to grow some corn and vegetables to supplement their diet, but there was a heavy reliance on meat. At least one raid had been required to replace the animals lost, and it had to be in England; with King Jamie on the march against Maxwell, raiding on the Scottish side of the border was not a viable proposition. With many of his best riders otherwise engaged, Alexander had enlisted the help of his neighbours for his raid; reiving parties involving members of several reiver families was nothing new in Liddesdale, and a combined group had carried out this highly successful one. Elliots, Armstrongs, and Nixons had all taken part. Liddesdale was still recovering from the effects of the attack by Bothwell, and while the number of men killed or wounded in the actual fighting had been relatively light, the valley could not afford to drop its guard. Sufficient riders had to remain behind to defend the valley in case of another attack.

Because of the recent skirmish with the Hetheringtons involving Big Jock, Malcolm and Robert in Dumfriesshire, Alexander mounted this raid against the Hetherington and Fenwick farms situated around Bewcastle. These English reivers had to learn that the Elliots were not going to sit by and let anybody think they could take liberties with them on either side of the border.

Now that they were almost home with their plunder, Alexander had time to reflect on the result. Much to his surprise, the raid had met with only token resistance and he was finding it difficult to understand how such a large raiding party seemed to have escaped the notice of the Border

Watchers, or why whoever had replaced Musgrave as Captain of Bewcastle, had not put in an appearance. The pickings had been rich, and he fully expected at least one hot trod to be mounted, but none had yet materialised. Had anyone told Alexander that the threat of a Spanish invasion of England was responsible for the lack of opposition to his raid, he would not have taken it seriously. Apart from those parts of England within raiding distance, and the frequent wars between England and Scotland, he knew nothing of the neighbouring country, and cared even less.

He didn't know that the English March Wardens had orders to be ready to send every available rider south to fight the Spanish if required; neither did he know that Lord Scrope had assumed that reiving had finished for the year and was, belatedly complying with the order from London. Because he didn't know, he put the lack of opposition to the raid down to good fortune, and as a result, Alexander, along with the rest of Liddesdale, failed to take full advantage. Having carried out one highly successful raid and returned to Liddesdale unscathed, he reasoned that he couldn't hope to be quite as fortunate again, and so, he decided that reiving was over until the following winter.

Privately, however, he admitted to himself that there was a second compelling reason behind his decision. He had still heard nothing of Big Jock or his two sons. Wondering if they were dead or alive continued to play havoc with his mind and several times during the current raid, he had found himself looking for them among his reiver band only to find that they were not there, and his worries intensified. Now he had yet another cause for concern. With the emergency involving Bothwell over, his wife had returned home from their daughter's family in England, and try as she might, Margaret could not disguise the fact that she was terribly afraid of what might have happened to her sons. The worry was beginning to show and Alexander feared that it might make her ill. As a reiver's wife, she fully accepted that death was a constant presence in her life, but the uncertainty was proving extremely difficult for her to live with.

Alexander noted that she tried hard to keep her worries from him and he chose not to comment on the fact that she seemed to spend more time than usual on her own; time, which he suspected, she spent in prayer. He had to do something, and there was only one way to resolve the problem.

Irrespective of whether the king and Maxwell were running wild in the area, he would ride into Dumfriesshire and discover the truth for himself. There were plenty of men ready and willing to ride with him but he knew that riding in there with a band of Liddesdale reivers, would be courting disaster.

He checked his weapons, gathered some provisions, saddled his horse and rode out alone.

Chapter 28

Big Jock sat on his horse poised for action and waited for Maxwell's men to ride into his trap. Knowing that the three riders he had sent after Rabbie were still missing, and had presumably run into some kind of trouble, would add an element of urgency to Tam's plans to join up with Maxwell, and Big Jock was in no doubt that joining up with his laird was exactly what Tam had in mind. In his view, that made their attempt to rescue Sandy much less of a gamble. Tam would still be on his guard, his instincts as a reiver would ensure that he was, but he would also be growing in confidence. He would soon be under the protection of his laird and out of danger, and the closer he got to Maxwell, the less wary he would become, but Big Jock knew that they could not afford to wait too long. It had come as a great relief to find that Tam had decided to keep his prisoners, especially Sandy, alive, presumably as hostages, but now that they had crossed the River Nith, that situation might soon change. It was imperative that he and Rabbie rescue Sandy before the reiver decided that hostages were no longer necessary and decided to unburden himself.

Now was the time to strike and the old reiver was satisfied that their plan was a good one. It had already worked well once and he saw no reason why it should not be equally successful again.

Maxwell's men were advancing in typical reiver formation. A single file with Tam in the lead holding tightly on to the rope attached to his prisoners' horses with Sandy, his prize hostage, forced to ride immediately behind him. One of his riders rode on each flank with the others strung out behind. If Big Jock Elliot should attempt a rescue, Tam clearly planned to use one Elliot to hold the other at bay.

"We're over here!"

The sudden shout brought them to an abrupt halt. Tam tried and failed to locate the source of the shout and was momentarily confused, but he was far too experienced a reiver to panic and react carelessly. He knew the tricks that the misty rain could play with sounds and he was not about to take chances. As far as he could tell, the shout came from off to one side and slightly behind, but he could not be sure, and he was not prepared to send any of his riders to search for it. He signalled to his men to stay where they were and tied the rope holding the prisoners' horses to his saddle to leave both his hands free. He drew one of the wheel lock pistols, which he had thought to load in case of further trouble from his prisoners, and checked the load.

The call came again: "Over here, Tam."

The reivers were now fully alert. They looked for a signal from their leader, but Tam signalled them to wait. They sat for several minutes to see if anything further happened. Nothing did, and the tension began to get to the already nervous reivers. Tam, too, in spite of his experience, began to feel the strain, but still he hesitated. Whoever was calling had failed to include the word his band used to identify themselves, but mention of his name meant that it must be someone who knew him. His men were becoming visibly uneasy and Tam knew that he had to act quickly or risk losing control.

In spite of the distortion caused by the mist, Sandy recognised the voice. He turned to Musgrave, the next prisoner in line, and mouthed 'get ready'. There was really no need for the warning, Musgrave had also recognised Rabbie Elliot's voice.

As Rabbie uttered the second shout, he and Big Jock began to inch forward. Rabbie, leading the spare horses, did nothing to disguise the sound of his approach. The noise hid any sound made by Big Jock, and the big man's presence went undetected. Tam had been about to send out a scout to investigate, but held up his hand and concentrated on the sound of the approaching horses. His men followed suit, they turned towards the sound and stared into the mist.

Tam visibly relaxed. "Tis jist the wan or twa riders, three at the most, but nae mair."

Suddenly, another shout, coming from closer to them, pulled him up sharply. "Watch out, Sandy. It's King Jamie, he's…"

There was a thudding sound followed by a strangled cry as if someone had been clubbed into silence. The, by now, thoroughly alarmed Tam, prepared to drop the rope holding the prisoners and make a run for it. Then several things happened at once:

"For Scotland and King James!" Rabbie yelled the war cry at the top of his voice. He led the riderless horses in a mad charge into the rear of the group and brought one rider down with a lance taken from one of the reivers killed earlier. The other reivers didn't hesitate further. They wheeled their horses and galloped off in a panic. Tam twisted round in the saddle to see what was happening behind, but immediately sensed danger from infront. He turned and saw a figure galloping out of the mist in front of him. He levelled the pistol and might well have shot Big Jock had the prisoners not taken a hand. When Musgrave picked up Sandy's signal to get ready, he inched his horse forward and dragged Cortez forward with him. As Tam levelled the pistol at Big Jock, there was enough slack in the rope for Sandy to kick his horse forward and barge into Tam's mount as he had done earlier with Cortez. The pistol ball went wide and Big Jock drove the point of his lance into the reiver's throat.

The remaining reivers had by now scattered in complete panic. As they disappeared into the mist, Big Jock signalled to Rabbie to let them go. They could never hope to find them all in these conditions, and risked being ambushed themselves. They set about releasing the prisoners. Rabbie cut the rope attaching Sandy's horse to Tam's, and dealt similarly with the cords binding his brother's hands. Sandy rubbed his tender wrists to restore the circulation, then leaned forward and freed his horse from Musgrave's mount.

Big Jock rode up to Musgrave, looked questioningly at the Englishman's bonds, and held up his dagger. "I canna decide whither tae cut ye free, or tae kill ye, Mister Musgrave. Can ye help me make ma mind up?"

Musgrave grinned but said nothing. He held up his hands inviting Big Jock to cut the rope, but the old reiver hesitated. He was wondering if it would not be wiser to keep the Englishman tied up, but he remembered that

Musgrave had been partly responsible for preventing Tam from shooting him. Moreover, the former Captain had been as good as his word and told Maxwell that his captives were Elliots and not Johnstones. It gave him sufficient reason to cut the Englishman's bonds.

He turned to Cortez, clearly prepared to free him too, but Musgrave put out a hand to stop him. As usual, the Englishman was busily calculating his next move and he felt that, for the moment, it would be in his interest to keep the Spaniard on a short leash. Since his wild ride over the Scots Dyke, nothing much seemed to have gone his way, but suddenly out of the blue, or out of the mist, things seemed to have taken a marked turn for the better, and by playing his cards with care he might yet turn the situation to his advantage. If he could persuade Big Jock to let him keep Cortez as his prisoner and take the Spaniard back to Scrope, his position as Captain of Bewcastle would be restored, not to mention pocketing a substantial financial reward.

Big Jock too, was unsure about whether he should release the Spaniard. He knew nothing about Cortez except the little Rabbie had told him, and he had learned a long time ago to be wary of anything out of the ordinary. Musgrave noted Big Jock's hesitation and was anxious to help the big man make up his mind. He thought that the best way to do that was to tell Big Jock the truth, not the whole truth, but an edited version of it.

"Leave him tied up, Jock," he said urgently. "All he ever talks about is some Spanish ships that are supposed to be landing somewhere around here. I don't know what it's all about, but he has his mind set on being there to meet them when they arrive. If we let him free, he'll be gone before we know it. Part of me would be glad to see the back of him, but if Maxwell catches him, he will want to know what happened to me and these two Elliots. This particular Spanish gentleman is part of whatever Maxwell is up to and he'll tell the bastard everything, and that's the last thing we want."

Sandy, who by now had had plenty of opportunity to observe the Spaniard, agreed with the Englishman. "Musgrave is right, Jock. He's been nothing but trouble all the way from Lochmaben, for us as well as for Tam. I think that the only reason Tam didn't kill him is that Maxwell is somehow mixed up with whatever these Spanish ships are coming here for. The other thing is that he thinks we're all English spies. He wants us dead and he'd be happy to let Maxwell do it for him. He's more trouble than he's worth and we'd be better off getting shot of him. As Musgrave says, we can't let him go so our best bet is to kill him here and ride on."

Sandy grinned and added, "If Maxwell wants to make anything of it, he can take it up with Tam."

Big Jock was surprised that Sandy was the one to suggest killing the Spaniard. The thought had crossed his own mind but he had expected the suggestion to come from Musgrave, or maybe young Rabbie, but whatever had happened to them since riding out of Liddesdale, had helped to turn the hiedsman's sons into real reivers. He fully accepted what they were saying about the Spaniard causing them trouble, and why they could not simply let him go. Once they set him free, there would be no knowing what he would do, where he would go, whom he might meet, or what he would tell them. Now that he had found the hiedsman's sons, Big Jock's only concern was to get them home to their father before something else untoward happened, and he was not prepared to risk having them taken prisoner again. Whether it was King Jamie, or Maxwell, who captured them would make little difference; next time there would be no escape. It was essential that he get them away from here without any further difficulties, and he decided that the best thing to do was to cut the Spaniard's throat.

He drew his dagger but again Musgrave intervened. The Englishman knew that, from the Elliots' point of view, killing Cortez was the obvious answer, but in order to take the Spaniard back to Scrope, he had to keep Cortez alive. He stood to reap a rich reward and was reluctant to let it slip from his grasp.

"Hang on a minute, Jock," he said thoughtfully. "Wouldn't it be better to hang on to him for a while? If we run into Maxwell, we're dead anyway, but if we were to meet King James, we could use him as a hostage. James would give a lot to know about those Spanish ships and we could use Cortez to bargain our way out."

Big Jock had known Musgrave for long enough not to trust him any farther than he could see him, but this Spaniard was right about one thing. There could be no longer be any doubt about Musgrave being an English spy. He would certainly have reasons of his own for holding Cortez prisoner and Big Jock guessed that Musgrave intended to sell the Spaniard to the

English. Not that such a thing bothered Big Jock Elliot; in Musgrave's position he would have been thinking along similar lines himself. His objective now was to see his hiedsman's sons safely home, and he could see that having Cortez as a hostage might well prove to be a help in achieving that.

Although convinced that the Englishman was not being completely honest about his reasons for keeping Cortez alive, Big Jock turned his back on the Spaniard and sheathed his dagger.

Cortez had no idea of how close he had come to losing his life, but when the big man turned away, his heart dropped. To his utter dismay, he remained a prisoner!

For a little while, this unexpected turn of events had given him hope that he would not have to wait until dawn before making his escape. He had confidently expected his rescuers to release him with the other captives, and immediately his hands were untied, he planned to make a run for it. He would never have a better opportunity to ride with a warning to the Spanish ships than while his liberators were busy congratulating themselves on the success of their rescue mission, and he would not even wait to offer them a gentlemanly 'thank you' for freeing him. Then came this unwelcome turn of fortune. The English spy intervened and Elliot had backed him up. As a result, the big man with the dagger poised to free him, had changed his mind. His earlier assessment had been correct. They were all English spies, and worse, he was now their prisoner! To a Spaniard, there could be no greater indignity.

Slowly, however, his frustration abated. He forced himself to set his loathing for the English spy, and his Scottish accomplices, to one side and concentrate on working out a new course of action. Somehow, he had to find a way of reaching the Spanish ships, and that had suddenly become more difficult. Even in his anxiety to warn the ships, the soldier in Cortez could not help but be impressed by the way that this big Scotsman had completely routed Tam and his band of ruffians, and by how ably the youngster had assisted him. He knew instinctively that escaping from them would not be as easy as it would have been from Tam and his rabble, and a glance around to see if his new captors were off guard following their victory, told him that they were not. None of them had dismounted; a sure sign that they were aware of possible danger and were fully alert. Their watchfulness, he knew, stemmed from a wariness of what might lie out there in the mist; in these conditions, that pistol shot would have carried for miles. They were certainly not ignoring him, and Musgrave for one, was making it plain that he was watching him. So, waiting until everyone was tired and making a sudden break for freedom, was no longer a viable option. He would have to think of an alternative.

The three Elliots waited anxiously, not knowing from which direction danger might come, but nothing happened and, gradually, they began to relax. Big Jock directed Sandy to dismount and arm himself, which he did. He picked up a discarded lance, and helped himself to a sword and scabbard from the body of one the reivers. He was about to remount when he paused and picked up the wheel lock pistol Tam had dropped when he fell, then went to the reiver's body and removed the other pistol, together with the remaining powder and shot.

He looked up at Big Jock. "It's no use leaving these for anyone else to find," he said.

He put one pistol in his belt and threw the other to his brother who deftly caught it. Rabbie looked the weapon over, got some powder and shot from Sandy, and proceeded to load it. He was pleased to have it back but not because he wanted to show it off as he previously had. His experiences over the last weeks had taught him that, for a reiver, firearms were not the answer to every problem and this time he wanted it back simply because his father had given it to him.

As he stuck the pistol in his belt, Rabbie grinned ruefully and turned to Big Jock. "It wouldn't have been much of a help to us here would it, Jock?"

Big Jock nodded his approval and turned to Sandy. "Take yon rapier as well."

Sandy removed the Spaniard's slender sword, ornate scabbard, and belt. He handed them to Big Jock and the old reiver examined them carefully. He regarded the rapier as nothing more than a fancy toy and he had never had any use for such a weapon but, while he wasn't interested in keeping it for himself, he recognised superb craftsmanship when he saw it.

Musgrave, who had watched Sandy collecting the weapons, rode up to Big Jock, still holding onto the rope holding Cortez's horse and pulling the

Spaniard along behind him. "I'm unarmed, Jock. If we get into a corner, I'll need something to fight with."

Big Jock looked at Sandy, who shook his head. He thought that the Englishman was probably lying and cast a knowing look at Musgrave's boot, suspecting that there was a ballock dagger hidden there. Most reivers carried them. He had carried one himself and, even if you never got a chance to use it, just knowing it was there, gave you confidence. Big Jock calculated that rescuing Musgrave from Tam was enough to settle any debt the Elliots owed the Englishman, and he decided that it would be wiser not to let him have his choice of the weapons that were left; arming him might cause unnecessary trouble later. He said nothing but handed Musgrave the Spanish rapier. The Englishman laughed. It was not what he had hoped for but it was better than nothing and it was clear that it was all he was going to get. He could possibly dismount and help himself, but he wasn't prepared to risk doing that for fear of having the rope connecting him to Cortez pulled from his grasp. On the other hand, if he happened to lose the Spaniard between here and Carlisle, the rapier would serve as proof of the story he was taking back to Scrope.

Drawing the sword from its finely worked scabbard, he made a show of wielding it, performing a series of intricate fencing moves in front of Cortez.

He waved it under the Spaniard's nose. "So this is what you were going to kill me with, is it? Well, not any more you're not. You missed your chance, Senor Cortez."

Cortez forced himself not to be provoked. He had become accustomed to the Englishman's insults and counselled himself not to respond. Musgrave's clumsy attempts to demonstrate his fencing skills were laughable to say the least, and the Spaniard took heart from the thought that he could easily best him in a duel.

Musgrave waited for a riposte, but when one was not forthcoming, he pressed on. He held up the rapier. "I'll get a good price for this in Carlisle. You'll like Carlisle, Senor Cortez, they have a lovely gaol there. It's well fitted for a Spanish gentleman, and they'll pay me handsomely for bringing you to grace it with your presence."

Far from feeling intimidated, Cortez felt his spirits lifting. The English spy, he thought, has overplayed his hand and said a little too much. Musgrave's admission that he intended to sell him in England had given the Spaniard the germ of an idea. He ignored the Englishman's gibes and carefully thought back over everything that had happened since he first encountered the man. The more he thought about it, the more he realised that Musgrave's capacity for getting under his skin had caused him to neglect looking for pointers to the man's true character. Looking back over what he had seen of the man, he concluded that Musgrave was not a full-time spy. This Englishman was essentially a mercenary, and that might offer him a way out of his current dilemma.

With some thought, Cortez also changed his mind about the three Scotsmen. The big man, 'Jock', who was clearly their leader, had not allowed Musgrave a weapon other than the rapier, which he obviously considered to be nothing more than a mere toy, and had he been in league with the English spy, he would have made sure that his friend was adequately armed. The Spaniard reluctantly admitted to himself that he had allowed his obsession with English spies to cloud his judgement, and he vowed not to make the same mistake again. Now thinking clearly, Cortez noted that Musgrave was pleased to have his rapier, not as a weapon, but because of its potential monetary value, and it presented him with an interesting new possibility. This Englishman would almost certainly be open to a bribe.

The realisation changed his perspective. Instead of wasting time thinking of ways to escape, he should be looking for ways of exploiting Musgrave's weak point. It was time to bring his skills as a diplomat into play.

"It will be much too late for you to sell anything at all by the time you eventually get me into England, Musgrave, if in fact you ever do. By then, England will be finished and the heretic Elizabeth will have lost her head."

For his part, Musgrave remained unimpressed, but he too, was thinking back over what had happened. From the way that the Spaniard had been acting, and from what he had been saying about Spanish ships, it was obvious that something important was about to happen and it might be worth his while trying to glean a little more information. Anything he could learn would help to make him a rich man.

Cortez did not expect to sway the Englishman with a single remark, he realised that it would be a long process but he had to start somewhere.

"You don't really think that I'm going to fall for that do you, Senor Spaniard? You'll have to do a lot better to make me think I can't take you back to sell to Lord Scrope."

The experienced Cortez guessed that Musgrave was attempting to make him reveal something more about the Spanish conquest of England. He saw this as proof that his change of tactics was beginning to take effect and decided to remain silent.

The Spaniard's silence came as a surprise to Musgrave. In the past, Cortez had always responded immediately to his gibes, and he had expected him to do the same again. His curiosity, however, had been aroused and he continued trying to provoke the Spaniard into divulging something more.

He introduced an element of mockery. "Look at yourself, Spaniard, with your hands tied, the prisoner of an Englishman. How could anybody even begin to think that an army of Spanish fops like you could invade England and depose our Queen Bess? She'll still be there long after you are an honoured guest in Carlisle Castle. And I'll be counting my money."

Cortez looked him in the eye. "There will be no English money for you to count," he said seriously. "But there will be plenty of Spanish gold. Not that you will ever see any of it."

In the meantime, Big Jock was becoming anxious. The king would surely have sent a large contingent of riders from Langholm after Maxwell, and while Jamie's army would probably stop and bed down for the night, their quarry would not. The canny laird and his riders were reivers to a man and would be happy to ride all night. Big Jock thought that Maxwell would lay an ambush for the royal troops, but he would lead Jamie further into the Galloway Hills before doing it, and the obvious route for the king to take was the one Tam and his riders had been on when he and Rabbie had caught them. If he was right in his thinking, large bands of Maxwell riders could be arriving here at any minute.

Sandy too, was feeling uneasy about delaying too long. If either Maxwell or the king caught them, there would be no question of holding them as hostages. For both factions, the time for that was long past.

He rode up to Big Jock. "We should be moving, Jock," he said in a low voice. He looked meaningfully back to where Musgrave and the Spaniard were still engaged in mocking each other. "And we'll have to ride fast. Those two will slow us down."

Big Jock motioned to Rabbie to join them. "Time tae be awa' hame," he said.

"The sooner the better," Rabbie said. "But we can't go back to Liddesdale by way of the Johnstones. We'd be sure to run into Maxwell or Jamie."

Sandy agreed. "The only way we'll get home is to ride north and then turn east."

The way his two young kinsmen were beginning to think and act was a cause of some satisfaction to Big Jock, but he made no comment other than, "Aye, it is, an' that way we'll no have tae use yon ford. Jamie'll soon have riders there."

Sandy was still worried about Musgrave and Cortez. He cared nothing for Cortez and, like Big Jock, he was happy that any debt owed to Musgrave was now paid. "We'll have a better chance without those two, Jock; they'll only cause us trouble."

Once again, Big Jock agreed. "Aye, it'd be best tae ride alane. We'll be awa' laddies, there's a bit o' the night left yet."

"What about Musgrave and the Spaniard?" Rabbie asked.

"Leave 'em be," Jock answered. "Musgrave has something on his mind an' he'll no be wantin' tae come wi' us. We canna leave their bodies here for Jamie tae find an' yon Englishman will ken how tae keep oot o' his way."

The others nodded and the three Elliots prepared to set off into the mist. As they were leaving, Big Jock turned to Musgrave. "We're awa'. Come or stay as ye will."

Jock was already sure of what the answer would be. He didn't bother waiting for a reply.

Chapter 29

Alexander Elliot rode hard through the misty night. He had chosen a route that would take him well north of Langholm and clear of the Debatable Land. It was important to be clear of the area before daybreak. He dare not risk running into any elements of the king's army still in the area following the battle with Maxwell; if he did, his quest would be over before it started. The Broken Men in the Debatable Land would not dare to molest a Liddesdale hiedsman, but the news that Alexander Elliot was riding alone toward Dumfriesshire would fetch a good reward from any number of other interested parties. And that meant it was necessary for him to avoid them.

These were certainly important considerations, but there was another even more compelling reason for choosing this particular route into Dumfriesshire.

If, and in Alexander's mind it remained an 'if', Big Jock and his sons were still alive and on their way home, they would surely be riding this way. Assuming that he was somewhere in Dumfriesshire, Big Jock would know that King Jamie had begun his campaign to deal with Maxwell, and he would have guessed what the laird was doing to counter the king's efforts to capture him. Alexander knew that Big Jock would avoid becoming embroiled in the struggle between the king and his laird, and if the big man had made contact with Malcolm and Robert, he would have ensured that they, too, steered well clear of trouble. He put himself in Big Jock's boots and was confident that the canny old reiver would err on the side of caution, assuming such an option was open to him. Big Jock would certainly want to avoid the Johnstones, who would certainly be riding with the king, and he would ride as far north as he dared before turning east for home. It was what any experienced reiver would do.

There was currently no bad blood between the Johnstones and Elliots, and under different circumstances, Alexander could expect to be the recipient of the best of Border hospitality. These, however, were not ordinary times. The Johnstones would side with the king, if for no other reason than James was out to arrest their archenemy, Maxwell. They would be on full alert for anything or anyone in the least suspicious, and a group of three Elliots riding out of Dumfriesshire would certainly count as being suspicious. At the very least, they would detain the three suspicious riders, and even if they did not, word of their presence would soon spread throughout The Borders, and before long, it would inevitably reach the ears of James and Maxwell. James would certainly not pass up the opportunity to bring three members of the notorious Elliot reiver family to justice and God alone knew how Maxwell would react. In either case, it would do nothing to help Big Jock and Alexander's sons get back home to Liddesdale. Big Jock would know this and would be riding home by a circuitous northern route. To the south and west was Maxwell country and the old reiver would certainly avoid going that way. All Alexander had to do was follow a reciprocal route and hope to intercept them.

It all sounded straightforward enough, but the Elliot hiedsman was far too experienced to indulge in overconfidence. Too much depended on what had happened to his sons since they left home, events that, worryingly, he had no knowledge of. Foremost in his mind, was the nagging thought that he did not know whether his sons were alive or dead, but he was perfectly well aware of how the odds lay. But he told himself that he could take nothing for granted, and his only option was to assume that they were alive, and act accordingly.

Undetected, he cleared the elements of the king's army remaining around Langholm and then forced himself to slow down. Frustrating as it was for Alexander, and as badly as he wanted to find his sons, now was a time for proceeding with extreme care. Big Jock, Malcolm and Robert would also be taking great care to avoid discovery and they, too, would be riding with extreme caution. As a lone searcher, by throwing caution to the wind and taking a direct route, he would virtually ensure that he missed them among the Dumfriesshire hills, especially at night; and Big Jock would certainly be riding by night. His years as a reiver had taught Alexander the dangers of riding carelessly into the unknown. Such rashness invariably led to death at the hands of either an enemy or the authorities, and in this case, it could easily cause the deaths of the three men he was trying to find. With this in mind, he began the long and time-consuming process of taking a painstakingly slow, zigzag path westward across a wide swathe of unfamiliar country.

Alexander had to accept that, even allowing for as many eventualities as possible, his hopes of finding Malcolm and Robert alive and well could still end in bitter disappointment. Nevertheless, he could no longer bear to sit on his hands in Liddesdale wondering what had happened to them, or watch their mother worrying, for one day longer. He simply had to discover for himself the fate of his sons.

***

Lochmaben Castle was under siege and the defenders, now under the command of Maxwell's brother, David, were putting up a stout defence. So much so that King James, anxious not to waste any time in his hunt for his errant laird, sent an urgent plea to Lord Scrope, Warden of the English West March, for siege artillery. The king's request left Scrope, now under orders from Walsingham, to hold all of his available forces in readiness to counter the threat posed by Spain, in something of a quandary. Agreeing to James's request would mean weakening those forces, but that in itself would make little difference. He did not envisage the large unwieldly siege pieces being of much use against the Spanish invaders. By the time they managed to haul the two heavy guns all the way from Carlisle to the south coast, the invasion would be over one way or another. The men required to fire the guns were, however, a different matter. Sending them to Scotland would be in direct contravention of his orders, something that, at sometime in the future, he might have to answer for.

On the other hand, how could he possibly deny such a request? There was a strong probability that James would one day wear the crown of England as well as that of Scotland, and then he would certainly have to answer for his failure to offer full support to his future king. Unable to resolve the political problems involved, he considered the advantages, or otherwise, to his own March. Complying with James's request, would at least have the advantage of helping to remove one potentially dangerous thorn from his side, Maxwell, and that proved to be the decisive argument. He came to a decision and sent the guns over the border to Scotland, accompanied by the men to fire them.

Scrope's decision spelled the end for resistance at Lochmaben Castle. With the English seige artillery he needed on its way, James left the siege in the capable hands of Sir William Stewart and set off to the west after his main quarry, the returned exile, Maxwell.

When the heavy English cannons arrived, Stewart set about battering Maxwell's stronghold into submission, but still the defenders held out. He concluded that if he were to follow his king's instructions to take the castle quickly, other, more devious, methods were required. He personally delivered a message purporting to come from James with a written promise guaranteeing the lives of the Captain of Lochmaben and his men in return for their immediate surrender. The promise of safe conduct aside, in the face of the English artillery, David Maxwell knew that he could not hold out for much longer. He agreed to Stewart's terms and surrendered the castle.

The promise of safe conduct, however, turned out to be worthless. As soon as it came to James's notice, he immediately repudiated Stewart's promise, and David Maxwell, together with five of his men, went to the gallows set up outside the castle gate.

Maxwell's castle at Caerlaverock fared no better. Easily captured by other elements of James's army, it left the laird without a firm base in Dumfriesshire. Due to the king's swift action, none of his three fortresses had held out for as long as Maxwell had hoped, and he had little option but to lure James further west, and sooner than he had originally intended. There, he knew he could count on local support and lay reiver-style ambushes. The prospects of forcing James to give up and return to Edinburgh after just a few ambushes, were practically non-existent, but that was not what Maxwell had in mind. His primary purpose was to hold James up until the Spanish ships arrived. After that, everything would change.

James would be obliged to repel the invaders; the laird would ride to his assistance, help to defeat the Spanish, and reap the resulting rewards, not to mention that Spanish gold. Time, however, was working against him. The early loss of his fortresses meant that he would have to keep up his game of cat-and-mouse with the king for that much longer.

Had Maxwell known that the possibility of the Spanish invasion force he was pinning his hopes on arriving on time was becoming more and more remote with each passing day, his confidence would not have been nearly so high.

***

The Duke of Medina Sidonia was once again in jubilant mood. His latest information confirmed that the bulk of the English fleet remained tied up in Plymouth. He briefly considered attacking the enemy ships while they lay in port but, and much to his second-in-command's frustration, decided against it.

De Recalde reasoned that, provided they struck quickly, only a small portion of the great armada would be required to keep the vast majority of English ships bottled up, while, in the meantime, the rest of the armada were free to sail unhindered up the Channel. Blockading enemy ports was, he argued, a tactic the English had used against them with great success, and here was an opportunity to pay them back in kind. He feared that the English would allow the Spanish ships to enter the Channel and then sail out from Plymouth behind them. Once that happened, the English would have the advantage of the wind gauge. They would enjoy the luxury of being able to make maximum use of the prevailing winds, while for the Spanish there could be no turning back. As Sidonia had also ruled out an invasion of the Isle of Wight, de Recalde knew that the armada was now committed to a single course of action. The Duke, however, was not in the least perturbed. This, he said, was precisely what King Philip had planned.

In the excitement generated by anticipating, and preparing for, the coming momentous events, the fate of ships bound for Scotland was totally ignored, but that no longer mattered. De Recalde had already concluded that they had been irretrievably lost in the recent storms.

Chapter 30

Musgrave and Cortez sat on their horses and silently watched the three Elliots disappear off into the Border mist. Neither made any effort to follow. Riding north was not something that suited either the Englishman or the Spaniard. Each had reasons of his own for wanting to take a different direction, and both were content to see the Elliots go.

For Cortez, going north would only take him further from his objective, that of finding and warning the Spanish invasion force before it landed and was annihilated by King James and a large Scottish army. He had given up any hope that their erstwhile ally, Maxwell, would keep his promise to support the invasion, and for Cortez, warning the Spanish ships had become his sole purpose in life. Moreover, he was perfectly prepared to die in the attempt. He did not, however, intend to let the urgency of his mission cloud his judgement, nor was he any longer going to allow himself to be distracted by the English spy's jibes. His hands remained tightly bound but there could be no doubt that it would be much easier to escape from one captor than from four. Especially now that he had discovered a large chink in the Englishman's armour.

There had been a moment when he feared that Musgrave would opt to ride off with the Elliots and drag him along, but the Englishman had not, and that came as a huge relief. What he had to concentrate on now was how best to exploit the English spy's apparent weakness: the man's inherent greed.

For his part, Musgrave had never seriously considered riding north with the Elliots. It took no effort whatsoever to work out what Big Jock had in mind. He would ride north until he was well clear of Maxwell and the king, and then turn east for Liddesdale. The route did hold some attractions for the Englishman. For one thing, it was safer, the only dangerous part being the ride to get clear of Maxwell lands, and in the event of an encounter with a hostile force, being with the Elliots would provide safety in numbers. Nevertheless, there were also serious disadvantages to riding with the three Liddesdale men. He would have to take his prisoner with him, which would slow them down, and at the first sign of trouble, the Elliots would simply dispose of Cortez. Big Jock would have worked out that the Spaniard was only valuable as a bargaining tool against the king, and in any encounter with Maxwell's riders, he would not hesitate to kill the prisoner himself rather than try to protect him. Musgrave also calculated that in north Dumfriesshire, there was every likelihood that Maxwell sympathisers would soon learn of the group of five strange riders and ambush them. The fact that the laird himself would be further west concentrating on ambushing King James, would make no difference.

The Elliots on their own, he thought, stood a good chance of riding through untroubled by the Maxwells, Johnstones or any of the other Dumfriesshire reiver families, but an Englishman and a Spaniard would certainly beg all kinds of awkward questions.

To Musgrave's mind, if he did happen to find himself cornered, it would be better if it were by the king rather than by Maxwell. With James, he could use Cortez as a bargaining tool. At some stage, he might have to dispose of the Spaniard himself, but to him, Cortez was now far more valuable alive than dead and he would try to postpone that particular option for as long as possible. It had occurred to him that he could sell what information he had already gleaned from Cortez to James as readily as he could to Lord Scrope, something, he told himself, he should have thought of earlier. It would not be quite as easy as dealing with Scrope but the king would pay just as handsomely for the Spaniard and everything he knew. James, of course, could not restore him to the Captaincy of Bewcastle, but at least he stood to gain something for his trouble.

Added to what his prisoner had said about Spanish ships, he had also mentioned something much more appealing to Musgrave's ears: Spanish gold. That was something no reiver worth his salt could easily dismiss.

First, however, he had to get clear of the probable path of Maxwell's flight to the west, and he turned their horses south towards the Solway Firth. He would have to hide out until he was sure that both Maxwell and the king had cleared the area, and riding south was the safest option. His one big problem was that he would have to either re-cross the river using the ford, or ride north in a wide circle around Dumfries, and both options were fraught with danger. Then there was Caerlaverock, which he envisaged would soon be under siege by the king, but he had every confidence that as long as this foul weather held, he could easily negotiate his way around that particular obstacle. He estimated that three or four more days of mist and rain would see him safely back in Carlisle, and in the meantime, Cortez's mention of Spanish gold intrigued him, and he felt compelled to try to learn more.

Cortez, meanwhile, although he dare not give Musgrave an inkling of what he was thinking, was getting desperate to find a way of locating and warning the Spanish invasion force about King James being in the vicinity with an entire Scottish army. It would be going totally against King Philip's orders, but the Spanish ships could not possibly land in the face of such opposition. His original plan had been to find the small port where he had landed with Maxwell, but now he realised that finding that particular port was not strictly necessary, and yet again, he cursed himself for allowing Musgrave's insolent attitude to interfere with his thinking. On proper reflection, he realised that there must be many other similar small fishing communities along this coast where he could steal a boat. It did not matter what kind of boat he stole, he was confident that he was a competent enough sailor to handle any craft he was likely to find in this remote area, and even in this weather, the Spanish ships would not be difficult to locate.

The Spaniard began to believe that his fortunes were starting to change for the better. As soon as Musgrave decided to ride in the opposite direction to that taken by the Elliots, he felt a surge of inner satisfaction and found it difficult to think of a more favourable turn of events. He guessed that when the Englishman judged that he had ridden far enough to the south, he intended to turn east for England. Cortez would have preferred to ride west, but south would do for now. He didn't know how long it would be before Musgrave deemed it appropriate to begin making his way home to England, but it might not be long, and so now was the time for him to begin working on the Englishman's mind with a view to persuading him change it.

He rode closer to his captor. "So, Englishman, you finally seem to have come at least partially to your senses. You have concluded that riding off to the north with those Scotsmen would not only lead you further from England, but also closer to death."

Musgrave's confidence was high enough for him to disregard the Spaniard's sarcasm. "It'll make no difference to you which way we ride, Senor Cortez. You'll still finish up in a cell in Carlisle Castle."

"You will never get me to Carlisle alive, Englishman, and even if you manage to get there alone, you will only be handing yourself over to a Spanish garrison. Then you will be the one in the cell awaiting an appointment with the scaffold."

The Spaniard's insistence on sticking to the same theme was beginning to have its effect on Musgrave and, almost involuntarily, he began to think that Cortez's words carried more than just a ring of truth. There could be no denying that the Spaniard himself believed them to be true, and the fact that he had mentioned getting him to Carlisle 'alive' had given the Englishman further food for thought. Would Cortez die rather than be taken to England as a prisoner? The Spaniard's every word and action since their first encounter all pointed to the answer being 'yes', which left Musgrave facing a problem he had not previously considered. He dismissed Cortez's claim that the Spanish would have taken Carlisle, but he began to doubt that arriving there with nothing more than a Spanish rapier as evidence, would be enough to convince the sceptical Lord Scrope; it certainly would not satisfy Walsingham. To have any chance of gaining a substantial reward, he not only had to get Cortez to Carlisle but also get him there alive. It was a sobering enough thought to make him look at his options from a different perspective, and this time, try not to allow thoughts of what rewards he might gain in England to cloud his thinking.

That, however, would have to wait. A new and more worrying problem was rapidly becoming evident. Almost unnoticed, the weather had begun to change. The persistent drizzle had ceased, the mist was lifting, and the sky was becoming perceptibly lighter. Soon it would be daylight, the summer sun would be up, and the misty gloom he had been counting on for cover would quickly burn off. It was no longer safe to ride by day and he would have to find a place to hide until dark.

He found a secluded spot among some rocks in a deep and narrow crevice eaten out over the centuries by a burn tumbling down from the hills and now swollen by the rain. Unknowing, he had hit upon a hiding place similar to the one where Big Jock and Rabbie had taken refuge just a few hours earlier. Since then, the burns had flooded but this secluded spot was still perfectly tenable. Musgrave chose to use such a hiding place for the same reasons Big Jock had; it provided excellent cover, and there was water and grass for the horses. There was nothing for the men to eat, but as a Borderer and a reiver, going hungry for a day or two did not cause him any great distress. He couldn't be sure what effect it would have on this soft Spaniard but, in truth, he really didn't care and decided not to waste time worrying about it. He led the way down the bank to the burn, gestured to Cortez to dismount, and motioned to his prisoner to sit. He took the length of rope recovered from Tam and tethered his prisoner to a clump of bushes. The horses had remained unsaddled for two days now, but being Galloway Nags they were used to such hardships and, trained for reiving, while they remained saddled they would not stray.

Almost immediately after landing in Scotland, Cortez had discovered that, due to his dress and manner, people tended to regard him as what Musgrave had described as a 'fop', and it was an impression he had chosen to promote. Diplomat he might be, but he had also been a brave and resourceful soldier, which was why de Recalde had chosen him to accompany Maxwell to Scotland. Nobody in this country even suspected that he might be anything other than what he appeared to be, and that included Musgrave, whose knowledge of the Spaniard's character and capabilities was sadly lacking. Cortez noticed that since their last exchange of words, the Englishman had remained uncharacteristically silent and he suspected that he had lost some of his earlier bravado. In the current situation, his feigned lack of experience would serve him well, and he set out to use his deception to further play on the English spy's mind.

"If you want to keep me alive, Englishman, you will have to find me something to eat."

Musgrave ignored him, but Cortez pressed on. "And what about these poor animals? They will never survive the journey unless they are properly cared for, and especially if you need them to carry you out of trouble. They will not be able to raise a gallop."

The Englishman again ignored him. As far as he was concerned, all the Spaniard had done was to reinforce his opinion that his prisoner was completely out of his depth in the rough and tumble of Border life.

Cortez guessed that the Englishman's mind was elsewhere and that allowed him a little time to think before interrupting his thoughts. He looked up at the quickly clearing sky. "The rain has stopped and it is going to be hot today, Englishman, or at least as hot as it ever gets in this godforsaken land. I can sleep through the heat of the day, but you will have to stand watch or else, in this clear weather, King James will find you. And then you will die."

Musgrave was certain that falling into the king's hands would be no more welcome to Cortez than it would be to him. James might hesitate to kill the Spaniard, at least until he had extracted all the information he could regarding the Spanish ships heading for Scotland, but that would put an end to any thoughts Cortez had of meeting and warning those same ships. Moreover, it had become patently obvious that these ships actually did exist; he could no longer dismiss them as a ruse by Cortez to divert people's thoughts.

The possibility of selling Cortez and his information to King James had given Musgrave an alternative to taking the Spaniard to England, but it was a dangerous option and did not hold quite the same attraction. On balance, it would suit him better to get the Spaniard back to Carlisle. If he took his prisoner to James, the king might well conclude that letting the Englishman off with his life was sufficient reward, while Scrope, Musgrave thought, would be more willing to pay. In Carlisle, he definitely stood to gain more, and there was the Captaincy of Bewcastle and the possibility of a second reward from Walsingham to take into account. Both of these options sounded equally tempting, but with a little thought, a new, and potentially equally rewarding, possibility entered his mind. Being satisfied that a fleet of Spanish ships would soon be arriving to land somewhere in this area, and that Cortez's concern for them was real, presented Musgrave with yet another tempting option. Tales of the fabulous wealth plundered from the New World and carried by Spanish galleons, had penetrated even into The Borders, and Cortez had said that these Spanish ships would be carrying gold. He was now sure that the ships actually did exist, and if the ships were real, then so was the gold.

The presence of Spanish gold held out a promise of riches far beyond anything Musgrave had yet imagined, and it suddenly struck him that this was what had motivated Maxwell to risk returning from exile in Spain in the first place. Neither Scrope nor Walsingham commanded purses that could begin to compete with Spanish gold, and even if they did, neither would part with any more than the absolute minimum necessary to pay him off. To Musgrave's reiver's mind, it seemed that King James, with a massive army at his back, was sure to be first to reach the gold and so be in a position to be generous with his rewards. By then, however, the Spanish would have already landed and any information he had gleaned from Cortez, would be worthless. It was patently obvious that if he wanted to get his hands on any of that Spanish treasure, he would have to take it for himself. That, however, seemed to a remote possibility, and he failed to see how, on his own, he could manage to achieve it.

Nevertheless, in spite of the problems involved, thoughts of riches beyond his wildest dreams began to prey on the Englishman's mind. As he began to imagine the almost unbelievable possibilities, his natural reiver's caution temporarily deserted him. They had a long day ahead of them before they could move, and he decided to try to use it to trick Cortez into telling him more.

He began by laughing off the Spaniard's last remark. "You don't want to meet King James any more than I do, Spaniard, but if we do, at least I'll have you to bargain with."

It was the Spaniard's turn to laugh. "You don't believe that the king will pay you for my dead body do you? And know this, Englishman: I will willingly die before I betray my country to either James of Scotland or your Lord Scrope."

The Spaniard's determination was clear, and Musgrave knew that he would have to keep a careful watch in case a desperate Cortez decided to make a death or glory attempt to reach the Spanish ships. Given the slightest opportunity, he might be prepared to throw caution to the winds and try to ride off, even at the cost of his life. Such a concept was beyond Musgrave's comprehension. This Spaniard seemed to possess a sense of loyalty to his king and country that the Englishman found difficult to understand, but he realised that, while he spent his time assessing the risks against the possible rewards, Cortez had a single objective in mind. He would do his utmost to warn the Spanish ships, or die in the attempt. There was, however, a flaw in that argument. Musgrave realised that, while Cortez was quite prepared to die, death would be a last resort. Dead, he could not possibly warn anybody. It would be worthwhile finding out more about what was driving Cortez, why warning these Spanish ships was so important to him, and more to the point, how much in Spanish gold he was prepared to offer in exchange for his freedom. Without some freedom of action, Cortez could not possibly warn the ships.

In order to make any kind of dent in the Spaniard's armour, the Englishman knew that he would have to adopt an entirely different approach, and he believed that he had found one.

"Don't take me for an idiot, Cortez. If you die, you won't be able to warn off those Spanish ships and stop them sailing straight into King James's arms."

Cortez was silent. Musgrave clearly had something on his mind and the best way of finding out what, was to wait until the Englishman had no option but to tell him. He leaned back against a smooth rock and closed his eyes as if intending to sleep.

Musgrave guessed that Cortez was not going to sleep, but neither did he intend to say anything more. The Spaniard was waiting for him to continue with what he had started, but the Englishman was loath to give him the impression that he had changed his mind about what he intended to do next. It was too early to let Cortez know that he might be prepared to negotiate some form of arrangement with him in exchange for some of that gold; that would give Cortez an equal say in where they went from here. As long as the Spaniard remained his prisoner, he held the upper hand, but Cortez showed little inclination to bargain, and was clearly leaving it up to him to make the next move. Musgrave had hoped that his prisoner would be anxious to strike an immediate bargain, but having waited for several frustrating minutes in which the Spaniard failed to say a word, he had to come clean and admit that he was considering altering his original plan.

"All right Cortez," he said testily. "How do I know that there really is any Spanish gold, and if there is, how do I know that you can get your hands on it?"

Cortez sat up leisurely. This was exactly what he wanted to hear and it was ample confirmation that he had been right about this Englishman's inherent greed. He was now effectively in negotiation with Musgrave, and on familiar ground, where his diplomatic experience would serve him well. It was highly satisfying but he was not about to let his satisfaction show.

He resumed his position against the rock and continued to look completely relaxed. "It is now you who is taking me for a fool, Englishman. You know that I do not have any gold with me here, but as King Philip's personal representative, I do of course have access to it, and I have authority to use it in any way I see fit. Paying you to set me free would be a legitimate use, and I would pay you more than you could hope to get from either Lord Scrope or King James for my dead body. But know this, Englishman, freedom does not mean a thing to me unless I can use it to find and warn our ships before they land in Scotland."

Musgrave had already worked out that in order to have any hope of getting his hands on some of that gold, he would have to help Cortez find the Spanish ships, and find them before either Maxwell or King James did.

"All right, Cortez. What do you have in mind? It better be good, because I think that the only thing that brought Maxwell back from Spain was that he knew those Spanish ships would be carrying gold."

Cortez knew that he had his man. He could afford to be more forthcoming. "I fear that you are right about 'laird' Maxwell. He persuaded King Philip to mount part of his invasion of England from here, but I'm afraid that what he really had in mind was stealing the gold he knew the ships would be carrying."

This news rather shook Musgrave. It was common knowledge, even in The Borders, that Philip of Spain would, one day, attempt to invade England, but no one suspected that they would land a force in Scotland as well. It was information he knew he ought to take back to Carlisle immediately, but that would mean giving up all hope of getting his hands on some of that Spanish gold, and anyway, he told himself, if he helped Cortez to warn off the Spanish ships it would amount to the same thing in the end. The threat of a secondary Spanish invasion in Scotland would be over. Nevertheless, it still depended on what Cortez had to offer.

The Spaniard decided that it was time to present Musgrave with a definite proposition. "I am prepared to reward you in return for your help in warning the ships about King James and his army being in the area. It would constitute a legitimate use of His Majesty's gold."

Musgrave believed that he had come out on top in the argument with the Spaniard, but he was careful not to appear too eager to accept Cortez's offer. "How much gold would you be prepared to pay?"

Cortez knew that he had Musgrave exactly where he wanted him, but he knew that getting into an argument over exactly how much he would pay in gold, would only prolong the discussion and give the Englishman time to think of alternatives. "That will depend on whether we are successful in getting a warning to the ships in time. If we are, you will be amply rewarded."

He paused before adding, "And it will certainly be more than you would get from either your Lord Scrope or King James for my dead body."

Cortez had once again pointedly remarked that he was fully prepared to die rather than be handed over to the king or to Scrope, and Musgrave believed him. With that in mind, he had nothing to lose but possibly much to gain by helping Cortez in his mission.

Musgrave could hardly resist; no real reiver could. Before accepting, however, he thought that pointing out some of the problems attached would help him to squeeze the maximum payment out of the Spaniard. He was beginning to suspect that Cortez was a much more resourceful man than his first impression had suggested, and he was confident that the Spaniard had already thought of a way around them, but he decided to mention them anyway to give the impression that he still had doubts.

"You're trying hard to make it sound easy, Cortez, but you know as well as I do that it won't be. If I know Maxwell, he still has plenty of riders left, and I suppose he knows where your ships are planning to land. The bastard will be there long before us, or the king, and he'll wait until they are well into unloading so that he can catch them cold and reive the gold.

And if James catches up with Maxwell first, it still won't make a blind bit of difference. Either way, we won't see any of your Spanish gold."

Openly outlining the severity of the obstacles that stood in their way, was almost enough to make Musgrave think again. Unless Cortez had a virtually foolproof plan for overcoming them, he might still be better off trying to get the Spaniard back to Carlisle. The lure of Spanish gold remained too strong for the reiver in him to resist, but he was determined not to appear too eager.

"So, how are we going to get over that problem, Senor Cortez? And we still stand a good chance of being caught before we even find the place where the ships are going to land."

Cortez knew that to be convincing, he had to have an immediate answer. "We don't wait for them to land," he said. "We find a boat and sail out to meet them while they are still at sea."

"A boat!" Musgrave's first thought was to dismiss the whole idea out of hand. His only experience of boats was in a coracle fishing for salmon in the River Eden, and in common with most men bred in the English West March, he had heard fearsome tales of the Solway Firth with its dangerous tides and currents. To the reivers, the sea was an alien environment; they confined their plundering to dry land and left robbing ships to the pirates. For Musgrave, accepting Cortez's proposal meant taking a step far into the unknown. He waved an arm towards the sea somewhere to the south.

"Are you mad, Cortez, that's the Solway Firth you're talking about. Nobody in his right mind would take a boat out there unless he was born and bred to it."

The Spaniard's response was immediate. "Nonsense, Musgrave! I could sail before I could walk or ride. There is not a boat or a ship that I cannot sail. I have been to the New World three times and compared to the Western Ocean, that is a mere pond out there. And, anyway, there are certainly fishermen along this coast who do it every day."

Musgrave was not convinced. "You might think you're the best sailor in the world, Cortez, but you wouldn't be the first to set out on that Solway Firth and never be seen again. And you might as well know now, I know nothing about boats of any kind, and I have no intention of learning out there!"

As far as Cortez was concerned, it made little difference whether the Englishman accompanied him or not; in fact, under the circumstances, it would be better if Musgrave did not. It was clear that the man was afraid of the sea and that could be dangerous in a small boat, but such considerations would have to wait. Before he could do anything at all, he had to get Musgrave to release him, and that meant persuading him to put his fears to one side. He sensed that it would be a waste of time telling the Englishman that as long as you knew what you were doing, going out in a small boat was perfectly safe; but there was still a way of getting the Englishman to set his fears aside.

He gave the impression that he had accepted the fact that Musgrave would not accompany him. "Suit yourself, Englishman," he said. "I will simply have to go alone. I clearly have to go to meet them before they land, or as you yourself pointed out, either Maxwell or King James will capture them and find the gold. Once I have warned them of the danger awaiting them ashore, I will return with a reward for you for releasing me. I'm prepared to give you my word of honour on that."

This solution was clearly the one Cortez preferred but, even though he had offered to give Musgrave his word, he doubted whether the Englishman would accept it.

Musgrave responded just as the Spaniard suspected he would. "Not on your life, Senor Cortez. What's to stop you sailing away with your friends and leaving me here with nothing?"

Cortes reacted with patently genuine anger. "I gave you my word, Englishman, and unlike you treacherous English, a Spaniard keeps his promises."

After a pause, he looked at Musgrave with obvious contempt. "The gold is on board the ships and if you are not prepared to accept my word that I will come back, then you will have to come with me. If they bring the gold ashore, it will soon be in the hands of either Maxwell or King James, and then, you will certainly get nothing."

Musgrave knew that he had little room left for manoeuvring. He suspected that a man like Cortez would actually do his best to keep his word, but it was a concept beyond his understanding, and a risk he found extremely difficult to accept. Even if the Spaniard did return with a bagful of Spanish gold, by that time this whole area would be alive with warring Scots. Maxwell and King James would surely be at each other's throats and he and Cortez would have more to worry about than gold. They would be lucky to escape with their lives.

Cortez had already anticipated this problem and knew that he had to find a way of overcoming it, or Musgrave might just decide to revert to his original plan and attempt to take him to England. He was aware that he could do nothing to allay the Englishman's fear of the sea, but he could do his best to help him overcome it.

"I find it strange that an Englishman should be afraid of the sea," he said pointedly, "and I suspect that you are merely using it as an excuse to increase your demands."

For once, Musgrave's personal pride, such as it was, was hurt, and it was his turn to display a moment of anger. "I never said I was afraid of the sea, Cortez. But I'm certainly afraid that when you bring me back here, I'll walk into the middle of a pitched battle between James and Maxwell."

Cortez remained the picture of calm. "I do not have to bring you back here, Englishman. I can take you and your gold to the other side of this bay, where you will be home in England. Or, if you prefer, you can come with me on one of the ships, and be landed somewhere in the south of England; or you could even come to Spain where you would be treated as a hero for helping in King Philip's great crusade against the enemies of the Holy Church."

Musgrave's head began to spin at this unexpected turn of events. Helping the Spaniard held out the exciting possibility of riches beyond his dreams, and a short trip in a small boat seemed to be a small price to pay; Cortez would not have suggested it if he had not been a competent sailor. However, he knew that he could not take his gold back to Carlisle. In a land populated by reivers, any show of sudden wealth would simply be inviting someone to take it from him. He dismissed the idea of going to Spain with Cortez; living the rest of his life in a strange land held no real attraction for him, whatever the promised comforts might be. The thought of going to the south of England where he could live like a lord was, however, something that did appeal to him. It would not matter whether it was under English or Spanish rule, the English would admire him for having stolen Spanish gold or the Spanish would thank him for his help in warning off their ships from landing in Scotland.

Almost without fully realising what he was doing, and in a complete departure from his usual cautious practice, he agreed to the Spaniard's proposal.

"All right, Senor Cortez, I'll give it a go. We'll sail out to warn your ships, but I want your word that you'll land me and my gold somewhere in the south of England."

Cortez nodded, careful not to let his inner feeling of relief and satisfaction show. "Very well, Englishman, you have my solemn word."

He held out his hands, inviting Musgrave to cut his bonds, but the Englishman had not yet been so blinded by the lure of future riches, that he had lost all of his inherent reiver instincts.

"Not on your life, Spaniard. I'm not setting you free until I need you to sail that boat."

It was no more than Cortez expected, but he had achieved most of what he had set out to achieve, and that was enough for now. He smiled and leaned back against his rock to rest until nightfall.

Chapter 31

Rabbie looked back into the dark and the mist. He was bringing up the rear and it was his place to ensure that nobody followed them. "There's still no sign of Musgrave and the Spaniard following us, Jock."

"They'll no be riding wi' us," Big Jock replied. "Yon Spanish man has some business somewhere around here, an' Musgrave thinks there might be something in it for him."

Big Jock knew that this short assessment was comment enough and he felt no need to elaborate further. His two companions both knew that trying to squeeze more information out of the big man would be a waste of time; he had said all that he needed to say, and told them all they needed to know.

From the heated exchanges between Musgrave and the Spaniard, Sandy had gleaned a little about what Cortez was doing in Scotland, but now that they were free of Maxwell's riders, he decided that it posed no danger to Liddesdale and, as such, it was no longer any of his business. He was happy see the back of both of them.

"We're better off without them," he said. "That Spaniard was blethering about Spanish ships landing around here, and I think that he is supposed to be meeting them. I bet that Maxwell is part of whatever is going on, but King Jamie will have something to say about the Spanish landing here in his country, and we wouldn't want to get caught with that Spaniard on our hands."

"Aye, laddie," Big Jock agreed. Sandy was right in thinking that whatever was going on between Maxwell and the Spanish was not their concern, but he also knew that they couldn't afford to ignore it entirely. It might have nothing to do with Liddesdale and the Elliots, but Sandy and

Rabbie had seen and heard more about both the Spaniard and Maxwell than was good for them, so the sooner they put Dumfriesshire behind them the better. They rode on for a while, still making their way northward to avoid getting too close to Dumfries. Then Big Jock suddenly called a halt, looked up at the sky, checked their surroundings and altered their course to the west into the Galloway Hills.

In response to a curions look from Rabbie, he said: "This weather's set tae lift soon. We'll need tae find a spot tae hide 'til dark an' we'll find better cover up an' by."

Again, there was no need for further explanation and his two kinsmen followed without question. They trusted the old reiver's skill at predicting changes in the weather and, as usual, it proved to be accurate. With the dawn, an orange glow lit up the eastern sky behind them bearing the promise of a clear summer's day, and once again, Big Jock resorted to his favourite method of finding concealment. They followed the line of a burn tumbling down from the hills and swollen by the rain. In the improving light, he spotted a north facing rocky overhang topped by thick furze sporting its summer yellow. They rode into the shelter of the overhang where he sat unmoving for several minutes with his senses alert to the slightest sign of danger. He heard nothing and dismounted, but motioned to Sandy and Rabbie to remain in the saddle while he scouted around on foot. They knew that he was carefully checking the lie of the land and were prepared to face any trouble that might suddenly arise. They also knew that Big Jock would want them to take flight at the first sign of danger, but in spite of their trust in the old reiver's judgement, neither was disposed to follow that particular course. Without having to waste time in discussion, each had made up his mind that, if necessary, he would stand and fight, at least until Big Jock was back in the saddle. In the event, however, the necessity for immediate action did not arise, and they relaxed.

The area around the base of the rock was well sheltered from the weather and Big Jock knew that when the sun rose it would be in deep shadow. Farther along, the path rose steeply towards the western hills and veered slightly away from the line of the burn. He could hear the sound of a waterfall and guessed that the path led around it on its way to the high hills. To the north, in front of the great rock, the far bank of the burn rose steeply and disappeared into a thick tangle of bushes. The hideout was deserted now but showed signs of having been used as a refuge by others, albeit not recently. Big Jock was not at all surprised that the place had seen previous use; with shelter, water and grass, it made for a refuge place no reiver would pass up. As such, local riders would know of it, but he was not overly concerned about that, he was confident that they had arrived here undetected, and with armies on the march in the area, nobody, other than those connected with Maxwell or the king, would be venturing far in broad daylight. The old reiver was as satisfied as he could be that they were safe from any but the most diligent searcher, and he motioned to his two companions to join him. They watered the horses, tethered them to some bushes and allowed them to graze.

Big Jock produced some more of his oatcakes and they washed them down with water from the burn. Although satisfied that they were safe from discovery, he left nothing to chance, and he clambered up onto the crag where he lay prone in the shelter of the furze. The spot proved to be a perfect lookout and he could see for miles to the north, east and south. The hills obscured the view to the west but he could still see far enough to give him ample warning of anyone approaching from that direction. He turned his attention back to the north, east and south. At first, the morning mist obscured his view, but the rising sun soon burned it off, and as the visibility improved, several farmsteads came into view, but they were clearly deserted. The men would be riding with their laird, Maxwell, and the families would have gone into hiding, taking everything they could carry with them. The sun cleared more of the mist and two groups of riders came into view far off to the northeast. The nearest band of about thirty riders were riding westwards towards the hills. They would pass close to his hiding place and for a moment, Big Jock feared that he and his two companions would have to move to avoid being discovered, but he soon relaxed. The band were riding hard, clearly intent on reaching their destination as quickly as possible, but on second thoughts, it seemed more likely that they were anxious to get away from someone or something behind them. They appeared to be unarmed and Big Jock guessed that they were Maxwell riders coming from Lochmaben, in which case the castle must have fallen and these men were the remnants of the garrison. If that was true, and Big Jock was sure that it was, they would have little time to waste searching for strangers.

Further to the east, another and, very much larger, group was marching south. Even at a distance, he noticed that, unlike the first group he had seen, this band included foot soldiers who marched with military precision behind a standard-bearer and a mounted officer, obviously a man of some importance to be leading such an army. Large groups of riders rode in front and in the rear at some distance from the main body. Big Jock guessed that they also came from Lochmaben, and were definitely not reivers. Jamie's men, he thought, who must have taken Maxwell's fortress, and were now on their way to join up with the rest of the king's army somewhere to the south. More importantly from Big Jock's point of view, they too, would be too intent on what they were doing to bother him and his two companions. To the south, the sun glinted off the waters of the Solway Firth but the distance was too great to allow him to see riders in that direction. He reasoned that if Lochmaben Castle had fallen, then Caerlaverock must soon suffer the same fate – if it was not already in the king's hands. Jamie was on the move and from the direction the troops from Lochmaben were taking, he was keeping his army well to the south of the Galloway Hills, which, Big Jock guessed, would not suit Maxwell at all. Laying ambushes of the size necessary to trouble the king, would only work if James led his men into the hills where their freedom of movement would be restricted.

At some stage, the king's army would have to cross the River Nidd and probably by the crossing Tam had used, but that was well to the south and Big Jock was not concerned. It would be several hours yet before they became a danger to him and the heidsman's sons.

With all of the activity taking place to the east and south, it occurred to him that the country to the north would soon be free of hostile riders and they would have safe passage through it. As long as the two groups he had seen kept to their current courses, and he could see no reason why they would not, he decided that he and the Elliot brothers could resume their ride north as soon as both bands were out of sight and there was no longer any need to wait for nightfall. They could resume their ride in a few hours, and in the meantime, they could get some badly needed rest. He scrambled down from the lofty lookout, told his two companions what he had seen, and that it would be safe to move in a few hours. While they waited, they should try to get some sleep, so they checked on the horses and settled down in the shelter of the overhang to rest.

Rabbie, in particular, was tired out from the exertions of the last few days, and fell asleep. Sandy too, was tired but he only managed to doze fitfully. Now that the troubles of the last few months were seemingly over, and they were on their way back to Liddesdale, he began to dwell on what had happened in Liddesdale since they left home, and his mind was alive with questions. Had his father received sufficient warning that the king was on the move? Had either Jamie or Bothwell, or both, attacked Liddesdale and, if an attack had come, had the tower house held out, and had his whole family survived? The questions kept on coming but remained unanswered. They ruined any chance of meaningful sleep and he had only just dropped off when Big Jock shook him awake.

After a short sleep, the big man glanced at the shadow cast by the rock as the sun gained height and moved around to the south. He allowed his companions to rest until he estimated that they could wait no longer and it was time for them to move. He shook Sandy and Rabbie awake and was heartened to see that, even before they splashed their faces with water from the burn and slaked their thirst, they checked their weapons, including the loads on the two pistols. Big Jock and Rabbie set about tending to the horses while, as a precaution, Sandy climbed to the top of the crag to check that there were no more bands of riders in evidence. Almost immediately, he came hurriedly scrambling back down.

"Jock, there's a band of about ten riders heading straight for us. They look like Jamie's men and they'll be on us in minutes!"

Chapter 32

Alexander began to thread his cautious way between Johnstone lands to the south and Douglas territory to the north. Like Big Jock, he sensed that the weather would clear, but not yet, and when it did, for him it would be something of a mixed blessing. Improved visibility would make Big Jock, Malcolm and Robert, easier to locate, but it would leave him exposed to the inevitable prying eyes. As an Elliot heidsman, being seen meant being recognised, which added considerably to the risks he was already taking. He might not be currently feuding with any of the leading local reivers, the Douglas, Graham, Irvine or Johnstone families, but with the war raging between Maxwell and the king, Border hospitality would be, albeit temporarily, set aside. On the contrary, there were many who would see a profit in taking and holding him for ransom. Nevertheless, there could be no turning back.

A voice from inside kept telling him that Malcolm and Robert were still alive and needed his help. He was practical enough to accept that this inner voice might well represent nothing more than a desperate search for hope, but it persisted, so he listened, considered, but rode on. So urgent was his need to find his sons that it drove him to take even greater risks. At this season, even while the mist and rain continued, Border nights were growing short and days long, and he was loath to waste all of those hours of daylight in hiding when they could be better spent searching for his sons. He was in the saddle until long after the watery sun rose, and again well before it set, seeking cover and rest only in the middle of the day. A sense of irony brought a rare smile to his weathered face. Such actions gave the lie to almost everything he had tried to teach his sons about the art of reiving. But if Big Jock and his sons were alive, and somewhere in Dumfriesshire, they would follow similar tactics in their efforts to get home to Liddesdale. Taking such risks, however, did have one advantage: it helped him to make better progress. Riding in daylight meant that it was not necessary for him to set such an exaggerated zigzag course in order to cover as much ground as possible, and soon he was nearing his first goal, Lochmaben Castle.

According to Big Jock, his sons' captors had taken them to the castle and he needed to check and see if they were still there. The only way he could think of doing this was to ride boldly up to the castle and demand to know what had happened to his sons. It was a risk, but it was unlikely that Maxwell would be there in person – he would still be busy luring King Jamie off to the west – and he thought that the threat of Elliot retribution would be enough to make whoever he had left to defend the castle to cooperate fully with him.

The further west he rode, the more the weather improved, and with it the visibility, which meant a greater need for caution. As a result, he was still some way from the fortress when he was disturbed to hear the unmistakable thunder of artillery. Although he knew that Jamie would attack the castle at some stage, he had expected the king to bypass it in his haste to arrest Maxwell and return to capture it later, so the sound of artillery came as an unpleasant shock. If his sons were still prisoners in the castle, they would be in as much danger from the guns as their captors. He was still trying to think of what to do next when the gunfire abruptly ceased. He listened carefully but heard nothing more. He waited, but all was still silent, so he took yet another chance and rode closer to see what was happening, and he came in sight of the castle just as the siege ended. He did as Big Jock had done and hid in the trees, now in full leaf, on the far side of the loch to watch. The garrison came filing out, and he was surprised that Maxwell's men had given up so soon. Then he realised why the defenders had little option but to surrender. The two great siege-pieces he had heard were in position in front of the fortress and, while Alexander was no expert on artillery, these guns were bigger than any he had previously seen. He guessed that this must be the heavy siege artillery he had heard about but never seen, and Lochmaben Castle certainly showed every sign of their having been put to effective use. Alexander's heart sank when he thought about how his own tower house would fare against such a bombardment should Bothwell ever get his hands on such powerful weapons.

He shook off that disturbing thought and turned his mind back to the present. A large body of the king's troops herded the men from the garrison into a group in front of the castle, and to his immense relief, there was no sign of his sons being with them. The nagging inner voice changed its tune and began whispering to him that his sons were dead, but again he refused to listen. Malcolm and Robert were alive and with Big Jock, and he would eventually find them.

He recognised the man who made what passed for a formal surrender, David Maxwell, the laird's brother. The prisoners were disarmed and made to sit with their hands on their heads, and he was surprised to see that the king's soldiers were treating them with a measure of leniency unusual in The Borders. Alexander could only surmise that the king had promised them their lives in return for an early surrender, and as if to prove the point, an obviously high-ranking officer came to address the prisoners. Alexander did not recognise him but he was sure it was not Jamie in person. He was too far away to hear what the officer said, but from his stance and tone, Alexander guessed that he was demanding to know where Maxwell was hiding.

Whoever he was, and what he was saying was, however, of little interest to Alexander who was more concerned about keeping his presence hidden from the king's army and evading capture as he rode away from Lochmaben. Having taken the castle, he hoped that the victors would relax and not bother to post too many sentries or send out scouts, but whoever the high-ranking officer was, he knew his business, and set a proper watch all around the castle. Alexander was compelled to remain in hiding for the night and he found a suitable hiding place in a small patch of bog by the side of the loch. It was cold, wet and uncomfortable, but that was nothing to an experienced reiver. Confident that he was safe from discovery, he tethered his horse and allowed him to graze, knowing that the well-trained animal would remain quiet. As a precaution, he kept his lance and his sword by his side as he rested.

All through the night, he could hear riders coming and going to and from the castle; messengers he thought, passing between the man who had taken the castle and the king. Early next morning, the scouts returned to the castle and he was able to leave his boggy hiding place. The king's men settled down to breakfast and the scent of roasting meat came to him carried on the breeze, and tempting as it was, he managed to ignore it. Like Big Jock, he never travelled far without a good supply of dried meat and oatcakes, and satisfied himself with that. When the troops had eaten, the prisoners were fed on what he thought would be scraps. It was surprising to find that any effort at all was made to feed them, but it confirmed his suspicion that they had been offered some form of safe conduct in return for their early surrender. What would happen to them now, he neither knew nor cared. His only concern was to get away from here and resume his search. He was at a loss to know how to do so, but whatever he did, he had to do it quickly.

He retrieved his horse, mounted, and prepared to do something he knew to be foolish, but there was nothing for it except to make a break out of hiding and hope to get away unscathed. He waited anxiously for an opportune moment to affect his escape, but was interrupted when a rider galloped up from the south and handed the king's senior officer a message. The officer called for attention and the king's army immediately became alert. Alexander's heart sank; he thought his opportunity had passed.

The officer read the message and spoke urgently to a small group of men Alexander took to be his senior soldiers. They began shouting orders and at first, he thought that the king's men were preparing to leave Lochmaben and go to join the rest of Jamie's army somewhere to the south or west. He could not be sure which, and he decided to wait until they left. When they did, he would be able to resume his search for his sons unhindered.

That, however, was not to be. There was a discernible change in attitude towards the prisoners by the king's men gathered outside the castle. What happened next confirmed Alexander Elliot's long-held loathing for kings and their ways.

As he watched, soldiers dragged several heavy beams out of the castle and began erecting what Alexander immediately recognised as a scaffold. The prisoners also recognised what was happening and there were shouts of alarm. Once the hastily erected scaffold was constructed, soldiers grabbed David Maxwell, tied his hands behind his back and stood him in front of the king's general who read out something from the message he had received from James. Maxwell's brother immediately flew into a rage and began shouting back at his captor. Although in hiding on the far side of the loch, Alexander was able to pick up the words 'safe conduct' and 'Stewart'. From what he heard, he guessed that the king's man was Sir William Stewart, and that Stewart was the one who had afforded Maxwell safe conduct, only to have it repudiated by James.

Alexander watched in angry frustration as King James's men hanged David Maxwell without even the pretence of a trial. It brought back memories of when, as a small boy, he watched from hiding with his father as James's father, James V, hanged Johnnie Armstrong while he, too, was supposedly under a promise of safe conduct. He had no reason to feel any sympathy for David Maxwell, but his loathing for the authorities, and especially for kings, returned. Only his determination to protect his sons from suffering a similar fate prevented him from joining in the protests. Two more of the prisoners were picked out at random, had their hands tied behind their backs and were manhandled over to where the lifeless body of their leader still hung limply from the scaffold. Soldiers cut David Maxwell down and attached two fresh ropes to the beam.

Fearing that the king's men were about to hang them all, the remaining prisoners rebelled. As a man, they made a break for where a group of horses were tethered. Several died in the attempt but some actually managed to reach the horses. They mounted and galloped off in a body leaving yet more corpses behind them.

With everyone else's attention firmly fixed on the fracas, Alexander grasped the opportunity to mount and ride for his life. The noise created by the escaping prisoners deadened the sound of his hoofbeats and in the confusion, no one noticed the lone rider galloping out of the woods on the far shore of the loch.

Clear of the castle, and satisfied that his flight had gone unnoticed, he stopped to allow his horse a breather. He wondered if Big Jock, wherever he was, had heard that the castle was under siege. If he had, Alexander was confident that the big man would have delayed before riding around Lochmaben, and that meant he was probably still somewhere south and west of here. He rode on towards the Galloway Hills, where he still hoped to find Big Jock, Malcolm and Robert.

On reflection, he decided that the siege and fall of Lochmaben had allowed him a breathing space. He was confident that, this far from Liddesdale, he would not be so well known, and anyone coming across a lone, armed rider would take him for one of the king's messengers and give him a wide berth. Nevertheless, he had to make sure, and he rode up a steep rise topped by some trees intending to stop and survey the surrounding countryside. He was almost at the crest when a rider dashed out of the trees and galloped off down the far side of the hill. Alexander noticed that he was unarmed, and took him to be one of the escapees from Lochmaben acting as a lookout. It came as no surprise that they would have someone riding behind to see if the king's men were following them; it was standard reiver practice. Alexander watched, and at the bottom of the hill, the rider joined a group of about thirty other unarmed riders that he recognised as the survivors from Lochmaben. He guessed that the lone rider had assumed that he was a scout sent out by Sir William Stewart to find them, and the whole band galloped off as soon as the man reported having seen him. He realised that there might well be some real royal scouts in the area trying to locate and recapture the prisoners so he rode into the trees to check behind, but saw nothing. Still, he felt that it might be dangerous to move just yet. In his hurry to find his sons, he had taken too many chances already. Then, as he watched the countryside behind, a large column of riders appeared heading south. Sir William Stewart had clearly received orders to leave Lochmaben. The king's men continued south and he was able to relax.

Stewart had decided not to waste time recapturing the Lochmaben survivors or, because he was the one who had promised them their lives, he was allowing the survivers to escape.

Alexander was relieved to see the back of them but the incident prompted him to stop and take stock. He knew that he had been extremely fortunate to get this far without arousing suspicion, and before he went any further, he had better review his options.

If Big Jock and his sons had ridden past to the north of Lochmaben while he was held up by the siege and its aftermath, then he had missed them anyway. On the other hand, if they hadn't already started out for home, they wouldn't be able to do so while both the king's army and Maxwell, who must still have a sizeable force of riders to call on, were in the area. The canny old reiver would not move until he was sure that they were not in danger from either side. So, where would Big Jock hide out while he waited? Alexander was sure that he could only head west into the Galloway Hills. The escapees from the siege were obviously heading there and he decided that he might as well follow. Even though they were not armed, there were enough of them to cause trouble for Big Jock and his sons, and if they did, he wanted to be on hand to help.

Alexander was aware that he was still relying on speculation. Once more, his common sense returned to mock him. It tried to persuade him that he was indulging in a fantasy, but he was no more prepared to listen now than he had been when he first set out from Liddesdale.

In spite of his stubborn determination, the nagging inner voice managed to score one victory: he conceded that from now on he must stop taking unnecessary risks. The chances were that the countryside was deserted but, although he had not seen any, and in spite of the king's men he had seen marching south, there could still be bands of James's soldiers searching for stragglers from Lochmaben. With the view over the immediate countryside, the trees at the top of the rise made for an obvious spot for a lookout; too obvious, he thought, as proved by the escaped prisoner who had hidden there. He decided to give up following the Lochmaben survivors and, instead, hide and rest until dark. For safety's sake, he moved further into where the woods and undergrowth were densest and found an ideal hiding place.

The day passed without incident but Alexander had too much on his mind to be able to sleep, and time dragged. With the clearer weather, nightfall arrived perceptibly later, but at the first hint of twilight, he could wait no longer. He mounted and rode westwards through the night towards the Galloway Hills. A new moon helped him make good progress and by daylight, he had entered the foothills. He stopped to rest his horse and work out exactly where he was. He had never previously ridden so far into Dumfriesshire and knew little of the geography of the area, but he knew enough to be aware that the Galloway Hills covered a large area and stretched as far as the sea. How far that was, he did not know, and for the first time since he made the decision to ride into these hills he was forced to accept the impossibility of a single rider searching every inch of them. He realised that he had been blindly overoptimistic and came close to cursing himself for a fool. Knowing Big Jock as he did, he was confident that the old reiver, assuming that he was still alive and somewhere in these hills, would be aware of the escapees from Lochmaben and would have avoided them. Big Jock would not want to ride too far west into Maxwell's lair and the presence of those men from Lochmaben would prompt him not to hide until he was certain that they were well out of the way. All Alexander had to do was to find that hiding place.

He searched around until the sun told him that it was past midday, but there was no sign of Big Jock or his sons. The enormity of the task he had undertaken without sufficient thought, again came back to haunt him, and he even considered giving up and going home.

To take his mind off his troubles, he continued to scout around the foothills and found a well-used path leading westwards into the hills. There was evidence of a group of riders having recently come this way and he realised that he had inadvertently discovered the route taken by the survivors from Lochmaben. They would be going to join up with Maxwell and would clearly know where to find the laird. He would do well to avoid falling foul of Maxwell but the presence of the escapees gave him at least a sliver of hope. Big Jock, assuming that he actually was in the area, would surely be aware of them too. He would be watching this path in case any more riders appeared, and Alexander decided that he could do worse than follow it himself. It was not much, but at least it provided him with somewhere to begin his search. Setting his doubts aside, he followed the route into the hills. He forced himself to travel warily, and his caution was soon justified when he heard a group of riders coming up behind him. They were riding hard, and making no effort to disguise their presence, so he had sufficient warning to move off the path and hide behind a clump of tall bushes. It provided scant cover and he had to dismount in order to make sure he was well out of sight. He need not have worried; the dozen or so riders that swept past were too intent on reaching their objective to worry about looking for strangers.

These were clearly the king's men and he knew that it would be too risky to follow them. He waited to make sure they were not the advance guard for a larger group and was about to retrace his steps and find another route into the hills, when a gunshot rang out.

The shot came from up ahead and was closely followed by a second. Even his limited knowledge of guns told him that these were pistol shots, but there was no indication of who might have fired them, or who their targets were.The Maxwell riders from Lochmaben were not armed, so it could not be them. The king's soldiers had passed by too fast for him to notice whether they carried pistols. All he knew for sure was that Malcolm and Robert had their pistols with them when they left home.

He threw caution to the winds and spurred his horse towards the sound. He simply had to find out who had fired those particular shots, and why.

Chapter 33

Sandy's report of the fast-approaching riders came as a blow to Big Jock. He realised that he had miscalculated badly, and the consequences were likely to be serious. The old reiver's assessment that they would not be bothered by any of the riders he had seen earlier had proved to be very wrong, and his mistake had landed not only himself, but also his hiedsman's two sons, in mortal danger.

What had happened was plain to see. A party of horsemen had been detached from the king's army he had seen marching south, probably to search the eastern edge of the Galloway Hills for any Maxwell riders the laird might have placed there as scouts. They were riding directly towards where he and the hiedsman's sons were hiding, and were certain to discover them. For a reiver of Big Jock's experience, it was the most basic of errors, and what had seemed like a safe haven had suddenly turned into a trap. His basic mistake had led them into this predicament, and it was up to him to find a way out. He had to find a solution, and find it quickly.

The approaching riders had spread out in order to search as much ground as possible, but were not so widely dispersed that they could not bunch up again at short notice. While these men may not be reivers, some of them would have clashed with reivers before and be familiar with reiver tactics. It was unlikely that they would know about this hidden reiver's retreat, but some of them would definitely follow the burn, and they would use the crag as a lookout just as Big Jock himself had. Life was about to become very dangerous for him and his two kinsmen. But there was no time to waste worrying about what was past, and he quickly reviewed his options. They were worryingly few.

If they stayed where they were, the oncoming riders were sure to spot them and assume that they were part of Maxwell's band, and there would be no point in arguing that they were not. The king's men would be in no mood to listen. Following their victories at Langholm and Lochmaben, their blood would be up and they would consider any unknown rider they encountered to be an enemy. They would attack with deadly intent without wasting time asking questions. Sandy had estimated that there were about ten of the king's riders coming, but Big Jock had faced bigger odds before. He considered making a stand here and trying to fight them off, but that would not solve the problem. As soon as the fight began, the leader of the king's men would send a rider back to inform the main party that they had located some of Maxwell's men, and reinforcements would soon be arriving in overwhelming numbers. The obvious solution was to run, but where to?

Big Jock briefly considered hiding in the furze on top of the crag but they could easily find themselves trapped up there, which would simply make a bad situation worse. Worse still, horses could not possibly climb that rock, and as there was not time to look for a suitable hiding place, they would have to leave them for the king's men to find. The soldiers would immediately begin a search for the riders, and the first place they would look was the top of the crag.

The obvious way out of this trap suitable for horses was the way they had entered, but the approaching riders were coming that way and the Elliots would ride right into them. Riding north up the steep bank that led up from the burn would leave them fully exposed, which would lead to certain capture. What lay ahead on the path that led west up and around the gorge was an unknown quantity, and riding in that direction meant that they would have the king's riders behind them and Maxwell's in front. They were in danger of getting caught between the two warring factions, and neither side would extend much of a welcome to strangers. Being Liddesdale Elliots would count for nothing with either the king or Maxwell; the first would arrest and hang them as reivers; the second would have some awkward questions for Sandy and Rabbie about their escape from Tam and his men, and Maxwell would make certain that they did not escape again.

Big Jock thought about asking his companions for their opinions. They were showing signs of having grown into competent reivers, but apart from the fact that there was no time for discussion, he blamed himself alone for getting them into this danger and it was up to him alone to get them out of it.

The path up and around the gorge did not look well travelled, but it was their only hope. They had to ride, and ride now, before the king's men came upon this reiver hideout and found them. He motioned urgently to Sandy and Rabbie to ride up the path while he followed close behind. The path was narrow and steep, too steep to allow for a full gallop, and they had to ride frustratingly slowly up in single file. Rabbie was first to reach the top and he dashed for the cover of the tall bushes he spotted further along the path. Sandy had just reached the top, but Big Jock had waited to make sure that they were safe before following. He was little more than half way up when there was a shout from behind. The leader of the king's men had sent a rider to follow the line of the burn and check out the area around the bottom of the crag. The man shouted the warning to his companions then aimed a pistol shot at Big Jock's retreating form. Sandy heard the shot and turned to see what had happened. He didn't hesitate. He drew his own pistol and shot the king's man out of the saddle. Big Jock reached the top and reined in his horse.

At the sound of the shots, Rabbie rode back to see what was happening. A second rider came galloping after the first. He reached the bottom of the path and Rabbie shot him while Sandy was carrying out the complicated business of reloading. Big Jock looked approvingly at the two brothers.

Their swift reaction to the crisis had not only reduced the odds, but had also bought them a little time.

"That'll hold them up for a wee while. They'll no be sure how many o' us are here. But we have tae ride."

They galloped along the unfamiliar path, which followed a narrow ledge with the dark and gloomy gorge on one side, and the hillside rising steeply up on the other, and was dotted with moss-covered rocks interspersed with sparse vegetation. There was nowhere to hide and so they kept on. Eventually, the path began to descend and Big Jock called a halt. He listened for sounds of the pursuit he knew must soon be nearing them, and picked up the sound of a raised voice issuing orders, but it was a little way off. After Sandy and Rabbie's swift action, he was sure that the king's riders would have to proceed with caution. They would not know how many well-armed men they were trying to hunt down. They would have sent a rider back for reinforcements, but whether they would wait for help to arrive was open to question. Big Jock thought not, but they had a short breathing space.

"We hef tae gang on a wee way."

Big Jock sounded unusually out of breath, and Sandy could not help but notice. He looked at the big man, but he seemed to have recovered. He saw no cause for concern, and, anyway, he had something more important on his mind.

"We can't go too far west, Jock, or we might run into Maxwell, but we can't turn back either, and God knows what's happening in the south. The Spanish soldiers that foreigner was telling Musgrave about, might have landed and be fighting Jamie."

Rabbie thought that he might have found a solution to their dilemma. "Like Jock said, the ones behind are worried that there might be a lot more of us, or they might think we're Maxwell riders leading them into an ambush. They'll have to follow us but they'll wait for more of Jamie's men before they come too close to us."

Sandy looked at Big Jock. "Rabbie could be right, Jock. If he is, we might be able to ride north while they're deciding what to do."

The old reiver thought about this for a minute. Rabbie could indeed be right, and it certainly bore thinking about. What he and Sandy proposed was fraught with danger, but then so was everything else he could think of. Big Jock, however, hesitated. He was trying to think of several things at once, and he knew that one more mistake would mean certain death for all three of them. Again, he felt much as he had when helplessly watching from the gorse as Maxwell's riders took Sandy and Rabbie as prisoners, but this time the crisis was of his making, and not due to a rash action by Rabbie. He was the one who had made a basic mistake and put Alexander Elliot's sons in danger. It was not like Big Jock to dwell on such thoughts, but to add to the problem of escaping from the king's forces, he was trying to deal with another, and potentially far more dangerous, complication.

He motioned to the others to watch the path ahead. As soon as their backs were turned, he reached under his jack and felt behind his back. When he withdrew it, his hand was wet with blood. The man who had fired a pistol at him as they made their dash up the path, had aimed well. The old reiver quickly wiped off the blood on his horse's mane. Sandy and Rabbie must not learn that he had been badly wounded.

The old reiver's obvious hesitation came as a surprise to Sandy. "If we ride north, we won't be any worse off than we are now, Jock," he urged. "At least we'll be heading home, but whatever we do, we don't have a lot of time."

He waited, but there was nothing forthcoming from Big Jock. Sandy looked at his brother and shrugged; the old reiver's reaction was totally out of character, but someone had to make a decision and make it now. He led them further along the path, which now led gradually downwards to where the ground levelled out and they could cross the burn. They crossed and found another old reiver's path leading north and followed it, with Sandy leading and Rabbie in his usual position guarding the rear. Between them, Big Jock rode in silence. For him to be silent was nothing new, but Rabbie was becoming concerned about the old reiver's demeanour. Big Jock seemed to be lost in his own thoughts, and Sandy noticed that he had begun to sweat. He sensed that something was seriously wrong, but he knew that if he asked what it was, the old reiver would only shrug it off, and it would be a waste of time trying to argue with him.

Here, at the edge of the Galloway Hills, the undulating countryside rose and fell with several stands of timber and clumps of gorse, interspersed by stretches of good grazing land. Summer shielings dotted the hillsides which, in peaceful times, would have housed people tending their stock, but in this turbulent summer, the shielings were deserted and the grassy hillsides were devoid of animals. Sandy briefly considered hiding in one of the huts as they had done back near the Debatable Land, but these were the first places any competent searchers would look. A little farther on, they reached the bottom of a hill with a flat top dotted with furze, and they followed the path to the top. It afforded a good view of the land ahead and Sandy called a halt. He dismounted and went cautiously forward to check the path ahead. On either side, the hillsides were steep, covered with dense growth, and not suitable for horses. The only way off the hill, apart from the way they had come up, was to follow the path which carried on down on the northern side. At the bottom of the hill, another clearly defined path leading east and west intersected the one they were following.

The horses needed a breather and Sandy decided that they could risk stopping for a short while. They dismounted, and ate some oatcakes. Sandy cast a worried look at Big Jock, who sat apart, ate nothing, and seemed lost in thought. He thought about approaching the big man in an attempt to discover the reason for his strange behaviour, but he feared that it would be a waste of time. In any case, they could not wait here any longer.

He went to recheck the path ahead before mounting, and a glance down the path told him that stopping for a rest had been a mistake.

Another group of about a dozen of the king's men had circled around to cut them off. They appeared to be waiting at the bottom of the hill, but as he watched, two riders left the group and were riding cautiously up the path to see what lay ahead. Sandy realised that they had not yet spotted him and his companions. If they had, the whole group would be charging up to either capture them, or drive them back into the hands of their friends, who must now be somewhere close behind them.

"There's another bunch of Jamie's riders waiting at the bottom of the hill," he said urgently. "They're coming this way, but they're sending two up first to check the path."

Rabbie quickly grasped the situation. "We can't go back, so we'll have to fight our way through. We'll have to kill those two when they get here and then try to take the rest by surprise."

He drew his pistol, but Sandy shook his head. "We'll do this as quietly as we can. We don't want to let them know we're here until we have to. After that, our only chance is to do what you said, Rabbie. We'll charge down through them and take the path to the east; if they think we're Maxwells, they won't expect us to go that way. But we'll get these two first."

He outlined how he intended to trap the two oncoming riders, and Rabbie nodded in assent.

Big Jock said nothing. He felt the blood running down his back from where the bullet had struck. So far, his jack had hidden the growing red stain, but soon it would show. He was sweating heavily and could feel himself growing weaker. He feared that he would soon faint from loss of blood and he knew that he could not stay in the saddle for much longer. Nevertheless, he was determined to hold on for as long as he possibly could. He knew that it would not be long before Sandy and Rabbie realised that something was seriously wrong with him, but while he still had some strength left, he was determined to do what he could to help them. It was important that they did not find out yet how badly wounded he was, or they would try to make allowances and care for him. That would mean that none of them survived.

Sandy, however, was becoming increasingly worried about him. He looked keenly at the old reiver while he explained what he had in mind. "Are you all right with that, Jock?"

"Aye Laddie," Big Jock replied, and raised his lance to show that he was ready.

To Sandy's relief, the thought of action seemed to shake the big man out of his lethargy. He motioned to Rabbie and Big Jock to move aside, and out of sight. They complied, and he rode back down the way they had come up the hill until he judged that he would be just out of sight when the two king's scouts reached the top. Then he turned around to face uphill. The king's riders rode onto the hilltop, more intent on checking the path ahead than noting their immediate surroundings. Sandy waited until they reached roughly the middle of the hilltop, then rode up into the open and feigned surprise and alarm at finding them there. His sudden appearance took the two riders by surprise but before they could raise the alarm, Rabbie and Big Jock rode up and brought them down with lances. They grabbed the two riderless horses to prevent them going back down the hill.

Using the same ruse recently employed by Big Jock and Rabbie, Sandy sent the riderless horses careering down the path and led the charge down after them with Rabbie close behind.

"Come on, and keep as far as you can to the right," he yelled.

The momentum generated by galloping down the hill with the two uncontrolled horses, carried them right into the startled group of king's riders and threw them off balance. Sandy fired his pistol into the middle of the group and galloped onto the path to the right. He heard another pistol shot, glanced around and saw Rabbie close behind. There was no sign of Big Jock.

He reined in and shouted to his brother, "Where's Jock?"

Before Rabbie could answer, a familiar voice carried above the shouts of the king's riders. On the charge down the hill, Big Jock realised that his hiedsman's sons had little chance of getting away unless he did something to hold the king's men up. He knew that he had not long to live, and for Big Jock Elliot, there was only one possible way to die. He knew what he had to do. At the bottom of the hill instead of taking the right-hand fork, he charged directly into the king's riders.

"Keep ridin'," he yelled. "I'll hold the bastards up."

Instead of heeding Big Jock's urgent shout, the brothers turned as one to help. The old reiver had already killed one man with his lance and knocked another off his horse with the hilt of his sword, but in spite of their losses, they were too many. The fight was soon over and Big Jock Elliot died with a sword thrust into his throat.

Sandy suddenly realised why the old reiver had acted as he had. He grabbed his brother's rein and urged him to ride. "He was as good as dead from a pistol shot before we charged down the hill."

As he said it, he realised that they had already delayed for too long. The leader of the king's riders was an experienced campaigner, and even before Big Jock died, he saw what was happening. While Sandy was pulling his brother away, he drew a pistol, rode up and aimed directly at Rabbie.

At point blank range, he could not possibly miss.

Chapter 34

Maxwell was becoming increasingly worried. His carefully laid plans continued to go awry. Riders from Caerlaverock and Lochmaben had reached him with news that both strongholds had fallen. He had not expected King James to attack Caerlaverock while Lochmaben was still under siege, and he was confident that Lochmaben would hold out at least until the Spanish invasion force arrived. But it was the manner in which his strongest castle fell that concerned him most. His brother, David, would not have accepted Sir William Stewart's offer of safe conduct had it not been for the unexpected arrival of English artillery, and that, coupled with the fact that James had repudiated Stewart's promise of safe conduct, meant that the king was in no mood to parley.

As events unfolded, it was becoming increasingly clear that harassing James in the Galloway Hills was going to prove more difficult than he originally thought. From local sympathisers, he learned that James had crossed the River Nith with a large force and was riding west along the coast. Another large force had left Lochmaben and was riding south, presumably to join up with the king, and if they turned west into the hills, then what? The more Maxwell thought about it, the more he worried that James might soon have him trapped between two forces. It was, after all, just what he would have done himself. The king, with an entire army at his disposal, could afford to split his forces while he, Maxwell, even with the advantage of knowing the ground, did not have sufficient men to fight off simultaneous attacks from two sides. James, he thought, must have an experienced reiver among his advisers and he could easily guess who that adviser was. Johnstone, the current March Warden. The thought of his archenemy being involved caused him to throw a rare fit of temper, but he eventually had to accept that, for the moment, there was not a thing he could do about it – except store it up for the future.

He continued to pin his hopes on the Spanish invasion, but that, too, was becoming ever more problematic. If his assumption regarding James's intentions was correct, he would have to move further west into the hills to avoid being caught in a trap, but being driven too far to the west meant that he could find himself cut off from Kirkcudbright, the proposed Spanish landing site. Unless the Spaniards arrived very soon, there was a danger that the king would have met and defeated them before he could ride to His Majesty's assistance, and that would put an end to his dreams of being reinstated as March Warden. Not to mention getting his hands on that Spanish gold!

In his anxiety, he began to regret his decision to send Cortez to Caerlaverock with the other captives. If he still had the Spaniard with him, he could hand him over to James and say that he had captured him trying to escape. It would not be much, but it would be something. He believed that his man, Tam, was smart enough not to risk getting caught in a siege at Caerlaverock and would now be riding west to join him. As an experienced reiver, Tam would not want to waste time guarding prisoners and would have already disposed of Musgrave and the two Elliots, but he had given the reiver instructions to keep Cortez alive. He comforted himself with the thought that Tam would bring the Spaniard into the hills with him and, with his usual optimism, he continued to pin his hopes on the Spanish landing on time.

Had Maxwell known that Tam was dead, while Cortez was still very much alive and planning to warn off the Spanish invasion fleet, his confidence would have suffered a severe knock.

***

In Carlisle Castle, Lord Scrope studied the latest urgent communique from Sir Francis Walsingham. It told him that the Spanish armada was entering the Western Approaches and the battle was about to begin. As he read on, Scrope's anxiety increased. He feared that the message would contain an order for him to send all of his available forces south to combat the invaders, but much to his relief, that was not the case. On the contrary, Walsingham ordered him to keep his forces intact at Carlisle.

The spymaster had learned that a Spanish galleon loaded with troops had foundered on the rocky west coast of Ireland. At first, Walsingham thought that the wrecked ship might be part of the armada and had wandered off course, but he soon dismissed that possibility. It was extremely unlikely that a single Spanish ship would have strayed so far from what appeared to be a well-disciplined formation. Instead, Walsingham feared that a second Spanish invasion force had sailed before the main fleet, and they would certainly not have entrusted such a venture to just one ship. There must be others, and if they had weathered the storm that caught the first ship, they were still at sea. The spymaster concluded that the Spanish planned to mount a second invasion in northwest England, and it would be the local March Warden's responsibility to repel it.

For Scrope, everything suddenly fell into place. The Spanish were not going to invade the English West March, but the Scottish one. And they were going to do it with Maxwell's help. He immediately dispatched a messenger to Walsingham outlining his fears and suggesting that Queen Elizabeth contact King James to inform him of what they suspected. He guessed that Walsingham's suspicious mind would conclude that James was in league with Philip of Spain, so he stressed that no king could allow an invasion of his country by foreign troops. He added that, as James was already in the field against Maxwell, he was ideally placed to deal with a Spanish landing.

Scrope was convinced that, while Walsingham was wrong about the location, he was right about the invasion, and as such, it rendered any news that came from Musgrave, if he was still alive, of no value whatsoever.

It meant that he had no further need for his spy. If Musgrave showed his face in the English West March again, he would find himself back in the dungeons at Carlisle Castle.

Chapter 35

Dusk was falling, and the balmy summer evening would very soon become a warm summer night. To begin with, the darkness would be relieved only by the light of the stars, but it would not be long before a full moon rose, and for several hours the night would be almost as bright as day. Musgrave and Cortez prepared to mount and leave their hiding place by the burn. The horses had rested, fed, and watered, but not the men, who had only peaty water from the burn to satisfy them. Not that Musgrave was particularly concerned; as a reiver, he had gone hungry before. He wondered how Cortez would cope, but he gave it no more than a passing thought. By now, he had come to realise that this Spaniard was much more than the soft diplomat he pretended to be, and the Englishman had a feeling that this was not the first time his captive had gone for days without food. Cortez would no doubt complain, but Musgrave thought that he would cope well enough.

With the king's army and Maxwell's riders both somewhere in the area, it was essential that they cover as much ground as possible before the moon rose. The main bodies of the warring factions would be camped for the night, but Musgrave knew that they would have to be wary of scouts sent out by both sides. A pair of riders found abroad here at night would be marked down as enemies.

"That river we crossed," Cortez asked. "Where does it enter the sea?"

The Englishman gave the Spaniard a hard look. "I don't know," he replied. "Somewhere to the south of here I suppose, but what has that got to do with finding a boat?"

The Spaniard thought that his meaning should be clear enough, but apparently not to this stupid Englishman. "There will be fishermen's boats moored in the estuary and it should be a simple enough task to steal one. These people do their fishing out at sea and they will have to have boats they can rely on. That is the kind of vessel we need: a boat capable of reaching His Majesty's ships before they land. I would have thought that was obvious, even to an Englishman."

Musgrave ignored the jibe, and when he failed to comment, Cortez added a pointed rider. "And one capable of carrying your gold."

Throughout the long, hot, day, Cortez had managed to get several hours sleep while Musgrave had been obliged to maintain a fitful watch. The Spaniard felt fully refreshed and was thinking clearly, but the Englishman had not slept for two nights, and his failure to understand why his captive had asked about the river meant that fatigue was beginning to affect his thinking. Being unsure of exactly where the king's army was, Musgrave originally thought that he could avoid them by riding north, then heading west before eventually turning south for the sea, but recent events had caused him to change his mind and he now considered riding south to be a much safer option. Maxwell would already be somewhere to the west, and if King James was following him with a large force, he would go north to the ford in order to get his army across the River Nith. He didn't like Cortez forcing him to question his original plan, but he couldn't disguise the fact that the Spaniard had made some valid points.

His tiredness, however, made him stubborn and he was determined not let Cortez outmanoeuvre him. "There are plenty of boats further west," he snapped. "And we won't have to sail so far to reach your ships."

"I'm sure that there are plenty of boats further west," Cortez replied calmly. "But we will have to avoid two armies to reach them. For myself, I would much prefer to be out at sea as soon as possible. I would imagine that neither King James nor the traitor Maxwell have any seaborne forces, and I will feel much more secure out there. You can take your chances on land if you wish, but I am going to find a boat as soon as I possibly can. If you kill me in the process, you will have to give up all hope of getting any of the gold I promised you from the fortune the ships will undoubtedly be carrying. Suit yourself, Englishman."

Mention of 'a fortune' was enough to jolt Musgrave fully awake. His reiver's mind could not find an argument against that, and in spite of being angry with himself for letting the Spaniard get the better of the exchange, he had no option but to reluctantly lead off back towards the River Nith.

Cortez looked up at the stars; as an experienced seaman, he knew that Musgrave was taking them towards the river and he smiled to himself. The Englishman had accepted the logic of what he said about the boats and he found it difficult to resist making further sarcastic comments, but he knew that it would do nothing to help the situation. His overriding priority was to warn King Philip's ships that they were sailing into a trap, but he could do little while he was still a prisoner, except try to persuade Musgrave to follow his line of thinking until they found a suitable boat. At that point, his captor would be compelled to release him.

When they finally got out to sea, he would dearly love to ditch this arrogant Englishman, but he had given his word, and to Don Juan Cortez that was sacrosanct.

After they had ridden a little further in silence, Cortez stopped and turned to Musgrave. "Do you think that King James will have crossed the river yet?"

Musgrave was becoming frustrated with the Spaniard. Cortez seemed to have a better grasp of the situation than he did. He could not see how it mattered whether James had crossed the river or not, but if Cortez had seen fit to bring the subject up, he must have a reason.

"Why?" he asked.

"Because we have to make sure that we are on the right side."

"What difference does it make which side we're on?"

"It makes a great deal of difference," Cortez replied.

All that achieved was to increase the Englishman's sense of frustration. Although he had the Spaniard's hands securely tied and was leading his horse, Musgrave feared that he was close to losing control of the situation. He was sorely tempted to ignore his prisoner's assertion that the king, having already crossed the river, would somehow affect his plans, but galling as it was, he knew that he could not afford to dismiss anything Cortez said. Still, he wanted to avoid putting himself in the undignified position of having to ask Cortez a question he felt he should already know the answer to, so he tried to work it out for himself; but his tired mind failed to respond.

He reined in his horse and hauled on the rope attached to Cortez's mount. He dragged his captive to his side, drew his dagger and held the point to the Spaniard's throat. "I know what you're up to, you bastard. You're trying to lead me into a trap. You only want to know which side of the river the king is on so that you can hand me over to him."

Cortez felt his own temper rising; being threatened with a dagger was an insult he would not normally tolerate, but this was a time for treading carefully. The Englishman, he guessed, was nearing breaking point and he feared that he might have been too eager to tease him, so he quelled his anger, kept his voice calm, and looked Musgrave squarely in the eye. "Why would I want to lead you into a trap that I was bound to get caught in myself? Surely you can see that I do not want to be captured by King James any more than you do."

"Why else would you want to know which side of the river he's on?" Musgrave demanded.

Cortez completely ignored the knife at his throat and continued to hold the Englishman's eye. "Think, Englishman."

"Think what?" Musgrave angrily interrupted.

Again, the Spaniard's temper rose, and again he had to fight hard to control it. "If you were a fisherman putting out to sea from here, and there was an army on one side of the river plundering anything they could find, where would you moor your boat?"

Musgrave's anger made it difficult for him to refrain from sinking his dagger into Cortez's throat. Even in his frustration, however, he was able to spot a rare opportunity to pay the Spaniard back in kind. "Armies don't usually cross rivers at night, so unless he crossed two days ago, he's still on that side. You should know that, Spanish man."

He laughed and followed up his jibe with another. "You're not such a clever bastard after all," he sneered. "You're nothing but a cocky Spanish popinjay."

Again, the Spaniard's temper began to rise, but he could see that the Englishman, seemingly satisfied with getting his own back, had calmed down. He ignored the obvious insult, which in any case he did not fully understand, and calmly reached up with his tied hands and firmly pushed Musgrave's dagger away.

"Look, Englishman," he said calmly. "This is not getting us anywhere. It is not helping me to reach the ships or you to get some Spanish gold. And if we keep shouting at each other, someone will hear us. We should stop and consider a proper course of action."

Musgrave sheathed his dagger. Tired and angry as he was, he could not escape the fact that the Spaniard was right. Nevertheless, he was not going to afford Cortez the satisfaction of thinking that he had no clear idea of what to do next, when in fact he did.

He tried to keep any hint of tiredness out of his voice. "All right," he said evenly. "If the boats are on the far side, we'll have to look somewhere else. We can't cross this river at the ford because James will definitely have men watching it. Even kings don't make that kind of mistake. So we're stuck on this side, and all we can do is what I said in the first place: ride west to find some other boats."

"When we reach the river, I will be able to tell the state of the tide," Cortez answered. "If it's ebbing, we will probably be able to cross further down. I imagine that these Scottish horses would not be able to cope with such a strong current, but we could always leave them and swim across ourselves. We will have to abandon them anyway when we find a suitable boat, so it will make little difference."

"I imagine that you can swim, Englishman?" he added as an afterthought.

As a law officer and reiver, swimming across a river was a skill Musgrave had never had to put into practise. As a boy, he could swim well enough, but that had been no more than a game of many years ago, and much different to swimming in a strong tide. Besides, he suspected that the Spaniard would not have mentioned it unless he was a more than competent swimmer himself and, as he would have to release Cortez's hands, the Spaniard would then have an advantage over him.

Rather than let Cortez see his fears, he voiced a different objection. "If the tide is coming in we could get carried a long way back up the river before we reach the far bank."

"If it is, we will have to wait until it turns and then we can use it to our advantage. That will happen soon, certainly well before daylight. We are not far from the sea now so we will have plenty of time."

Musgrave felt his anger rising again. "You bastard, Cortez, you've known all along where we are. Why else would you say that it's not very far to the sea?"

Cortez pointed up at the seabirds wheeling above. "They are telling me," he said.

The Spaniard had an answer for everything and Musgrave felt that he was in danger of getting completely out of his depth. And in more ways than one. To make matters worse, he could not avoid a sense of fear of what he faced creeping into his mind, and it added to his feeling of angry frustration. Cortez must have known from the start what would be involved and had deliberately kept the details from him, but what riled him most was the thought that, although Cortez was his prisoner, the Spaniard had been in charge from the very start. He had been cleverly manipulated all along by a bloody Spaniard who was every bit as devious as Lord Scrope back in Carlisle, and to help relieve his frustration, Musgrave roundly cursed the pair of them. He was beginning to have serious regrets about having fallen in with the Spaniard's scheme in the first place, but realised that he had come too far to turn back now.

He was on the point of simply killing Cortez and riding away, but the lure of Spanish gold remained far too strong.

There was nothing for it but to accept that Cortez had tricked him just as Scrope had, and all he could do was follow the Spaniard's lead and see it through to the end. He consoled himself with thoughts of all that gold, and it persuaded him to set his fears aside. Obtaining that level of riches was bound to have risks attached, but then so did everything else he had ever done, but this time the possible rewards were greater than any he had ever dreamed of, and without thinking further, he agreed to Cortez's proposal.

"All right, we'll do it your way, Spaniard. We'll swim across the Nith if we have to. But if there's no gold at the end of this, you're a dead man."

Cortez ignored the threat. They reached the river, turned south, and followed a well-beaten path along the bank. Stretches of mud were beginning to appear along the river's edge and even Musgrave could tell that the tide was beginning to go out.

"It will not be long now, Englishman, before we reach the boats." Cortez announced.

"Won't these boats be guarded?"

"The fishermen are certain to have people watching their boats, but they will also be watching for King James which will confuse them. They will be simple fishermen and, if they challenge us, we should be able to frighten them off for long enough to steal a boat."

Musgrave again made no comment. It all sounded so easy, but for a reiver, the prospect of exchanging his horse for a boat was still an alien concept and not something to be treated lightly. Now that the time had almost arrived, he was finding that what he had actually agreed to was becoming less and less attractive, but the lure of the gold drove him on.

Soon they saw several small boats drawn up on the opposite bank and a few larger craft anchored out in the river. Cortez's heart thrilled at the sight. Some of them were more substantial-looking craft than any he had expected to find here. "So King James's army has already crossed and is on this side of the river, but I doubt if we will run foul of him here. He must know that even Maxwell will not risk being caught with his back to the sea."

Musgrave knew that the Spaniard was right but would not give him the satisfaction of telling him so, and he merely grunted in agreement.

Cortez ignored him. "There appear to be some excellent craft moored out there." His newfound enthusiasm almost dispelled Musgrave's fears, but the Spaniard's next remark brought them flooding back. "All we have to do is swim out as far as the first suitable vessel. With the king on this side, the owners will be over there. They will never suspect what has happened until it is too late."

The Englishman remained silent, lost in his own thoughts, while Cortez continued to study the river. It occurred to him that he had once again allowed Cortez to trick him. He hoped that there might be small boats on this side of the river as well and they could avoid swimming in that dangerous current simply by using one to take them out to a larger one. He looked carefully up and down the riverbank, but much to his disappointment, there were no boats of any kind moored on this side of the Nith. Apart from the ones moored in the river, the only boats in sight were those drawn up on the far bank. To avoid swimming across to reach them, they would have to go back upstream and cross by the ford, and that would now be under guard by the king's soldiers. Even so, he considered telling Cortez that he had changed his mind about swimming. He thought about simply giving up, but the lure of all that shiny gold would not allow him to.

Cortez interrupted his thoughts. "The tide is not as strong as I feared and we can easily swim in that. Once we have located a suitable craft, we can start upstream and let the current carry us down to meet it, and once we are aboard, we can let it carry us out to sea. If we do this quickly and quietly, anyone watching will think that the boat has slipped its mooring and is drifting out on the tide. But we will be gone before they have time to react."

He looked at Musgrave. "Time to release my hands, Englishman."

For Musgrave, they had reached the critical point. Releasing his prisoner now would confirm that he had decided to go along with Cortez's suggestion, and that would mean handing complete control of the situation over to the Spaniard. If he went on from here, there would be no turning back.

It was a decision he would rather not have to make, and he decided to put it off for just a little longer. "Not yet, Spaniard. As soon as I let you go free, what's to stop you riding off and leaving me here. I can't do this on my own, but I bet that you could."

This time, Cortez made no attempt to disguise his anger. "My word will prevent me riding off, Englishman. It may mean little to you, but to me it represents a sacred oath! If you suggest that it does not, I shall challenge you on the field of honour."

Musgrave could see what giving his word meant to a man like Cortez, and he realised that the Spaniard meant what he said. He was quite ready to fight Cortez, but not until after he had his hands on that Spanish gold, and to demonstrate that he was still the master here, he tried another ploy to avoid having to set the Spaniard free.

"It might come to that, Cortez, but I don't have to let you go until we find the right boat."

Cortez, however, had a counter argument. "I have been tied up for days now and have lost all feeling in my arms. Once they are free and the blood begins to flow back into them they will start to hurt, and it will take some time for the pain to subside. In such pain, I will not be able to swim, and I will find it impossible to sail even the smallest boat. Do you want to drown us both?"

With great reluctance, Musgrave was obliged to concede the point, he had suffered that particular pain himself, most recently from Lord Scrope, and he knew what the Spaniard would go through. He drew his dagger and cut Cortez's bonds. The Spaniard tried to flex his fingers but they were completely numb and refused to budge. He tried moving his shoulders in a circular motion and, slowly, he found that he could move his arms in more than one direction. With the movement came the pain as the blood began to circulate. He tried not to let the Englishman see just how painful it was, but it was difficult not to utter a few groans. Eventually, he was able to shake his arms and rub them vigorously, which made him feel better.

The Englishman looked on impassively, doing nothing to alleviate the Spaniard's pain. When he felt that Cortez was able to ride with ease, he led off to the south.

They rode in silence. With his hands free, Cortez was able to relax in the saddle and pay more attention to things other than the river and the seabirds. He was surprised to find such a balmy night here in Scotland. It was more reminiscent of the climate on the Mediterranean coast of his native Spain than a country so far north. Apart from the gentle lapping of the water, the riverbank was deathly silent and he found the strange sweet scent of the furze pleasant but quite heady. The only drawback was the myriad of annoying, tiny insects buzzing around his head. They might have been difficult to bear had he not experienced worse in the swamps of the New World.

The swarms of midges did not bother Musgrave; in warm summer weather following the mist and rain, they were a constant in a Borderer's life. What was really playing on his mind was the prospect of swimming out to a boat and then sailing out to sea, but he dare not let the Spaniard see just how nervous the thought was making him. If he pulled out at this late stage the Spaniard, now that he had his hands free, would simply leave him and go on by himself. Cortez had given his word that he would share the gold with him, but it occurred to the ever-suspicious Musgrave that if it came to a choice between keeping his word to an Englishman and warning the Spanish ships, there could be little doubt about which option the Spaniard would choose.

They rode on and soon the boats moored in the river came into plain view in the moonlight. There was no sign of activity either on the bank or in the boats. Cortez heaved a huge inner sigh of relief and lifted his eyes upwards to give thanks. The one thing he had feared, and decided not to tell the Englishman, was that the fishermen too, would take advantage of the receding tide. The fact that they had not, meant that something had persuaded them to remain on shore, and while that might be the war between Maxwell and the king, he prayed that their reason for not sailing on the tide could also be due to the presence of Spanish ships out at sea.

Musgrave's nervousness was beginning to grow. Normally a brave fighter ready to face any man in battle, his doubts were beginning to grow and his confidence wane. The thought of abandoning his horse, swimming out to board a boat, and sailing off to God knows what, was starting to play on his mind. To steady his nerves, he concentrated on all that Spanish gold and somehow managed to keep his voice calm.

"What about these?" he asked.

"They would not remain afloat for long in the western ocean off the coast of Spain," Cortez replied. "But in this sheltered bay they will be perfectly adequate."

Musgrave suspected that the Spaniard was making a disparaging remark about the quality of Scottish boatbuilding, but it meant little to him. He told himself that if the Spaniard was the experienced sailor he claimed to be, he would never go out to sea in a less than perfectly seaworthy boat, and the Englishman drew strength from the thought.

"What now?" he asked.

"We go for a swim," Cortez replied. "And if we move quickly, there will still be time for the tide to carry us a good way out to sea before it turns."

The Spaniard sensed that allowing the Englishman time to think would increase the fear he was clearly attempting to hide. He had given Musgrave his word that he would reward him with gold from the Spanish ships, but that was before he realised how frightened the Englishman was of boats and the sea. To Cortez, this was a totally irrational fear, and he found it impossible to predict how the Englishman would react when it came to making a final decision. He thought that it would be all too easy to push Musgrave over the edge, at which point the Englishman might simply give up and ride away, which would suit Cortez fine but he knew that it would not be as easy as that. Musgrave was still armed with his rapier and that vicious looking dagger, and Cortez had no doubts that if pushed too far, Musgrave would use the weapons, if only out of spite.

Nevertheless, His Majesty's ships were somewhere out there, and he would spare no effort in trying to warn them of the danger they faced on land. If that required him to break his word, then so be it.

He scanned the water carefully and judged tide and distance. Without a further word, he rode a little way back upstream and dismounted. He removed his hat and fancy doublet, then sat and took off his boots. He began to walk down the muddy bank hoping he would not suddenly find himself caught in quicksand.

At the water's edge, he turned to Musgrave. "It is now or never, Englishman!"

With that, he waded into the river.

Chapter 36

"Die, you Maxwell bas...." The king's officer never finished the sentence. The gleam of anticipation at the prospect of killing one of Maxwell's reivers suddenly turned to one of shock as the lance pierced his body and sent him tumbling from his horse.

The rest of the king's men, joyfully congratulating themselves for having killed someone they thought was one of Maxwell's riders, were stunned into silence as a rider came galloping up the path, brushed Sandy and Rabbie aside, and drove their leader out of the saddle with a lance. The newcomer wheeled his horse around and yelled at the two Elliots.

"Ride!" Alexander Elliot shouted as he led his sons in a frantic gallop away from the scene of the skirmish with the king's troopers.

There had not been time for him to retrieve his lance from the body of the man he had killed, and he felt naked without it. But there could be no going back for it. He had been extremely lucky to arrive in time to help his sons, and even luckier get away, and a lance, even a favourite one, was a small price to pay. His principal concern now was how the king's men would react. With half their number, including their captain, dead or wounded, and being in some confusion about exactly who and how many had attacked them, Alexander thought that they might wait for reinforcements before attempting to hunt them down, but he was not entirely confident that would be the case. The king's men would assume that he and his sons were Maxwell riders, and would spare no effort to catch and hang them. That, however, was only one of his worries.

There would almost certainly be someone among the king's riders, possibly a Johnstone, who would recognise Big Jock, and that could cause even further trouble for Liddesdale. If Big Jock's body were to be recognised, Jamie would jump to the obvious conclusion that the Elliots were in league with Maxwell, and he would attack Liddesdale in overwhelming force once he had dealt with his renegade laird. But that would have to wait for future consideration; his immediate problem involved gettting away from the Galloway Hills with his sons, and without being killed or captured by either the king's troopers or Maxwell's reivers.

He urged his sons to spur their horses to greater efforts. They followed the path he had taken into the hills, but they could not remain on it for long. There would certainly be more of the king's men ahead and he hoped that they would have ample warning of their presence in order to have a chance of avoiding them. They galloped on until Alexander guessed that they were nearing the edge of the foothills and would soon be out in open country. It went against his reiver's instincts to ride out there in daylight unless he absolutely had to, so he called a halt to give the horses a breather. He held up a hand for silence and listened. There were no audible sounds of pursuit, but that did not mean that they weren't being watched or followed.

"They're takin' it easy," he said. "We'll have time tae hide 'till dark."

He rode on at a canter and motioned to his sons to follow. They complied without a word, knowing that this was not a time for lengthy explanations. After riding on a little further, Alexander picked up the sound of a burn running over stones. It was somewhere to the north and not very far away, so he called a halt again and signalled to his sons to dismount.

"Up there, an' dinna' leave too much sign." He pointed up a scrub-covered bank topped with furze.

Sandy instinctively knew what was required and led his horse up the bank trying not to disturb the undergrowth any more than was necessary, and Rabbie followed his brother's example. As Alexander watched, he felt a sense of satisfaction that his sons had reacted well and did what he asked of them without question; being in the company of Big Jock in whatever dangers they had recently faced had clearly taught them a lot. When they disappeared over the crest of the bank, he rode up the opposite slope leaving a clear trail. Near the top, he turned east and rode along for a little way, taking care to avoid being skylined on the crest, then rode back down again. He made his way back along the path, dismounted, and followed his sons up the northern bank, rearranging the scrub behind him. It was not perfect, but it was the best he could do. He hoped that laying a false trail and trying to hide the real one would at least delay their pursuers long enough to give him and his sons a breathing space.

Once over the crest, he remounted and rode down to the bottom of a small valley where the burn rippled musically down from the Galloway Hills, but there was no time to admire the scenery. On the opposite bank, the land rose again up to another ridge topped with a stand of trees. He looked for his sons but there was nobody in sight. At the water's edge there were tracks left by a single horse leading upstream and, puzzled, he followed them cautiously until he spotted Rabbie sitting on his horse in the middle of the burn, unconcernedly reloading his pistol. He was about to ride up and give his son a piece of his mind for being so careless when he heard a rider behind him. He turned and saw a grinning Sandy approaching.

Rabbie looked at Sandy with a wry smile. "That's my last shot," he said.

Sandy nodded. "I have only two left."

Alexander was about to remind his sons that running out of powder and shot was one of the reasons he disliked firearms, but held back. He had lost his own lance and, besides, he was pleased with the way his sons were reacting. Without a word from him, they had known exactly what to do and had done it well, well enough to fool even him. Rabbie had acted as decoy while Sandy waited to spring an ambush. Yet again, he noted how much they had learned since he last saw them; they had grown into efficient reivers, and he sensed that he could rely on them to help him find their way back to Liddesdale. He kept his pride hidden but nodded in understanding. Since the escape from the king's soldiers, he had said no more than a few words to his sons and, irrespective of how each might be feeling inside, there had been no outward demonstrations of emotion at their reunion.

The loss of Big Jock would begin to play on the minds of all three soon enough, and for the moment, there was no time for displays of sentiment, explanations or recriminations. They had to concentrate on getting back to Liddesdale.

Alexander had a plan in mind, but from the way his sons were reacting to the situation, he decided that it would be worthwhile asking for their opinions. "What d'ye think?"

Rabbie thought about what Big Jock might have done. Thinking about the old reiver brought a lump to his throat but he quickly suppressed it. "We should try to find somewhere to hide out and rest until dark."

He looked at the lengthening shadows. "It won't be too long 'till it gets dark, but wc can't spend too much time looking. If we take too long about it, we're in danger of running into either Jamie or Maxwell. Those trees up there look as good a place as any."

Alexander nodded and looked questionably at Sandy.

"Rabbie's right," Sandy said. "And when it gets dark we should ride north. Jamie's army will be all over the hills to the west looking for Maxwell, but he'll have left riders between here and Lochmaben in case the laird breaks out and tries to get his castle back. And I wouldn't put that past him."

His father had not thought about Maxwell trying to retake Lochmaben but, for a reiver, it made perfect sense. "Ye're right," he said. "We'll ride north and take the lang way hame."

They entered the burn and rode a little way upstream, but instead of riding north, Alexander turned and led them back up the bank that overlooked the path out of the hills. "They'll think that we'll gang as far north as we can before dark."

Just under the crest, a clump of small ash trees set in a tangle of blackthorn offered the promise of cover. It looked impenetrable but something in Alexander's reiving experience prompted him to take a closer look. He dismounted and went forward on foot. His instincts served him well and he soon discovered that this seemingly uninviting clump of vegetation was in fact a well-prepared reiver hideout with a clearing in the centre where a few men and horses could hide, and a concealed opening facing down the slope to the path for a quick exit. It was not perfect, and an experienced searcher would soon spot it as Alexander had done, but it would solve their immediate problem. He signalled his sons to dismount and led them into the cover, then motioned to Sandy to go back up on foot to check what was over the crest of the ridge. In spite of the seriousness of their predicament, it gave him great satisfaction to see that, once again, his eldest son knew exactly what was required without asking questions.

Sandy crept forward to the top of the ridge and hid in the furze. He waited and listened, then inched his way along the crest in the direction of the trees until he found a more open spot that afforded him a view over the surrounding countryside. To the north, the foothills continued to undulate for several miles with gently rising hills interspersed with deep valleys, most with a burn running through them. Beyond that, the country began to flatten out into more heavily populated farmland. He turned his attention to the east and stiffened as he saw a group of a dozen or more riders on top of the ridge not far along from where he lay hidden. His first thought was that his father's attempt to disguise their passage had given them no more than a minimum breathing space; the leader of the king's men obviously knew his business and had enough men at his disposal to cover several options. As Sandy watched, however, he noticed that they wore coloured tabards over their breastplates, presumably to identify them as Jamie's riders, but lowering sun glinted off their helmets. He was surprised that they would be guilty of such a basic error. The reflected sunlight would betray their position, and it was a mistake no reiver would ever be guilty of making. It confirmed his first impression that these were the king's men and not Maxwell's. These were not experienced soldiers, and that might help the Elliots' cause. The riders left one of their number on the ridge hidden in the trees, and rode north to the crest of the next one. Once again, they left a man there in a small stand of firs while the others continued to ride north to leave yet another man on the next ridge. Puzzled, Sandy wriggled back to where his father and brother waited and told them what he had seen.

Rabbie was first to voice an opinion. "They're setting up a string of watchers, like the March Wardens do."

"Aye," his father agreed. "They call it a picket line. But it means that we canna use yon trees."

"They wouldn't be sending out so many watchers for us," Sandy said. "They must be on the lookout for Maxwell."

Alexander thought about this. "Aye," he said. "In case the laird tries tae ride back tae Lochmaben. Ye were right aboot that."

Rabbie looked around him, and then turned to his father. "We might as well stop here until dark. I don't think the watchers can see us, but they might spot us if we move around."

His father agreed. "Ye're right. We'll leave as soon as it gets dark, and try to be far enough away before the moon."

Sandy looked at his father. "I'll go back up to keep a watch."

It was more of a statement than a question and he left without further comment. As his father watched him go, it was on the tip of his tongue to warn him to be careful but he checked himself. He was again amazed at how well his sons had developed their skills as reivers, almost to the point where he hardly recognised them. One of Alexander's secret worries had always been how his family, and his reiver band, would fare when something happened to him, as it inevitably would. He desperately wanted either Sandy or Rabbie to follow him as heidsman, and he occasionally mentioned this to his wife, Margaret, when he considered that she was mollycoddling them. Now, however, their conduct in the current desperate situation had served to lift that particular concern from his mind.

He thought in terms of 'when' something happened to him, rather than 'if'. Reivers seldom lived into old age, and it was something he suspected Big Jock was aware of when he charged into the king's soldiers without a hope of survival. Now that he was no longer worried about his sons' suitability to follow his example, he hoped that when his time came, he would emulate his old friend. That was a suitable end for a reiver, and particularly an Elliot reiver.

He also noted that for the first time he could remember, he had begun to think of his sons as 'Sandy' and 'Rabbie' rather than Malcolm and Robert, and he thanked Big Jock for that.

Sandy's sudden and breathless return broke into his thoughts. "They've finished setting their watchers and the rest are coming back this way. They're spread out and they'll be here well before dark, so they're bound to spot us. We'll have to ride through them if we want to go north, and if we go east those watchers'll see us!"

Chapter 37

As he watched Cortez prepare to swim out into the river, Musgrave's doubts about the wisdom of taking part in what he was beginning to regard as a hair-brained scheme, multiplied. In his reiving career, he had stolen just about anything he could lay his hands on, but never a boat, and although he had been in small boats to get him across rivers or to catch fish, he had no experience whatsoever of the sea. Like all born reivers, what he did not understand he did not like, but he refused to admit, even to himself, that his apprehension stemmed from a fear of the sea. As his doubts, and his fears, multiplied he could not bring himself to dismount and join the Spaniard in the water. Rather than admit to being afraid, he began to question the Spaniard's chances of actually reaching one of those boats. Cortez might be a competent sailor, but what was he like as a swimmer, and it seemed to the Englishman's tired mind that the tide was gaining in strength.

Musgrave was a man who had frequently faced death without flinching, but this was different. The thought of swimming out into the River Nith, and then sailing out into the notorious Solway Firth, generated a level of fear unlike anything he had ever experienced. To allay his fears, he convinced himself that nobody, including Cortez, could swim out there without drowning.

His confidence evaporated, and with it the lure of Spanish gold.

He began to concentrate on the negative aspects of what Cortez proposed, and what, he was loath to admit, he had agreed to. In an effort to make excuses, he convinced himself that the Spaniard had tricked him into releasing him with false promises of Spanish ships and gold. That there were Spanish ships out there could not be denied: if there were no ships, the

Spaniard would not have abandoned his horse and be preparing to swim out into the estuary, steal a boat, and sail out to meet them. And warning them had been the sole focus of Cortez's life since they had left Lochmaben as prisoners. One of those ships might well be carrying gold, and although Cortez had given his word, Musgrave's tortured mind now began to entertain some nagging doubts. Cortez might well keep his word, but there was no guarantee that the Spanish captains would be ready to honour it. The more he allowed the thought to develop, the more he became convinced that Spanish captains would be extremely reluctant to hand over some of their king's gold to an unknown Englishman, especially if Cortez told them that he was an enemy spy.

In his confusion, he convinced himself that Cortez was luring him out into the river, not to steal a boat, but to drown him! Something that the Spaniard, who was clearly the stronger swimmer, would have little difficulty in doing. The prospect of Spanish gold rapidly receded, and he cursed himself for a fool for having fallen for what he was now sure was really another of the Spaniard's tricks.

Now convinced that Cortez had known all along that the Spanish captains would never stand for rewarding an English spy, and now intended to kill him out there in the river, made Musgrave angry, and the anger banished any remaining thoughts of gold. The bastard was playing him for a fool, and he made up his mind that Cortez was not going to get away with it. He decided that this devious Spaniard would pay dearly for taking him for a fool.

He dismounted and drew his dagger. "You bastard, Cortez," he yelled. "You've been lying to me all along. Well it's not going to work."

Cortez eyed the dagger, laughed, and moved further out into the river estuary. That was the last straw. Losing all sense of fear, Musgrave removed his boots and stepped into the water, intending to catch the Spaniard and cut his throat. He was going to kill this devious bastard, and do it now, before Cortez could swim further out into the river.

The Spaniard felt the tide moving around him and he was having difficulty staying on his feet, and he could wait no longer. It was time for him to go. He relaxed and allowed the tide to carry him downstream towards the moored fishing boats.

Musgrave saw what was happening and made a lunge to stop him, but as soon as he moved, he felt the sandy bottom shift under his feet. He lost his footing and plunged headlong into the water. He thrashed about trying to regain his feet, and in the process swallowed several mouthfuls of dirty, silted up river water. Thinking he was drowning, he panicked and tried desperately to regain his feet. He failed and all he achieved was to make a bad situation worse. The tide caught him and he thought his life was over.

Then, without him knowing it, the same tide that had almost taken his life gave it back to him. It swung him round and washed him up onto a sandbar jutting out from the shore and gradually emerging as the river level dropped with the outgoing tide. He lay on the sand for several minutes before he realised that he was actually going to survive.

After what seemed an age, he recovered sufficiently to desperately scramble ashore.

***

Cortez was well out in the estuary before he took a moment to turn on his back to see Musgrave lying on the sandbar. He couldn't tell whether the Englishman was dead or alive, but either way he was clearly not in a position to join him in stealing a boat. In the meantime, he was relieved of any obligation to the Englishman.

He turned his attention back to the problem at hand and found that he needed to move further out into the estuary or risk the tide sweeping him past the fishing boat he had selected and out to sea. It required several strong strokes before he judged that he was on the correct course and by then the tide had taken him almost up to the small craft swinging gently on its anchor rope. A few more adjustments and he was able to reach out and grab the prow, which was facing upriver into the outgoing tide. He worked his way along the side and hauled himself aboard.

His initial impression was of the stink of rotten fish, but that was only to be expected. Otherwise, he was relieved to find that the boat was in all respects ready for sea. He found both sail and oars stowed on board, together with a neat roll of nets, and some fishing lines neatly laid out along the length of the boat. A collection of other fishing gear was tidily stored under one of the seats. The fishermen who owned this vessel had clearly left everything ready for sailing, probably at dawn, and a glance at the sky told him that he had no time to lose. A quick inspection revealed that as well as the anchor, there was a line attaching the boat to the shore and, for a moment, he almost regretted not having Musgrave and his dagger with him, but he put that out of his mind. He searched through the fishing gear and to his relief found a sharp gutting knife. Although razor sharp, the knife was small and not designed for cutting through mooring ropes, so it took what seemed an age of sawing before the line parted and the boat was swinging on its anchor. After that, it only took a moment for him to haul up the anchor from the sandy bottom and the boat moved off, stern first, on the tide.

As the boat began to pick up momentum, he heard shouts of alarm from the shore. He hunkered down out of sight, hoping that the fishermen would think that the boat had simply come adrift from its moorings, but quickly realised that they would soon discover that the mooring rope had been cut. That would tell them that their boat had been stolen, and as many men as could be mustered quickly, would set out as fast as they could to retrieve it and catch the thief.

For the moment, however, he was content to let the tide carry him stern first down the estuary and out into what he imagined must be the Solway Firth, but when the boat began to slow down and turn beam on, he knew that he had come as far as the tide would take him. There would still be a tide running out in the Firth but it would not be as strong or as fast as in the river mouth, and before long, it would turn. Until then, he intended to make full use of it. He dumped the nets and other fishing gear over the side to give him more room to work the unfamiliar craft, but when he inspected the sail, he found it to be disappointingly rudimentary, nothing more than a single square sheet of canvas. Knowing that in this part of the world the prevailing wind was from the west, he had to accept that, with such a basic rig, sailing into the wind would be difficult and take far too much time. If he wanted to find the Spanish ships quickly, he would have to use the oars, and again, he briefly regretted not having Musgrave with him. The man might be afraid of the sea, and be a woefully incompetent sailor, but he would surely have been able to handle an oar. However, he could do nothing about it now, and he would have to do the best he could on his own.

By now, dawn had broken and signalled the start of another fine summer's day. That meant that visibility would be good and finding the ships, that by now must surely be nearing their destination, should not present too much of a problem. But no sooner were his hopes raised, than they were cruelly dashed. Out to the west, an early morning sea mist was rolling in, and unless it burned off quickly, it would obscure his view of the ships. He put out the oars to straighten the boat, keep it on course, and make as much speed he could manage, but as he turned the boat around and faced back towards the rivermouth, his heart sank. Three boats similar to the one he was in were exiting the river, each manned by several clearly very angry fishermen intent on recovering their stolen boat. With several experienced men to work the oars, they would soon catch up with him.

He had nothing he could use as a weapon save the gutting knife, and perhaps an oar, so there was no hope to fighting them off. He briefly thought that he might be able to bribe them with offers of Spanish gold, but he doubted that any of these men could speak English, and certainly not Spanish. And even if they could, they would be in no mood to listen. Their minds would be set on one purpose only: recovering their boat and throwing the thief who had stolen it into the sea. His only hope was the fog bank. It was still rolling in and he rowed frantically towards it. Unless he reached that all-enveloping fog before the fishermen reached him, his whole mission to warn the Spanish ships was doomed. Although an experienced sailor, Cortez was a man more used to being rowed than to rowing, and he found the unaccustomed labour not only exhausting but also extremely painful. Soon his hands were blistered and bleeding from gripping the roughly fashioned oars. He redoubled his efforts but the fishermen continued to gain on him at an alarming rate. He was never going to reach the fog bank in time to hide, and he was almost collapsing with exhaustion when the first of the fishing boats caught up with him.

The boat drew alongside and one of the men shouted angrily at Cortez in a language he failed to recognise. He let go of the oars and picked up the gutting knife. One of the fishermen held the side of the boat while another leaned over and reached out for him. He moved away, threatened the man with the knife and the fisherman hesitated. There was a dull thud as a second boat drew up on the other side and bumped into his. He felt a rough hand on his shoulder and struck out blindly with the knife. That brought forth a howl of pain and rage and won him a brief reprieve, but he knew that he could not hold them off for long. The third boatful of vengeful fishermen arrived and he knew that he would soon be overwhelmed. Further resistance would be useless.

He was about to give up and attempt using some of his diplomatic prowess and try and explain who he was by using a form of sign language, when one of thc fishermen shouted in alarm. The man stood up and began frantically pointing towards the nearing fogbank.

Cortez turned to look in the direction the man was pointing. The shape of a larger boat powered by several oarsmen loomed out of the mist and came straight at them. This craft was crewed by men clad in sailors' dress, and it carried several other armed men wearing the uniform of Spanish soldiers. Fluttering from its stern was the flag of Spain and Cortez's heart leapt as he recognised a Spanish captain's seaboat. A man in the bow was throwing a weighted line into the sea then pulling it up, carefully examining it, and calling out to an officer standing in the stern. Cortez knew that they were taking soundings to see if there was sufficient depth to accommodate larger craft, and that meant that bigger ships were waiting somewhere out there in the fog. He realised that he had rowed much further out into the Firth than he thought and, had he been able, he would have fallen to his knees to give thanks. He had found the Spanish ships!

The sight of the unfamiliar flag, uniforms, and firearms, alarmed the fishermen. They stopped and looked uncertainly from one to another, seeking guidance from each other. Cortez took advantage of the reprieve. He stood up, waved, and began shouting in Spanish at the top of his voice. At first, the Spaniards failed to hear him, but they saw him waving and steered warily towards him. Soon his voice began to reach them. Still too far off to distinguish the actual words, they recognised their own language and picked up speed.

That was enough for the fishermen. They turned their boats around and rowed away in haste.

As the Spanish boat drew near, Cortez began to explain who he was and demanded that they take him to the senior officer on the Spanish flagship, but the junior officer in charge of the Spanish boat, and who clearly knew nothing about Cortez's presence in Scotland, eyed him with open suspicion. In truth, as Don Juan Cortez stood in the little fishing boat, his appearance did nothing to mark him out as a man of importance. He was bootless, hatless, and unarmed; what clothing he was wearing, was still wet through from his swim out to steal the boat, and his usually neatly trimmed hair and beard were a knotted tangle of dirty strands. The sea mist was now swirling around them and caused the temperature to drop significantly, and after having worked up a sweat from rowing, the cold began to eat into his tired and hungry body and he stood there shivering. His lacerated hands were beginning to hurt, and he began to berate the young officer. His Majesty's ships were sailing into a trap and he must warn the fleet commander of the danger awaiting his troops if they landed in Scotland. If the officer did not do as he ordered, Don Juan Martinez de Recalde, second in command of the great armada sailing to invade England, would hear of it.

The young man bristled at being shouted at and ordered about by someone who stank of fish, but the man spoke Spanish like a gentleman, and this told him that there might just be some truth in what he was saying. Besides, he was now as far from his ship as he dared to go without risking getting lost in the fog, and he decided that his safest course of action was to take this ruffian back to his ship's captain, but under close guard. He had Cortez unceremoniously hauled out of the fishing boat, thrown into the bottom of the Spanish craft, and they rowed back the way they had come into the mist to find the Spanish fleet. On the way, Cortez attempted to question the officer about the ships, their captains, and the senior officer, but the young Spaniard was keeping as far from the smell of rotten fish as he possibly could, and was not keen to engage in conversation with its source.

After what seemed an age to the increasingly impatient Cortez, they came alongside the massive hull of a Spanish galleon. His demand to speak to the captain immediately, met with total distain, and he stood fuming in the boat while the officer clambered up the rope ladder to make his report. The young man first reported the results of the soundings and discussed them with the captain before even mentioning anything about their encounter with the highly suspicious Spaniard seemingly being attacked by some fishermen. The attackers had fled and he had taken the Spaniard prisoner.

At the mention of the prisoner and his demands, the captain's whole demeanour changed and he ordered the officer to bring the man on board immediately. The young man started to protest that the prisoner stank of fish, but thought better of it and went to carry out his orders. The captain knew who Cortez was, and why he was in Scotland, but he had expected to meet de Recalde's representative ashore with a Scottish army waiting to support a Spanish landing. But Cortez being found at sea, and in such strange circumstances, could only mean that something else had gone awry with what was already an ill-fated expedition. Unlike his junior officer, he ignored the smell of fish while Cortez quickly explained what was happening in this part of Scotland, and the danger of the landing force falling foul of King James's entire army.

Cortez suggested that the ships wait until James had dealt with the treacherous Maxwell, and gone back to Edinburgh. At that point, they could land unopposed, and be across the border before the English realised that they faced a second invasion. The Spanish captain shook his head. Off the west coast of Ireland, the three ships that left Spain ran into a severe Western Ocean storm. One foundered on the rocky coast, and he had not seen anything of the other one since; at best, it had returned to Spain badly damaged; at worst, it had suffered the same fate as the first.

Without any prospect of support ashore, there was little or nothing his one shipload of soldiers could accomplish, and Cortez had to face the unpalatable truth. This part of King Philip's grand scheme to invade England was doomed to failure. The captain hid his relief at the abandonment of an enterprise he considered doomed from the start.

In the the officer's quarters, Cortez bathed and was fitted with some new clothing. He tried to rest, but plagued by thoughts of what might have been, sleep refused to come. He had an account to settle with a certain 'laird', not for himself, but on behalf of King Philip, and he asked the captain to put him ashore.

The captain, however, had already had quite enough, and was not ready to take any further risks. He turned his ship around to sail down the Irish Sea and join the main armada in the English Channel.

Chapter 38

Alexander Elliot looked at his sons. He did not have to look hard, as a glance told him that they were well aware of the danger they faced. For the second time in a single day, a seemingly secure hiding place could, at any minute, turn into a trap. They had a group of the king's men bearing down on them, but they dare not move or the watchers on the hilltops would spot them. In spite of the danger, however, both looked calm and fully prepared for whatever happened next, and Alexander felt a sense of relief tinged with an element of pride. His sons were proving to be well worthy of bearing the name of Elliot, and for that, he made a silent gesture of thanks to Big Jock. But for the moment that was by the way, he had come a long way to find them and take them home, and he was determined to complete the task. All that was required was working out a way of achieving it, and doing it quickly.

Sandy was first to break the silence. "We'll wait until they're almost on us and then break through 'em. If we time it right, we should be able to take 'em by surprise and be away before they know it."

Alexander looked doubtful. "Ah'm nae sure," he said. "But I canna think o' anythin' else."

Rabbie thought he could improve on his brother's basic solution. He was reluctant to mention it because it might involve a long explanation to his father later, but he knew that it was a good idea and in spite of having to admit that he had not exactly followed the plan the last time they employed it, he felt that he must mention it. "Why don't we do like we did when we met the Hetheringtons? We ride off in different directions and meet up again when we're in the clear."

Even in such a tight corner, Sandy could not resist a grin. "It didn't work that time," he said, but then he softened the blow. "But it worked well against Tam and Maxwell's riders."

Their father listened and, although he knew that what they proposed was a tried and tested reiver tactic, he didn't like the idea of the three of them splitting up. For one thing, he feared that none of them knew the Galloway Hills well enough to know where to find a secure meeting place, and with Jamie's army spread all over the area, they could not be sure of finding each other again. On the other hand, he was confident that each of his sons was capable of getting back to Liddesdale on his own, and a lone rider might well have a better chance than a group of three. And there was another fact to be borne in mind. Neither Sandy nor Rabbie was widely known outside of Liddesdale, whereas he, like Big Jock, was instantly recognisable.

The recurring thought that someone among the king's riders would certainly recognise Big Jock's body, had begun to play on his mind and recent developments served to increase his feeling of concern. Once the news that Big Jock Elliot had been killed in Dumfriesshire got back to Jamie, the king would assume that the Elliots were in league with Maxwell, and not only the Elliots but the whole of Liddesdale.

Time was short and he could find only one solution to the problem. A solution he knew he would have to keep from his sons.

He made up his mind and looked at Sandy and Rabbie in turn to make sure that he had their full attention. "We'll dae that," he said. "But when we ride we'll gang doon tae the path at the foot of this hill. When I give the word, Sandy ye ride doon tae the bottom an' head west. Then turn north when ye get the chance, an' ride for hame. The watchers will have their eyes on Sandy so ye, Rabbie, ride east before they ken what's goin' on."

"And," he added with great emphasis, "we canna stop for anythin' until wan o' us gets hame."

Rabbie looked puzzled. "But surely we have to join up again somewhere before we ride back to Liddesdale."

"No!" His father was adamant. "We have tae keep ridin' an' we canna stop for anythin'."

He was about to explain further but was interrupted by Rabbie. "You're not saying that if one of us gets into trouble, the others can't ride to help him?"

"I am."

Again he was about to explain, but for a second time he was interrupted by an incredulous Rabbie who was finding it impossible to accept that his father of all people would simply ride off and leave one of his sons, or any other Elliot for that matter, in danger. Especially after having ridden all this way to find them.

He began to show signs of reverting to his old wilful self. "After everything that's happened, I'm not going to ride off and leave you or Sandy to fight Jamie's riders on your own."

Alexander, in turn, began to show signs of exasperation with his younger son. "Ye will if I tell ye tae, Robert." Hoping that use of his given name might help his son realise just how serious he was.

As Sandy listened, he became increasingly anxious. He had seen how close the king's riders were, and they would be getting closer by the minute, yet his father and brother seemed to be more intent in engaging in a private battle of wills. He was convinced that their father would not have insisted on them splitting up without having a very good reason for it, and he had hoped that Rabbie would at least allow their father to explain, but it seemed that his brother and father continued to rub each other up the wrong way. He desperately tried to think of why his father was so adamant that they couldn't stop for anything, and he thought that he could understand at least part of it. He was aware that his thinking might not be accurate, but he could see that Rabbie was about to continue with the argument and he knew that he had to intervene.

"Shut up the both of you!" he hissed quietly but sharply. "You'll let Jamie's riders know we're here."

He turned to his brother. "Look Rabbie. You know that Da would never say anything like that without a good reason, so for Christ's sake let him explain." He looked at his father. "You want us to take a message to Liddesdale, is that it?"

Alexander, who was already regretting losing his temper with Rabbie, looked gratefully at Sandy. "Aye," he said. "There'll be Johnstones and others ridin' wi' the king an' if wan o' them sees Big Jock's body, they'll ken who he is. Word will get back tae Jamie, an' he'll get the idea that the Elliots are ridin' wi' Maxwell. He'll ride on us after he's done wi' yon laird, an' we have tae warn Martin o' Braidley."

He paused to make sure that his words had sunk in. "If we ride together, we might get caught together. We stand a better chance alane, as lang as we don't stop for anythin'."

He was confident that Sandy would heed him so he turned and looked steadily at Rabbie. "An' this time someone has tae get word tae Liddesdale. So nae stoppin' for anythin'. All right, Rabbie?"

Even before his brother had admonished him, Rabbie was having second thoughts. Sandy was right. Their father would never have suggested what he had without a very good reason, and the reason Alexander had just outlined was certainly a good one. To make matters worse, Rabbie still felt that he had let Liddesdale down once before, but all he could do now was put that behind him and do what was required of him this time around. It was not in a reiver's vocabulary to apologise, and his father would probably think less of him if he attempted to do so, but he could feel the hiedsman's stern gaze on him and had to make some sort of acknowledgement.

He looked his father in the eye. "All right," he said.

Alexander turned to Sandy, who simply nodded. He nodded back and was satisfied that he could rely on both his sons. They could still easily come to grief, but not if he could help it, and to that end, he had thought of a way of not only assisting his sons' escape, but also avoiding Jamie's inevitable destruction of Liddesdale. His plan was not yet fully formed, but even if it had been, he would not have dared breathe a word of what he had in mind to either Sandy or Rabbie.

Sandy crept forward one last time to check on the progress of the approaching riders and came hurrying back. The king's men had reached the bottom of the little valley and begun the climb up the opposite side of the ridge to where the three Elliots waited. They would be here in minutes.

Even in the excitement of the moment, neither brother could fail to notice that, for the first time they could remember, their father had not addressed them by their full given names, and it had the effect of reinforcing the seriousness of their current situation.

Alexander paused to see if Rabbie protested that he had been handed the easiest task, but there was no protests and so he continued with what he had to say. "Ye'll have the best chance o' breakin' oot and ye should be hame first. So dinna stop for anythin' 'til ye get there."

Rabbie nodded and both brothers looked questioningly at their father. He knew what they wanted to know. "As soon as yon riders top the bank, I'll lead them south an' lose them after dark. That will no be lang noo."

They could hear the king's riders coming up the hill behind them. There was no more to say. No unnecessary farewells or warnings to be careful. Alexander mounted and his sons followed suit.

Alexander could wait no longer. He looked at Sandy. "Ride!"

Sandy spurred his horse and burst out of the bushes. The thorns snagged his jack, but he was not seriously hampered, and galloped freely on down the hill. Alexander waited until Sandy was halfway down then slapped the rump of Rabbie's horse and sent him on his way.

Alexander's timing was almost perfect. Sandy was at the bottom of the bank and galloping west; Rabbie was over half way down before a shout of alarm came from the watcher on the ridge to the south. He only had to wait another few moments before the first of the king's riders topped the ridge behind him. As they came into view, he burst out of cover and tore down the hillside. Reaching the bottom, he paused to glance back, hoping that the men behind had recognised him and mistakenly thought that the watcher's shout referred only to him. They had, and they bunched up to give chase. Another quick glance told him that none had broken off to chase after either Sandy or Rabbie. He crossed the path and galloped up the hill on the far side, followed by several pistol shots. The shots all went wide and he was confident that he could gain enough time for his sons to get well away.

The watcher on the ridge who had raised the alarm, was alive to the situation. He shouted again and waved frantically but failed to attract the attention of the men chasing Alexander. He gave up trying, left his post and started down the hill to intercept Rabbie. He reached the point where a burn running down the hillside turned and followed the path off to the east. There he turned and waited until the onrushing Rabbie reached the path. He held his lance ready to drive it through the fugitive's body. Rabbie had seen the danger and reached for his pistol, but heeding what his father had told him, he kept it out of sight until the last minute. He had one shot left and had to make it count. He held the weapon hidden until he had almost reached the point of the spear before raising it and firing at point blank range. The soldier slumped in the saddle but was not dead. Rabbie's momentum carried him level with the badly wounded man and he snatched the lance from his dying hand. He pushed the trooper's bleeding body out of the saddle into the burn, and the heavy fall was sufficient to kill him. Rabbie jumped off his own horse and quickly removed several pieces of equipment, including the breastplate with the tabard still attached, from the now dead body. He picked up the helmet and attached it to his saddle. After a quick glance around to make sure that there were no other immediate dangers, he mounted the dead soldier's horse, took up the reins of his own Galloway Nag and set off along the path out of the Galloway Hills.

The watcher on the opposite crest was much slower to react as the trees he was hiding in obscured his view, and by the time he realised what was happening, it was too late. His companion lay in the burn with a red stain polluting the clear water and the man who had shot him was fast disappearing to the east. The fugitive who had broken to the west was by now out of sight, and the whole troop of his fellow royal horsemen were chasing the rider escaping to the south. Either from a sense of duty, or self-preservation, he decided to remain where he was and resume his watch in case something else untoward occurred. He was aware that the man with the pistol must have taken his dead colleague's horse, but had missed seeing Rabbie taking the breastplate and helmet.

Rabbie rode hard until he was sure that he was not being followed, then slowed down to give his horse a breather. He was conscious of the fact that there may well be more of the king's riders ahead, so he donned the breastplate and helmet he had taken from the watcher's body. There was a neat round bloodstained hole in the breastplate and tabard close to where the wearer's heart would have been, and he noted with surprise that the armour had failed to stop the pistol ball. In spite of the bullet hole, however, it was still serviceable and he hoped that it would ease his passage home. At least it partially covered up his dishevelled appearance. If he could pass himself off as one of King Jamie's messengers, he should be able to ride unhindered out of the hills and through Johnstone territory, now controlled by the king's army, and perhaps even across the Debatable Land. As long as nobody bothered to look too closely.

Almost unnoticed, night had crept up on The Borders and the darkness was thickening. Now well past the line of watchers on the ridges, he rested until the moon rose and then resumed his journey home.

***

Unlike his brother, Sandy got away unchallenged. He reached the path and, heeding his father's words, rode west with every ounce of speed he could squeeze out of the Galloway Nag. When he neared the place where Big Jock had died, he had to slow down and move with caution in case the king's men were still there, but the scene was deserted. There was no sign of their recent encounter with the king's men, so when the soldiers left, they must have taken Big Jock's body with them, which meant that his father's fears were well founded. Someone had recognised the old reiver's body and they had taken it to show Jamie. It was now even more important than ever to get a warning through to Liddesdale.

Sandy set off again with renewed determination, but he knew he could not stay on this path for too long. He was riding into unknown territory where two possible dangers lay in wait for him: Maxwell's reivers and King James's soldiers. He did not have anything similar to the flimsy disguise Rabbie had acquired, but he still had to make sure that neither Maxwell nor the king caught him. If he ran into Maxwell, the laird would recognise him and finish the job he had ordered his man, Tam, to carry out; the king would take him for a Maxwell rider and kill him on the spot. That would be better than Jamie finding out he was an Elliot, but either way, he would fail to get that vital message through to Liddlesdale.

He left the path and, in spite of the need for urgency, decided to find a place to hide until nightfall when the darkness would conceal him. As soon as it did, he turned north and rode cautiously through the night trying to get as far as possible before the moon rose and lit up the hills. Then he would work his way to the northeast to skirt around Lochmaben and follow the route his father had taken from Liddesdale.

***

Alexander continued to lead his pursuers south as he had told his sons he would. The fact that the watchers and the group chasing him were wearing tabards meant that they were wary of being mistaken for Maxwells. They would be working to a definite plan, and he thought that might suit his purposes. He felt confident enough that at least one of his sons would get through to Liddesdale, but it was up to him to make certain that they did. Things could still go very wrong, and in case they did, he had something in mind that he hoped would help. He did not intend to follow the plan he had outlined to Sandy and Rabbie, and instead of doubling back when darkness fell, he intended to find a secure hiding place for the night. In the morning, he would set in motion the scheme he had hatched for saving Liddesdale.

He knew that what he planned would probably cost him his life, just as what Big Jock did had cost him his, but he hoped that it would not only increase his sons' chances of getting home to Liddesdale, but also prevent an attack on the valley by the king.

Chapter 39

It took Musgrave some time to recover from his brush with death. Gradually, he became aware of his position and managed to drag himself off the sandbar. He sat on the riverbank and waited for his shattered nerves to settle down and, eventually, he felt sufficiently recovered to stand up and move around.

The opportunity to go with Cortez was now gone, and with it the chance of getting his hands on any of the Spanish gold, and the loss of the gold hurt him more than any physical damage he had suffered. His anger at Cortez returned, and venting his frustration had the effect of bringing him back to reality. He knew that he should reassess the situation and look for possible alternatives, but what, he asked himself, did he have to gain now that the gold was gone. The disappointing answer was precious little. There was Cortez's rapier, boots and doublet, and the horse the Spaniard had been riding. But that still fell woefully short of what he had hoped for when he first rode over the Scots Dyke.

Looking out into the moonlit estuary, he saw someone he assumed to be Cortez moving about in one of the boats. As he watched, the boat began to move on the tide, heading for the open sea. It was almost out of sight when there was a commotion on the far bank where several clearly very angry figures appeared. The fishermen waded out into the water, clambered aboard three other craft, and set off after the Spaniard.

The scene reminded Musgrave of a hot trot. "Go on," he shouted. "I hope they drown you, Cortez, you Spanish bastard."

He felt better for having vented his feelings, but that soon gave way to a sense of shame – an emotion that until now was completely alien to him.

Hard as he tried to avoid doing so, he finally accepted the uncomfortable fact that, for the first time in his life, he had given in to fear and failed to accept a challenge. It was an unpalatable thought made worse by the still persisting suspicion that he had somehow allowed Cortez to get the better of him. Even if the fishermen caught up with him before he found the Spanish ships, the Spaniard would die knowing that he had at least tried his very best; whereas he, Musgrave, had failed miserably.

He looked around for someone, anyone, to blame and vent his anger on. But there was no one, and in frustration he cursed everybody, and again, venting his anger helped to dispel his tiredness, but he was still unable to think clearly.

Still in something of a quandary, he put on his boots, gathered up the oddments of equipment, caught up his horse and mounted. Feeling more at home in the saddle, he found that he could begin to think like a reiver. He calmed down and his reiver instints returned to remind him that reivers did not dwell on past mistakes. That kind of thinking only led to further disasters.

There was no longer any point in wasting time thinking about Cortez and his hair-brained scheme, and difficult as it was for a born reiver, he had to accept that thoughts of Spanish gold were no longer relevant. His fate was now back in his own hands. So, what to do next?

He was, of course, on the wrong side of the river and in extremely dangerous territory, but unlike the perils of the sea, this was the kind of danger he had faced and overcome many times before. Now back on familiar ground, and no longer subject to the temptation generated by thoughts of Spanish gold, he found that he could think more clearly and re-examine his options. He could go west into the Galloway Hills and find Maxwell, or let Maxwell find him, but that would lead to too many difficult questions regarding Cortez, Tam, and the Elliots. On the plus side, he now had some solid information about a Spanish landing in Scotland, and with Cortez's boots, doublet, and rapier to back it up, this could prove to be extremely valuable information indeed. But who best to sell it to? There were only Scrope or King James. Both options, however, presented their own special problems. Selling to Scrope meant making his way to Carlisle, but without knowing what fate awaited him there, that could be risky. The

English March Warden was already aware of some trouble north of the border involving Maxwell, but in Musgrave's view, it was a safe bet that he knew nothing about a Spanish landing in Scotland. With the Spanish rapier to back up his story, he should have enough to convince Scrope that he had carried out the task the warden had sent him over the border to perform, but he suspected that instead of rewarding him, the devious Scrope might simply decide to return him to a prison cell. On the other hand, approaching the king while he was in the field against Maxwell, was also fraught with danger. With their hands full hunting Maxwell, the king's men would be more likely to kill him out of hand rather than take him to talk to James.

After some further thought, he decided that while his information was of value in Carlisle, it would be worth more in Edinburgh. He no longer held Cortez as a present for the king, but he still had a plausible story backed up by the Spanish rapier, doublet and boots. All he had to do was find the right man to tell it to, and with the whole king's army in the area, that man should not be too difficult to locate. He thought that the best place to find one of the king's senior officers who might be prepared to take him seriously, rather than kill him out of hand, was at Caerlaverock, which would by now, be in the king's hands. One obvious advantage of going there was that it would save him having to avoid Maxwell's former fortress as he would have to if he decided to return to Carlisle. His best course of action was to ride boldly into the castle and relate his story to the senior officer there. If the garrison commander believed him, and he could see no reason why he should not, he could expect to receive a large reward for such valuable information. And, he told himself, a king's reward would be far greater than any likely to be on offer in Carlisle.

A lot depended on whether Cortez managed to warn the Spanish ships before the fishermen caught up with him. In a reversal of his previous thoughts, Musgrave hoped that the Spaniard would actually find the ships. On balance, no invasion at all was better than an early invasion. By the time the king realised that the Spanish were not landing, he, Musgrave, would be long gone, but if the Spanish had already landed, his information would be worthless. It was, he decided, a risk worth taking and he made up his mind accordingly. Caerlaverock it would be.

One problem, however, remained. How to get back across the river undetected? A glance told him that the tide had turned and was coming in. This time, swimming was no longer a viable option, and although he had already made up his mind, he was glad to have a legitimate excuse for dismissing it. Thinking of that, reminded him of what Cortez had said about the fishermen; if they were on the far bank, then the king's army must be on this side. That being so, the king must have already crossed with his army, but he would have left men to guard the ford. Dawn was breaking and making it too dangerous to cross in daylight, and he reluctantly decided that he would have to hide and wait for nightfall. Then, for once, his fortunes changed for the better.

He noticed the mist gathering out to sea, and even with his limited knowledge of such things, he knew that it would soon roll inland along the river. All he needed was for it to reach as far as the ford, and for him to get there before the sun burned it off. It was a risk, but the kind of risk he was accustomed to taking and he didn't hesitate. He waited for the mist to reach him, then leading the second horse, he followed it upstream. As he approached the ford, he slowed down and gazed into the fog, searching for the soldiers the king was certain to have left to guard the crossing in case any of Maxwell's riders escaped and decided to hide in the Debatable Land. He failed to locate the main group of James's men but to his relief, he noted that there were only two sentries on duty on each side of the river. They did not seem to be taking their guard duties seriously, but there was still no way of getting across without alerting them. He considered releasing the second horse and using it as a decoy, but he was reluctant to lose any part of the meagre profit he had left to show for his recent efforts.

He drew a deep breath and spurred his horse into a gallop. He charged up to the ford, yelling at the top of his voice, "King's messenger, make way for the king's messenger!"

The ruse worked. He splashed across and galloped off eastwards as if heading for Lochmaben. Once out of sight of the ford, he turned south to the coast, and on reaching it he turned east for Caerlaverock

He rode close to the Solway coast. The sun had burned off the mist but Maxwell's former stronghold was still not in sight. He knew that before long, someone would see him and question who the lone rider was, probably one of the patrols from the fortress sent out to provide a warning of any potential attack. The likelihood of an attack was practically nil, but if the man in command of the garrison knew his business, he would not take chances. Musgrave thought that it would serve his purpose better if the garrison commander was an experienced soldier; he needed a man capable of making instant decisions. To add a further element of credibility to his story, he increased his pace and rode at a gallop. He must make a good impression on whomever he spoke to at Caerlaverock, so it was essential that he demonstrate a sense of urgency in getting his information to King James.

If Musgrave was worried about the officer commanding the garrison at Caerlaverock knowing his business, he took heart from the fact that the man leading the patrol that intercepted him certainly did. In spite of his vigilance, they caught him completely by surprise.

There was no warning and none of the usual challenges, or any other sign that they had discovered him. He was completely unaware of their presence until he suddenly found himself surrounded. They were still not right on him, but with riders in front, riders to the side, and riders behind, there was no possibility of escaping them. Not that he wanted to escape, but had he wished to do so, his only option would have been to make a break towards, and eventually into, the sea. Musgrave found himself caught in what amounted to a reiver ambush. The man who had set it had clearly dealt with reivers in the past and may even have been one himself, and that, as far as the Englishman was concerned, was not a bad thing. This experienced soldier was not likely to act without thinking. A less experienced man would not have thought to lay such an effective trap, but instead, might have opted to kill him first and think about it later. There was every chance that this man would take him to a senior officer, which was exactly what Musgrave had in mind.

Once he was sure that his captive could not escape, the king's man made a further demonstration of his competence by sending out some of his men to make sure that Musgrave was alone. The Englishman sat quietly and showed no sign of resistance as the king's soldier rode close to him, took hold of his rein and handed the lead rope of the spare horse to one of his men. As he began to lead his prisoner off to Caerlaverock, he turned to look more closely at his captive. He said nothing but Musgrave detected a brief look of surprise crossing his face. It was gone almost as soon as it appeared, but it was enough to give Musgrave food for thought. It was not beyond the bounds of possibility that a man with a wealth of experience in chasing reivers would recognise the former Captain of Bewcastle. The fact that he immediately spoke quietly to one of his men and sent the rider ahead to Caerlaverock, seemed to indicate that he at least harboured some suspicions regarding the identity of his prisoner. Musgrave had planned not to say anything about his being a former English officer, or about being sent into Scotland by Lord Scrope, but if he had been recognised, it would be better to avoid suspicion by coming clean and telling the truth about who he was. And just in case that did happen, he decided to begin laying the groundwork for his plan immediately.

He rode forward to speak to the rider leading the king's patrol. "I have some vital information, which must reach King James as soon as possible."

The soldier didn't deign to reply. He merely nodded in satisfaction as Musgrave's accent confirmed his suspicions regarding his prisoner.

They rode up to the castle at Caerlaverock. The fortress, with its unique triangular layout, had been in the possession of the Maxwell family for over two centuries but was currently in the hands of King James. And it was his royal standard that now flew from the top of one of the towers standing at each of its three corners. They crossed the drawbridge over the moat and entered the castle compound through an imposing gateway. The soldier in charge ordered Musgrave to dismount while the men guarding him remained mounted. As he got down from his horse, he tried to retrieve the Spanish rapier from where he had tied it to the saddle without anyone being any the wiser, but his ruse did not escape the leader of the king's men's notice. Neither did Cortez's boots and doublet. The soldier removed them from the Spaniard's horse and once again, a look of surprise flashed across his face. He said nothing, but merely grunted and went to report to his commanding officer, taking the Spanish rapier with him.

Musgrave was made to stand and wait, but as time dragged on, he decided to reinforce the importance of the news he carried by shouting impatiently at the men guarding him in a voice loud enough to be heard throughout the castle.

"Unless someone has the brains to listen to me soon, this castle will be overrun by a Spanish army."

None of the king's soldiers took any notice, so he turned his attention to checking his immediate surroundings. Musgrave was no stranger to fortresses; over the years, he had visited more than he wanted to remember, especially those such as the castles at Lochmaben and Carlisle where he had first-hand knowledge of the dungeons. His first impression of this particular castle was one of military orderliness with everything carefully stored in its proper place. There were no bits and pieces of discarded equipment lying around as would be expected of an army in the field, and he noted how well turned out the mounted men who guarded him were. Both men and horses had been prepared as if they were forming a formal escort for someone of very high rank, and the soldiers on guard at the gate, as well as those patrolling the castle battlements, displayed an equal level of military correctness. Caerlaverock, Musgrave guessed, was under the command of a man who was a stickler for proper military discipline. But that made little difference to him, his immediate future lay in that man's hands, whoever he might be.

Before he had time to speculate further, the old soldier who had led the king's patrol reappeared. He motioned his prisoner to follow him up a spiral stone stairway and ushered him into an office similar to the one occupied by Lord Scrope at Carlisle. Musgrave found himself facing a young man wearing an ornate uniform and felt an immediate pang of disappointment. This officer was clearly not an experienced military man, but bore every sign of being a young aristocrat merely playing at being a soldier.

Musgraves's already dishevelled appearance had not been improved by the dried mud still clinging to him from his adventures on the riverbank, and the officer eyed him with obvious distain. "What is the Captain of Bewcastle doing all on his own on this side of the border, and without any prior notice to the authorities here?"

The Englishman now knew for sure that the old soldier had indeed recognised him and there was no point in denying who he was, but having taken an immediate dislike to the young man, he decided not to make it easy for him.

"I'm no longer Captain of Bewcastle."

At this, the officer turned to question the soldier, but Musgrave interrupted him. "I used to be Captain of Bewcastle, but now I perform other duties for Lord Scrope. He sent me here to find out what Lord Maxwell was up to since his return from Spain, and as for prior notice, I was given to understand that His Lordship would contact the March Warden, and as far as I know he has."

The local March Warden had not, of course, been informed, but Musgrave guessed that the officer wouldn't know that, and the young man's obvious confusion told him that he was right. The officer, however, considered that this prisoner had questioned his authority, and his dignity would not permit him to accept that. He was no longer sure of his ground but he was determined to re-establish his superiority, and to this end, he pressed on with the same line of questioning.

"You say you were sent on official business, but you didn't see fit to announce your presence yourself. Why not?"

To Musgrave this was all totally irrelevant, but again he had a ready answer. "I was captured and held prisoner by Lord Maxwell, so I couldn't announce myself to anyone. This is the first chance I've had to see anybody in authority."

Although Musgrave had been at pains to assure the young man that he actually was 'someone in authority', it was as if the officer hadn't heard a word; or if he had, he completely ignored it. "Rubbish! If you or your superior had seen fit to follow protocol, all of this would be unnecessary. As it is, I'm afraid that I will have to verify your story with the English Warden before we can take this matter any further."

In spite of having ruffled this pompous young fool's ornate feathers, the interview was not going to Musgrave's liking. This toy soldier was clearly a political appointee, someone given a commission by King James to curry favour with some rich and influential family, and appointed to the command of the captured fortress rather than being trusted with an active role in the hunt for Maxwell. Now, faced with a situation requiring him to make a real decision, all the young fool could do was rely on his privileged upbringing for guidance, and as a result, he became obsessed with protocol to the exclusion of everything else. The Englishman felt his temper begin to rise. He was tired and hungry, and after all he had been through, this idiot was going to ruin everything for him by contacting the English Warden. He had no doubt that Scrope would deny any knowledge of him and leave him to his fate, and in the meantime, he feared that unless he did something quickly, the prospects of gleaning a rich reward for his information about the Spanish would disappear into thin air.

It was time to take things into his own hands. He pointed to the Spanish rapier on the table and shouted at the young man. "Do you know what that is? It's a Spanish rapier. I took it off a Spaniard who came here with Maxwell to prepare for a Spanish landing in this part of Scotland in support of their invasion of England. And if you don't inform King James that Maxwell is in league with the Spanish, the king will have a much bigger fight on his hands than he thinks."

He paused for breath and continued. "And if you don't do it quickly, you'll have both Maxwell and the Spanish knocking on the door of this castle. And they definitely won't ask for your formal permission."

All Musgrave's aggressive stance achieved was to make the king's officer angry. The young aristocrat was not accustomed to having his authority questioned by someone of much lower social standing, and he certainly did not appreciate it coming from this insolent Englishman. He stood up, with his face growing red with indignation. The soldier who had brought Musgrave to Caerlaverock had been listening to the exchange and, while he did not fully trust the Englishman, he realised that there must be at least some truth in what he was saying, and if it was true, there could well be some important issues involved. His experience prompted him to risk offending the officer's beloved protocol, so he stepped forward and picked up the rapier. It took no more than a cursory inspection to convince him that at least this part of Musgrave's story held a degree of truth.

He turned to his commanding officer. "It's definitely a Spanish weapon like he says, sir, and I found some other foreign things on a second horse he was leading. These things are not easy to come by around here, and we should find out how he got them. Maybe we should listen to what he has to say for himself."

The young man's dignity would not allow him to accept having his authority questioned by inferior people like these, and for someone like him that took precedence over everything else. He became more determined than ever to re-establish his superiority.

"I'm well aware of what it is sergeant," he snapped. "But surely you can see that both this and the other things you saw must have been stolen. It doesn't prove anything other than that this man is a thief."

Musgrave was becoming desperate. Unless he could make this idiot listen to, and believe, his story, all of his hopes of gaining a reward here in Scotland were in ruins. It seemed that he had made a grave mistake in coming here instead of going to England, but it was too late to correct it now. All he could do was make one more attempt to get his point across to the officious young officer behind the desk.

"That's all beside the point, sir. If you fail to warn King James about Maxwell and the Spanish, you will be held responsible for what happens."

This was too much for the aristocrat turned soldier. In his mind, what Musgrave said about his being held responsible amounted to a threat, and he was not accustomed to giving in to threats! "I will not be threatened in this way by anybody, Musgrave. If you were a gentleman I would challenge you, but I do not fight duels with common thieves. If you threaten me again I'll have you hung as a spy."

Musgrave half wished that the young man would challenge him so that he could teach the arrogant clown a lesson, but that would get him nowhere. All he could do was to continue piling on the pressure in the hope that he might eventually get through to the idiot.

"I can only tell you what I've seen and heard. Whether or not you believe me, and act on it, is up to you."

"I certainly do not believe a word you say, Englishman. Do you think that you can play me for a fool? I simply refuse to contemplate that King Philip of Spain, a man I have met socially by the way, would countenance mounting an invasion of Scotland, a land ruled by his friend, King James VI. And from what the sergeant here tells me, even as Captain of Bewcastle you were nothing more than a common thief. This is clearly an English plot, and if I were going to report anything to King James, it would be just that. But unfortunately the king has returned to Edinburgh."

This was something Musgrave had not considered. It had been yet another mistake, and one that could cause a major setback to his prospects.

To rectify the situation, he desperately needed this pompous young idiot to report to somebody with the sense to listen.

"Report what you like," he replied. "As long as whoever the king left in charge knows about the danger he faces from the Spanish."

Although Musgrave did not know it, he had just made a third miscalculation. King James, thinking that the hunt for Maxwell was as good as over, had decided to return to Edinburgh and left Sir William Stewart in sole charge, and this young officer was loath to report anything at all to Stewart. In the young man's view, Stewart, a person he also viewed as his social inferior, was the man responsible for leaving him stuck here in this isolated fortress while Sir William rode off to grab all the glory for himself. The longer he remained here in Caerlaverock, the more his resentment of Sir William grew, and he had begun hatching plots to use against Stewart. One of these centred on the fact that Stewart had borrowed English siege artillery to use against Maxwell's castle at Lochmaben, and it followed that he must have friends in England. The more he thought about it, the more he convinced himself that Stewart was secretly planning something behind the king's back. That something involved the English, and now he had reason to believe that the English March Warden, Scrope, and this man, Musgrave, were participants in the plot. Until he knew more, he was not about to contact Stewart, or send him a warning about something as ridiculous as a Spanish invasion. It was time to reassert his authority and put a stop to this nonsense.

He sneered at Musgrave. "A Spanish invasion of Scotland? I've never heard such a ridiculous suggestion. But there is something afoot and I will certainly look into that."

He turned to the soldier. "In the meantime, throw this thieving Englishman in the cells."

The sergeant hesitated. He had recognised Musgrave and was aware of his chequered record as a law officer and reiver. But that was nothing unusual in The Borders. The Englishman could well be lying, but that Spanish rapier was difficult to dismiss. It might not mean much to this young man, who would have seen plenty of such fancy weapons on the Edinburgh social circuit, but it would still be worthwhile finding out how Musgrave had acquired it. He also knew Maxwell, and he was convinced that there was nothing the devious laird would not do to further his own ends, and that could well include helping the Spanish to land troops in Scotland to support their invasion of England. The very reason he and his commanding officer were here in the west of Scotland was because Maxwell had escaped from exile in Spain, and he must have had Spanish help to do that, but he knew that trying to point this out to his incompetent superior would be a complete waste of time. This so-called officer, whom he knew to be nothing more than a political appointment by the king, would not listen to anything he preferred not to hear.

So, all he could do was stand to attention. "Yes, sir."

Musgrave's entire plan was unravelling around him, and his desperation showed on his face. The sergeant feared that the Englishman might attack the young officer and, although he had no more time for the pretend soldier than Musgrave had, he could not stand by and let the Englishman harm his superior officer. He called in two of his men who grabbed the Englishman by the shoulders and manhandled him out of the officer's presence.

Outside, Musgrave was marched back down the stone steps, across the castle compound and through a door leading into a large space laid out as a barracks. The sergeant dismissed his men and turned to Musgrave. "I'll have tae lock you up, but first I'll hear what ye have tae say. If I think there's anythin' in it, I'll send riders tae check."

The approach came as a complete surprise, but it served to pacify Musgrave. "What about that young fool upstairs?" he asked.

The soldier merely shrugged his shoulders. "Forget about him. Just tell me how ye came by all this Spanish gear."

It was as much as Musgrave could hope for. "All right," he said, "but first I could do with something to eat. Something better than you serve in the cells."

For the first time, Musgrave saw the old sergeant grin. He called to one of his men to fetch some food and a drink for the Englishman, and they sat at a rough table while Musgrave ate greedily and told his story between mouthfuls. He had already decided that the nearer he kept to the truth the more believable it would be, so he told the sergeant everything except for the part played by Big Jock and the two younger Elliots. Instead, he said that he and the Spaniard had escaped when the Maxwell reivers guarding them had panicked when they spotted a large group of the king's soldiers. When asked about how he came to find out about the Spanish invasion, he explained about Cortez trying to enlist his help by bribing him with Spanish gold, but stressed that he didn't believe that the Spaniard would, or even could, keep his promise. It was only when Cortez stripped off his boots and doublet, left his horse and rapier, and swam out into the River Nith to steal a boat to go and meet the Spanish ships, that he finally believed his story.

The experienced sergeant was well aware that Musgrave would not have told him the whole truth, but what he had said was convincing enough to warrant further investigation. In view of the attitude of the idiot left in charge of Caerlaverock, it was up to him to find out more, but he would have to tread extremely carefully.

"All right, Musgrave," he said at length. "I'll send a couple o' men to try and check out yer story, but I'm not goin' to take the chance of sendin' them too far. If they're away too long I could be in trouble, and ye'll have to stay in the cells as the bairn up the stair ordered."

The only thing Musgrave could think of that might help him regain some kind of control, was to advise the sergeant. "Get your riders to ask the fishermen at the mouth of the Nith if they're missing a boat. That won't take them too long."

The sergeant nodded. He ordered two men to ride to the rivermouth to talk to the fishermen.

Musgrave was escorted down to the castle dungeon, glad that he would finally get some much-needed sleep. Meanwhile, the sergeant went to report to the garrison commander that he had the Englishman securely locked up.

Chapter 40

The moon rose, signalling that it was time for Rabbie Elliot to remount and resume his attempt to carry a vital warning to Liddesdale. Conscious of what his father had said about the need for urgency, he was determined not to waste any time, and now that he had acquired a second horse, he should be able to set a steady pace by frequently changing mounts. Since first entering the Galloway Hills with Big Jock, they had worked their way north far enough to enable him to cross the River Nith without having to use the ford, and barring accidents and delays, he estimated that he could easily reach Liddesdale within two days.

The moon was still high as he exited the foothills and entered open country. He splashed across the Nith and was in Johnstone territory, now effectively under the control of the king. He stopped to change horses, took a deep breath, and rode on. If either the Johnstones or the king's soldiers stopped him, he would have to rely on the breastplate, helmet and tabard, together with the distinctive harness on the horse he now rode, to back up his pretence of being a messenger in King James's army. If questioned, he would say that he was on his way to Langholm with a dispatch. It seemed to be straightforward enough but he was well aware that it was the flimsiest of disguises, and if his ruse failed, he was already a dead man. He pushed that disturbing thought to the back of his mind and rode with all the confidence he could muster. He worked his way south and east in the hope that he would enter the Debatable Lands south of Langholm. By daybreak, he had reached the undulating countryside he remembered from his eventful journey from Lochmaben to Caerlaverock, and by midday, he guessed that he was well on his way to the Debatable Land. What happened when he reached there would depend on how much daylight remained.

He thought that his best chance of getting through without falling foul of the bands of Broken Men who infested the area, would be during the brief period of darkness between sunset and moonrise, but that was by no means a guarantee of safety. These men owed allegiance to no one and would be attempting to profit from the turmoil currently swirling all around them. No lone rider, irrespective of whether he was a Maxwell, a Johnstone, or even one of the king's troopers, could expect safe passage should he be discovered; even being recognised as a Liddesdale Elliot would not be enough. Rabbie did not enjoy the reputation or standing of either his father or Big Jock, which meant that he was vulnerable to attack by these desperate men. His only alternative would be to ride north of Langholm, a route that would not only take longer, but would also increase the risk of capture. Langholm was in the king's hands and Jamie's men would be everywhere.

As if to reinforce that fear, his sharp reiver's eye caught a glimpse of a colourful flag, unmistakably one of the king's standards, which, at first glance, seemed to be floating in the air and moving across his path. Rabbie guessed that it was carried by a group of horsemen hidden from sight in a shallow gully. He was confident that he hadn't been seen, and his first instinct was to hide, but he decided that this could be the first of many such groups of soldiers he would meet and he couldn't possibly hope to evade them all. It was time to brave it out and put his disguise to the test. He left the Galloway Nag out of sight and rode openly on the 'king's horse' to the edge of the gully in plain view of the troop of a dozen or so riders of King James's cavalry. He had been careful to choose a position that would give him a good head start should his ruse go badly wrong and, happy that he had, he stood in the stirrups and waved to attract attention.

"Which way tae Lochmaben?" he called out to the leader of the troop.

The leading trooper looked up in surprise, saw who had called out, then turned and said something to his men. Rabbie feared that he was giving orders for his men to arrest the stranger, but the remark seemed to cause some amusement and he guessed that the captain was making fun of a new recruit who was too green to find his own way. Rabbie, who might once have taken offence at such a thing, didn't mind in the least.

The man pointed to the north. "Lochmaben is that way," he shouted back. After a short pause, he pointed to his backside and added, "and yer arse is down there."

That brought forth peals of laughter from the king's riders. Rabbie didn't wait around to take issue with them but waved his thanks and rode off in the direction indicated by the king's man.

When he was certain that the group was well out of the way, he returned and collected the Galloway Nag, crossed a burn and resumed his original route. He knew that he had been fortunate to meet a troop of soldiers led by an officer more interested in showing off to his men than in questioning an unknown rider, and he could not hope to be so lucky again. He decided to slow down and ride with more caution. It would add to the time it took to complete his mission but increase his chances of spotting any more of Jamie's men before they saw him. He managed to evade one more group and was beginning to feel that he was in the clear when, suddenly, it seemed as if his luck had run out.

Nightfall was imminent and he was almost in sight of the Debatable Land when he spotted another group of the king's men riding from north to south and showing unusual vigilance. He managed to hide, intending to wait until they had ridden on, but, to his dismay, they simply rode a little further south before turning and retracing their steps. Puzzled at first, he watched and then realised what they were doing; they were patrolling the border of the Debatable Land, presumably to prevent any survivors from Maxwell's band from riding to hide among the Broken Men or one of the reiver families somewhere to the east. If that was true, and he was sure that it was, there would be other groups linking up with this one to ensure that they covered the entire length of the Scottish half of the Debatable Land. The king's men clearly intended to keep up their watch all night and he thought that his chances of stealing past them, even in the dark, were extremely low. This totally unexpected obstacle required him to rethink his original plan, and he had almost decided that he would have to retrace his steps and take the long way home north of Langholm, when he had an idea. There would be risks attached, but then there were risks attached to whatever he did, so he decided to give it a go.

He again relied on the tactic that had by now become almost second nature to him and found a place to hide in a gully by a burn where he could spend the night. What he planned to do would not work in the dark, or even in moonlight. Contrary to his recent practice, this time he actually wanted to be clearly visible. He dismounted, watered his horses and allowed them to rest and graze, then refreshed himself with water from the burn. He could barely remember when he had last eaten, but the excitement generated by what he was about to attempt, banished all thoughts of hunger. In spite of the need to reach Liddesdale as soon as possible, he settled down to wait out the night. Sleep was out of the question and time dragged its feet. The night seemed interminably long until, finally, dawn began to turn to early morning and it was time to go. He gambled that the riders of king's patrols, having kept up their watch all night, would not be fully awake. He prepared to ride but he knew he could only use one of the horses. Leading a spare mount would slow him down. The Galloway Nag, bred for reiving, had almost unlimited endurance but did not have a high turn of speed; the horse he had taken from the king's watcher was faster but did not enjoy the same level of stamina. He opted for speed.

He divested himself of the cumbersome breastplate, helmet and, reluctantly, the lance. Pretending to be one of the king's men would not help him here, a lone rider; even a king's messenger, would have no business entering the Debatable Land. He mounted and rode cautiously to a ridge overlooking what he judged to be the edge of the Debatable Land and stopped. One of the king's patrols was approaching from the north. A shout went up. They had seen him. He hesitated as if in surprise, then spurred the horse into motion and galloped down the slope and into the Debatable Land. Once he was sure that he was into the disputed territory, he turned to see if the king's men intended to follow him. They did. The leader of the patrol clearly had orders to apprehend anyone seen riding into or out of the Debatable Land, and had dispatched three of his men to apprehend the unknown rider. Rabbie's plan was working. The Broken Men would steer well clear of any situation involving a number of King James's soldiers and so he would not have to worry about them. All he had to do now was to keep ahead of his pursuers until he reached the River Esk, which he knew ran diagonally across the Debatable Land. It would not be easy but if he could cross it as far to the east as possible, he thought he would be safe.

They were gaining on him and he urged the horse to greater efforts. He had to be out of the Debatable Land before they caught up with him. Only then would he be safe. It was unlikely that the three king's men would cross the Esk and venture into the lands of the reiver families; if they did, they could not be sure of getting out alive. He still had to outrun them and that was becoming more unlikely by the minute. He dared not look back again but concentrated on what was ahead. With his heart pounding, he squeezed every last modicum of speed from his horse and galloped desperately on. A pistol shot from behind sent a ball whistling past his head, and was enough to tell him that they were gaining on him. He almost gave up hope and began thinking of how best to fight for his life. His pistol was empty. He was out of powder and, having discarded his lance, he had only his ballock dagger. It was hopeless. They were almost on him by the time he reached the River Esk.

Then the mad race ended with such suddenness it took Rabbie completely by surprise.

On the far bank, were a band of heavily armed riders partially hidden in a stand of trees. To his immense relief, he recognised the riders. They were Armstrongs and, to Rabbie's delight, a few Elliots who recognised him were riding with them. King James's riders saw them and immediately gave up the chase. He was home!

***

Compared to his brother, Sandy had a much less eventual journey home, but his chosen route meant a longer ride requiring much greater care. There were hostile riders all around him and he was constrained to riding at night and hiding as best he could during the day, but he constantly reminded himself of the importance of getting his father's warning through to Martin Elliot of Braidley. He expected either his father or Rabbie to get there before him as they were taking a much shorter route through the Debatable Land, but that way was fraught with danger and it might still be up to him.

In case anything prevented his father or brother from getting through, and he could think of several possible ways that things could go badly wrong for them, he had to be the one to make certain of reaching Liddesdale. His responsibility was to get through irrespective of how long it took.

Like his brother, he waited for moonlight before making his way cautiously north. He knew little about the country north of the Galloway Hills except that it was Douglas territory. Up there, he would be a long way from home with no real knowledge of the country or the dangers it might hold. Still, the way things currently were in The Borders, it would be safer than making his way home via Johnstone territory. In spite of the need for urgency, he knew that he had to err on the side of caution.

On the first night of his ride, he kept to low ground and managed to avoid all human contact. He hid during the day and was relieved not to be disturbed. To his surprise, he saw far fewer riders than he expected and the only reason he could think of for that, was that most of Jamie's army must have moved further to the south and west. Therefore, on the second night of his journey, although he was still in the Galloway Hills, he decided that it would be safe to edge his way further east. In the early dawn, he almost came to regret that decision. To the east, he spotted several small bands of the king's riders, but his caution paid off and he went undiscovered. At first, he put his success at evading them down to good fortune, but then he realised that they were all marching south, which reinforced his thought that something important was happening down there. He took a chance and rode to the top of a broom-covered hill from where he had a better view of the countryside to the east. The morning sun had risen high enough for him to see without shading his eyes, and from the north east, where the fortress of Lochmaben lay, he could see what appeared to be yet more of King James's army marching south with banners flying. The riders he had seen earlier were patrols sent from the main body.

Sandy could only guess at what had caused the king to move what must be his entire army south, but the most obvious answer was that Jamie had finally cornered Maxwell and was intent on inflicting a crushing defeat on his errant laird, in which case the king could afford to weaken the garrison at Lochmaben Castle. Sandy felt that he could change his tactics and take a faster route home, but he had the disturbing thought that his father and Rabbie, having taken the southern route, might still be in the area controlled by the king. If they had not managed to get away by now, they would have great difficulty in avoiding what amounted to a significant part of the king's army, and his first instinct was to turn around and ride to look for them. But he knew that he could not. Even if he found Alexander and Rabbie and helped them home, his father certainly would not thank him for it. His task was to carry the warning to Liddesdale, and he must allow nothing to stop him.

He waited until the king's soldiers were out of sight before riding openly for home. He followed roughly the same route his father had taken when he rode to find his missing sons and circled around north of Lochmaben. Two days later, as he entered the hills to the north of Liddesdale he spotted a large group of riders. To his relief, he recognised them as men from Liddesdale sent out to find him and escort him home. Meeting these riders answered his first question. Rabbie had already reached Liddesdale safely and delivered his father's warning. In answer to his second question, however, the riders admitted that his father had not yet returned. Alexander's late arrival was causing some concern but they had every confidence in their heidsman, and Liddesdale had received his warning about a possible attack by King James. Bands of riders were once again out watching for any aggressive move by the king, and this time, unlike when Sandy, Rabbie and Big Jock had performed a similar duty, they rode out in strength in case their hiedsman needed help. And if that meant riding into Dumfriesshire, they were quite prepared to do it.

At Alexander's tower, their mother made very little attempt to conceal her joy at having both Malcolm and Robert safely home. Once the reunions were complete, they looked forward to the return of their father. But having waited for nearly a week without any news, it became increasingly clear that something serious must have happened to delay the hiedsman and Sandy feared that, with their father still missing, Rabbie might once again suffer pangs of conscience and blame himself for what had occurred.

He could easily imagine his brother still feeling that had he not been so stubbornly set on chasing after the Englishman, Musgrave, none of this would have happened. He knew that it was up to him to reassure his brother that he was not responsible for the actions of either Maxwell, Musgrave or King Jamie. He took Rabbie aside and found that he was right about him still harbouring a deep sense of guilt. He realised that trying to persuade his brother that he was blameless, would be a waste of time and so, he adopted a different approach and forcibly reminded Rabbie of what was really at stake here. Feeling guilty about something that had already happened would be of no help to their father now, and would only make things worse for everybody. It was best that they kept what had happened strictly to themselves. Until the heidsman returned, his riders would look to his sons to lead them. It would do no good whatsoever to let people know that one of them blamed himself for their father's loss, and consequently start a spate of dangerous rumours that would soon spread far beyond Liddesdale. Eventually, Sandy managed to convince his brother that what had happened should remain their secret and it was a sign of Rabbie's growing maturity, that he accepted his advice and was prepared to put Liddesdale first.

They waited for a further anxious two days after Sandy's return before Martin Elliot of Braidley rode up to the tower to break the dreadful news. Alexander Elliot had been captured by Jamie's men and was a prisoner at Caerlaverock. Presumably to await execution as a reiver.

Chapter 41

In Carlisle, Lord Scrope was having sleepless nights. A constant barrage of messages from Walsingham was giving him nightmares. The spymaster kept appraising him of the situation and expressing confidence in an English victory, but a victory that was possible only if he, Scrope, remained alert and defeated the expected secondary invasion on the north coast of his March.

It was not Walsingham's messenges alone, however, that interfered with his sleep. Based on what he had learned, and had guessed, about Maxwell and King James, he had taken the important decision to ignore the spymaster's assessment. He staked his future, and with it his head, on the supposition that the secondary Spanish invasion would take place, not in the English West March, but in Scotland, and he laid his plans accordingly. This plan called for him to keep his meagre forces at Carlisle and prepare to march against a combined Spanish and Scottish invasion force at a moment's notice.

He reviewed his prospects of success but found only further cause for loss of sleep. If he was right and England prevailed as Walsingham predicted, he would be a hero; but if he was wrong and the Spanish landed in his March, even if England prevailed, he could still lose his head for disobeying Walsingham. If England lost, it would not matter much either way.

He had no time to spare a thought for the man he had sent into Scotland. Whether his former Captain of Bewcastle was alive or dead was immaterial; Musgrave had outlived his usefulness, and if he ever returned to Carlisle, he would find himself back in the castle dungeon.

***

Far to the south of Carlisle, the 130 ships of the great Spanish Armada carrying 30,000 men, 180 priests, and thousands of barrels of wine, entered the English Channel. Immediately the enemy ships were in sight, a series of beacons sprang to life all along the south coast. This early warning system was the one aspect of the English preparations that worked well, and the entire country was soon on the alert and standing to arms to repel the expected invasion. Nevertheless, experienced heads in England knew that not all the preparations were equally effective. In spite of urgent pleas from her advisers, Queen Elizabeth's noted penury would allow for nothing more than the minimum supplies of men and material.

There were, however, also reasons for concern on the Spanish side. To de Recalde's dismay, the Duke of Medina Sidonia again stubbornly refused to attack the English ships anchored in Plymouth Sound. An experienced commander would have seen that, with both wind and tide against them, the English would find themselves trapped in the great harbour. Instead, Medina Sidonia, adhering rigidly to King Philip's plan, continued up the Channel and his planned rendezvous with the Duke of Palma off The Netherlands coast.

The English, under Lord Howard of Effingham, supported by Admirals Drake, Hawkins and Frobisher, eventually managed to escape from Plymouth, and profiting from their good fortune, were now behind the armada with both wind and tide in their favour. The battle proper began, and the more manoeuvrable English ships harried the Spanish all the way up the Channel in a series of hit and run attacks, refusing to allow them to resort to their favoured tactic of closing with, and boarding, enemy vessels. But the armada sailed on in classic crescent formation with the larger and slower ships in the centre surrounded by the lighter faster vessels, and in spite of expending copious amounts of powder and shot, the English failed to break the formation. De Recalde again attempted to get Sidonia to land a force on the Isle of Wight but was again overruled, and the armada sailed past an inviting and lightly defended invasion site. De Recalde despaired as another opportunity was lost, but in spite of their tactical mistakes, the Spanish had lost very few ships and he began to take heart. The great crusade to rid England of its Protestant Queen might just succeed after all.

His optimism soon proved to be misplaced. With no word coming from the Duke of Palma regarding his readiness to cross the English Channel and mount the invasion, Medina Sidonia decided to enter Calais to wait for news. De Recalde's heart sank. In a complete reversal of what had happened earlier, the Spanish now found themselves trapped in port, and at the mercy of whatever the English decided to do; and what the English did decide to do, proved to be decisive. Under Admiral Drake, they attacked the anchored armada with fireships, forced them to escape the port in complete disorder, and won a decisive victory over them at the Battle of Gravelines. The great crusade was over.

The Spanish fled up the Channel and into the North Sea. It was their only possible escape route but it was far from being the end of their troubles; it took them around the perilous north coast of Scotland and down the rugged west coast of Ireland, and there they lost half their ships as storms drove them to destruction on the rocky shores.

As second in command, de Recalde had little time to spare for thoughts about what had happened to the Scottish element of King Philip's grand design. If the king's scheme to land troops there was successful, and if the bandit, Maxwell, was as good as his word, then it might have helped, but he doubted it. He was not responsible for allowing Maxwell to return to Scotland or for agreeing with the devious Scotsman's plan to mount a second invasion of England from there with the Scotsman's help. King Philip had taken the decision in person, and de Recalde had no reason to blame himself.

What he was responsible for, however, was sending Don Juan Cortez to keep Maxwell in line. If that element of the grand plan had also failed, and he fully expected that it had, he prayed that Cortez had somehow survived. His duty now was to save his ship and the men who sailed in her. He concentrated on that, and so was unaware that his prayer had already been answered.

***

Maxwell, too, was a worried man. He had riders posted all along the Solway coast on the lookout for Spanish ships, but so far, none had appeared. The king's army was advancing ever closer and he was being pushed further and further west. If he went too far west he would be cut off from Kirkcudbright, the proposed Spanish landing site, and his scheme to defeat the invaders and ingratiate himself with King James, would end in abject failure. Instead of being hailed as a hero, he would probably be hung from the walls of Edinburgh Castle, and even if he managed to evade the hangman's noose, his chances of ever being reinstated as a March Warden would be reduced to nil. His time was running out; men who had joined him from local reiver bands simply for the plunder he had promised, were not prepared to risk their lives in a battle with either the Spanish or King James, and certainly not based on Maxwell's vague promise of Spanish gold. They were giving up and going home; as reivers, they did not live on promises, but on plunder they could see and feel. Soon, all he would have left were the members of his own reiver family.

If all else failed, Maxwell thought that he could hide out indefinitely in the hills and forests of Galloway, and survive on the spoils of some basic reiving in the rich farmland to the north, but his days as a feared reiver lord would be over. For Maxwell, that would be unbearable, but giving up now was unthinkable. He had come too far and paid too much. So far, the enterprise had cost him his three fortresses, but in spite of the many setbacks, he was determined to get them back. He continued to place his faith on a Spanish landing and, even if he was no longer in a position to support the king, there was a distinct possibility that James might be satisfied with having beaten off a Spanish invasion and take his army back to Edinburgh. With his designs on the English throne, the king might well choose to bask in the glory he would gain from helping to defend his future realm and forget about what was happening in his own country.

Unfortunately for Maxwell, he soon found that this was nothing more than wishful thinking. To his complete dismay, his watchers reported that a single Spanish ship had been seen entering the Solway Firth shielded by an early morning sea mist, but when the mist cleared the ship was gone. The Spanish invasion he had staked his future on, was over before it had even begun.

Whether or not the king learned of the lone Spanish ship was immaterial; even if James returned to Edinburgh now, he would leave Sir William Stewart to clear things up in his West March, and Maxwell knew Sir William of old. That man never gave up, and he would not rest until he had him, Maxwell, in chains.

Chapter 42

Alexander Elliott decided to put the plan he had kept secret from his sons into action.

He had found his sons alive and well and helped them to escape from King James's soldiers. They were still in grave danger, not only from the king's riders but also from Maxwell. Even if the laird himself were to be killed or captured, hundreds of his followers would escape and be free to carry on reiving. They would also be looking for revenge for their failure, and ready to exact it from anybody and everybody. That, however, was a constant in The Borders, and Alexander had a much more pressing concern on his mind: the one involving the death of Big Jock.

He was convinced that Big Jock had given his life so that Sandy and Rabbie would have a chance to escape. Such a noble sacrifice by his old friend was one for which he would be eternally grateful, but thinking about that would have to wait. A more important issue was that he found it impossible to believe that the old reiver's body would escape recognition, and the discovery of such a well-known Elliot in the Galloway Hills would lead the king and his advisors to jump to the conclusion that the Elliots were in league with Maxwell. Once James had dealt with his errant laird, he would turn his attention to teaching the Elliots a lesson, and that would inevitably involve the whole of Liddesdale. This, Alexander realised, would not be one of Jamie's, or Bothwell's, periodic forays to curb the activities of the Liddesdale reiving families, but with his blood up following success against Maxwell, the king would set out to finish the job once and for all. James would ride into the valley with his entire army, and following the recent battle with Bothwell, Liddesdale would not be strong enough to withstand such an attack. Alexander knew that it was up to him to do his best to prevent that. But how?

Back in the hideout while concentrating on ways of escaping from the king's riders, the problem was still troubling his mind, but by the time they had split up and broken away from the king's riders, he had found what he believed to be the only solution. He had seen enough of the way his sons had developed into men who could stand on their own two feet to be confident that they could make their own way home, and carry a warning to Liddesdale for him. His responsibility was to provide them with a suitable diversion, but more than that, he had thought of a way of ensuring that even if both Sandy and Rabbie failed to reach home, he could still prevent King Jamie from sacking Liddesdale. It was a drastic solution, and one that he knew he had to keep secret from his sons, but he was sure he could carry it off, and if he could, it would have the added benefit of ensuring that Big Jock's death had not been in vain.

There was an enormous risk attached to what he was proposing to do, but it was a risk he was fully prepared to take.

When he had explained his own role in the plan for escaping from the king's riders, he told his sons only what he thought they would readily accept. He would make his break to the south, double back north, and when night fell, ride for home. He had not told them an outright lie, and under different circumstances he might have felt uneasy about not telling them the whole truth, but in this situation that was impossible. He knew that if he explained his whole scheme, he would never be able to persuade them to agree with it and they would waste time trying to argue him out of it. That would mean that their chances of death or capture by the king's riders would increase to a virtual certainty.

As it was, his sons had simply nodded their agreement, quite confident that their reiver father could easily give his pursuers the slip in the dark, double back, and make his way home.

The king's riders, alerted by Sandy and Rabbie's sudden break out of the bushes, spurred forward. They were almost on Alexander when, with a wild reiver yell, he burst out of the bushes, careered down the hill, crossed over the burn, and galloped up the incline on the far side. At the crest of the ridge, he reined in and turned round to make sure that the majority of the king's riders were following. To his satisfaction, he found that they were. The leader of the pursuers was clearly an experienced officer and Alexander guessed that he was following a strict plan. The officer's orders were probably to search out and capture one of the scouts Maxwell was bound to have in the area, alive if possible, and he naturally thought that the three men he had surprised must be the scouts he was looking for. He sent two riders after the man riding west into the Galloway Hills, but with a warning that unless they caught him quickly, they were to turn back. That was still very much Maxwell territory and he did not want to lose men needlessly, or worse, have them held as hostages. The man riding east he effectively dismissed, the watcher on the nearest hill seemed to have him well covered, and in any case, he was heading away from his reiver friends and into an area completely controlled by the king. The man riding south was a different matter; there was something vaguely familiar about him and he assumed that he had seen him with Maxwell while the laird was still a March Warden. If he was right, his quarry must be an important member of the rebel army and he concentrated his efforts on capturing him.

It was everything Alexander had hoped for and he concentrated on leading them south. His plan was working and he had given his sons a fighting chance. The rest was up to them.

The further he chased his quarry south, the more certain the leader of the king's riders became that he could catch him. Sir William Stewart was assembling a large army on the narrow plain between the hills and the coast in preparation for his final drive to capture Maxwell, and by nightfall, the officer was satisfied that the only way his quarry could escape was by doubling back in the period of dense darkness between nightfall and moonrise. He halted the pursuit and stationed his men in a line across the most likely route his quarry would take if he attempted to double back on him. To cover sufficient ground, his men had been spaced further apart than he would have liked but there was no need for them to hide; it was better for his quarry to see them and get the impression that every possible route back was securely blocked. He lived through a couple of anxious hours before the moon rose, and once it had, he doubted that the Maxwell man he was chasing would attempt anything.

Alexander, however, in spite of what he had told his sons, did not intend to turn back. He did carefully scout a little way in that direction to make sure that the man chasing him did as he thought he would, and was on the lookout for such a move. Satisfied that he would not be disturbed, he settled down for a few short hours' sleep. Sleep, however, would not come and he spent the night fretting over what would happen in the morning. A voice kept telling him that he could not trust the people he planned to meet and reminded him of the treachery he had witnessed after the recent surrender at Lochmaben. But he refused to listen. There was still time to change his mind and make his way home, which he had every confidence he could do, but he had a responsibility to do everything he could to ensure that his sons got home safely, and as an Elliot hiedsman, he bore a duty to the whole family, particularly those in Liddesdale. He was well aware that there was plenty of scope for his plan to go completely awry, but he had no choice but to adhere to it.

It was still dark when he mounted, although the stars told him that dawn was imminent. It was necessary to get a head start in case his pursuers took up the chase at first light, and to fall into their hands before he put the rest of his plan into operation, would spell disaster. He rode south towards the sea, always aware that his pursuers were part of a much bigger and well-organised army. He kept a careful lookout for the other patrols the commander of the king's forces would inevitably have in the area, but at this time of the early morning, they were not keeping the most diligent of watches and he managed to evade them with ease. As dawn broke, his keen reivers' nose picked up the smell of peat smoke and soon afterwards he could smell cooking. The amount of smoke and the strength of the smell pointed to there being a sizeable army encampment close by, and he dismounted and inched his way towards it. Soon he could see their banners against the lightening sky and riding a little further forward and he spotted the sentries. To his satisfaction, they were all foot soldiers. By now, he was as close as he could get without them seeing him, so he remounted and galloped past the startled guards straight into the encampment as if he belonged there. He halted in the middle of a large open space set among the impressive array of tents, horse lines, wagons, artillery pieces, and stores.

All of which pointed to this encampment housing a major element of King James's army.

It took only a minute for the king's men to react, and Alexander found himself surrounded by a squad of four soldiers, all of them armed with long-barrelled firearms.

"My name is Alexander Elliot," he said to the man who seemed to be the most senior among them. "And I have important information for whoever is the hiedsman here."

A man ran off and reappeared with an officer. Alexander was aware of most military ranks by name, but that was the full extent of his knowledge. He had no idea of how to distinguish one rank from another but this man seemed to be important enough for his purposes.

The officer looked up at him. "You're Alexander Elliot you say? The reiver from Liddesdale?"

"I am."

The officer was clearly sceptical. "If that's true, what are you doing here in Galloway?"

"I'm lookin' for ma sons, Malcolm an' Robert. They were taken for hostages by Maxwell."

Alexander could see that the officer didn't believe a word, but that was no more than he had expected. The man clearly knew his name, but that was known and feared all over The Borders. Nevertheless, the chances of finding him here in the middle of the war between Maxwell and the king were remote to say the least.

"And did you find your sons?" he asked.

"I did."

"Then I have to ask you again, what are you doing here?"

"I have something tae say tae the hiedsman here."

The man's calm assurance and the fact that he had been unable to rattle him, was beginning to annoy the officer. "I don't believe a word you say. The real Alexander Elliot would never be stupid enough to ride openly into one of His Majesty's encampments. So, if you value your life, you had better tell me who you really are."

"I'm Alexander Elliot o' Liddesdale. An' if ye value yon fancy uniform ye're wearin' ye'll find someone who knows me, so that I can gi' him ma news."

Other men were by now gathering to see what was happening. As the officer was about to order Alexander taken prisoner, he heard an astonished voice behind him: "Christ! That looks like Alexander Elliot."

The officer turned and demanded to know who had spoken. A man who was not wearing the king's uniform, stepped forward. Asked how he knew this man was the infamous reiver, the man replied that he was a Johnstone rider and he had seen Elliot on several occasions at Truce Days. This was enough to convince the king's officer. He ordered Alexander to dismount and give up his weapons. Alexander hesitated, giving up his horse and arms was not something a reiver did readily, and inwardly, he began to harbour doubts about the wisdom of what he was doing. He thought about making a break for freedom, but it was clear that he would not live to reach the entrance to the encampment. He fully expected that whatever happened he would die within the next few days, but he must at all costs remain alive until he had done what he came here to do, which left him with little option but to comply.

The officer turned to his men. "I have to report this. In the meantime, guard him well."

He strode off, leaving Alexander surrounded by an increasing number of curious, but alert, king's soldiers. He did not have long to wait. The group of soldiers suddenly began to drift away, leaving only the men guarding him. The reason for their sudden loss of curiosity became immediately apparent. Approaching them was an imposing figure Alexander remembered from Lochmaben, Sir William Stewart.

The man who commanded the king's army instantly recognised Alexander, and came directly to the point. "I must admit, Mr Elliot, it comes as something of a surprise to find someone like you in my camp and without a band of your thieving kinsmen. Are the Elliots in league with Maxwell now? At one time or another you have been allied with just about every other reiver family in The Borders."

"We're no' ridin' wi' Maxwell," Alexander answered.

"So why else would you be here in Maxwell territory?"

Alexander pointed at the officer who had first questioned him. "Like I told him, I came to find ma sons after that bastard Maxwell took them as hostages."

"Then where are these sons of yours now?"

"On their way hame. They got away frae Lochmaben when you took the place wi' the help o' the English."

Stewart laughed. "You mean to tell me that two young boys managed to escape from someone like Maxwell. You'll have to do better than that, Elliot."

Alexander realised that Stewart was testing him. Sir William knew more about what had happened at Lochmaben than he was prepared to say, but he wanted to see if this reiver was telling him the whole truth. Alexander, however, thought that he could make this work in his favour by giving him the opportunity to play his trump card.

"They had the help o' Big Jock, an' the Englishman, Musgrave." He paused for effect before adding: "An' there was a Spanish gentleman there too."

Sir William's surprise showed. "A Spaniard? What on earth would a Spaniard be doing here?"

"From what I heard, he came here frae Spain wi' Maxwell. They're expectin' some Spanish ships tae come wi' soldiers tae help him against King Jamie."

This answer had the desired effect. Sir William's face clearly showed that the mention of a Spaniard and Spanish ships had come as something of a shock. He knew about Big Jock Elliot being in the area, and he had heard something about the Captain of Bewcastle having escaped from Carlisle after being caught reiving, but the Spanish? That was something entirely new to him. To cover his confusion, and to give himself time to think, he decided not to mention it just yet.

"Ah yes. Big Jock. I heard about him. He was killed in an attack on one of my patrols. You were also involved, and if you are not in league with Maxwell, why attack the king's men?"

Alexander shrugged his shoulders. "We thought they were Maxwell riders, an' anyhow it was your riders who attacked us first. I suppose they took us for Maxwell men too."

To Stewart this made sense enough. He was satisfied that it was highly unlikely for the Elliots to be in league with Maxwell, but two questions still required answers. One concerned that mysterious Spaniard; the second, and equally mystifying, was why would a reiver with Alexander Elliot's record of plundering on both sides of the border, ride openly into a royal encampment seemingly without a care in the world. He strongly suspected that these two puzzles were connected but he needed time to work out how.

"Keep this man under close guard," he ordered. "I'll speak with him again after breakfast." With that, he turned on his heel and strode off to his tent to consult with his senior officers.

The royal army encampment, being merely a temporary one, did not include a guardhouse and Alexander had to remain standing out in the open guarded by a group of armed soldiers, and if the idea was to make him lose patience and do something rash, it was not going to work. He was conscious that he had been extremely lucky to find such a high-ranking member of the king's army at the first time of asking, and he knew that mention of the Spaniard, had definitely aroused Sir William Stewart's interest, which was more than it might have done with a junior officer. In addition, the longer the king's commander took to mull it over, the better it would be for Alexander who hoped that it would divert Stewart from delving too deeply into what the Elliots were doing in Maxwell territory. His hopes that any assumptions Stewart might have made about the Elliots being in league with Maxwell being discarded, were looking better; and any delay bought that much more time for Sandy and Rabbie to get safely home.

There was, of course, another reason for his patience. A reiver riding boldly into the midst of the king's army could hardly expect to escape with his life, irrespective of how important the information he carried, and he was content to wait for however long it took Stewart to make up his mind.

Sir William eventually sent for him. He and another man, Alexander recognised as Laird Johnstone, were waiting for him in Stewart's ornate tent, presumably to ply him with further questions. Alexander was, of course, familiar with who and what Johnstone was. In the true tradition of The Borders, and although currently the local March Warden, Johnstone was, like Maxwell, a reiver lord. Knowing the history of the years of bitter feuding between the Maxwells and the Johnstones, it came as no surprise to find Johnstone riding with the king, but there being currently no bad blood between the Elliots and the Johnstones, the two men simply nodded cordially to each other. Sir William was well aware of both men's history as reivers but he had something more important on his mind than the relationship between two well-known reiver families.

He looked sternly at Alexander. "Tell me again what you know about this Spaniard, and his association with Maxwell."

Alexander again recounted what he had gleaned from his sons.

When he finished, Johnstone spoke for the first time. "So you didn't see him yourself?"

"No," Alexander replied, and added testily, "But my sons are no' given tae lyin', so I know what they said is true."

Sir William sensed trouble brewing. Inter-family feuds had flared up over less, and he decided to nip this one in the bud. "Do you know what might have happened to him after he left your sons?"

Alexander shrugged. "All I ken is that he was taken prisoner by yon Englishman, Musgrave."

"And what do you think Musgrave did with him?" Johnstone asked.

"Ye ken yon Captain o' Bewcastle as well as I dae. He's a canny bastard an' whatever he does he'll make sure there's something for himsel' in it."

Sir William took some time to digest this. Eventually, he came to a decision. "All right, Elliot, Colonel Johnstone and I will look into this matter further, and while we do, you will be securely held in Caerlaverock. I will be marching west to deal with Maxwell once and for all, and I will ensure that I have sufficient force to deal with any help he gets from Spain."

Alexander could not help smiling at the thought of Stewart addressing the reiver lord as 'Colonel' Johnstone, but he supposed that, while in the service of the king, the laird had to be honoured with a suitably senior military rank.

Sir William called back the guards. Alexander was ushered out of the tent by Johnstone and again made to stand and wait under guard. While he remained calm on the outside, internally he was beginning to grow anxious about the briefness of the initial interview. He had expected a much more in-depth questioning and he had even entertained a slight hope that an extended session with Sir William, might give him an opportunity to negotiate a safe passage back to Liddesdale based on his volunteering the information about the Spaniard. But it was not to be, and although he had always known that it was at best an extremely slim hope, he was nevertheless disappointed.

All around him, the king's army were preparing to move out and mount the final thrust against Maxwell, and Sir William would soon be leaving with them. He would want to be the one to strike the final blow. Amid all of the activity, Alexander felt as if they had forgotten all about him, and that this was the best chance he could expect to get if he decided to make a break for freedom, but tempting as it was, that would spoil everything. If he did somehow manage to escape, it would only increase the risk of an attack on Liddesdale. When Stewart came to recapture him, as he surely would, he would come in force. So he stood patiently and waited, prepared to stand there for as long as necessary. Riders came and went, and he passed the time by trying to guess what orders they might be following, but the results of his speculation did little to excite his interest. He watched idly as another small troop of riders galloped into the camp, but suddenly realised that this time they were showing much greater urgency than usual. The man in charge spoke briefly to the officer who had first questioned Alexander. The officer listened and immediately led the rider away to Sir William Stewart's tent. He was clearly the bearer of important news and Alexander's heart sank. He feared that either the king's soldiers or Maxwell's reivers had killed or captured one of his sons.

He was still worried when 'Colonel' Johnstone stalked out of Sir William's tent showing every sign of being an angry man. He assembled a sizeable troop of his own riders, including the men who had just ridden in. He directed Alexander to mount and led the way out of the camp, still clearly not a happy man. Alexander could easily guess the reason for Johnstone's anger. He would have set his heart on riding with Stewart to witness the capture of his archrival, Maxwell, but instead, Stewart had ordered him to escort Alexander Elliot, a man he bore no particular grudges against, to Caerlaverock; and there was not a thing the frustrated March Warden, now 'Colonel', could do about it. In this instance, the honorary rank of ‘Colonel’ had not worked in Johnstone’s favour; it obliged him to follow his commander’s orders.

Even so, Alexander thought that it must have taken a powerful argument on Sir William’s part to persuade Johnstone to ride to Caerlaverock and the only reason he could think of was that they already knew a great deal more about the Spanish than they were saying.

The briefness of his meeting with Sir William seemed to back up that theory, and an extremely worried Alexander feared that the information could only have come from his sons.

Chapter 43

Musgrave's cell door opened, the sergeant entered and thrust a bowl of thick broth into the prisoner's hands.

"Drink that quick, somebody wants a talk wi' ye."

The Englishman was grateful for the hot soup. This was not the first time since he had locked Musgrave up in the dungeon that the soldier had surreptitiously supplemented his prisoner's meagre rations, but was careful to do so behind the young garrison commander's back.

Probably due to the young aristocrat's obsession with protocol, conditions here were much better than Musgrave had experienced in either Carlisle or Lochmaben. The cell was clean and the straw was fresh, but a castle dungeon was still a castle dungeon and the food served here was no better than in any of the others. Not knowing for how long he would remain incarcerated, the last thing the Englishman wanted to do was to get his supplier of extra food into trouble so he drank the broth quickly and handed the bowl back to the sergeant.

For nearly two days since he locked Musgrave up, the sergeant had been a worried man. He had been as good as his word and sent riders to talk to the fishermen at the mouth of the River Nith, but having no wish to end up in the dungeon with the Englishman, he dare not risk the garrison commander finding out that he had acted behind his back. He had given his men strict instructions to be back by early the following morning, which should have given them ample time to ride to the Nith, question the fishermen, and ride back. That, however, was almost two days ago and still the riders had not returned. Musgrave could see that the soldier was worried, but the man's anxiety did not rub off on him. To his mind, the delay to the sergeant's riders could only mean one thing: they had discovered something important, and that implied that the fishermen had confirmed his story about Cortez stealing a boat to sail out and warn the Spanish ships. He tried to console the sergeant by telling him this, but the soldier replied that if that had been the case, one of his men would have come back to report it, and soon he would have to face the problem of explaining to the garrison commander why two of his men were missing.

This morning, however, the sergeant seemed to be in a much lighter mood and Musgrave thought that the riders must have returned. There had been a disturbance late last evening with the arrival of a large band of horsemen accompanied by a loud authoritative voice issuing orders, and shortly afterwards someone had been marched down to the dungeon and locked in a cell. The prisoner must have been someone of importance because the guard had been strengthened, which prevented the Englishman from communicating with his new neighbour.

"Are they back?" he asked. "And did they find out that I was telling the truth?"

"They came back last night with Colonel Johnstone and a whole troop o' his own riders, and they brought a prisoner," the sergeant answered. "But my lads were sent oot again wi' some o' Johnstone's men before I had a chance to ask them, so I don't know what they found oot. Anyway, there must be somethin' big goin' on, big enough for someone like Johnstone tae be sent here."

That there was 'something big' going on could mean anything, and Musgrave needed more information. "Do you think that they might have found out that I was telling the truth about the Spaniard?"

The sergeant merely shrugged. "I dinna ken, they don't tell me everythin'."

It was clear to Musgrave that he was not going to get anything out of the sergeant and he gave up trying. Like Alexander Elliot, he grinned at hearing Johnstone addressed as 'Colonel'.

"Johnstone? Would that be Lord Johnstone the March Warden?" he asked.

"Aye it would be," the sergeant answered.

Musgrave's spirits rose. He knew Lord Johnstone and, more importantly, Johnstone knew him and could vouch for him. That idiot in command here would have to listen to him now. His plans were back on track.

"So the clown in charge wants to see me again, does he? He'll have to listen now, but I don't suppose he'll bring himself to apologise for locking me up without good reason."

"It's not him that wants tae talk tae ye," the sergeant replied. "The bairn was sent back tae Edinburgh tae be wi' the king. Colonel Johnstone is in command here th' noo."

There was a definite note of relief in the sergeant's tone as he gave Musgrave the news about the young aristocrat, and the Englishman's pleasure clearly showed on his face. He had not expected things to move so far or so fast, but he felt that at last there might be someone here who would listen and, just as importantly, someone he could bargain with.

"You won't be sorry to see the back of him," he said. "I heard the commotion last night, and with all these guards around, that new prisoner must be someone important."

During the night, he had tried to think of who could be important enough to warrant the extra guards, but no one came to mind and he put the increase in the guard down to the young garrison commander's obsession with military correctness – an increase in the number of prisoners required an equal increase in the number of guards. Now, having heard the sergeant's story, he could think of several likely possibilities, but what would suit him best was for this new prisoner to be a Spaniard. It might even be Cortez, but that was far too unlikely. From what he knew about that particular Spaniard, Musgrave was sure that he had escaped, or died in the attempt. However, when the sergeant told him who the prisoner actually was, he couldn't have been more surprised if it had been Cortez.

There was a definite note of satisfaction in the sergeant's voice as he uttered the prisoner's name: "That reiving bastard, Alexander Elliot."

"Alexander Elliot?" Musgrave exclaimed. "What was he doing in this part of the world?"

The sergeant shrugged his shoulders. "All I heard is that he came tae look for his sons. Johnstone didn't talk to me personally aboot it, but it could be true. We've been after that thieving bastard for years. Then all of a sudden he turns up here, and he'd have tae have a good reason for doing that."

It was evident that the sergeant did not care much for reivers, but his hatred did not seem to extend to law officers who rode on both sides of the narrow line separating the reivers from the authorities. With that in mind, the Englishman wondered how he would feel about having to take orders from a known reiver lord like 'Colonel' Johnstone, and the answer was, 'not well'. That was certainly something well worth remembering and Musgrave stored it away in case it came in useful later, but there was one more piece of information he still needed.

"Were Elliot's sons taken prisoner as well?" the Englishman asked anxiously.

"No, just him," the sergeant replied.

Musgrave heaved a sigh of relief. If Sandy and Rabbie had fallen into the hands of the king's men and had revealed how, and why, they came to be in this part of Scotland, together with what had happened since, it could spell serious trouble for him. So far, he had said nothing about them, yet it seemed that Johnstone was aware of their presence in Dumfriesshire and that information could only have come via their father. He decided that when he met Johnstone he had better include them in his account of events. However, several things he had gleaned from the sergeant still did not ring true. Musgrave knew enough about Alexander Elliot to accept that the hiedsman would certainly risk his life to help his sons, but he would still have expected the vastly experienced reiver to avoid capture, especially as it seemed his two sons had escaped without him. It would be nice to know the details of Alexander's capture, and what he had actually told Johnstone, but finding that out would prove to be difficult.

"Is there any chance of having a word with Elliot before meeting your colonel Johnstone?" he asked hopefully.

"Nae chance," the sergeant answered.

One of the first orders 'Colonel' Johnstone had issued was to ensure that Musgrave and Elliot were not to talk to each other. He did not want them comparing notes and concocting a joint story, so the sergeant, thinking that he had said enough to the prisoner already, and probably more than he should have, called two of his men and they escorted Musgrave out of his prison cell to meet the new garrison commander, 'Colonel' Johnstone.

***

In his cell deep in the castle dungeon, Alexander Elliot picked up snippets of the conversation between the sergeant and his fellow prisoner. He was not near enough to hear everything, but he was near enough to pick up Musgrave's distinctive English accent, and the sound of that particular voice lifted a great load off his mind. It must have been Musgrave and not his sons who had informed the king's army about the Spanish invasion, so there was still a good chance that Sandy and Rabbie had safely reached Liddesdale. However, if that were true, it meant that his own chances of survival had suffered a severe setback. Now that Sir William Stewart knew about the Spanish, Alexander could hardly use the information to negotiate his way out of Caerlaverock. He might never see Liddesdale again, but as long as Sandy and Rabbie were safe, he was ready to face whatever fate held in store for him. As a reiver, he had lived all of his life with the harsh reality that his next raid could well be his last. In common with all men who followed the reivers' way of life, he was aware that even if he did not die during a raid, or in a feud, he lived with the constant danger of death or capture by the authorities. And death in battle was preferable to being hanged for reiving.

Alexander had always sworn that he would meet his end with his lance in his hand rather than with a rope around his neck, and he hoped that would still be possible, but there remained one more dark cloud on his horizon. If the story spread, as it might in The Borders, that he had simply surrendered to Sir William Stewart, his enemies could use the knowledge to bring shame on the Elliot name, irrespective of the reasons behind it. He made up his mind that if this proved to be the end, he would not give the authorities the satisfaction of seeing him hang. When the opportunity arose, he would follow Big Jock's example and sell his life dearly.

***

'Colonel' Johnstone looked up as the sergeant ushered Musgrave in and pointedly returned his attention to studying the dispatch Sir William Stewart's rider had brought in early this morning. He made the Englishman stand and wait, but Musgrave's long association with Lord Scrope had prepared him well for such treatment.

Johnstone was not actually studying the dispatch in front of him. He already knew what it contained and while Stewart's orders regarding how the situation at Caerlaverock must be handled were not entirely to his liking, he decided that it was in his interest to follow orders, at least until Maxwell was caught, tried, and hanged. At that point, he would be released from the king's service, return home, and resume his life as both March Warden and reiver lord. In the meantime, he had to consider how best to put those orders into practice, and to help with that process, he went over recent events in his mind. He now knew that the threat of a Spanish invasion hatched by Maxwell, and discovered by Musgrave and Elliot, was very real, but for whatever reason the invasion had not materialised. The two riders sent out by the sergeant to speak to the fishermen at the mouth of the River Nith had immediately struck gold and the plan hatched by Maxwell was uncovered. With so many of the king's soldiers in the area, the threat of a raid by Maxwell and his reivers had receded and the fishermen had returned to occupying both banks of the river. They were eager to talk to the riders about their stolen boat and the strange events that had unfolded when they set out to recapture it, and they told the sergeant's riders about the boatful of soldiers who rescued the thief, and the unfamiliar language they spoke. Having recovered their boat, they followed the foreign soldiers at a safe distance until a large vessel flying a flag they did not recognise suddenly appeared out of the mist. At that point, they gave up and turned tail for home.

The sergeant's riders knew that they had discovered something of great importance and decided not to return to Caerlaverock as ordered by the sergeant. They knew that the sergeant would have trouble persuading the young garrison commander to act and, instead, they decided to report what they had learned to a more senior officer. Night had fallen and they had to wait for daylight, but they set out at dawn to find Sir William Stewart's camp and report the news to him, which they duly did. On their return to

Caerlaverock, they received a severe reprimand from their sergeant, but they knew that this was more to do with the anxiety they had caused him than it was for not following his instructions to the letter.

For his part, 'Colonel' Johnstone rued the fact that he had been unlucky enough to be in Sir William's camp when Alexander Elliot rode in. The king's senior commander, working on the premise that it took one reiver to fully understand another, had ordered him to sit in on his interview with Elliot, but the subject of reiving never came up. They heard Elliot's story, asked a few questions, and then ushered the reiver outside so that they could discuss the situation in private. Stewart asked Johnstone's opinion on whether there could be any truth in what Elliot claimed was happening and the warden offered the opinion that while Maxwell was in Spain, he could well have persuaded King Philip to send a force to Scotland in support of an invasion of England. Johnstone's intention had been to blacken his archenemy's name, but he little suspected that in doing so he had also ruined his own chances of being present at Maxwell's eventual capture.

The two riders from Caerlaverock arrived, reported what they had learned from the fishermen and confirmed what Elliot had told them, and from there events moved on apace; but not to 'Colonel' Johnstone's liking.

The threat of a Spanish invasion had been very real, but from what the fishermen said, it seemed that the danger might be past. Nevertheless, Stewart was not a man to take unnecessary chances and he decided that he would bring forward his march west to capture Maxwell, confident that if Spanish troops did land to join up with the renegade laird, his force was strong enough to deal with both. Johnstone, although he could not openly admit it, hoped that the Spanish would land. It would add one more nail to Maxwell's coffin and he desperately wanted to be there to see it happen, but Stewart had something else in mind for 'Colonel' Johnstone. Something that came as very unwelcome news to the March Warden.

Sir William decided that the fewer people who knew about the Spanish threat the better, so rather than brief another officer, he would send Johnstone to Caerlaverock to interview Musgrave. Johnstone knew that protesting would not only be a waste of time, but falling foul of Stewart could also have a detrimental effect on his plans for the future. When Maxwell was either dead or in prison, and Johnstone, having reverted to being March Warden, set about plundering the Maxwell lands, he did not want Stewart making a nuisance of himself by settling any old grievances. He looked forward to having the whole of Dumfriesshire at his mercy and falling out with Sir William could easily put that in jeopardy. So, all he could do was swallow his disappointment and do as directed.

Now he sat in the fortress at Caerlaverock as the garrison commander, with Musgrave patiently standing in front of him. As with Alexander Elliot, he knew Musgrave of old and he had no particular reason to hold any grudges against the Englishman. As Musgrave suspected, the 'Colonel' was not studying the dispatch in front of him, but it was not, as he thought, with the intention of keeping the Englishman waiting. He was making sure that, in deciding how to deal with this particular situation, he had thought of every conceivable angle. Eventually, he was ready.

"Right, Mister Musgrave. I want you to go over everything, and you can start with why Lord Scrope sent you into my March. And I warn you not to leave anything out like you did with the sergeant there. If you don't already know, I can tell you that we have Alexander Elliot in the cells here."

Johnstone's warning was unnecessary; the Englishman was already wary of how much the 'Colonel' had gleaned from Alexander, and equally wary of what the fishermen had told the sergeant's riders. Was Cortez dead, or had the wily Spaniard escaped to warn his friends? It would be nice to know what the fishermen had seen, but whatever it was it had certainly stirred the king's army into action. So apart from confirming the story currently circulating in The Borders that he had escaped from Carlisle Castle, which would have meant admitting that a condition of his release was that he act as a spy for Scrope, he told Johnstone the whole truth about what had happened since he crossed the Scots Dyke.

Johnstone stopped him a few times to clear up some points, mostly concerning the Elliots, and he seemed particularly anxious to establish whether Alexander Elliot had been with his sons from the beginning.

When he finished his story, Musgrave waited for Johnstone to say something, but when the 'Colonel' failed to comment, he spoke up for himself.

"Can I go back to Carlisle now?" Musgrave asked.

"Not yet," Johnstone replied. "You'll have to stay here for a little longer. Then we'll see."

As far as Johnstone was concerned, Musgrave was relatively easy to deal with. Sir William Stewart had decreed that the Englishman would not hang as a spy, which, in effect he was, but detained as a witness against Maxwell. Only after the traitor had been duly tried and executed, would Musgrave be released. In the meantime, the 'Colonel' was to hold him under guard, and Johnstone considered that the easiest way to do that was to send him back to the cells. Life in the dungeon would also serve to remind the Englishman that he was not in a position to play any more of his usual devious games.

Chapter 44

In his cell, Alexander waited to answer whatever questions 'Colonel' Johnston might decide to throw at him. He fully expected that he would have to endure some form of physical torture in order to force him to provide the answers best suited to the warden's purposes, but he resigned himself to the fact that in the end, it would make little difference what answers he gave. His captors, be they Johnstone's riders or King Jamie's soldiers, would have to show that a captured reiver had received some rough treatment. The law, as applied in The Borders, demanded nothing less.

In this particuar situation, Alexander decided that telling the truth would serve him best. Only the truth could save Liddesdale from King Jamie's wrath and all he could do was answer truthfully, hope the 'Colonel' believed him, and then convince the king that the Elliots were not in league with Maxwell. He felt that Sir William Stewart had believed him when he asserted that he had ridden into Dumfriesshire alone to find his sons, but who knew about Johnstone? Would the warden believe him, or would he even want to believe him? In spite of being currently in the service of King James, Johnstone would be intent on furthering his own ambitions, and his priorities might be directly opposed to those of Stewart. Alexander was resigned to the fact that if it took some pain to convince Johnstone that the Elliots were no threat to those ambitions, he would settle for that. He was under no illusions about what would happen once Johnstone had finished with him. There might be a trial of sorts, but he doubted it, and even if there was, the verdict was already in and the sentence already handed down.

As he thought about that, he became more determined than ever to follow Big Jock's example and die like a true Elliot.

Torture, however, was not what Johnstone had in mind for Alexander Elliot. Dealing with Musgrave had been relatively straightforward, but a prominent member of the Elliot family called for an entirely different approach. Sir William Stewart's orders were to take the notorious reiver to Jedburgh, where he would face trial and hang within sight of Liddesdale. The objective of these orders was to teach the other reivers in the valley a lesson, but Johnstone also suspected that holding a trial at all had more to do with King James's designs on the English throne than on any notion of justice. Stewart had not specifically mentioned torture, but the 'Colonel' had no doubts that it was expected in order to reinforce the message. In Johnstone's view, that was all very well for Stewart and the king, but while he had no compulsion whatsoever about hanging a reiver, he would prefer not to be associated with the torture and death of Alexander Elliot. Soon he would be the unopposed master of the whole of the Scottish West March with all of Maxwell's lands at his mercy, and the last thing he would want was trouble from a vengeful Liddesdale.

If Alexander, or any other Elliot, was to be tortured before being tried and hanged at Jedburgh, it would be better if his blood was not on Johnstone's hands. His problem was how to avoid being involved in the death of such a prominent Elliot without falling foul of either the king or Sir William Stewart. It would require careful thought before he was certain that he had found a solution to this dilemma, and was ready to interview Alexander Elliot.

As he was marched out of his cell by the sergeant, Alexander noticed that he seemed to warrant a much stronger escort than Musgrave had, and although he had not been able to distinguish their words, he had heard the sergeant chatting quite amiably with the Englishman. In puzzling over the apparent different treatments meted out to him and Musgrave, he came up with two possible answers. One was that the sergeant had developed a particular hatred for reivers, which would be understandable; a soldier with his length of service would have crossed swords with reivers in the past and have good cause to hate them. The second reason was that Musgrave had told Stewart and Johnstone something of such importance that it merited him receiving special treatment. He could do nothing about the first possibility, and while the second seemed to have some merit, if the

Englishman had contradicted his story regarding his search for his sons, it could herald disaster. He would simply have to tread carefully and hope.

As things developed, it was Alexander's earlier supposition that proved to be true. The sergeant had learned to hate the reivers and regarded Musgrave as representing the forces of law ranged against them. Musgrave's special treatment resulted not from anything he had told Stewart or Johnstone, but from King James's desire to keep on friendly terms with the English. In this regard, Maxwell and Elliot must face a proper trial before hanging, and that required calling witnesses. Stewart was intent on using Musgrave as a witness in both trials and he cautioned the 'Colonel' to treat the Englishman as a 'guest' rather than a prisoner, but to ensure that he remained in Caerlaverock.

Alexander knew nothing of this when he was finally brought before Johnstone by the sergeant. Having escorted the prisoner to the 'Colonel', the soldier was surprised to be curtly ordered out with his own men and told to check on their 'honoured guest', leaving just two of Johnstone's own riders to guard the prisoner. The sergeant's suspicions were immediately aroused and he began to wonder what game this erstwhile 'Colonel' was playing. He remembered that in spite of being in the king's service, Johnstone was as much reiver as March Warden and he decided that he would be wise not to trust his new commander too far.

As if to confirm the sergeant's suspicions, Johnstone's first question had nothing to do with either Maxwell or the Spanish. "Tell me about what happened to Big Jock?"

In a day of surprises, this was the most unexpected of all and it took Alexander several moments to recover. He failed to understand how the question had any bearing on the situation and, when he eventually answered, he adhered to his plan to tell Johnstone nothing but the truth. He told the 'Colonel' everything he knew about how Big Jock had met his death, with an emphasis on the fact that the old reiver had given up his life to help him and his sons escape. The story of Big Jock Elliot's death would soon be spreading across The Borders, and he was attempting to make sure, or as sure as he possibly could, that it was passed on with at least some degree of accuracy. He expected the 'Colonel' to remind him that several of the king's men had also died in the fracas and to demand an explanation for that, but Johnstone did nothing of the sort. He merely nodded and made a single surprising comment.

"That was a good way for a man like Big Jock to die."

If this caused Alexander's surprise to increase, then Johnstone's next remark amazed him. He looked the prisoner directly in the eye before speaking.

"It's a lot better than being hanged for reiving, and I hope that you're not thinking of doing something like that yourself."

"So I'm to be hanged, am I?" Alexander's answer was simply for the sake of having something to say and gain a little time to think. He failed to understand why Johnstone would want to bring up the subject of Big Jock's death, and what the 'Colonel' meant by his comment about him doing the same thing himself. He had already made up his mind that he was marked down to die by hanging and had decided that it would be better to follow his old riding companion's example and die in the saddle. Johnstone, he thought, knew the ways of the reivers and must have already guessed that if possible, Alexander Elliot would prefer to die fighting rather than tamely submit to death on the scaffold. That, however, did not explain why the 'Colonel' had chosen to bring the subject up at this particular time, or indeed, bring it up at all.

In answering Alexander's question about his being hanged, Johnstone seemed reluctant to admit that the sentence was a foregone conclusion, and it was evident that he chose his words with extreme care.

"That's what Sir William Stewart and King Jamie will want."

Still mystified by Johnstone's interest in how Big Jock died, Alexander decided not to pursue the subject of his own death any further. The temporary 'Colonel' was after all a March Warden and would soon return to that role, and as such, he should have a great deal to gain by being directly connected with the hanging of a reiver as notorious as Alexander Elliot. But that did not seem to be the case. On the contrary, it seemed to Alexander that Johnstone was intent on distancing himself from complicity in his death. He clearly had something entirely different in mind, and Alexander badly wanted to find out more, but he doubted if the 'Colonel' would be prepared to enlighten him.

In the event, he was denied an opportunity to gain any more information. The 'Colonel' sent one of his men to fetch the sergeant, and when the soldier entered, Johnstone again mystified Alexander by looking directly at him instead of the soldier as he issued his orders.

"Take the prisoner back to the cells, sergeant. He has told me everything I need to know. In the morning, I want you to assemble an escort to take him to Lochmaben. There is very little chance of you running into trouble on the way there, so use some of my men to make up the escort. It will save weakening the garrison here. From Lochmaben, you will be taking him to Jedburgh by way of Langholm for trial, and there can be little doubt about what the sentence will be. The garrison commander at Lochmaben will provide you with fresh horses and a strong escort of the king's men."

The sergeant hesitated before acknowledging. He was clearly considering questioning the orders, which, in his experience were unusual in the extreme. He would have expected a reiver with Elliot's reputation to have been hanged by now, but before he could make a protest, Johnsone decided to enlighten him.

"For political reasons, it has been decided that the prisoner should be properly tried, as Laird Maxwell will be."

The sergeant had little choice but to accept his orders, but he failed to hide a worried frown. In his experience, 'political reasons' invariably spelled trouble for soldiers, and Johnstone's next comment did nothing to ease his fears.

"Remember that after Langholm you will be passing close to Liddesdale, so make sure you choose your escort with care from experienced soldiers. And tell them to keep their eyes open."

A puzzled sergeant escorted an equally puzzled Alexander back to his cell. Both were highly suspicious of what game Johnstone might be playing, but especially the sergeant. In spite of the fact that Elliot had apparently told the 'Colonel' everything he wanted to know, there was not a single mark on the prisoner, and the thought of a reiver revealing anything at all without being tortured was almost beyond his comprehension. Nevertheless, as long as Johnstone bore the rank of Colonel in the king's army, he had no choice but to follow orders.

In his cell, Alexander too, was racking his brains trying to understand what lay behind Johnstone's strange attitude towards him. Johnstone had been at pains to impress on Alexander that sending him to Jedburgh for trial, followed by the inevitable death by hanging, was none of his doing, and furthermore, he had treated his prisoner almost as a friend. On the other hand, while giving orders to the sergeant, he had done his best to conduct himself in true military fashion. He had, however, rather spoiled this effect by letting Alexander, a prisoner, know what those orders were. Particularly the part about passing close to Liddesdale. Then the truth dawned on him. Johnstone was in effect offering him an alternative to the scaffold. As 'Colonel' he could do little, but as a March Warden he was making it possible for him to be rescued by riders from Liddesdale, or die as Big Jock had done! Why Johnstone would do this was not important, but for Alexander it was enough to know that he had a choice. He realised that there was no possibility of Johnstone having revealed his true thoughts to the sergeant, and so, when his opportunity came along, as he was sure it would, he would have to deal with the soldier himself. Nevertheless, he was determined to make the most of the alternatives Johnstone had suggested.

***

When the sergeant, who was clearly not his usual amiable self, took Alexander Elliot back to the castle dungeon, he released Musgrave, took him to the barrack room, and ordered some food from the kitchens. The Englishman was hoping to ask some of the questions that had suddenly become highly relevant to him, and which he badly needed answers to, but the sergeant appeared to be completely distracted, and he sat in silence while Musgrave ate.

By now, the Englishman had had time enough for the implications of what Johnstone had told him to sink in. With all chances of making any sort of profit out of his time in Scotland, he was happy to give evidence about Maxwell's involvement with the Spanish. He owed the laird something for ordering his riders to kill him, and he blamed Maxwell for costing him the large rewards he had originally expected, but he was not at all happy about the time it would take before the trial could begin. Knowing what he did about Maxwell, he guessed that it could be a long time yet before the the king's men captured the canny laird, and until then, he would have to get used to life in a castle dungeon. Whether here in Caerlaverock or in Edinburgh would make little difference, the prospect was not a pleasant one.

He eyed the sergeant and his two guards and it was evident that, while on the surface they might treat him as an important witness, he was nonetheless still a prisoner. Johnstone was making sure that he remained at Caerlaverock until it was time for him to testify at Maxwell's trial. A trial that he was sure would take place in Edinburgh and be presided over by the king in person. It crossed his mind that Scrope's attitude towards him might soften once he knew that his former captain had given evidence against Maxwell, but he doubted it. Once a Spanish invasion was no longer a threat, any of the information he had gathered would be worthless.

Musgrave realised that yet again, his carefully laid plans had come to nought and this time there seemed to be little he could do about it. He could see that the sergeant had something on his mind, but he decided to ignore that and try and engage him in conversation in the hope of picking his brain and finding something that might help him decide what to do next.

He attempted to engage the sergeant with a seemingly casual remark. "What happened to the things I had when I came here? The two horses, the Spanish clothes, and the fancy sword?"

The soldier, however, still wasn't listening, and Musgrave had to repeat the question. "It's a' bein' held for evidence," was the eventual answer.

"Will I get any of it back?"

The sergeant merely shrugged and Musgrave was not in the least surprised. Both men knew that the Englishman would never see any of his loot again. After Maxwell's trial was over, it would probably find its way into Johnstone's tower house, assuming that it ever reached the trial, and there was no point in protesting. In The Borders, it was the way of things and in his days as a law officer, Musgrave had sometimes been similarly careless with evidence himself.

He changed the subject. "How long do you think it will be before they catch Maxwell?"

Again, the sergeant merely shrugged, but Musgrave persisted. "Will you let me know when he's caught?"

"I won't be here," the sergeant answered shortly, making it clear that he was none too pleased about leaving Caerlaverock.

Musgrave became concerned. Without the sergeant, his supply of good food might dry up. He was about to press the matter further, but before he could, the soldier decided to explain.

"I have orders tae take Elliot to Jedburgh to be hanged. But ye don't need to worry, ye'll be kept here as a witness against Maxwell."

This really did surprise the Englishman. "I thought Alexander would be hanged here."

The sergeant did not attempt to hide his disappointment. "So did I, but they say that he has tae be tried first at Jedburgh."

The venom in the sergeant's next remark took Musgrave aback. "Anyway, if I get the chance, the reiving bastard won't live long enough tae see a trial."

Musgrave returned to his cell wondering if, after the trial, he was also destined to face a similar end and not live to see either Bewcastle or Carlisle again.

Chapter 45

Johnstone was pleased with his solution to the problem of complying with Sir William Stewart's orders while at the same time safeguarding his own position. He would send Alexander Elliot to Jedburgh by way of Lochmaben and Langholm, which, he would argue, was the best route available. It included two castles controlled by the king, and he did not have sufficient force to risk crossing the Debatable Land and entering Liddesdale. For the most dangerous part of the journey, close to Liddesdale, the prisoner would have a much stronger escort; one made up of the king's soldiers. His own men would not be involved, and should anything untoward occur on that leg of the journey, it would not be his responsibility.

Even though the king controlled the country north of Liddesdale, there was still a distinct possibility that the Elliots and their allies, the Armstrongs, would attempt to rescue such an important hiedsman, and even if that failed to materialise, being so close to home would provide Alexander with the opportunity of making a break for freedom. Johnstone was relying on the prisoner being either rescued by the reivers of Liddesdale or dying in an attempt to escape, and it did not matter which. In either case, the king's soldiers would have to bear full responsibility and he would not have to bear any of the blame. It even crossed his mind that if Alexander escaped, and it was suggested that he was complicit, he would gain some valuable allies in Liddesdale who could be relied upon to guard his rear when he set about exacting revenge on the Maxwells. In the unlikely event of his having to answer further questions, he would argue that he had simply been following Sir William Stewart's orders.

Johnstone smiled to himself; he could not think of a more advantageous position.

In his cell, Alexander spent the night deep in thought. If things worked out as he hoped, he would be dead before many more days had passed, so there was little point in trying to sleep. He had worked out what was behind Johnstone's strange behaviour at the interview, but it did not solve the whole puzzle. The 'Colonel' had clearly been pointing out ways for Alexander to escape the hangman's noose, but while he knew the 'what', he could not think of the 'why'. In the end, he decided that it did not matter much either way, and he concentrated on working out how best to take advantage of it.

In the early hours of the morning a horse clattered into the courtyard, and shortly afterwards the sound of cheering rang through the castle. Alexander spent several minutes trying to work out what had caused the commotion, and the most likely solution seemed to be that King Jamie's men had finally caught up with Maxwell. Johnstone's riders were celebrating the good news, and none, Alexander knew, would be cheering louder than Johnstone himself. In reality, however, it meant little to him; he had other things to think about and what happened to Maxwell was no longer of any interest to him.

Musgrave too, heard the cheering, and like Alexander, he could guess the cause. The king's army had taken Maxwell, but, unlike Alexander Elliot, Maxwell's capture meant a great deal to the Englishman. Knowing the laird's reputation for keeping himself out of trouble, he had been certain that Maxwell would have held out for much longer. In fact, he had seriously entertained the thought that the king's army could never take the fugitive laird alive. In the meantime, he had changed his mind about having to spend a long time here in Caerlaverock where, although housed in a cell, he was an 'honoured guest' rather than a prisoner in anticipation of his giving evidence at Maxwell's trial. With plenty to eat, and ample time to make plans for the future, he was now less concerned about how long it took to bring Maxwell to trial. As if on cue, however, the sergeant came to confirm that Maxwell had indeed been arrested, and to Musgrave it was not altogether welcome news. With Maxwell now in the king's hands a trial must be imminent, and he would have to leave the comfort of Caerlaverock for whatever awaited him in Edinburgh.

He began to consider what this change in circumstances would mean for him and it raised some worrying questions. The speed of Maxwell's arrest and the manner of the rebel laird's capture did not seem to fit with what he knew about Maxwell; to Musgrave's mind, the laird's arrest appeared to have been all too easy.

He suspected that, having given in so easily, Maxwell would have something up his sleeve to ensure that his future did not involve a hangman's noose. And the thought disturbed the Englishman. If Maxwell somehow managed to avoid the scaffold, and it became known that Musgrave had been prepared to give evidence at his trial, he would have made a very dangerous enemy indeed. The more he considered Maxwell's long record as a reiver lord, and his many narrow escapes from frequent brushes with the authorities, the more Musgrave became convinced that escape was a distinct possibility. If the laird could talk his way out of exile in Spain then nothing was impossible for him, and from Edinburgh it was a long way back to England, with little chance of escaping Maxwell's vengeance on the way. He became convinced that his only chance of ever reaching home was to avoid going to Edinburgh in the first place. Not giving evidence at the trial was his only option for ensuring his personal survival, and he set about thinking of ways to of achieving it.

'Colonel' Johnstone had already been woken up by the noisy arrival of Sir William Stewart's rider and knew at once that something of importance had happened. He jumped out of bed, grabbed the dispatch from the messenger, quickly read through it and went to join his men. In spite of his position as garrison commander, he could not resist joining in the celebrations. Stewart had captured Maxwell far sooner than he, or anyone else, expected. The news came as music to Johnstone's ears, and he did not share any of Musgraves's doubts about the laird managing to talk his way out of the noose. For him, the arrest portended an end to his term of service to the king, and he could enjoy an early return to the lucrative position of March Warden. Any feeling of disappointment he felt about not being present at his enemy's arrest, quickly disappeared.

After his initial sense of elation had abated, however, he remembered that Stewart's rider had also carried a second dispatch. He read it and decided to alter his recently laid plans.

Sir William had decided to deliver Maxwell to King James in person. He would take his prisoner to Edinburgh escorted by a large contingent of the king's cavalry, and 'Colonel' Johnstone's orders were to have his star witness against the laird, Musgrave, taken to Lochmaben to join Stewart's party there. His archenemy was on his way to Edinburgh in chains by way of Lochmaben, and Johnstone could not resist the temptation to go and witness the hated Maxwell's ignominious downfall for himself. He decided to take personal charge of the escort taking Alexander Elliot to Lochmaben, and take Musgrave with him. He would wait there for Stewart, and try to persuade Sir William to allow him to accompany him and Maxwell to Edinburgh. Being present at the trial and execution, would be something to savour for years. At Lochmaben in the meantime, the sergeant would revert to the original plan and take Alexander Elliot to hang in Jedburgh.

It would mean that he would be leaving Caerlaverock without a senior officer to command the garrison, but that would work in his favour. When he resumed his position as March Warden, it would be relatively easy for him to occupy Maxwell's castle and expand his own territory south to the Solway Firth.

In his cell, Musgrave had already concluded that his best chance of avoiding Maxwell's trial was to escape back to England. It galled him to be going back with absolutely nothing to show for all his trials and tribulations in Scotland, but it was better than risk having a vengeful Maxwell hunt him down. He doubted if he would ever be reinstated as Captain of Bewcastle while Lord Scrope remained as March Warden, but he could always return to reiving.

The sergeant eventually brought Musgrave the news. Sir William Stewart was taking Maxwell to Edinburgh by way of Lochmaben, and Musgrave was to join them there. They would be leaving at dawn with an escort led by Colonel Johnstone in person, and they would be taking the reiver, Elliot, with them to hang at Jedburgh. The sergeant's news served to compound Musgrave's problems. Going to Lochmaben with a notorious reiver like Alexander Elliot for company meant that the escort would be strong and doubly vigilant, especially with Johnstone rather than the sergeant in charge. It would make avoiding going to Edinburgh all the more difficult.

Chapter 46

They left on schedule at dawn with an escort made up of Johnstone riders plus the sergeant and three of his troopers, and led by the 'Colonel' in person. The party included the prisoner, Alexander Elliot, with his hands tightly bound, and Musgrave; also a veriable prisoner, but with his hands free. Johnstone's men were just as jubilant as the 'Colonel' at the prospect of seeing the hated Maxwell in chains, and he had tried to include them all, leaving only the original small garrison, less the sergeant and the three troopers, behind at Caerlaverock. None of the Johnstone riders had any particular bone to pick with either Alexander or the Englishman but when Musgrave tried to engage one of them in conversation hoping to gain some useful bits of information that he could turn to his advantage, his attempts resulted in failure. He received a similar rebuff from the usually talkative sergeant, which he ascribed to the fact that the soldier was not anxious to appear too familiar with an Englishman in front of his 'Colonel'. Having failed to get anything out of the escort, he rode close to Alexander Elliot and tried his luck with him.

"What happened to Sandy and Rabbie and Big Jock after we were forced to split up?" he asked, adding a note of concern to his voice.

"The two boys are awa' hame, an' Big Jock is deed," Alexander answered sadly.

Musgrave knew better than to enquire too deeply into the old reiver's death, but felt that he had to say something. "I'm sorry to hear that, Alexander. Big Jock was one of the best."

"Aye, that he was." With nothing else to occupy his mind until they reached Lochmaben, Alexander decided that he might as well pass the time of day with the Englishman and outlined for him the circumstances of Big Jock's death.

After a pause, Musgrave resumed the conversation: "You have two fine sons there, Alexander. I'd like to see them again, but it looks as if we're both headed for a trial; me to testify against Maxwell, and you to be hanged in Jedburgh."

Alexander gave the Englishman a determined look. "I'll no hang at Jedburgh or anywhere else. An' I canna see Maxwell being hanged either. He's too canny for that."

Musgrave was aware that the hiedsman wasn't referring to having an accident on the way to Jedburgh. Either Alexander expected to be rescued by his reiver friends before he reached the scaffold or, he realised with some surprise, the reiver was planning to make a break for freedom and didn't expect to get away alive. The more he thought about it, the more Musgrave became convinced that if Alexander failed in an escape attempt, he would be happy to emulate Big Jock.

The sergeant rode in silence, clearly not a happy man. With Johnstone having taken charge, and with responsibility for the prisoner having passed to the 'Colonel's' own men, he found himself with nothing to do but think. He had time to remember the men, many of them friends, he had lost in skirmishes with the reivers, and the endless hours spent in fruitless searches for the raiders in the bitter Border weather. As the memories came back, his hatred for the reivers, and particularly for the Elliots, grew and he became more determined than ever to make sure that Alexander was one reiver who would not escape justice. He decided to make certain that Elliot did not live to reive again, and he was not content to place his faith in the hangman. He had seen too many reivers cheat the noose in the past. He fingered the pistol nestling in his saddle holster, but he realised that he could not use it here in front of the Johnstones. However, once they left Lochmaben for Jedburgh, he would be in charge of an escort made up of the king's soldiers, and that was when his opportunity would arise. He was convinced that the reivers of Liddesdale would mount a rescue attempt and he did not intend taking on a whole reiver army, but he would have men stationed to give him ample warning of an attack. The minute he got the word that a rescue attempt was imminent, he intended to kill Elliot, bolt back to the safety of Lochmaben and blame the reivers for the death of his prisoner.

He turned and saw Musgrave and Alexander talking in an apparently friendly way, and it had the effect of fuelling his resentment. He rode between the two intending to split them up, but in doing so, he picked up Alexander's last remark and couldn't resist a sneering riposte directed at the prisoner.

"You're right about not being hanged in Jedburgh, Elliot, you won't live that long."

He checked that Alexander's bonds were still secure and rode away, feeling that he had scored a telling point and totally forgot about Musgrave.

Alexander dismissed the sergeant's barbed comment from his mind, but it was not lost on the Englishman. It set Musgrave's mind racing. There could be something of advantage to him in this.

He looked seriously at the reiver. "That bloody soldier is set to do you in, Alexander. And he'll do it somewhere between Lochmaben and Jedburgh, unless the riders from Liddesdale can snatch you away from him."

Alexander had no intention of waiting until the men from Liddesdale attempted to rescue him, as he knew they would. Even a failed attempt would give the authorities yet another excuse to ravage the valley and ruin all he had achieved by giving himself up to Sir William Stewart. A successful escape attempt would have the same result. The king would send an army to find him. Death by the sergeant's pistol was much more to his liking.

"Ah'm a deid mon anyhow," he answered.

This was confirmation enough for Musgrave. Alexander did plan to make a break for freedom and die in the attempt. What he failed to understand, however, was why the man's mind was so set on dying, and the only way to find out was to ask. He lowered his voice so that the riders around them couldn't hear.

"But why should it be that way, when you have a good chance of getting away? Big Jock got me and your sons out of a couple of tight corners back there in the hills. And you must have done something like it yourself to get Sandy and Rabbie out."

Alexander noted the Englishman's use of the familiar form of his son's names and knew that Musgrave was trying to encourage him to accept whatever proposal he had in mind, but events had progressed far beyond any need for such tactics, and he ignored it.

"Jamie would send an army tae get me back," Alexander answered sadly. "An' so soon after the fight wi' Bothwell, we canna stand anither attack."

So that was it, Alexander was going to give up his life to protect Liddesdale from an attack by King James. The nobleness of the gesture was completely lost on Musgrave, but the idea of the reiver making a break for freedom, held out real possibilities for him. If he could help Alexander Elliot to escape and get back to Liddesdale alive or dead, and without losing his own life in the process, he would gain valuable friends in the valley who would help him get back to England. Not only that, the Elliots would owe him a debt which they would be bound to honour, and having such powerful allies in Scotland, would be of immense help when he resumed his own reiving career. It could provide an answer to his problems, but first he had to persuade Alexander that he was wrong about the king attacking the valley.

"James won't attack Liddesdale now," he said with some conviction. "He'll be too tied up with trying and hanging Maxwell, and with preparing to become King of England, to worry about you. Besides, nothing will have changed. He can raid Liddesdale anytime he likes, and with you there, they'll have a better chance of beating him."

Alexander knew the Englishman well enough to be wary of anything Musgrave said, but he had to admit that this particular thought had not occurred to him, and it definitely made sense. However, it would make no difference in the end. From what that soldier said, and the way he said it, he doubted if a break for freedom stood even the slightest chance of success.

Musgrave waited for a reply but when one was obviously not forthcoming, he carried on. "I'm supposed to give evidence at Maxwell's trial, which I didn't expect to happen for months yet. Anyway, they caught him too quick for my liking and I'm sure that the bastard is playing some game or other that will get him off. And then I'll be left in the lurch."

Until now, Alexander had given little thought to Maxwell, but Musgrave's argument made him take notice. He was well aware of Maxwell's reputation for trickery and the Englishman was probably right, but then the former Captain of Bewcastle could be equally devious himself. The Englishman clearly had something on his mind, and while it would not stem from any great concern for anyone else's wellbeing, Alexander decided that he might as well hear him out.

"Aye," he answered, "yon laird is good at games, but so are ye, Musgrave. Ye're after somethin', so spit it oot."

By now, Musgrave had made up his mind that his best chance of survival was in throwing in his lot with Alexander. To his way of thinking, if they made a break together, and made it soon, they had a good chance of getting away. He guessed that Johnstone would not make too much of an effort to stop them because he and his men would be too intent on getting to Lochmaben to gloat over Maxwell. The only ones they had to worry about were the sergeant and his three troopers, and with luck, the vengeful soldier would concentrate on killing Alexander, leaving him free to ride into the Debatable Land and over the Scots Dyke. As far as Elliot was concerned, well, Alexander had already made up his mind to die.

Having failed to take advantage of the opportunity offered by Cortez, Musgrave was not about to let this one pass him by.

"Look, Alexander, there's nothing in this for me anymore, and I was thinking of coming with you. Two of us will have a better chance than one, and if we don't make it, well, for me it will be better than being hunted down by Maxwell, and for you it will be better than hanging."

Alexander knew that Musgrave would be concentrating on saving his own skin and would abandon him as soon as they got clear or, and much more likely, sacrifice him in the process. Even so, escaping with Musgrave might not be such a bad idea, and it began to grow on him. Like the Englishman, he knew that the sergeant would concentrate on killing him, and would almost certainly succeed. He could not hope to outrun the pistols the soldiers carried. Furthermore, 'Colonel' Johnstone had taken on personal responsibility for escorting him to Lochmaben, and escaping from him might not have the same consequences as escaping from the king's men. Bearing in mind what Musgrave said, Jamie might well send his

March Warden into Liddesdale to rearrest him rather than come himself, and Alexander cursed himself for not thinking of this before. He had been too intent on convincing the king that the Elliots were not in league with Maxwell, and with following Big Jock's example, to allow any other thoughts to enter his head. It made sense for him to go along with the Englishman.

The sergeant gave them a suspicious look and rode closer to make sure they weren't still chatting in friendly terms, and rode between them so that they couldn't say anything without being overheard.

Musgrave thought fast. He was sure that he had convinced Alexander to go along with his scheme to make a break for freedom, and the best time and place to make such a break was here and now. The further south they made their break, the shorter the distance to the Scots Dyke and home. But he had to find a way of communicating it to the reiver.

He looked past the sergeant and pointed to the east. "That's the Debatable Land over there, sergeant. The Broken Men are in there and I wouldn't want to get on the wrong side of them. But they won't bother the king's men unless you're foolish enough to ride in there."

The sergeant turned to look in the direction the Englishman was pointing. Musgrave managed to catch Alexander's eye and the Elliot hiedsman nodded to show that he understood what the Englishman was getting at. He lifted his reins to indicate that he was ready to do his part. Musgrave guessed that the sergeant was aware of the agreements governing the Debatable Land, and he continued to distract the soldier.

"And there's no danger of riders from Liddesdale coming from there either, so you don't have to watch that flank. If the Elliots try to save Alexander, they'll come from the west and try to drive you into the Debatable Land, and if you let that happen, another band of riders will have a perfect right to come at you from Liddesdale. You'd do well to send riders out to the west and I'm surprised that Johnstone hasn't done it already. He's done enough reiving himself in the past to know what will happen."

It sounded plausible enough to the sergeant, but one thing worried him. "Why would ye be telling me this, Musgrave?"

"You did me a favour with extra food while I was in the cells at Caerlaverock," Musgrave answered. "But that's not the real reason. If they come to rescue Elliot, they won't let anyone stand in their way and they won't take prisoners. They won't spare anybody, including me, and I'm unarmed. So why don't you go and have a word with Johnstone. Tell him that he's supposed to get me to Edinburgh alive to testify against Maxwell, and the least he can do is to give me something to defend myself with."

The sergeant, although not entirely convinced by the Englishman's reasoning, rode off to talk to Johnstone and an argument developed between the two. Alexander smiled to himself and silently applauded Musgrave's quick thinking. He couldn't have done better himself.

He looked at the Englishman and yelled, "Now!"

"Now!" Musgrave yelled back. He turned his horse and galloped for the Debatable Land with Alexander close behind.

Chapter 47

Johnstone's riders were all watching the heated exchange between their laird and the soldier, but there was a yell of alarm from one of the sergeant's troopers. The soldier turned in alarm, saw that the reiver, Elliot, and the Englishman were attempting to escape. He immediately gave chase, yelling at his troopers to follow.

Johnstone's men looked at the laird for guidance and he hesitated before telling them to stay where they were. It was not turning out exactly as he planned, but he could turn things around to his advantage. What happened to Alexander Elliot was of little concern; the reiver's death or escape would be the responsibility of the king's sergeant and his men, and he could argue that there were enough of them to recapture two unarmed prisoners. Musgrave, however, was a different matter. Johnstone needed him alive to ensure that Maxwell got his just deserts, and he had to concentrate all his efforts on recapturing the Englishman.

Alexander glanced back and saw that the soldiers were gaining. They would soon be within pistol range. Johnstone and his men were further back. He spurred the horse in desperation and shouted to Musgrave to increase the pace. Alexander had started out this morning not only prepared to die, but also prepared to welcome death, but the thrill of the chase changed all of that. All of the reiver's instincts for survival he had developed over half a century of raiding, came flooding back. All thoughts of death left him as he spurred his horse towards the Debatable Land, and beyond that, Liddesdale. But, with his hands tied he could not hope to get the best out of his horse.

Although there was no well-defined border, they knew they were into the Debatable Land. So did Johnstone. He ordered his men to stop and called to the four soldiers to do likewise. The sergeant ignored his 'Colonel' and kept up the chase. Johnstone gave little thought for Alexander but was determined not to lose the prime witness against Maxwell, and so, he called his riders back. His riders looked at their laird in surprise, but Johnstone knew exactly what Musgrave would do once he had given the sergeant the slip, as he surely would. He felt that he had made enough of a show of supporting the king's men but his main objective was Musgrave. He turned his men around and headed for the English border.

With his hands tied, Alexander inevitably began to lose ground and the soldiers continued to gain. The sergeant thought that they were within effective pistol range. He drew his pistol and his men followed suit. Four shots rang out as one. Musgrave sensed rather than saw two of the balls strike Alexander who slumped forward but remained in the saddle. He was clearly hard hit and without his rider's desperate urging, his tired horse began to slow down.

The Englishman decided that it was time to leave. He knew that the sergeant would be too intent on finishing Alexander off to take any notice of him. He turned his horse and rode south towards the Scots Dyke and England.

Alexander did his best, but he was bleeding badly and his strength was ebbing away with his blood. The sergeant eagerly spurred forward to make sure that he could never recover, but one of the troopers called out in alarm and the three troopers hung back. The sergeant ignored them. He drew level with Alexander and reached for his sword. As he grasped the hilt, two shots rang out and he fell from his horse, dead before he hit the ground. So intent had he been on Alexander that he had failed to notice Sandy and Rabbie Elliot ride up with a large group of riders. The troopers, who had seen them coming, turned tail and galloped out of the Debatable Land.

In the meantime, Musgrave, satisfied that the sound of the pistol shots would have kept any of the Broken Men well out of the way, and that neither Johnstone's riders nor the king's men were following him, slowed his horse for a badly needed breather. He resumed his journey south at a leisurely pace and reached the Scots Dyke. He was about to cross when he found himself surrounded by armed riders who seemed to have come out of nowhere.

"You have an appointment in Edinburgh, Mr Musgrave, and I'd hate you to miss it." Johnstone had guessed that the Englishman would abandon Alexander Elliot and had laid a trap accordingly. Whether or not the sergeant and his men caught Alexander, was of little importance to him.

Chapter 48

Sandy and Rabbie rode one on either side of their father, doing their best to support him. A rider was sent ahead to tell Martin Elliot of Braidley that they had found Alexander, but that he was badly wounded. Martin of Braidley knew that the hiedsman had been a prisoner at Caerlaverock, but as Alexander had not yet been hanged, he guessed that he would soon be moved. He was planning a rescue attempt, but did not know when the authorities intended to move the heidsman from Caerlaverock, and he decided to send riders to watch the fortress rather than endure an anxious wait for news. Sandy and Rabbie volunteered to do it with a band of riders, but Maxwell's early capture had caused their timing to go awry. In the event, that had proved fortunate.

They arrived in the Debatable Land just in time to wrest their father from the king's men.

They stopped at the first homestead they came to in Liddesdale, intending to leave Alexander to rest and recover. The hiedsman, however, was not having any of it. The women of the house stemmed the bleeding, and cleaned and bound their hiedsman's wounds, as they had done for many other wounded reivers. But Alexander knew that he was dying.

By a strange twist of fate, his end would be brought about by a pistol shot, but unlike his old friend, Big Jock, he intended to die at home in his own tower house.

"Tak' me hame," he managed to tell his sons.

After a quick conference, they agreed. They commandeered a wheeled cart and gently placed Alexander in it on a bed of hay. After a tortuous journey during which he lost consciousness several times, they eventually got him home to his own reiver's tower.

There, surrounded by his family, and knowing that he was leaving his reiver band in capable hands, Alexander Elliot finally cheated the hangman.

Historic Footnotes

Queen Elizabeth finally died in 1603 and the Act of Union united the crowns of England and Scotland. James VI of Scotland became James 1 of England and with the formation of the United Kingdom, the border between the two countries ceased to exist. Although violent upheaval followed for several years, it spelled the end of the Border Reivers.

Previously Published Works:

The Last Coachman (2010)
ISBN 978-1-84897-088-5

This Bitter Land (2011)
ISBN 978-1-84897-173-8

Shake Hands with a Connaught Ranger (2013)
ISBN 978-1-84897-286-5

An Tánaiste – The Heir (2017)
ISBN: 9781848978379